He survived—but only because
he did what he had to do.

He hates the memory of it; hates that any of it ever happened; hates that he can't change the past, or seem to forget it.

Most of all, he hates that it isn't over, even now, and never will be. And so, Jeremy is doomed to carry around the anger and hurt forever.

And he can't tell anyone the whole truth. Not even his wife.

Lucy doesn't know the rest. She doesn't grasp the extent of what he's capable of doing . . .

She doesn't know what else you actually did.

And now that he's built a life for himself, with a wife he loves and a baby on the way, he has more to lose than ever before.

Nothing—*no one*—is going to take that away.

And he can never be tempted to tell anyone what he did.

That voice, *her* voice, it echoes through his head sometimes, even now.

She's dead, and yet he hears her still . . .

By Wendy Corsi Staub

HELL TO PAY
SCARED TO DEATH
LIVE TO TELL

Coming Soon
NIGHTCRAWLER

"I will render vengeance to
mine enemies..."

WENDY CORSI STAUB

HELL TO PAY

AVON

An Imprint of HarperCollinsPublishers

AVON BOOKS
An Imprint of HarperCollins*Publishers*
10 East 53rd Street
New York, New York 10022-5299

Copyright © 2011 by Wendy Corsi Staub
Excerpt from *Nightcrawler* copyright © 2012 by Wendy Corsi Staub
ISBN 978-0-06-189508-1
www.avonbooks.com

First Avon Books mass market printing: October 2011

For my godparents: Aunt Mickey and Uncle Lorrie.
And for my aunts and uncles:
Aunt Rita and Aunt Marian,
Uncle Sam and Uncle Ron,
who have been there for me all my life.
And for Mark, Morgan, and Brody, with love.
With special gratitude to Laura Blake Peterson,
George Catalano, Theresa Gottlieb,
Brooke Johnson, Nanci Kennedy, Bob Mackowiak,
Lucia Macro, Wendy Nevid, Paula Santo Donato,
Dave Schudel, Chris Spain,
and last alphabetically but far from least, Mark Staub.

Whoso sheddeth man's blood, by man shall his blood be shed.

—Genesis 9:6

Prologue

Bridgebury Correctional Facility
Massachusetts

Something is wrong.

Lying awake in her bunk in Cellblock B, she senses it even before she hears or feels it.

Later, looking back on this moment—something she will do every day for as long as she lives—she'll acknowledge this flash of prophecy that saved her life. She'll wish she could share the incredible story with the world.

But she can't.

This memory, like the others that will continue to haunt and inspire her, will be her secret. No one, other than Chaplain Gideon of course, will ever know about the premonition that kept her from dying in her bed on a cold New England night.

All around her, the others are sound asleep in their cells. They'll never know what hit them.

For her, though, the awareness strikes out of nowhere, like one of her ferocious headaches.

Yes, something is wrong . . .

The perception is so strong—so *earth-shattering*, she'll wryly think later, with no one to appreciate the clever wordplay—that her eyes fly open and she braces herself for . . . something terrible.

She fully expects to find someone looming over her bed. It wouldn't be the first time.

But it isn't that. It isn't about her at all.

No, this is bigger—much bigger, rushing at her like a subway train: distant rumbling; the ground begins to shake. Instinctively, she dives off the bed and rolls beneath the steel frame just as the first chunk of mortar lands on the floor beside it.

A bomb?

No—that would be a single explosion; perhaps a series of them. This is an endless detonation, and as the world crumbles all around her, she knows. She *knows*.

It has come to pass, just as the Bible foretold in the Book of Revelation.

. . . and there was a great earthquake, such as was not since men were upon the earth, so mighty an earthquake, and so great.

Huddled in a fetal position, she stays under the bed as brick and concrete rain down. Metal beams and iron bars groan and collapse, reducing the impenetrable fortress to rubble. The bunk is still standing, having been factory-welded into indestructibility to prevent it being dismantled and used as a weapon.

She can hear the others' terrified screams in the face of God's fury, but she herself remains calm. Panic would trigger a flight response; were she to budge from under the bed, she'd surely be crushed to death in an instant.

Deep down, she knows she's meant to be spared. She won't die. Not here. Not now.

At last, the shaking subsides.

She opens her eyes to a stinging cloud of dust. She can hear wailing car alarms, sirens, moans and shrieks of the trapped and dying. Dust clogs her lungs so that she can barely breathe, but she's in one piece. Alive.

She feels her way out from under the bed, squirming through the debris until she's standing. The cell floor is cracked and littered with wreckage, and there, beside the bed that shielded her, is her precious dog-eared Bible.

Trembling, she picks it up, clasps it to her chest.

The dust has begun to settle, falling strangely cold and wet. She tilts her head back and for the first time in years, sees the wide-open night sky, swirling with snowflakes.

Richard Jollston has been predicting it for decades.

But when it actually happens—when a major earthquake strikes his native New England—he isn't even there to witness it firsthand. No, he's a continent away, safe and sound in California of all places, sitting at the hotel bar nursing a stiff bourbon and water after a grueling day of conference presentations.

"Shit," the young bartender mutters, and Richard looks up from his drink to see the kid gazing at the television screen mounted high above the top-shelf liquor—top shelf, in this modest hotel, being Jack Daniel's.

"What's going on?" Richard squints at the

blurry montage of images and captions. Only one is discernable: the enormous, distinctive "Breaking News" graphic.

Back in the old days, before the ubiquitous cable news crawls and headline-generating reality TV–star scandals, a special report might have generated serious notice among the cluster of people seated at the hotel bar. But tonight, after a cursory glance, most go back to their conversations. Only the bartender is watching the TV, and now—because unlike the others, he's sitting alone—so is Richard.

Too bad he can't see a damned thing, having stopped in his room to take out his contact lenses before coming down to the bar. He's been wearing them only a few weeks and hasn't gotten used to them yet.

Terribly nearsighted, for years he'd resisted contacts. But it's hard enough to reenter the dating scene after divorcing your high school sweetheart at forty-two. He'd figured out pretty quickly that most single women aren't interested in a bespectacled, asthmatic, perpetually penniless seismologist.

Not that they're any more interested in an asthmatic, perpetually penniless seismologist in contact lenses.

"Earthquake," the bartender informs Richard as he peers at the TV screen. "Major one."

"Where?"

"Near Boston."

"What?"

"Yo, that shit is messed up, right? Whoever heard of an earthquake there?"

"There was an estimated 7.0 quake in New Hampshire in 1638, a 6.2 off Cape Ann in 1755," Richard rattles off, "a 7.2 off the southern coast of Newfoundland in 1929, and a—"

"Yeah? How do you know? Were you there?"

Ignoring the bartender's smirk, Richard says simply, "It's my life's work."

He's spent over twenty years analyzing historical seismic activity in the Northeast—and the better part of the last decade warning public officials, private administrators, the media. He told anyone who would listen that the aging infrastructure of most New England cities, along with modern coastal construction built on landfill, simply could not withstand a quake of the magnitude seen in 1755. And that the area was long overdue for another.

Convinced that a series of minor recent tremors were actually foreshocks, he'd even created a seismic hazard map of the most vulnerable South Shore zones, indicating private homes and municipal buildings that were at risk.

Now that the inevitable has come to pass, are any of them left standing?

And oh, dear Lord . . .

Sondra.

Richard fumbles for his cell phone in the pocket of his tweed blazer. It starts ringing before his hand even closes around it.

"Hello?"

"Go ahead and say it," his ex-wife greets him, and he's so relieved to hear her voice that it takes him a second to regroup and address her greeting.

"Go ahead and say what?"

" 'I told you so.' Seriously, go ahead."

Any other time, he'd be tempted to say it . . . about a lot of things.

But right now, he's just glad to know she's alive. They may be divorced—which wasn't his idea— but he still cares about her. Probably more than he should, considering all the nasty things she's done.

But as his late mother liked to tell him, no one is all good or all evil. There's a little of both in everyone.

"Even you?" he'd asked, unable to fathom even a hint of evil in his sainted mother.

"Even me."

If there was, he never glimpsed it. But he saw plenty of Sondra's evil side these last few years— and it got the better of their marriage.

"Are you okay?" he asks her now.

"I am, but . . . it was so scary. Buildings are collapsed everywhere, Rich."

"Around you?"

"No, over toward Bridgebury."

Bridgebury. Pretty much ground zero on Richard's "map of doom," as one reporter had referred to the document he'd made public time and again.

"The power is out here so my sister is following it on the news in Vermont," Sondra tells him, "and she's been texting me updates. She said there are fires, too."

"Broken gas lines. Don't light any matches until you know—"

"Too late. I had to light a candle. I couldn't find the big flashlight. But don't worry, the house is still standing, in case you were wondering."

He was—but does it even matter? The house,

a vintage Cape in Taunton, is all Sondra's now, along with half his pension. He got the big flashlight, though. Terrific.

He also got a third floor walk-up in Quincy—hardly the "bachelor pad" of his dreams.

"Where were you when it happened?" he asks his ex-wife.

"Sleeping. It woke me up."

Right. It's past midnight on the East Coast. All those people sound asleep in houses, hospitals and nursing homes, prisons . . .

How many, Richard wonders, have been crushed to death in their beds?

Lush snowflakes fall through jagged holes in what's left of the prison roof, dusting her gray-streaked hair and making her shiver despite the blanket wrapped around her shoulders.

Still clutching her Bible, she picks her way around a heap of bricks and over yet another half-buried, bloody body in an orange jumpsuit.

So many of them, dead . . .

But you've survived. You are the chosen one, a prophet.

Freedom is so close—just a few more yards, and she'll have made it past the ruins that mark the outermost wall of the collapsed prison.

Hearing a groan, she looks around to see a guard, one she knows all too well. He works the perimeter of the prison and was the first, though not the last, to rape her. When it started, she was still pretty, still slender, still naïve enough to believe the abuse would stop if she lost her looks and her figure.

It didn't.

The only saving grace was that she couldn't get pregnant. She'd known for years that it was medically impossible for her to bear a child.

The guard is lying on the ground in what used to be the prison yard, his arm pinned beneath a boulder-sized chunk of masonry. Face contorted in agony, he writhes in a futile effort to free himself.

"Please," he begs her. "Please help me."

Stepping closer, she regards the situation, wondering what to do.

Ah, Deuteronomy: *I will render vengeance to mine enemies.*

She reaches toward the guard.

"Thank you." He exhales and his eyes flutter closed in anticipation of relief.

Pulling his pistol from the holster at his hip, she takes aim and fires.

Fragments of skull, flesh, and brain scatter into the drift of dust and snow at her feet.

"Thy will be done," she whispers, satisfied.

Hurrying on toward the woods behind the prison, she's about fifty yards away when she hears the deafening explosion.

Whirling around, she sees that the prison—what's left of it—is engulfed in flames.

For a long moment, she allows herself to stand and watch, a wondrous smile playing at her lips, the words of the prophet Isaiah ringing in her ears.

For, behold, the LORD will come with fire . . . to render his anger with fury, and his rebuke with flames of fire.

Then she steals into the night, clutching the gun in one hand and her Bible in the other.

CHAPTER ONE

One year later
The Ansonia, New York City

Nothing like a hot bath on a cold November night, Sylvie Durand muses, as hot water runs into the tub and the bathroom fills with the scent of Chanel bubble bath. A glass of Haut-Brion waits amid flickering white votives beside the tub, and Edith Piaf croons over the recently installed surround-sound speakers.

Music piped into the bathroom—it was the perfect birthday gift from her grandson, Jeremy, who installed the wiring in less time than Sylvie takes to put on makeup for an evening out.

"There, Mémé—now you can listen to your music while you relax in the bath. It'll be just like a spa," he told her.

He's grown into a wonderful man, Jeremy. To have overcome such tragedy in his young life . . .

He'd been given up at birth by his unwed parents, winding up in the foster care system. After several troubled placements, he was one of the lucky school-age children who found his way into a loving adoptive home. Sylvie's daughter Elsa and her husband, Brett, had their hands full—Jeremy was a troubled child—but they adored him. They were devastated when he was abducted from their backyard as a seven-year-old.

Sylvie—like the rest of the world—assumed he'd fallen victim to a child predator and would never come home again. She was right—and wrong.

She shakes her head, remembering the terrible day she'd learned that Jeremy had been murdered overseas not long after his abduction—and that his own birth father, the powerful and famously pious New York gubernatorial candidate, Garvey Quinn—was responsible.

Less than a year later, Jeremy turned up alive after all.

It was a miracle. They can happen, Sylvie has learned. But one miracle in a lifetime is more than anyone should hope for. She learned that the hard way a few years ago, when her lover Jean Paul became ill.

Humming along to "Mon Dieu," she admires her reflection in the mirror above the sink.

Just this morning at the salon on Madison Avenue, as she was leaning back in the sink chair to be washed, the new shampoo girl commented, "You know, I was expecting to see facelift scars, but you don't have any."

"Pardon?" Sylvie decided that she would never become reaccustomed to brash American manners.

Having lived in New York most of her adult life, she'd returned to her native France for over a decade after rekindling a teenage romance. Adapting to her native culture had been surprisingly easy, but the homecoming wasn't meant to be permanent. Her heart may be in Paris, but her daughter and grandchildren—not to mention her own fabulous apartment—are not.

And so, after Jean Paul passed away, Sylvie settled back in on the Upper West Side. That wasn't nearly as seamless a transition as she'd anticipated. Maybe she's simply too old to deal with change.

American culture feels foreign to her even now; she's perpetually caught off guard by this penchant for barging into strangers' lives with such audacity. Europeans tend to respect each other's privacy.

"It's just that your skin is so beautiful, and your bone structure is amazing," the shampoo girl continued, massaging Sylvie's temples, "I mean, I shouldn't be surprised—I know who you are— but I figured you must have had some work done. It seems like everyone does, especially in your business."

"Not I," Sylvie replied haughtily, though she was secretly flattered by both the praise and the recognition of her stellar career.

The shampoo girl refused to leave well enough alone. "I thought that was why you always go around wearing those hats with the little veils— to cover the scars."

Sylvie was speechless at the audacity—so much so that she couldn't point out that she's been wearing hats with blushers for decades. They were— and remain—her personal signature.

Now she turns her head from side to side, her legendary blue eyes narrowed as she studies herself in the misty mirror. Yes, the porcelain complex-

ion and facial bone structure that made her one of
the world's first supermodels have certainly with-
stood the test of time. And her hair, freshly dyed a
becoming shade of brunette, looks as natural as it
did when she was strutting the runways.

No wonder the handsome waiter mistook her
and Elsa for sisters just the other day, when they
were out to lunch with Elsa's daughter, Renny, a
student at NYU.

"Would you like to order dessert?" the waiter
asked Elsa, turning to her after Sylvie had ordered
the crème brûlée, "or shall I just bring two spoons
for your sister's?"

Sylvie—though never fond of sharing dessert—
would have gleefully gone along with it, and with
the waiter's mistaken assumption about their
relationship, had her outspoken granddaughter
not nipped it in the bud—probably because she
thought the waiter was flirting with her mom.

He might very well have been. Elsa is strikingly
beautiful even in middle age—nearly as beautiful
as Sylvie herself. But her marriage to Brett Cavalon, having weathered many a storm, is stronger
than ever.

"Actually, they're mother and daughter," Renny
promptly informed the waiter, "not sisters."

"Is that so? Well, I sure can see the family
resemblance in all three of you."

As soon as he walked away, Renny rolled her
eyes and sipped the pinot noir she'd glibly ordered
as a newly minted twenty-one-year-old. "He's so
full of crap."

Sylvie scolded, "Renny! Such language at the
table!"

"Oh, it could have been worse, Maman." Elsa grinned. "She could have said he's full of—"

"Elsa!"

Her daughter laughed, and Sylvie shook her head. *Americans.*

"I didn't mean he was full of crap because he thought you were sisters, Mémé," Renny told Sylvie, who couldn't help but be as pleased by her granddaughter's French term of endearment as she was displeased by the repetition of the offending word. "But he's all 'I see the family resemblance.' Meanwhile, I'm adopted."

"Well *I'm* not," Elsa pointed out, "and you actually look more like me, Renny, than I look like Maman."

C'est vrai, Sylvie thought. While they were adopted years apart from the foster care system, and don't share blood with their mother or each other, Elsa's grown children do resemble her *and* each other. Both Renny and Jeremy have dark eyes and dark hair. Renny's complexion is on the olive side compared to Elsa's fair skin, and Jeremy's eyes are darker than his mother and sister's, so dark they're almost black.

Ah, such a shame that Sylvie's blue eyes—which Frank Sinatra himself once told her were bluer than his own—will die with her.

But not, God willing, for a long, long time. She's feeling good, despite getting around with a cane these days: a handcrafted walking stick, imported from the century-old Fayet in France.

And yes, her cardiologist is always telling her to go easier on the butter and cream, but Sylvie has no intention of obliging. She's svelte as ever,

despite butter and cream, wine and chocolate—
all the pleasures of life, which she'll continue to
enjoy to its fullest, *merci beaucoup*.

"*Mon Dieu*," laments the great Piaf over the
bathroom speaker, and begs God to let her lover
stay with her a little bit longer.

Such a sad song. Sylvie thinks of Jean Paul as
she turns away from the fogged-over mirror. Such
a painful loss.

And yet, life goes on. She has much to look
forward to. Thanksgiving in a couple of days.
Christmas next month, and she's spending it with
friends on the Côte d'Azur.

And when she returns to New York, if all goes
well, she'll be a great-grandmother at last. Jeremy
and his wife, Lucy, are expecting.

"The kids have been through so much," Elsa
said at lunch the other day. "Will you offer a
novena that nothing goes wrong again, Maman?"

"But of course."

Lucy's two lost pregnancies—the first, a late-
term stillbirth—were a lot to bear. God willing,
there won't be a third. Sylvie, who attends daily
Mass at Holy Trinity, is a strong believer in the
power of prayer, as is her granddaughter-in-law.

Sylvie is impressed by Lucy's unshaken convic-
tion that she will be blessed with a child.

After all she's been through—the tragedy that
marked her childhood, and the heartbreaking
miscarriages—she's been remarkably resilient.

A woman like Lucy can survive anything. Sylvie just hopes she won't be tested again in the
months ahead.

Poking a fingertip through the frothy layer of

bubbles into the steaming tub, she decides the water temperature is just right. She turns off the tap, fits a shower cap snuggly over her fresh coiffure, and uses the sleeve of her robe to wipe a small window into the mirror.

Checking her reflection to ensure that her hair is neatly tucked beneath the shower cap, she glimpses a flutter of movement reflected in the filmy glass. Frowning, she wipes a wider swath.

Reflected in the mirror, a robed, hooded figure stands behind her.

The sight is so shockingly out of place that Sylvie blinks, certain it's a trick of the light.

Slowly, she turns.

She isn't alone.

The cloaked intruder swoops upon her, hands outstretched—ominously wearing rubber gloves, Sylvie realizes in horror.

"Mon Dieu!" Edith Piaf sings, reaching the crescendo as the gloved hands push Sylvie down, down, into the full bathtub. She thrashes and gasps, sucking hot water into her lungs.

I can't breathe . . . I can't breathe . . .

Panicked, she struggles futilely to free herself from the strong hands that hold her face submerged.

Drowning . . . I'm drowning . . . Mon Dieu . . . Mon Dieu . . .

Climbing the stairway to her second floor apartment, Lucy Walsh Cavalon—who not so long ago regularly ran the New York Marathon—is pretty sure she's about to collapse from sheer exhaustion.

"Stay strong, Lucy—stay strong!" her father used to shout from the sidelines when she was on the middle school track team.

Stay strong, she's been telling herself for the last twenty minutes. *Stay strong.*

But her fatigue isn't due to running—or even walking, really, despite the five blocks she briskly covered from her office to Grand Central and three more blocks from the train station home.

No, what did her in was standing on her feet in the aisle of an overheated train for the duration of the forty-minute commute from midtown Manhattan to Westchester County.

It's a Wednesday—matinee day on Broadway, when the Metro North trains are crowded with the usual commuters plus chatty suburbanites clutching theater *Playbill*s. Lucy can always find a seat anyway, if she leaves the office with enough time to spare.

Being super-organized, that's something she manages to do most nights without any problem.

But this was one of those frustrating days when nothing was within her realm of control: the phone kept ringing and e-mail kept popping up and she was running late. The train, extra-jammed with matinee-goers, was standing room only. And no one, not even the retirees who can usually be counted on for more gentlemanly behavior than their thirty- and fortysomething counterparts, offered to give up a seat for Lucy.

You'd think someone would have noticed that I was pregnant and on the verge of keeling over.

Then again, if anyone knows better than to count on the kindness of strangers, it's Lucy. You have to take care of yourself out there, because nobody else will.

The thing is, I'm not just trying to take care of myself. I have a baby to protect now. Again.

Please, God, let this baby be born. Please . . .

She crosses herself and says a quick prayer.

Ever since a pregnancy test confirmed the new life she's carrying, she's felt terrifyingly fragile—not that she'd confess that to anyone, even her husband. Jeremy is worried enough for both of them. She reassures him every chance she gets.

Yet it's unsettling for a woman who's always prided herself on being in control of her own fate to accept that that really isn't the case.

"God is in control," Father Les, her parish priest in Westchester, counseled her after her last miscarriage. "We can't question why bad things happen. We can only accept that they do, and trust in God's plan for us."

She's been trying to do that. She really has. Trying to grasp that motherhood might not be a part of God's plan for her.

But it might be. Please, let it be.

She was reluctant to even tell anyone about the pregnancy this time. Her mother, her brother and sister, her in-laws, her best friend—none of them knew until the first trimester was safely past.

Safe? There's no such thing as safe. Not until you're holding a healthy newborn in your arms.

The first time she was pregnant, Lucy carried all the way into her sixth month before she started bleeding.

Blood . . . all that blood.

She shudders, forcing the memory from her

thoughts, having trained herself long ago to fixate on future dreams, not past nightmares. She's
safely past the six-month mark now.

It doesn't mean nothing can go wrong. It just
means the baby is getting stronger and stronger.
Some babies born at this premature stage survive.

Aching and yawning, she trudges up the last
few steps, wishing she could just crawl into bed
and not set the alarm.

Maybe she really should, as her husband keeps
urging, consider taking an early leave from her job
as a network administrator. Between the stress-
ful commute, and the regular pressures of corporate America, and dealing with the daily chaos in
Manhattan—which will be more crowded than
ever with the holiday season upon them . . .

"But what if they decide I'm on the mommy
track and get rid of me altogether? We count on
my salary," she points out whenever Jeremy starts
down that road.

"We can get by on mine."

Not really. He's a youth counselor at a group
home in the Bronx. Overworked, underpaid.

"Or we can borrow money from my parents if
we need to," he suggests.

Maybe, but Lucy's in-laws aren't exactly rolling
in dough. While the Cavalons won a sizable damages settlement years ago, what isn't being held in
trust for Renny was lost in a series of bad invest-
ments, or used for living expenses back when
Brett was forced into early retirement from his
nautical engineering job.

"Let's just see how it goes," Lucy keeps telling
Jeremy. "Plenty of women work through preg-

nancy with no problem. And it's not like I'm slaving away in a factory or something. All I do is sit at a desk . . ."

. . . for eight hours a day troubleshooting with frustrated employees whose computer systems aren't working the way they're supposed to . . .

Still, she's really good at what she does, makes decent money with good medical benefits, her job is stable, and she generally works a regular forty-hour week. Things could be a lot worse.

I just have to stick it out until maternity leave.

Please, God, let me get to that point this time.

Statistically, the odds are stacked against her carrying a baby to term after multiple miscarriages. Still, at twenty-nine, she's relatively young. Her obstetrician told her to be hopeful—and extra-careful.

Thank goodness for the long Thanksgiving weekend coming up next week. Her old, hyper-industrious, nonpregnant self would have seized the opportunity to take a trip, or get things done around the house. But aside from eating turkey at her mother's house a few miles away, all she plans on doing from Wednesday night until the following Monday morning is sleeping. She's pretty sure Jeremy won't mind. It'll give him a break from constantly telling her to sit down and take a break.

An envelope is taped to their apartment door at the top of the stairs. Plucking it off as she stomps the slush from her boots, Lucy sees that it's addressed to *Mr. and Mrs. Jeremy Cavalon* in handwriting she doesn't recognize.

Odd.

The building, a duplex, is kept locked. No one

should be able to get in here other than the first floor neighbors, or—

Carl Soto?

Having torn open the envelope and spotted the landlord's signature, Lucy quickly skims the typewritten page. Her eyes widen in dismay.

This can't be right . . . can it?

Rereading, she sees that it is, indeed, an eviction notice giving her and Jeremy just thirty days to vacate the apartment. That's it. No further explanation.

So much for sleeping, Lucy thinks grimly, resting a hand on her rounded stomach.

When it's over, Sylvie Durand's limp body, now stripped of the white bathrobe, lies facedown in the bathtub, partially obscured by a foamy drift of perfumed bubbles. The wineglass sits undisturbed, the candles remain aglow, and Edith Piaf croons a new song.

"Thy will be done." With a satisfied nod, still wearing the surgical gloves, she swiftly takes off her hooded cloak, soaked in the struggle. After hanging it on a hook beside Sylvie's dripping robe, she picks up the thick white bath towel Sylvie had lain out on the heated towel bar.

The label is familiar—Le Jacquard Français.

Long ago—before she'd been condemned to using thin, scratchy prison-issue towels—she herself had lived in a grand home whose marble bathrooms were stocked with fine European linens.

Now that home—and everything in it—belongs to someone else.

Not, however, to the Cavalons. It was sold before they won a sizable portion of her family's assets in the damages settlement.

Back when that happened, her attorney, Andrew Stafford, relayed the news gingerly, as though he thought she might explode in anger or grief at the news that Jeremy Cavalon and his adoptive family had been awarded what should rightfully have belonged to her.

She didn't explode. She clenched her handcuffed fists so hard her nails drew blood from her palms. But of course, Andrew couldn't see her hands. He could only see her face, and she was an expert at masking her emotions. She remained as stoic as she had the day Andrew told her that Jeremy had married Lucy Walsh.

Yes, Jeremy and Lucy were still out there in the world, living their lives, while she was caged like an animal.

Every time she allowed herself to think of them, helpless rage would well up inside her. She knew then—as she knows now—that there is nothing to do about it but wait for Judgment Day, when Jeremy and Lucy—and the others, too—will get what they deserve. Yes, justice at the hands of the Almighty upon his return to earth.

The earthquake heralded the beginning of the end, the imminent arrival of the Messiah. Now Judgment Day is almost upon them, and she—as a prophet, and a true believer—will be rewarded at last.

She surveys Sylvie Durand's waterlogged corpse. Having made good and sure to slam the woman's head hard against the edge of the tub, she's not worried about anyone suspecting foul play.

An elderly woman, living alone, slips getting into the bathtub, bangs her head, is knocked unconscious, and drowns. A terrible accident, the medical examiner will conclude. But the kind that happens every day.

Pooled water on the floor and spatters on the walls and mirror are the only signs of a struggle. She easily obliterates them with the thick, absorbent towel. After draping it over the hook with the other soggy things, she opens a linen closet.

The shelves are stacked with neatly folded white towels identical to the soggy one. That's how it is in wealthy households like Sylvie's—and her own, long ago: everything belongs to a luxurious linen set, no mix-and-match.

With her gloved fingers, she lifts a towel from the top of the nearest pile and drapes it over the heated towel bar. Then she rolls the wet things into a tight bundle and tucks it beneath her arm.

Better to risk taking the bathrobe and towel than to arouse suspicion should someone show up here unexpectedly and discover the wet evidence. Surely the Cavalons will be too caught up in grief and shock to notice anything is missing.

After taking one last look around the bathroom, she slips out and closes the door behind her.

CHAPTER
TWO

"Wow—how many more boxes *are* there?" Lucy asks, holding the door open for Jeremy as he lugs two more heavy-looking cartons into the apartment.

"Trust me, you don't want to know."

He's right. She doesn't. It'll only make her feel even more guilty.

She watches him heave the boxes onto the polished herringbone wood floor beside stacks of others. "I wish I could help you."

"Don't even think about it." He brushes a hand over the raindrops beaded on his close-cropped dark hair. "You know what Dr. Courmier said."

He's talking about her new OB-GYN, who specializes in high-risk pregnancies. Her former doctor referred her after the second miscarriage.

"Dr. Courmier has said a lot of things," she points out to Jeremy.

"Including 'no heavy lifting till the baby comes.' "

Yes. She knows.

She knows what could happen if she disobeys; knows only too well what might very well happen anyway.

Yet Lucy has never been the kind of person who sits by watching as someone else takes care of things. She can't help but feel guilty that Jeremy's literally had to shoulder the weight of this forced move from Westchester down to his late grandmother's apartment on the Upper West Side—in a miserable December downpour, no less.

She wishes they could have afforded to hire movers, but their finances are pretty dire this month, especially with the holidays looming next week.

Luckily, her Christmas shopping is done—and has been for months now, one of the perks that come with being hyperorganized. She buys things on sale, wraps them, labels them, and puts them away until the holidays.

If that weren't the case, she and Jeremy probably wouldn't be exchanging gifts with each other or anyone else this year, given their bank account balance.

She really hopes they'll be able to save some money, living here for a while. It would be nice to catch up on the bills before the baby comes.

Seeing Jeremy start toward the door again, she says, "Why don't you at least wait until my brother gets out of work? He said he'd come over and help."

"Nah, that's okay."

"His office is right off Columbus Circle."

"Yeah, but—"

"It's only two subway stops away, and—"

"I *know* where he works!" he snaps, and Lucy clamps her mouth shut.

Sometimes, especially when he's tired, Jeremy lashes out unreasonably.

Okay. So he's only human. She does the same thing herself. Who doesn't?

Still . . .

Somewhere in the back of her mind, there's always a shred of a reminder that her husband once had anger issues so severe that twice he'd nearly taken a life with his bare hands.

La La Montgomery's life.

Both times, in fact.

The first time, they were both children—Jeremy newly adopted out of foster care and adjusting to life with the Cavalons. The incident happened at the country club where he was taking junior golf lessons. Apparently, La La—a spoiled Daddy's girl—was teasing Jeremy, and he snapped, swinging his club at her, striking her in the face and head.

La La was rushed to the hospital, stabilized, and intubated—a medical necessity that helped save her life, but tragically, her voice would never be the same. Once a gifted vocalist who had dreamed of growing up to be a star, little La La would never sing again. Thankfully, reconstructive surgery gave her a nose, cheekbones, a jaw. A whole new face— just as Jeremy bought himself a new face after he fled California, not long before he found his way back into La La's world. Into her arms. Her bed . . .

That's ancient history, Lucy reminds herself. She can't bear to think of the two of them together any more than she can bear to think about the way it ended—with Jeremy inflicting an attack that was strikingly similar to the first one.

But that was strictly a heroic effort to save his sister's life after La La went crazy and tried to kill them both.

Crazy—now *there's* a loaded word.

There are so many ways—so many reasons—a person can become lost in the haze of madness. He can inherit mental illness from a family member, as Garvey Quinn reportedly did from his grandmother. He—she—can suffer damage to the frontal lobe of the brain, as La La Montgomery probably did when Jeremy struck her with the golf club thirty years ago. A person can lose touch with reality in the wake of a trauma, like poor Elsa Cavalon, years ago after Jeremy was kidnapped. Or a person can self-medicate to take away the pain and get caught up in the madness of addiction, like—

No. Don't think about her. *That was just too awful.*

Really, it's miraculous that anyone in Lucy's world has managed to stay sane in the wake of all that's happened to them over the years.

"How can one family survive so much pain?" Lucy's friend Robyn once asked her.

She just shrugged and said, "Look at the Kennedys."

"That's your answer? 'Look at the Kennedys'? C'mon, Lucy."

"What do you want me to say? What do you want me to *do*—go around wallowing in misery?"

"You have every right to wallow. Trust me, if I were you, I'd be wallowing. Most people would."

Maybe. But Lucy doesn't wallow. She just tries not to dwell on it. Any of it. So much pain . . .

Right now, back to his sweet, gentle self, Jeremy jangles his key chain. "Listen, the U-Haul is double-parked, and I need to get it back up to White Plains before rush hour. Anyway, I don't want to bug Ryan—he's got enough going on right now between the new job and the new girlfriend."

Lucy's brother has fallen head over heels in love—pretty much overnight.

"I really think she's The One," he told Lucy.

"How can you say that about someone you've only known for a few weeks, Ry?" she asked, worried that Ryan, who had never been in a serious relationship, was jumping into this one too quickly and headed for heartbreak.

"Well, we all can't be lucky enough to fall in love with someone we've known forever, the way you did."

"I haven't known Jeremy forever."

"You met him when you were fourteen, so—"

"I was *fifteen*."

"Sorry, you're right. That makes a *huge* difference."

Lucy rolled her eyes, feeling as though she and Ryan were kids again, bickering about some stupid thing that didn't even matter.

But this *does* matter. Not only is Ryan finally involved with someone, but he hasn't introduced her to the family yet.

"Thanks, but no thanks," Ryan said when he turned down Lucy's invitation to bring his girlfriend over for dinner. "Maybe over the holidays."

"It'll just be me and you and Jeremy on Christmas Eve this year," she reminded him.

It's been her tradition to host a seafood dinner for her family before they all go to midnight Mass. But right after Thanksgiving, her mother and stepfather—Sam was newly retired—headed to a condo in Florida. They're planning to stay through January. Lucy's sister, Sadie, and Sam's son, Max, both away at college, will be joining them there for the holidays.

It's Lucy's first Christmas apart from them all, though she and Jeremy will, as always, drive to New England to spend Christmas Day with his parents and Renny. And then there's Ryan . . .

"You *are* planning to come here on Christmas Eve, right?"

"I'm not sure yet."

"What do you mean?" It's bad enough that the rest of her family has bailed on the holiday this year. "I'm inviting both you and Phoenix," she said, "if that's what this is about."

"Thanks. I'll have to let you know."

Lucy figures Ryan must be putting off the introduction to his girlfriend because he thinks Lucy will find fault with her.

"Well, I'm sure you will," Jeremy said mildly, when she mentioned that theory to him. "I mean, you already had an issue with her name."

"Phoenix? All I said was 'What kind of name is that?'"

"Okay. But let's face it, you can be a little hard on people—and so can your mom and Sadie."

"It's not that we're hard on people. We're just slow to trust anyone new. Can you blame us?"

Of course he can't—he's the same way. After what they've been through—all of them, including Jeremy—it's a miracle they've managed to live relatively normal lives over the past decade and a half.

When Lucy was fourteen, her father, Nick, left her mother for another woman. Then he became entangled in a lethal web spun by politician Garvey Quinn, who engineered the murders of Nick Walsh and his mistress, and the abduction of Lucy and her siblings. Fortunately, they were quickly rescued.

Not so for Jeremy, whose fateful connection to Garvey Quinn resulted in his own kidnapping as a child. He was left for dead overseas, "rescued" by a pedophile, and kept isolated in California until he was twenty-one. That was when the man Jeremy knew as "Papa" died, and he found his way home at last.

No—not *home*. First to La La Montgomery, the victim of his childhood attack. She forgave him, seduced him, then obsessively began hunting down anyone she believed had wronged Jeremy in childhood, blaming them all for his act of violence that had destroyed her vocal cords.

Lucy met him shortly afterward, as he was coming to terms with finding that he had not just one family, but two: the Cavalons and the Quinns.

Lucy never thinks of the latter without a pang of regret. The Quinns, more than anyone else, lived a charmed life before Garvey's unthinkable crimes came to light. And look what happened to them afterward, one by one . . .

There but for the grace of God, Lucy thinks whenever Marin Quinn and her daughters, Caroline and Annie, come to mind.

Lucy met the girls only once, years ago. It was Mom's brilliant idea that they should all get together for a mother-daughter lunch in Manhattan: Lauren with Lucy and Sadie, Marin with Caroline and Annie, and Elsa with Renny.

"Why doesn't Ryan have to go?" Lucy remembers grumbling when she found out about it. That was during one of her adolescent rebellious stages—which, by contrast to what Mom later went through with Sadie, weren't very rebellious at all.

"Ryan would feel out of place with all those girls. Sam is taking him fishing."

That was a disaster, as it turned out. Fishing was something Ryan and Dad used to do together. He resented his mother's then-boyfriend trying to take his father's place, and he let Sam know it.

The girls' lunch was also pretty much a disaster. Mom had reserved a tatami—one of those small private dining rooms—at a Japanese restaurant. That didn't go over well with Renny, who was claustrophobic. She melted down in a panic attack, and they had to leave early. Sadie wanted to follow her lead, but Mom insisted that they stay.

Annie Quinn, the younger of the two sisters, was sweet and shy—and allergic to pretty much everything on the menu. She was overweight, and self-conscious about that, Lucy could tell. Later, Marin told Mom that food was Annie's drug of choice.

Famous last words, Lucy would think years later, in retrospect.

And then there was Caroline.

Lucy expected to relate to her in a fellow-big-sister way, but she was a difficult person to know—much less like.

A spoiled Daddy's girl who had been spectacularly deserted by her father—though Garvey would never have left her willingly—Caroline was alternately prickly and withdrawn that day at lunch. It was obvious that she blamed her mother for what had happened to them—which made little sense to Lucy—but it was Caroline's contempt toward her younger sister that Lucy found hardest to take.

By then, thanks to the press, she—along with everyone else in the world—knew that Annie had been conceived as a savior sibling for her critically ill sister, but rejected by Garvey when in utero testing showed she wasn't a match.

Caroline had grown up mirroring her father's indifference toward Annie, and it turned into blatant resentment after their lives fell apart.

Fiercely protective of her own younger siblings, Lucy tried to give Caroline the benefit of the doubt. Who knew—maybe she'd have behaved the same way in Caroline's shoes. She had been through so much . . .

But by the time that disastrous lunch date was over, Lucy knew she didn't want to spend any more time with Caroline Quinn. Luckily, Mom was of the same mindset. And anyway, both Quinn girls went away to boarding school that fall, and after that, to distant colleges. They rarely came home. Who could blame them?

Marin still came around, though, to visit the Walshes. With Jeremy.

Lucy had a tender spot for Jeremy, as did her mother, and he gradually became a fixture in their household. Six years older than Lucy, darkly handsome with haunted eyes, he had a lot of pain to work through—but then, so did she.

He was like a big brother as she navigated her high school years. They were both in therapy, trying to work through the past—though Jeremy's issues were far more complex than her own.

They stayed in touch by e-mail and phone when they simultaneously attended college—a hundred and fifty miles apart, with different majors and circles of friends. Already in his mid-twenties by then, Jeremy stayed in New York, tending to his mother, attending Hunter College, earning undergrad and graduate degrees in social work.

Lucy went to Rensselaer Polytech and stayed there through graduate school, emerging with a master's in computer science, summa cum laude. She returned to the city to start working, and somewhere along the way, realized she had fallen in love with Jeremy.

Now, he pauses on his way to the door to rest a hand on her belly. "How are you feeling, Goose?"

Goose: his longtime nickname for her, evolved from the distressingly unromantic—at least, in her teenage opinion—Lucy Goosey.

But it grew on her—just as Jeremy did.

"I'm feeling great," she tells him.

"I thought you were nauseous."

"I am—I feel like I could vomit any second." Though her morning sickness had subsided after the first trimester, she's been feeling queasy again lately.

Jeremy raises an eyebrow. "Wow, vomit. That *is* great."

"It's a good sign. It means the pregnancy is going strong."

Jeremy, who had cried with her when she started spotting last time—and the time before—and held her hand when the doctor confirmed both miscarriages, says nothing, just kisses her on the cheek.

"You're sweet," she tells him, and he wraps her in his arms and nuzzles her neck.

"How about if we go christen our new bedroom?"

"Right now? I'm nauseous, and you're in the middle of unloading a truck, remember?"

"Yeah, yeah. Later, though. Tonight."

"Maybe, if I can stay awake long enough."

"I've got a brilliant idea—why don't you take a nap? I'll leave the door to the hall propped open while I go down for another load so you don't have to get up and let me in."

She grins. "A nap doesn't guarantee I'll be able to stay awake later."

"Yeah, well, no nap pretty much guarantees you won't, so . . . you just go rest and nest, Goose Girl." He disappears into the hall.

Lucy gladly leaves the circular foyer, with its crystal chandelier, seventeenth-century paintings, wall-sized gilt-framed mirror, and French Classical Baroque chairs.

The large oval living room, too, looks more like a palace than a starter home, cluttered with Jeremy's late grandmother's gilt and marble Louis XIV furniture, velvet upholstery, and tasseled draperies.

What Lucy wouldn't give to swap out the fancy furniture for some shabby-chic Pottery Barn stuff.

But the move isn't permanent. Even if they were in love with the sprawling, old-fashioned place—which they are not—they'd never be able to afford it.

Made up of several flats that were combined

over the years as the original tenants moved out, this is one of the largest apartments in the historic Ansonia, and worth a fortune. Elsa would probably already have it on the market, had her mother's sudden death not coincided with Lucy and Jeremy unexpectedly finding themselves evicted from their Westchester duplex.

The timing couldn't have been worse—or better, depending on how one looks at it.

Certainly, Sylvie's death was disturbing. She hadn't been getting any younger, but she was hardly a frail old lady, either. No one expected her to drop dead out of the blue, the victim of a tragic accidental fall and drowning in her own bathtub.

In one of life's cosmic coincidences, it happened just as Lucy and Jeremy learned they'd have to move. While they're not thrilled about moving into the apartment where poor old Sylvie Durand died in a tragic fall, this is the least complicated solution to their immediate housing dilemma. The place is all theirs, rent-free—for the time being, anyway.

Lucy just wishes she knew why Carl Soto had kicked them out of their apartment in the first place. Unfortunately, the lease revealed that he was well within his rights as a landlord, and he had no legal obligation to explain, though of course Jeremy left him a couple of messages about it. He didn't bother to return the calls. *Coward.*

Well, he'd better return their security deposit now that they're out. They're counting on that money to help pay for extra expenses they've had the last few weeks: the truck rental, Christmas, doctor visit co-pays and prenatal vitamins, the flowers and a decent black suit for Jeremy for his grandmother's funeral . . .

"I have a suit," he'd said, as Lucy stood beside him in front of his open closet door the morning of the wake, shaking her head.

"It's old and gray and completely out of style. Sylvie would roll over in her grave if you wore that to her funeral."

They both smiled at that, knowing it was true, and he agreed to get something nice.

Lucy plops down on the couch—as much as one can "plop" onto a Louis XIV sofa—and reaches for the cup of tea with lemon that waits atop a coaster on the marble-topped coffee table.

Situated on a far-flung wing of the H-shaped building, this place is so still compared to their former second floor apartment on a busy Westchester thoroughfare. There are plenty of windows—many embellished by the building's trademark wrought-iron Juliet balconies beyond the glass. And yet, high above Broadway, insulated by century-old stone and plaster, these rooms are known as being virtually soundproof. Even with the door open, there's not a hint of sound from the building's carpeted corridors.

Lulled by the silence, Lucy leans her head back with a yawn.

Is it a good sign that she's even more tired now than she was in past pregnancies? Does it, like the morning sickness, mean the hormones are stronger this time around?

Oh, come on—who isn't *tired in the middle of a major move?*

She still can't quite believe that they're living in the cold, impersonal city, the last place she really wanted to start a family. Having grown up in a suburban house with a big backyard and neighbors and friends she'd known all her life, she wants the same thing for her own child.

But it makes sense to eliminate the long commute, and to live close to Dr. Courmier's office—and to New York–Presbyterian Hospital, where she'll be delivering the baby if all goes well. She and Jeremy are already enrolled in a childbirth preparation class there after the holidays.

Plus, as long as they can live here rent-free for a while, they'll be that much closer to saving a down payment on their future house in the suburbs.

That's what they both want: picket fence and all. A normal life, the kind Lucy had until she turned fourteen and her father moved out. The kind Jeremy experienced fleetingly with Elsa and Brett before he was snatched away.

Normal life. You can strive for it, you can actually achieve it, but even then, there are no guarantees.

Lucy closes her eyes. The baby gives her stomach a hard kick, and she smiles.

Please, please, please God . . . let this baby be born . . .

Suddenly, the silence is broken by a sound in the front hall.

"Wow," Lucy calls out, "that was quick!"

No reply.

She must have been mistaken. Or dreaming—had she fallen asleep?

Maybe. It's so peaceful here.

Then she hears a floorboard creak, and her eyes snap open. "Jeremy?"

Silence.

Frowning, she stands and returns to the circular entryway. The door to the hall is still propped open, but there's no sign of Jeremy.

Hmm. Maybe pregnancy is doing strange things to her hearing, as well.

About to head back to the couch, she spots a foil-wrapped plate sitting on the welcome mat and bends to pick it up.

Christmas cookies, she sees, taking a peek. Sugar-sprinkled cutouts in various shapes that represent the Nativity: a star, a lamb, a manger, a stable . . .

The plate is warm. No note or card, though, and she's positive she didn't hear a knock or a voice announcing a visitor.

"Hello?" Sticking her head out the door, she expects to see a neighbor heading back down the hall, but it's empty. Whoever it was seems to have just dropped off the plate and run away.

Oh well. A home-baked treat fresh from the oven—it was a sweet, welcoming gesture from someone, and Lucy is sure she'll eventually find out whom.

Maybe the city isn't so cold and impersonal after all, she decides, thoughtfully biting into a cookie.

Carl Soto's footsteps echo on the hardwood floor as he walks back through the empty apartment, having concluded that he's satisfied with the way the tenants left it and he can return their security deposit. Good. One less thing to worry about.

He'd been concerned that they might trash the place before leaving. A young married couple, they didn't seem like the type, but hey, you never know. Especially under the circumstances.

Evicting the Cavalons hadn't been easy—wait, that's wrong. It *had been* easy. Frightfully easy. All it took was a letter, drafted off a template downloaded from the Internet. He hadn't even owed them an explanation, according to the terms of the lease.

Good thing, because the only one he had probably wouldn't have sat well with them.

But what would they—or anyone—have done, in his shoes? It's hard to say no when you're flat broke and someone's waving a fistful of cash at you. Even if it's a total stranger who came out of nowhere with a bizarre request.

"Are you Carl Soto?" she'd asked, stepping out of the shadows that cold autumn night as he left his latest night job at the gas station.

"Yeah. Do I know you?" He peered into the darkness, trying to make out her features. He thought she might be a hooker, though they didn't usually frequent this particular stretch of Westchester Avenue. Besides, a hooker—though he'd met his share—wouldn't know his name. And even on a frigid winter night, a hooker wouldn't be bundled from head to toe in some kind of flowing, hooded garment.

"No, you don't know me," she said. "But I need a favor from you."

When she reached into the folds of her cloak,

he braced himself, figuring she was going for a weapon, about to mug him.

Ha—quite the opposite.

She pulled out a thick stack of bills. Hundred-dollar bills, he saw, when she rifled them in front of his nose.

He instantly lost interest in figuring out what she looked like, forgot about the cold and how tired he was, about his hands that stunk like gasoline, about how much he hated having had to take a second job to make ends meet . . .

"I'm guessing you might be able to use some spare cash," she said, and though he couldn't see her face, he heard the smile in her voice. It unsettled him, but he was too mesmerized by the money in her hand to care that she might be a little . . . *off.*

"Who can't use spare cash?"

"Thought so. This is yours if you let me move into your apartment over on Post Road. The upstairs apartment."

Somewhere in the back of his mind, he knew this had to be some kind of scam. Or maybe a practical joke. His friend Lee was always playing them. Lee, who had told him he was nuts to have bought the old building as an investment property almost ten years ago.

"That old place is going to need endless maintenance, Carl," Lee had said. "It's going to suck you dry."

Lee was right about that. Carl would have sold it long ago, if anyone had been buying in this market.

As Lee pointed out, "Who'd want to live in that old place when they're putting up all kinds of brand-new high-rise condos downtown? You'll be lucky if you can get decent tenants."

He was right about that, too. But those high-rise buildings were expensive; the rent on Carl's place was right in line with the young married couple's budget and in walking distance to the Metro North train station. They'd lived in the apartment for almost a year; it had been vacant for well over a year before that.

And now he was supposed to believe that people were coming up to him on the street throwing money at him and begging to live there?

Something snapped inside him as he stared at that wad of money. He was no fool.

"Too bad, you're outta luck," Carl told the cloaked stranger, expecting his friend Lee to jump out at them any second, laughing at his stupid joke. "Someone's already living there."

"I'm serious, Carl."

"I'm serious, too. Someone's living there."

"Ask them to leave. I need to move in within the month."

"*What?*"

"You heard me."

He hesitated, gazed longingly at the money, then at the bushes at the edge of the parking lot. There was no sign of Lee. And she really did sound like she meant business.

"Who are you? And why—"

"My name is Mary. Look, I'll pay you double what you're getting for rent on the apartment for a year. Up front. In cash."

"But . . . why?"

"Sentimental reasons. I lived there when I was a little girl. I'll give you an extra five right here on the spot for keeping your mouth shut. You can't tell anyone about this."

"Five bucks?"

"Five hundred." She peeled off five bills and held them out to him.

"You want me to believe that you're going to just hand me five hundred dollars right here if I get rid of my tenants and let you move into my apartment."

"Exactly."

"But . . . why?"

"I told you."

Yeah, she lived there as a kid. So what? Sentimentality is worth thousands of dollars?

Even now, weeks later—with the five hundred bucks long since spent, and a hefty cash deposit in hand once he'd delivered the eviction notice—he doesn't quite believe her.

Oh well. Does it matter?

He'd been able to quit his night job, pay off some bills, even bought a plane ticket to fly down to North Carolina for his oldest granddaughter's First Communion in May.

Who says money can't buy happiness?

Hell, enough money can buy just about anything, Carl Soto muses, stepping out into the hall and locking the apartment door securely. Anything at all.

After wearily depositing the final damp cardboard box with the others, Jeremy finds Lucy in the living room, thumb-typing on her phone's keypad. Wearing jeans and one of his old chambray shirts with the sleeves rolled up, she's sitting with her sneakered feet tucked beneath her, heedless of the upholstery. Effortlessly pretty, with her long brown hair held back in a simple ponytail, Lucy looks about a decade younger than she is, fresh-faced and carefree.

Carefree . . . If only that were really the case.

She looks up expectantly from her phone. "Well? Is that everything?"

"Yeah, the truck is empty. Finally."

"Good." She pats the seat beside her and he sinks into the sofa.

"Do me a favor and shoot me if I ever threaten to buy another book. What I just moved could stock an entire library."

"It wasn't just books."

"No . . . but there were a lot of them. And they weigh a ton."

"We probably should have just put them into storage with our furniture. It's not like we'll have much time to read once . . ." She trails off momentarily before concluding, ". . . once we're not taking the train to work anymore."

That isn't what she originally intended to say, Jeremy knows.

Once the baby comes was probably more like it, but Lucy doesn't like to talk about that.

So different from her first pregnancy, when all they did was speculate about their future child, and what parenthood would be like.

Even the second time, they were optimistic—if cautiously so.

But now, it's as though neither of them wants to voice their hope.

"I'd just be happy if you're able to get a seat on

the subway in the mornings," he tells her, and she snorts.

"I doubt that."

"Then I'm going to start riding with you."

"How's that going to help?"

"I'll tell every jerk who doesn't give you a seat to bug off. Only I won't say *bug*."

Lucy grins.

"I'm serious. You can't stay on your feet all the way to work every day."

"It's not that far. I'll be fine."

"I just wish . . ." It's his turn to hesitate before shifting gears. ". . . I wish the subway weren't so crowded during rush hour."

What he'd meant to say was that he wished she didn't have to work. But she does have to, and he knows it—even though he's foolishly tried to convince her otherwise. As if she doesn't know the bills are piling up and they can't pay them as it is.

Why, oh why did he follow his heart a decade ago, convincing himself that he was meant to be a social worker, helping kids who were lost souls, as he once had been? Why didn't he think in practical terms and choose a career that paid more money?

He can't even support his pregnant wife. Hell, if it weren't for his conveniently dead grandmother, they'd be out on the street.

All right, their parents would never have let that happen, but still . . .

It's so hard to look at healthy, vital Lucy, who has always done everything exactly right, and imagine that anything could go physically wrong.

Yet it has, twice before. And though the doctor more or less told them the double miscarriages might have been a cruel fluke, Jeremy isn't sure he can accept that. There might be something they're missing, something that can be done to prevent it this time. Something, anything . . .

God, I hate feeling helpless.

"Want me to come with you to drive the truck back up to White Plains?" Lucy asks him.

"No, you stay here and rest."

"All I've been doing is resting." She sets her phone on the coffee table and picks up a foil-covered plate. "Want a cookie?"

"Where did you get them?"

"Someone left them for us."

"Who?"

"I have no idea."

Jeremy frowns. "Wait . . . what do you mean?"

"I found the plate by the door. I guess one of your grandmother's neighbors must have left it—you know, welcoming us to the building."

"My grandmother kept to herself. The only neighbor of hers that I've ever even met is Chiara Ronzoni."

"You mean the opera singer?"

"She must be eighty years old by now if she's still even alive. And if she is, I guarantee you that she's not baking cookies for us," Jeremy tells her, remembering that Elsa called the two women dueling divas, and for good reason.

"Well, whoever made them . . . they're great."

"You mean you *ate* them?" He gapes at Lucy in alarm.

What the heck is she thinking, eating cookies

from God-knows where? Have the pregnancy hormones clouded her judgment?

"I saved you some. Geez, don't look at me like that—I was hungry."

"That's not what I'm— Come on, Lucy, we're in the city. You don't just—"

"I *know* where we are," she interrupts, and the gleam in her light green eyes makes it very clear that she hasn't forgotten the way he cut her off earlier, when she was telling him about her brother's office.

He felt terrible the moment he snapped at her. He always feels terrible when he gets angry.

Most of the time, he can keep his temper in check using techniques he learned long ago, in anger management therapy. Thankfully, the occasions he's found himself truly flying off the handle have been few and far between—very rarely in recent years, and never in Lucy's presence.

Sometimes lately, though, he feels like the deep, dark well of anger inside him—fed by the stress of the move, his grandmother's death, the third pregnancy—has been transformed into a bubbling hot spring.

According to his shrink, Dr. Kitzler, that's not out of the ordinary, especially for someone who's suffered as Jeremy has.

"Overreactive anger often stems from long-suppressed rage," he told Jeremy. "All those years of abuse have taken their toll on you."

All those years . . .

Being shuttled from foster home to foster home, then finding a loving family at last, only to be snatched away, abandoned in a foreign country, and ultimately condemned to spending the remainder of his childhood with a sick pedophile who forced Jeremy to call him Papa . . .

He survived—but only because he did what he had to do.

He hates the memory of it; hates that any of it ever happened; hates that he can't change the past, or seem to forget it.

Most of all, he hates that it isn't over, even now, and never will be. There was never closure—Papa was never charged with abuse. No one even knew about it when he was still alive. Not that he had a circle of friends or family. He kept the residents of the small California town at arm's length. But they knew who he was. They'd have been shocked to learn that the mild-mannered man who waved to his neighbors and tipped the paper boy every week was a dangerous pedophile.

When Jeremy finally had a chance to tell his story to the authorities, long after Papa died, there was nothing anyone could do about it. Not even any evidence that it happened.

And so, Jeremy is doomed to carry around the anger and hurt forever.

And he can't tell anyone the whole truth. Not even his wife.

Lucy does know what he did to La La Montgomery—how he attacked her the first time, when they were children, and again when he smashed her skull with an andiron that day she kidnapped Renny and tried to kill Caroline.

Lucy knows all that, but she doesn't know the rest. She doesn't grasp the extent of what he's capable of doing . . .

She doesn't know what else you actually did.

Even Dr. Kitzler never knew.

Knew—past tense.

Jeremy hasn't been to therapy in a few years now.

He stopped going not long after he and Lucy were married. He was happy then—so happy. He convinced himself that the euphoria would last forever.

But gradually, life got back to normal. The honeymoon was over, as they say. Troubling memories began to pop up again, along with the familiar anger—and guilt.

Guilt—over what he did, years ago—is the most dangerous emotion of all.

For all those years of therapy, he carried the overwhelming burden into—and right back out of—every session, and he worried that he might spontaneously confess.

His own social work training told him enough about ethics and confidentiality to know that he has to tread carefully when it comes to discussing his past with anyone, even Dr. Kitzler.

The "least harm" principle would come into play if he spilled his secret, and it would be up to Dr. Kitzler to decide whether to keep Jeremy's confidence, or turn him in. If the psychiatrist decided that the least harm would come from the latter option, Jeremy would lose everything.

And now that he's built a life for himself, with a wife he loves and a baby on the way, he has more to lose than ever before.

Nothing—*no one*—is going to take that away.

He can never risk therapy again. He can never be tempted to tell anyone what he did.

"Are you okay?" Lucy asks, and he realizes she's watching him closely.

"Sure. It's just been a hell of a day. I'm tired and hungry."

"Here—have a cookie." Lucy offers the plate again.

He takes it from her and she starts to smile, then frowns when he sets it on the marble coffee table.

"Goose, you just don't go eating stuff when you don't know where it came from, like . . . like . . ."

"Snow White?" she supplies when he falters.

"Snow White?"

"She ate an apple poisoned by an evil queen in disguise."

"Then I'm sure there wasn't a happy ending."

"Really? You don't know? I can't believe you really aren't familiar with Snow White."

"Yeah, well, my childhood wasn't exactly filled with fairy tales."

Lucy stiffens. "I know that. I'm sorry."

Of course she knows. Why remind her?

Yet every once in a while, when someone mentions some kind of mundane childhood experience that Jeremy was denied, he still feels a stab of resentment. Even though he's come to terms with the fact that he was robbed of his childhood. That he'll never get it back. He'll never be like everyone else.

And it's certainly not that he wants—or needs—pity. He never did, and especially not after all these years, from Lucy or anyone else.

Anyone else . . .

That voice, La La Montgomery's voice, echoes

through his head sometimes, even now. She's dead, and yet he hears her still.

I've done everything you're too weak to do. I've punished them all for what they did to you, and this is the thanks I get?

She'd said he was weak, called him a coward. But he faced her down, and he won, and he thought he'd never be afraid of anything ever again.

He was wrong about that.

Whenever he sees the rare glimmer of uncertainty in his pregnant wife's eyes, Jeremy is terrified.

You can't screw this up. You can't.

Mustering a smile, he stretches a hand toward the plate and lifts the foil.

"What are you doing?"

"Having a cookie."

Looking relieved, Lucy smiles back at him. "You sure you want to take a chance?"

"Why not? I'd say the odds are pretty good that there's no evil queen hanging around here."

Watching them bite into the cookies she left for them, she smiles smugly to herself.

"They have no idea," she tells Chaplain Gideon. "Absolutely no idea they're being watched."

Thanks to decades' worth of furniture and artwork that fill Sylvie Durand's apartment, the tiny cameras were easy to conceal in every room, transmitting images directly to her computer screen. She'll be able to see what they're doing, hear what they're saying, any time of the day or night.

This particular camera—the one that clearly broadcasts the image of the Cavalons sitting in their living room—is concealed in the scroll-work of an elaborate antique folding screen that sits directly across from the couch. They'd have to be looking for it to find it—and even then, it wouldn't be easy.

She watches Lucy brush crumbs off her hands and ask Jeremy, "Are you sure you don't want me to ride back up to White Plains with you to return the truck?"

"No, I want you to stay here and rest up so that I can have my way with you when I get back."

"Have your way with me? Who are you, Rhett Butler?"

Watching them share an intimate laugh, disgusted by the turn the conversation has taken, she coils her hands into fists.

Sometimes, the urge to destroy Jeremy and Lucy Cavalon is so powerful that she must pray for self-discipline. Soon enough, they'll realize that there is no safe haven in this world—or in the next—now that Judgment Day is imminent.

It had all happened just as she'd been promised it would, back when she was in prison and Chaplain Gideon was her only visitor, coming nightly to read the Bible with her. It was all there in black and white, every detail. If you read the Bible with care, you would know what was going to happen, and what you were supposed to do.

Chaplain Gideon is the only one in the world who knows she didn't die on the night when—as foretold in the Bible—the Tribulation began with a great earthquake.

The prison collapsed and burned, rendering most victims' charred remains unidentifiable. No one could have realized she wasn't among them.

"So what do you think?" Lucy is asking Jeremy, who's munching a second cookie. "These are pretty good, right?"

"I bet the poison apple was pretty good, too."

"They're glib," Chaplain Gideon whispers. "Both of them. Look at them."

Yes. You'd think they'd have learned, all those years ago, never to let their guards down.

Killing them both, right here and now, would be so easy for her . . .

"But Lucy must be allowed to live," Chaplain Gideon reminds her, whenever temptation threatens to get the best of her, as it has in the past.

Yes. He's right. Lucy Walsh—who is carrying the Messiah in her womb—must be allowed to live—for now.

She's late.

It figures: late on the one day Ryan finally managed to get out of the office and actually make it to his and Phoenix's regular meeting spot with time to spare.

Most nights, she's already here waiting for him.

Now, standing on the northwest corner of Seventh Avenue and Fifty-sixth Street, holding an open umbrella and a cellophane-wrapped bouquet from the Korean market, Ryan keeps an eye on the south and east. Phoenix will be coming from that direction; the company where she works as a corporate accountant is located in the East Forties.

"I just like the West Side better," she said over the phone earlier, rebuffing his suggestion that he meet her at her building for a change. He'd love to take her to his favorite piano bar, Mimi's, over on Second Avenue, or maybe for tapas at Solera on Third . . .

"We'll do that someday. No rush," she told him. "We have all the time in the world."

"Excuse me, sir . . ."

Ryan turns to see a heavyset couple in fanny packs and wet hooded parkas. Tourists—the city is crawling with them right now. They're here to see the Rockefeller Center tree and skating rink and the Rockettes and the department store windows—all the magic of Christmas in New York. All the magic the locals avoid because the streets and sidewalks are clogged with out-of-towners.

"Do you know where Radio City Music Hall is?" the woman asks him, as her grouchy-looking companion wrestles with a soggy map.

"Sixth Avenue and Fiftieth Street." Ryan points across Seventh. "One block over, take a right at the next corner, walk down six blocks, and you'll see it across the street on the left."

"Didja hear that, Mel? It's that way. I told you!"

Mel turns the map sideways, then upside down. "Says here it's on Avenue of the Americas."

"That's the same thing as Sixth Avenue," Ryan tells him. "We just don't call it that."

"No? Why not?"

"They changed the name to Avenue of the Americas years ago," Ryan explains, "but it never caught on."

"How come?" asks Mel, who apparently comes from a place where the citizens call the streets by their official names, unlike these unruly New Yorkers.

Ryan shrugs. "I guess we're just creatures of hab—"

"Come on, Mel!" the woman shrieks, grabbing her husband's arm. "The light just turned! Let's go!"

Ryan smiles to himself, shaking his head as the man allows himself to be dragged into the crosswalk, off to see the Christmassy sights of Manhattan with his frenzied wife.

Maybe someday that'll be me and Phoenix— middle-aged, married . . .

What will Ryan be like in twenty years?

He can't help but compare himself, as he often does, to his own father. Handsome and vibrant advertising executive Nick Walsh was at the top of his game when he was killed.

What would he think of an anxiety-plagued, world-weary son who stopped growing taller halfway through his teens, can't seem to hold on to a job, and still lives at home with his mother?

At least Ryan has had the house to himself lately, with Mom and Sam still away for the winter. Maybe, by the time they come back, he and Phoenix will be ready to move in together.

But as his older sister has been saying for as long as he can remember, you can't count on much of anything in this world.

He and Lucy have led vastly different lives since the family tragedy. Hers has been charmed by comparison; somehow, she's managed to rise above whatever life has thrown at her.

The unexpected eviction notice is a perfect example. Lucy and Jeremy barely had time to digest the news before they found themselves moving—rent-free—into a palace of an uptown apartment.

To be fair, Jeremy's grandmother had died to make that possible.

And then there were the two miscarriages . . .

Okay, okay . . . not so charmed after all.

Lucy's had her share of problems. They all have.

Sadie finally straightened herself out and is in college, having been scared straight after seeing firsthand that drugs can kill. But for a while there, poor Mom had her hands full, and Sadie's teenage troubles put a terrible strain on her relationship with Sam.

So did mine, Ryan acknowledges uncomfortably. As an adolescent who'd just lost his father, he hardly welcomed a new man into the household. Thank God Sam was patient with him—with all the Walshes, really. He hung in there by Mom's side through all the tough stuff, and now the two of them are finally enjoying life together.

Ryan wonders what his mother is going to say about Phoenix.

He wants to think she'll be happy he has a girl-friend, considering that she asked him just last summer if he's gay.

"What would you do if I was?"

"You know it wouldn't matter to me."

Yeah. He knew that. But—

"It's just that you haven't dated anyone in so long . . . and I thought you might not want to come out of the closet because you were worried about what I'd say. But believe me, Ryan, I wouldn't—"

"Mom," he said, amused despite his dismay,

"I'm not gay. I'm just a loser no one wants to date."

That didn't go over very well. Naturally, his mother did her best to build up his self-esteem. She's an expert at it by now—Mom, his faithful cheerleader.

I believe in you, Ryan . . .
Chin up, Ryan, you're doing great . . .
Hang in there, Ryan, it'll get better . . .

It wasn't always this way. Before he lost his father, Ryan was a well-adjusted, confident, athletic kid. He was the man of the house after Dad moved out, the one who looked out for his mother and sisters. He had friends, "went out" with girls the way you do when you're thirteen . . .

Then the bottom dropped out of his world. His father was murdered, and Ryan came perilously close to losing his own life as well. In the end, he'd survived—but not wholly.

At first, it was as if he still lived inside the shell of the boy he'd once been, though his heart was shattered and his soul had lost its vitality. But as time went on, even the shell began to crumble, until he no longer recognized himself in the mirror.

The emotional stress took a mighty physical toll—he bit his nails until they bled, his skin perpetually broke out, his height spurt ground to a halt, he lost—and then gained—too much weight, going from scrawny freshman to dumpy senior.

His friends either developed a morbid fascination with the gory details of his own kidnapping and father's death, or eventually turned their backs on him, fed up with his gloominess. The only friend who might have actually stood by him—Ian Wasserman—was forbidden by his mother to hang around with Ryan anymore.

Janet Wasserman wasn't just the town busybody, she was utterly paranoid. She seemed to think that the tragedy that had struck the Walsh household was contagious and might follow Ian back to the Wassermans' huge brick house over in Glenhaven Crossing.

By the time Ryan graduated high school, he trusted no one other than his mother and Lucy and Dr. Rogel, the child psychiatrist who taught Ryan coping mechanisms that never really helped.

His grades suffered; he got into college by the skin of his teeth, and almost flunked out before dropping out—only to return when he realized he'd never make anything of himself without a degree.

Hell, he hasn't made much of himself anyway. He's quit, been fired, laid off—and never felt a great loss about any of it. Career failure paled by comparison to what he'd lost in the course of his life.

This latest job—in the benefits administration department of a large corporation—isn't any more promising than any of the other random corporate entry-level jobs he's had.

He just can't seem to figure out, even after all these years, who Ryan Walsh is or what he wants or where he belongs.

Maybe this would have happened to him anyway. But he—and Mom—blamed his troubles, and Sadie's, too, on what Garvey Quinn had done to their family.

The fallen politician had died of a massive

heart attack in a West Virginia federal penitentiary while serving a life sentence for his crimes.

There have been plenty of days in the past fifteen years when Ryan feels as though he, too, has been sentenced to live out his days in hell.

But that changed when Phoenix came along and fell in love with him. It's too good to be true, and yet . . .

It *is* true. She loves him. He loves her.

Again, Ryan looks anxiously at his watch.

Where *is* she?

The text from Carl Soto comes through on her phone just as she's headed out the door.

> **Apartment vacated. You can move in whenever you're ready.**

She smiles and hits the delete button.

Oh, Carl. I'm not going to move in. It was never about that.

I just wanted to make sure that Jeremy and Lucy moved out.

And now they're right here . . . right where I want them.

CHAPTER
THREE

Several days later, reminding herself yet again that vomit is a very good thing, Lucy kneels on the cold tile in front of the toilet seat in the bathroom where Sylvie Durand drowned.

So morbid . . . but will she ever think of this room in any other way?

It's not like she ever saw Jeremy's grandmother lying dead in the bathtub—her housekeeper is the one who found her—but Lucy pictures it every time she walks through the bathroom door. Or races through, as the case may be—and has been these last few mornings.

Standing behind her, Jeremy gently holds her long hair back from her face and says, "This is brutal."

No, brutal was losing two babies.

This is *normal*.

She'd tell him that if she wasn't busy dry-heaving.

When it's over, she gets shakily to her feet.

"Are you okay?" Jeremy hovers, holding her elbow.

"Yeah, fine." She flushes the toilet, and reaches

for her toothbrush yet again. Third time this morning. She barely made it out of bed without running to throw up.

Jeremy stands by, watching her worriedly as she brushes her teeth. "That can't be good for the baby. I'm worried that you aren't keeping enough food down."

"I'm okay." She wets the toothbrush again. "It's really just been in the mornings."

"No, you got sick the other afternoon, too, remember?"

Yes, she remembers—the day of the move. Jeremy left to drive the truck back to White Plains and she spent her first hour alone in the new apartment huddled miserably on the bathroom floor.

"That was probably just because I ate too many of those sugar cookies. Or who knows, maybe they really were poisoned," she adds teasingly, and her eyes meet his in the mirror above the sink. "I'm totally kidding, Jeremy. I was feeling sick before I ate the cookies."

"I know."

Finished brushing, she reaches for a towel to dry her mouth. "Anyway, you ate them, too, and you were fine."

"I know," he says again, but his dark eyes still look uneasy. "I just wish we knew who brought them here. You'd think by now someone would have mentioned it."

"We haven't even run into any of the neighbors yet, though."

"Yeah, that's the point. They all seem to keep to themselves."

"It's the city. What'd you expect, someone to come pulling a welcome wagon down the hallway?"

"No, I just . . ." He shakes his head. "You'd think if someone came by with cookies, they'd want to hand them right to us. Or if they did leave the cookies for whatever reason, they'd eventually come back to introduce themselves and say, 'Hey, I'm the one who brought the cookies.' It's bugging me."

"I don't know why. It's really no big deal."

"Maybe it's because . . ."

"What?"

"Because it's happening *here*. You know?"

"Here in New York?" Lucy isn't following.

"No, here in the Ansonia. In this apartment. This is where my mother and Renny were when she came after them at one point, back when . . . it happened."

It . . .

She . . .

Jeremy doesn't have to define his pronouns. Lucy understands exactly what he's talking about, and whom.

Nonetheless, she's surprised he brought it up.

They never really discuss La La Montgomery, who'd seduced him when he emerged from his abusive childhood as a scarred and vulnerable twenty-one-year-old—then gone on a murderous rampage to torment his foster and birth families because she'd decided they'd failed him.

"You know, my mother and Renny were trying to find someplace to hide that day because Mom had a feeling someone was after them, but no one believed her," Jeremy says now—perhaps more to himself than to Lucy. "They thought she was just paranoid, because of what had happened to me when I was little. No one realized she was right until it was too late and my sister had been kidnapped."

Lucy wonders, suddenly, if he's trying to tell her that he's feeling like Elsa did back then—as if an invisible threat is lurking.

But . . . that *is* paranoid.

After all, Garvey Quinn is dead. He can't hurt them now—and neither can La La Montgomery.

"We're okay," she says softly, and touches Jeremy's arm. "No one is out to get us anymore. That was a long time ago, and it's over."

He looks at her in surprise, and she realizes she must have read him wrong.

"I know that, Goose," he says. "And anyway, I would never let anything happen to you."

She smiles, but his words bring hollow comfort.

They both know that there are some things you just can't control.

Waking up, Ryan rolls over lazily to find an empty pillow next to his own.

"Phoenix?" he calls, and hears the shower running in the bathroom down the hall. He sits up and swings his legs over the edge of the mattress, noting—as he has ever since he started seeing Phoenix—that his mornings waking up in his childhood bedroom are probably numbered.

At his age—twenty-seven—he should probably be relieved about that. And on some level, he is.

It's about time you got a life.

But deep down inside, he feels . . .

Wistful? Afraid?

A little of both, maybe?

He can't quite put his finger on the problem. Here he is in love with a terrific woman who loves him in return. Everything should feel right in his world at last, but he can't seem to shake the nagging feeling that it's just the opposite.

Maybe it's that it happened so fast.

He and Phoenix bumped into each other—quite literally—on the street, just like in a romantic movie. His mood was bleaker than the blustery fall weather that night as he headed for the train at Grand Central after work, facing a lonely evening in the quiet suburban house. She came around a corner and crashed right into him, spilling coffee all over him.

She was so apologetic and distressed that he instantly felt sorry for her.

Overweight, with plain features, Phoenix wasn't the kind of woman any man would give a second look. Not on the streets of Manhattan, where every other pedestrian is a sophisticated, glamorous beauty.

Yet there was Phoenix with her hands all over him—blotting the coffee spill, but still . . .

There was something about her from that first moment that struck a chord of familiarity deep inside him.

"It's because we're soul mates," she said when he confessed, weeks later, how he'd felt as though he already knew her the moment they met. "I felt the same way. Our hearts recognized each other."

It might have sounded clichéd, coming from

someone else. But from her, those words were magical.

As they stood there that first night, Ryan splashed with coffee, she insisted that she wanted to pay his dry cleaning bill. Ryan expected that, but he wasn't sure quite how to handle it.

"Do you have a business card?" she asked when he faltered. "I'll call you later and you can let me know how much it is."

"I don't, I . . . I just started a new job."

"All right, then just give me your number or your e-mail."

She was so close he could smell her perfume and the coffee on her breath. "Really, it's okay . . ."

"Look, this is crazy. Either you let me pay for your dry cleaning or you let me buy you dinner."

He was so taken aback by that offer that he just stood there gaping at her.

She laughed. "I'll take that as a yes. Okay?"

"No, I—"

"You don't want to have dinner with me. Listen, I get it. That's fine."

"No! I didn't mean—"

"Great. Then you do? Are you in a hurry to catch a train? Because we can do this another time . . ."

"No!" he said, yet again. "I'm not in a hurry."

"Good. I'm not either. My name is Phoenix."

"What is it?"

"Phoenix. Phoenix Williams. With a last name like that—it's the third most common one in the United States—my parents wanted an unusual first name."

"Is that where you're from, too?" he asked her. "Phoenix?"

"People ask me that all the time. I think they expect me to say no, but the answer is yes. Arizona born and bred."

"What are you doing in New York?"

"My company transferred me. I'm an accountant. I've only been here a few months."

Ten minutes later, he found himself sitting across a linen tablecloth and flickering candle from her, feeling more comfortable than he ever had with a woman.

Phoenix did most of the talking that first night. It turned out she'd just gotten out of a difficult relationship back in Arizona. Her ex, she said, was a macho, controlling, insensitive jerk.

"Just like everyone else I've ever dated," she told him, sipping her red wine. "I'm so sick of men like that."

I'm not like that! Ryan wanted to tell her—but of course, he was too tongue-tied.

Anyway, he didn't have to say it. She just seemed to get him. She made everything so easy for him.

That, he'd always heard, was how it was supposed to be when you met the right person. You would just *know*.

She told him she was falling in love with him on their third date, and he told her he loved her in return. He barely remembers the details—they were drinking champagne that night, much too much of it, and he was giddy.

The next morning, he woke up feeling like he'd dreamed the whole thing. But Phoenix was there in his arms, and it was real.

Physically, she isn't the kind of woman he'd ever

imagined being attracted to. Her body is lumpy, and she doesn't bother with makeup. Unlike the other females in Ryan's life—his mother, his sisters—it's almost as if Phoenix simply doesn't want to bother to take care of herself, to make herself as attractive as possible.

But what matters most is how special Phoenix makes him feel. After all, beauty is only skin-deep—and anyway, beautiful women aren't exactly beating down Ryan's door.

Down the hall, the water turns off. He hears Phoenix open the door to the linen cupboard.

Oops—did he remember to fold the towels that were in the dryer the other day? Is the linen cupboard empty? If it isn't, are the towels that are there even presentable?

He never cared about that sort of thing before—that's Mom's department, and she's been wrapped up in decorating her Florida condo these days. But Ryan did go out and buy some nice new towels and sheets for his bed right before Phoenix first came home with him.

She doesn't stay over often enough for his taste, and when she does, it's her idea.

He keeps thinking it would be much more convenient for them to go to her place—she lives in the city—but she shares a one-bedroom with a roommate who, by the sounds of it, never goes out.

Worried about the towels, Ryan jumps out of bed and hurries down the hall calling, "Phoenix? I'm sorry, there might not be any—"

The bathroom door opens and there she is, wrapped in a towel. It's an old one, bottom of the barrel—the edges are a little ragged and so faded that it's hard to tell what color it once was—white? Beige? Gray?

"Sorry," he tells her, and pauses to drink in the sight of her damp, naked skin.

"For what?"

Good question. Oh. Right. "All the decent towels are still in the laundry."

"It's okay, Ryan. I knew this wouldn't be the kind of house that has perfect towels . . . all matching."

It's such an odd thing to say, Ryan thinks. Almost an insult—or is it?

She smiles at him, and he feels better.

"Growing up, that's the way my house was," she goes on, walking past him on her way to his room. "Perfect, perfect, perfect. My mother had to have everything perfect. All the towels had to match."

"Actually, I do have matching towels." Taken aback, he follows her down the hall. "They're just in the laundry, but I—"

"I wasn't happy there." She talks over Ryan as though she didn't even hear him. "I hated that house, in the end."

"Why?"

She doesn't answer him, just steps into his bedroom and reaches for the small overnight bag she'd brought with her yesterday.

Seeing the faraway look in her eyes, he wonders—as he often does—about her childhood.

"What happened before we met doesn't matter," she tells him, whenever the subject comes up. She doesn't like to talk about her past any more than he likes to discuss his own, so he doesn't press her.

She's told him that she was an only child, and lost both her parents years ago—but years apart. In return, she knows that Ryan's father died when he was twelve, his mother remarried, and he has two sisters, a brother-in-law, and a step-brother.

She's been in no hurry to meet any of them.

"No offense—I'm just not used to being around family," she said when he suggested that they go to dinner with Lucy and Jeremy. "I'd rather ease into meeting them—maybe at Christmas. You understand, don't you?"

"Of course I do."

At the time, he meant it.

But the more he thinks about it, the more it bothers him that she's not interested in getting to know his family.

They really need to discuss that—along with a lot of other things. But this weekday morning isn't the right time to analyze their relationship; they both have to get to work in the city.

Absently watching Phoenix get dressed, he thinks about his mother and Sam; his sister and Jeremy. Those are successful relationships he respects, and they seem to give each other space.

Ryan is in foreign territory now. He just doesn't know what's normal for him to do, to feel—or what isn't normal.

Normal.

That's all he's ever wanted. He had it, once—so long ago you'd think he'd have forgotten what it felt like.

But he remembers it all, a series of vivid moments he replays in his head so that he won't ever lose them. He remembers mornings waking up in this room and knowing that his parents were right there if he needed them, and his sisters would probably annoy him before the day was out by hogging the bathroom or touching his stuff. He remembers playing sports on sunny days and going to school and riding his bike around the neighborhood. He remembers having friends and knowing how to talk to them, even the girls. He remembers feeling safe, always.

But normal exited Ryan's world when his father did—and, like Dad, it never returned.

So now, with Phoenix—all he wants is to build a new life.

Yeah? Are you sure about that, pal?

Maybe what he really wants is to rebuild the old life.

Pulling a T-shirt down over her head, Phoenix catches his eye and smiles.

He smiles back, reminding himself that he's on his way.

Everything is going to be fine. He just has to make sure he doesn't sabotage his own bright future by getting stuck on the depressing past.

"Is it supposed to snow today?" Phoenix asks, cutting into his thoughts.

"I don't think so."

"Are you sure?"

"Not positive. We can catch the weather on the *Today Show* before we leave."

"Good," Phoenix says, surveying her reflection in the mirror above his dresser, "because I don't like surprises."

* * *

It's been one hell of a roller-coaster year for Richard Jollston.

A year ago, he was a lonely, ordinary, newly divorced guy with a decidedly unsexy career as a seismologist.

Now look at him: wedding ring back on his finger, riding through Manhattan in a limo, making the morning talk show rounds to publicize his new book.

New best-seller, he corrects himself, having learned just last night that *I Told You So* will be debuting next week on the venerable *New York Times* best-seller list. Talk about a perfect Christmas present.

"I think that went really well, don't you?" he asks Kristina, the publisher's PR rep accompanying him on this book tour.

"Absolutely." Tapping away on her iPhone, she doesn't look up. "Good idea to hand out bookmarks to the production staff. And I like the way you handled that question about whether your prediction about the Bridgebury quake was entirely based on science."

He laughs. "Do you think they knew I was kidding?"

"When you told them you'd had a biblical vision? Definitely."

Maybe the interviewers knew he was kidding, but Richard is well aware that there are plenty of religious zealots out there in the world who are convinced the Bridgebury earthquake marked the beginning of the end. Quite a few of them have sent him e-mails or turned up at his book signings, prattling on about the Tribulation and the Rapture and the Second Coming.

Richard doesn't buy into any of that dooms-day hogwash, but he's perfectly willing to humor those who do—as long as they buy his book.

"Okay, I just tweeted to the world that you're on your way to your next live interview." Kristina tucks her phone away. "Oh, and I liked how you mentioned in the interview that you have thou-sands of Twitter followers. I'll bet you'll have a few thousand more before the day is out." She smiles at him.

Richard admires her straight white teeth.

If he weren't back together with Sondra, he'd definitely be interested in mixing a little plea-sure with business here. But things are going well with his ex-wife—rather, as of last summer, his *ex*-ex-wife—and he doesn't want to jeopardize his remarriage for a fling with a pretty twenty-five-year-old who probably wouldn't have given him the time of day a year ago.

Probably?

Heck, even Sondra wouldn't give him the time of day back then.

But the Bridgebury quake gave Richard a new lease on life. On the heels of local New England reporters, the national and international press picked up on the fact that he had basically pre-dicted the catastrophe—right down to the sever-ity and the epicenter's general location.

Never mind that his prediction was based on straightforward seismological statistics. Every-one loves a story about a hardworking average Joe turned superhero just by doing his job, and it had been a while since the last one, so the time was ripe. The next thing Richard knew, he had a book deal, an agent, and a slick new wardrobe, and Sondra was back in his life.

"Just a couple of pointers for the next interview," Kristina says, and he thinks, *Uh-oh—what'd I do wrong this time?* He'd remembered to sit on the hem of his suit coat to keep it from riding up at the collar, and he'd been careful to tame his Boston accent and enunciate his A-Rs—*are* instead of *ah*; *Harvard*—his alma mater—instead of *Hahvahd*.

"Don't worry—you did great." Kristina touches his arm as though she's reading his insecure thoughts. "One thing you might want to do in the next interview, though, is clasp your hands in your lap so that you don't fidget. Oh, and don't mention where you're staying while you're here in New York."

"Did I do that?" He thinks back over the interview. It's a blur. It was live, and he was nervous—fidgety, apparently.

"You just mentioned the hotel in passing, when she asked if you were having a good time in New York."

That's right. He had. He couldn't help it—the whole world knows that actors and rock stars stay at that hotel. The paparazzi are always staking it out, snapping pictures of celebrities coming and going.

"It's just a good idea to keep things like that private, Rich." Rich. He loves that she calls him Rich. He loves that she's helping to *make* him rich. And famous.

"Why? Are you afraid the lobby might be swarmed by groupies later?" He's kidding—more or less. Just like he was kidding about the biblical vision.

Yes, and he hopes she knows he's kidding and that he doesn't think he's a big star or something. Although . . .

"Stranger things have happened," she tells him. "You don't want to take any chances. There are plenty of nutty people out there."

"Yeah, and I'm sure they're all busy stalking real celebrities," Richard says with a laugh, to show that he's humble.

"And you, my friend, are on your way. Now, let's go over the bookseller dinner we've set up at Smith & Wollensky later tonight. I hope you like steak . . ."

"Definitely." Richard leans back against the leather seat, loving life.

Walking along a dreary inner city block lined with row houses, Jeremy is struck, as he is every year during this season, by the holiday decorations.

Wreaths hang on battered front doors, strings of lights are stapled around windows with bars on them, and a plastic manger scene sits on one broad stoop, defying theft.

Meanwhile, he and Lucy have decided this year that they aren't even going to put up a tree—a break in tradition. In years past they've always had one, and decked the apartment with lights and poinsettias, too.

Lucy likes to go all out with the decorations because they host her family for a traditional seafood dinner on Christmas Eve before midnight Mass.

When everyone leaves for church, Jeremy stays back and cleans up the kitchen mess and the crumpled wrapping paper, waiting for Lucy's safe return in the wee hours.

It bothers his wife, he knows, that he won't go to church, even on Christmas with the family, but she doesn't push him on it. She's not the type. Secure in her own faith, she leaves his faith—or lack thereof—up to him.

It isn't that he doesn't believe in God. He even talks to God, sometimes, in his head.

"That's what prayer is," Lucy told him once, long ago. "You're praying, Jeremy."

"Then I'll just keep doing it in private," he said, mindful of all that news footage of Garvey Quinn coming and going from church, and shaking hands with religious leaders. Making a big show of his faith while hiding the fact that he'd disobeyed the ultimate commandment.

Thou shalt not kill.

Well, Jeremy isn't a hypocrite. He knows what he did. He *owns* what he did. And he doesn't go to church.

He thinks about all those letters Garvey Quinn sent him from prison. He opened the first one. It was addressed, *Dear Son* and signed, *Your Loving Father.* In between were pages and pages of barely coherent rambling about how Garvey was the chosen one, and Jeremy, as his direct descendant, had a responsibility to repent and become a true believer before Judgment Day . . .

Jeremy threw it away.

The letters kept coming—thick letters, pages and pages presumably filled with the same religious rhetoric. He wouldn't know. He threw them all away, unopened.

He passes an elderly woman pushing a wire cart filled with packages, a drunk sleeping it off in the shadow of a stoop, a group of school-age truants loitering on the corner. They stop talking as he approaches, and he sees them eyeing him.

"Morning, guys," he says.

They don't greet him in return, remaining silent as he passes, but then they resume their talk.

He crosses over to the next block, checks the address on the nearest row house, then consults the open appointment book in his hand. The one he's looking for is just a few doors down.

Reaching it, he finds that the metal-reinforced front door to the place is propped open with a small piece of wood.

Not a good thing. Not safe. Anyone can walk right into the vestibule from the street.

Jeremy does, and is glad to see that at least the interior door is closed and locked.

He presses the intercom button for apartment 2B, and after a few moments, a male voice answers with an unintelligible word.

"Jeremy Cavalon from the Bruckner Center to see Mr. Purtell."

Another unintelligible word, and then the door buzzes open, admitting him.

He finds himself in a dark hallway—worn linoleum, ancient-looking umbrella stroller folded and propped at the foot of the steep staircase. He can hear the Kinks' "Father Christmas" playing behind one of the closed doors down the hall.

In any other setting, he might appreciate it. In this one, the lyrical irony is grimly depressing.

He climbs the stairs. At the top of the flight, he finds the stout, elderly resident of 2B waiting in the open doorway of his apartment. He's wearing a green plaid flannel shirt beneath a red cardigan sweater that has a moth hole on the sleeve and is at least a size too small, the buttons straining to close over his stomach. What's left of his white hair is combed over his bald spot, and he's clean-shaven, though he missed a few spots of gray beard. Clearly, he's made an effort for this visit—and his expression is wary, indicating he knows what's at stake.

"Mr. Purtell? I'm Jeremy. I work with your grandson at the group home."

"Dylan is a good boy."

"He *is* a good boy. And he wants to come live with you."

"I want him here."

If only it were that simple, Jeremy thinks, as the man escorts him over the threshold into a tiny apartment that smells strongly of cleaning fluid. The carpet and furniture are threadbare and the television is enormous—not new, high-tech enormous, but hopelessly outdated enormous. Enormous enough that there's plenty of room on top for a small plastic crèche.

In one corner of the room sits an artificial Christmas tree, missing a couple of branches and more than a few nylon "needles."

Following Jeremy's gaze, Mr. Purtell says, "I'll light that on Christmas, if Dylan's here."

Jeremy, comprehending in that one sentence that the man can't afford the added electricity it would take to plug in the tree every night, nods and smiles.

"Have a seat." Mr. Purtell gestures at the sagging couch. "It folds out into a bed," he adds proudly. "That's where Dylan will sleep. Can I get you something? Some Pepsi?"

Jeremy, who rarely drinks soda, let alone at nine-thirty in the morning, smiles and nods, grasping how important it is to Mr. Purtell that he accept his hospitality.

He so wants his grandson here with him. With Dylan's father long gone and his mother—Mr. Purtell's daughter—jailed on drug charges, the old man has so little to offer the boy, other than love.

But sometimes, Jeremy thinks, lowering himself onto the lumpy couch, love is more than enough.

When her phone rings, Lucy is sitting at her desk gobbling down a chicken wrap she bought from the deli adjacent to her office building's lobby. It's far from her favorite place for lunch, but it'll do in a pinch.

This is quite a pinch—she's got ten minutes to eat it before she goes into a meeting.

There was a time when she'd have skipped lunch altogether on a busy day. Not anymore. She even managed to work in all the key food groups: protein, dairy, whole grain, vegetables, fruit, chocolate . . .

Yes, chocolate. A very important food group, as far as Lucy is concerned. She couldn't resist picking up a small Kit Kat along with the apple she bought for dessert.

She picks up the phone. "Lucy Cavalon."

"You know, it's funny," a familiar voice greets

her, "but I still always expect you to say 'Lucy Walsh.'"

"Too bad I don't have caller ID at work," she tells her brother, "or I'd answer with my maiden name just for you."

"It's okay. I'll get used to it."

"You think? It's been years since I got married."

"Maybe you'll always be little Lucy Walsh to me."

Happy to hear the teasing tone in his voice, she returns, "That's *big* Lucy Walsh to you, little brother. So what's up? Why are you calling me at work?"

"I actually left you a message last night and you never called back."

"I never got a message from you."

"Yeah, that's because I'm a total idiot."

"Who can argue with that kind of logic?"

"Seriously, I left a message on your old number in White Plains," Ryan tells her. "I thought I was dialing the cell. The voice mail picked up, by the way, so I didn't realize—didn't you guys disconnect the phone when you moved?"

"We did, but the voice mail there will work until the end of the month. I'll give you the new number at Sylvie's apartment."

"Don't give it to me now. I'm at work and if I write it down I might lose it."

Her brother's lack of basic organizational skills never ceases to frustrate Lucy.

But then, that's just Ryan. He'll never change.

"If you need me, it's best to just call my cell anyway," she tells him. "And please don't lose this number, because it's unlisted."

She crumples the remains of her wrap—a sliver of cheese, some stray avocado and chicken chunks—in the cellophane it came in and tosses it into the garbage can beneath her desk. Immediately, she regrets it. By about four o'clock, the smell is going to get to her. Her nose has been as sensitive as her stomach these last few days.

Another good sign.

Ryan clears his throat. "Listen, are you going to be home later?"

"You mean later, after work? Yeah. Why? Want to meet for dinner?"

Until recently, she and Ryan had a standing weekly Thursday dinner date near Grand Central before catching their separate trains back to Westchester—just the two of them, since Jeremy always works late coaching for the youth basketball league on Thursdays.

The weekly dinners fell off right around the time Lucy and Jeremy got the eviction notice—which coincided not only with his grandmother's death, but with Ryan meeting Phoenix.

Lucy can't remember who canceled the first Thursday, or the second—or why she and her brother seem to have assumed, from there on in, that their weekly dates were history. Maybe because they're no longer living in the same area. Or because there's a special woman in his life now.

All she knows is that she really misses seeing him. There are very few people in this world who get where she's coming from. Ryan is one of them.

"Actually," he says, "I thought maybe I could come over and see your new apartment."

"That would be great. Are you bringing Phoenix?"

The answer is a prompt, terse "No."

"She's more than welcome."

"Thanks, but . . . she's busy."

"What about Christmas Eve? Did you ask her about—"

"Lu, I have to run. I'll see you at six-thirty, okay?"

Lucy hangs up the phone, checks her watch, and notes that she has time to eat her apple or her chocolate bar, but not both.

Suddenly, though, she's lost her appetite for either.

Why doesn't Ryan want me to meet his girlfriend?

Is it about me, or is it about her?

Enraged, she shuts down the computer with an abrupt click of the mouse, then picks up the loaf of Italian bread she'd been eating and stands to pace the herringbone hardwood floors.

She's seen enough. *More* than enough.

She tears off a chunk of bread with her teeth, chews, swallows.

It was just as she suspected: Richard Jollston has a huge following on the Web. She never even heard of the man until today, when she happened to catch his appearance on one of those morning programs.

Fury swept over her when she realized what he was talking about: the Bridgebury quake.

Chaplain Gideon started in immediately, telling her what she had to do, shouting so loudly that she could barely make sense of what Richard Jollston was saying.

But she heard him say he'd had a biblical vision about the earthquake—*her* earthquake—and that he now had thousands of followers.

When she plugged his name into the search engine, she was appalled at what came up.

The man is being hailed as a phenomenon. He's written a book trumpeting this vision and now he's right here in New York City, promoting it.

Who does he think he is?

And who do *they*—his followers—think he is? The messiah?

"He must be stopped," Chaplain Gideon tells her.

She takes another savage bite of the bread.

"He *will* be stopped. I'll stop him," she whispers, Jeremy and Lucy Cavalon—and Lucy's idiot brother, Ryan, too—momentarily forgotten.

CHAPTER
FOUR

"Well, it's about time!" Lucy exclaims, opening the door to Ryan.

"What do you mean 'it's about time'?" He gives her a brief hug as he crosses the threshold. "I told you I'd be here at six-thirty. I'm ten minutes early."

"Five," she corrects in that efficient big-sister way, and he rolls his eyes in that annoyed kid-brother way.

"What I meant," she says, "is that it's about time you came to see the new place."

"Haven't you only lived here a couple of days?"

"Yeah, but you work right in the neighborhood. I thought you'd pop over before now."

"I've been busy. So have you."

"How do you know that?"

"When are *you* not busy?" His dark eyebrows rise above the wire frames of his glasses, and she can't help but smile.

"Good point. I've definitely been busy."

Beneath his open overcoat, Ryan is wearing a dark blue suit and a patterned tie that doesn't quite work with his striped shirt.

"Where's Jeremy?" he asks.

"Still at work, coaching basketball. It's Thursday, remember? Game night?"

"Oh yeah. I forgot."

She holds out her hand for his overcoat as he shrugs out of it. He gives it to her, and she sees a tear in the lining. Typical Ryan. He always manages to look thrown together, even now.

Somehow, she'd thought having a woman in his life might have changed him.

For a split second, Lucy finds herself remembering how she'd insisted that Jeremy get a new suit for the funeral, and thinking that Ryan's girlfriend shouldn't let him go around in a shabby coat and a shirt and tie that don't match.

Okay, that's ridiculous.

This isn't the fifties. Ryan is a grown man. He should be perfectly capable of taking care of himself.

He should be—and he probably is—but he doesn't do it.

And that's his own fault, not the fault of his girlfriend.

His fault, and Mom's. As far as Lucy's concerned, their mother enabled him, so disturbed by her son's newfound insecurities, so eager to see him heal, so fearful of seeing him fall, that she made sure he always had a safety net—usually her own outstretched arms.

Her coddling didn't do Ryan any favors.

Then again, who am I to judge? Maybe I'll be the same way with my own son or daughter.

Somehow, though, Lucy doubts it. She has little patience for people who let things happen to them, as opposed to *making* them happen.

She and Jeremy are planning to raise a strong, self-sufficient child capable of withstanding anything life hurls his or her way. *Just like Mommy and Daddy.*

"So how are you feeling?" Ryan asks her.

"Pregnant. How about you?"

"Not pregnant." He grins, and for a moment, Lucy glimpses a flash of the impish kid brother he'd once been.

All of their lives—hers and Ryan's, Mom's and Sadie's—had been altered by what happened to them fifteen years ago. But Ryan changed more than any of them.

Sadie—she had her share of troubles. But through it all, her personality never changed. She was always the same kid: stubborn, precocious, introspective.

Not Ryan. He changed drastically. Long gone is the carefree boy he'd once been. Riddled with self-doubt, old before his time, he's been struggling for years now to maintain the most basic elements in life; things that once came readily to him: friendships, romance, intellectual and physical health . . .

Sometimes, Lucy is so frustrated by her brother's inability to get his life together that—despite being critical of their mother's Ryan-smothering—her own protective instinct kicks in. She finds herself wanting to do it all for him, to take charge of his life and run it as efficiently as she has her own. Not that he'd dream of letting her.

Close as they've been over the years, Ryan has built an impenetrable wall around himself. When he was a kid, before their lives fell apart, he wore his heart on his sleeve; these days, most of the time, she has no idea what he's thinking. Scary, because she knows he's more connected to her than to anyone else in this world . . .

Well, he *was*, anyway. Now, presumably, Ryan's girlfriend is his closest confidante. Lucy only hopes the mystery woman treats her brother as well as he deserves to be treated.

"So, are you going to show me around?" he asks expectantly.

"Sure, come on in."

"This is a great building."

"Yeah . . . a lot of famous people have lived here."

"Such as . . . ?"

"Such as Rachmaninoff and Toscanini, Babe Ruth and Jack Dempsey, Sarah Bernhardt and *moi*," Lucy tells Ryan, in a perfect imitation of Jeremy's lovably narcissistic grandmother, who once said exactly that.

Will she ever think of this place—this palace, really—as home? For the last few days she's been more or less tiptoeing around, feeling as though prowling through someone else's house—or perhaps some after-hours museum is more like it.

"Prepare yourself to be wowed." She leads her brother through the circular foyer into the hall. "I can say that without bragging because I had nothing to do with any of this. It's all Sylvie."

"I believe it. Hey, how come that window is frosted over?" Ryan points to an opaque pane on the wall.

"It's an air shaft. Some of the apartments are built around them. My mother-in-law said people would open the pane in the summer to get a cross breeze years ago, before there was air-conditioning. Except Sylvie never did because she thought roaches would crawl in from the neighbors' apartments."

"Nice." Ryan tugs at the window and it raises easily, bringing in a gust of cold December wind. "You really should keep this locked."

"I thought it was."

He lowers it again and runs his fingertips over the wooden sill. "It doesn't even have a lock, see? But you can tell there used to be one. I wonder why Sylvie took it off?"

"I have no idea, but at least no one can get in. We're way above the street."

"Unless they want to creep along the ledge from one of the other apartments, like the roaches." Ryan raises the window again and together, they peer out. "It's like being inside a big chimney."

"Yeah, one with a hundred windows lining it."

"Have you met any of your neighbors yet?"

"Not exactly. One of them dropped off cookies the day we moved in, but I don't even know who it was." Lucy shivers. "I'm freezing. Come on. I'll show you the rest of the place."

Ryan closes the air shaft and she leads him through the living room and dining room, knowing she sounds like a museum docent as she points out some of Sylvie's more fabulous artwork and antiques.

Lucy and Jeremy's own belongings—books, electronic equipment, a few knickknacks—seem out of place amid the grandeur. Still, she stubbornly persisted in unpacking and displaying it all in an effort to make the apartment seem homier.

"I feel like we should be tiptoeing around and whispering," Ryan comments as she leads the way back to the kitchen after showing him the whole place—all two thousand square feet of it. "It's so quiet here. You can't hear any noise from the hall or the street. I don't even feel like I'm in New York."

"Yeah, I know. The apartments are supposed to be soundproof. I guess it takes some getting used to. I kind of miss noise."

"You know, you guys could have moved in with me." It's not the first time he's made the offer, pointing out that she has as much right to live in their childhood home as he does.

"Thanks, but it would be a little crowded once Mom and Sam get back from Florida, and Sadie and Max are home from college . . ." *And once I have the baby.* "Anyway, the commute would be a lot longer from Glenhaven Park. This place is fine—for now. Even if it is a little . . ."

"Stuffy?" Ryan supplies.

"Exactly."

"I just want to know who's going to keep this place clean. Dusting all this stuff would take an entire day."

"I know. Sylvie had a housekeeper, but Jeremy and I can't afford one. I guess we'll just have to live with dust and cobwebs for a while."

In the kitchen, she offers him a Corona, which he accepts, and Lucy wishes she could have one, too.

Never a heavy drinker, she did used to enjoy an occasional beer after work with Jeremy, or happy hour at La Margarita with her friend Robyn, whom she's seeing there tomorrow night.

But she won't be drinking margaritas. It's been over a year since she's touched a drop of alcohol, having spent that time either pregnant, trying to get pregnant, or recovering from a lost pregnancy.

Abstinence is the least of her worries at the moment. Still, every once in a while, after a particularly hard day at work, she wouldn't mind something stronger than tea.

She puts the kettle on and opens one of the custom cherry cupboards, taking out a clear glass mug. Then she measures loose tea from the tin into a strainer.

Ryan leans against the polished granite countertop, watching her. "What is that?"

"Tea."

"I thought tea came in bags."

"Not the good stuff. Want to try this?"

"Nope. What is it, herbal?"

"Regular old decaf. I can't have herbal tea while I'm pregnant."

"Why not?"

"Too risky. I read that there are herbs that can induce a miscarriage."

"Really? Do you think that's why . . . ?"

"No! I knew about that going into my first pregnancy. I never touched herbal tea. I was so careful about everything, but . . ." She sighs and shakes her head.

"Don't blame yourself, Lucy. You know better than that. Sometimes things just happen. You can do everything right, and you still just never know."

"Right. But I have to take charge of the things that I can."

"You've always been good at that."

She looks up at Ryan, surprised to hear the sincerity in his tone. He usually gives her a hard time about being a control freak. At the moment, though, he's almost looking at her with admiration.

"Sit down," she tells him, gesturing at the stools along the breakfast bar. She busies herself cutting a lemon into wedges. After a few moments, she asks, "So . . . what's up with you?"

"What do you mean?"

"I mean, you're *here*."

"I wanted to see the new place."

"But what else? It's a Thursday and I don't think you really forgot I'd be here alone. I feel like you want to talk to me about something."

He looks down at the beer bottle sitting on the counter, rolling it back and forth between his palms. Watching him, Lucy wishes things didn't have to be so difficult for him. The poor guy really needs a break.

"It's her, right? Phoenix?"

Ryan looks up sharply. "What makes you think that?"

"I can read minds, remember?"

When they were kids, there was a time when she had him—and Sadie, too—actually believing that.

Ryan's bittersweet smile tells her that he hasn't forgotten those days—and that somewhere deep down inside, he might just still buy into her alleged psychic abilities.

"What is it, Ry? Trouble with Phoenix?"

"Not really."

Yes, really.

She can tell. "Are you sure about that?"

He hesitates. "It's not her, exactly. I guess I just feel like no matter what I ever do, it's like there's some big, heavy dark thing hanging over my head. Like my life is supposed to be hard. And now that something good—something *great*—is finally happening to me, I feel like something's going to go wrong. Like it's got to. Do you know what I mean?"

"Yes."

"When do you stop feeling that way?"

Maybe you don't, Ryan. Maybe you never stop feeling that way.

But Lucy won't say that—even if it's the truth—because, quite simply, she just doesn't operate that way. She doesn't *do* second-guessing, or misgivings, or anything that falls remotely into wishy-washy territory.

Ryan needs her strength more than he needs her empathy.

They've *all* needed her strength, all her life. Even Mom, who was shell-shocked after Daddy left, once told Lucy, "When it comes to you and me, I'm never quite sure who's taking care of whom."

Mom was strong. But sometimes, Lucy was stronger—even as a kid. Stronger than all of them. Even Daddy.

Stay strong, Lucy. Stay strong.

I did, Daddy. I was. I am.

Yes, and if *he* had taken his own advice and been strong enough to resist temptation, he never would have left Mom and started the deadly chain reaction that led to his death.

"Lu?" her brother prompts.

She realizes he's waiting for her to say something—and not about their father's failings.

"Look, Ryan, you need to do everything in your power to stay in charge of your own life. If you love Phoenix, and she loves you, then make it work."

"That's so . . . *you*." He shakes his head. "You make it sound easy. You make it *look* easy. Everything you do. Even the hard stuff. I wish I could be more like you, Lu."

"We all have our problems, Ry. Even me." She tries to say it lightly, but it doesn't come out that way.

"I really think everything's going to work out for you. With the baby, I mean."

She swallows over the sudden ache in her throat. "I hope you're right."

"What about me? Do you think it's going to work out?"

"For you?"

"For me and Phoenix."

She wants to lie and tell him that she's sure it will. It's what he wants to hear. But what good would that do?

"It's hard for me to say without meeting Phoenix. I want to believe in this for you. Maybe when I get to know her, I'll have a better sense of whether this is right for you. As it is, all I've got to go on is what you say."

And what you're saying isn't all that encouraging.

"Yeah." Ryan sighs. "Half the time I just wish I knew what she was thinking."

"It's so funny—I was just thinking the same thing about you."

"That you wish I knew what I was thinking?" he asks in surprise. At her nod, he says, "I'm telling you exactly what I'm thinking. That I want things to work out for me and Phoenix. We're soul mates—that's what she said."

"Really?"

He nods. "The moment we met, there was something about her that seemed familiar, and she said she felt the same way about me. She said it's because our hearts recognized each other."

"Really." Lucy can't help but think that's either a very sweet thing to say, or a load of bull, and Ryan isn't the kind of guy who'd be able to tell the difference.

"But sometimes," he goes on, "she kind of shuts down, and gets all withdrawn, and I don't know why."

"Well, if it's any comfort—everyone does that," Lucy assures him, her thoughts again going to Jeremy.

He's never given her any reason to worry that he might break down again someday, or commit another violent act . . .

And anyway, what happened in the past stemmed from a childhood of abuse and neglect. He's had years of therapy, and medication, too, and not a single violent incident since that second attack on La La fifteen years ago.

Still . . . there are times when he's a million miles away, and she can't help but wonder what's going on in his head.

"Trust me," she tells Ryan, back in the sage older-sister mode. "Everyone needs space."

"Even you guys?"

"Are you mocking me?"

"No! I'm serious."

She peers at his face. He does look serious. Dead serious.

"Yeah. Even us. I love Jeremy, and he loves me, but we get moody and we argue and believe me, we don't want to spend every waking minute together. He has his stuff and I have mine."

"Do you ever feel like you have no clue what he's thinking about?"

"Sure, sometimes."

Then again, she usually knows what he's thinking about: the past. Sometimes she wonders if he'll ever be able to let it go.

For the most part, he's moved on, yet every Friday morning, he still feels duty-bound to go to Parkview.

Not last week, though, she recalls. *Or the week before that.*

She'd been surprised when he twice opted out of his weekly visit, but didn't want to question his decision to skip it or make a big deal about it, lest he feel guilty.

Maybe the break in routine is a sign that her husband is trying to loosen those ties at last—or at least, lessen the overwhelming sense of obligation to a woman who, while she might once have been as much a victim as he is, caused him so much pain.

"Lu?"

She looks up to see her brother watching her, undoubtedly waiting for more sage sisterly advice. Ha.

"Look, Ry, knowing what someone else is thinking—that's not the point. It's never going to happen. You need to make sure you have more going on in your life than just your relationship, and then it won't matter so much."

"I do," he replies, then, shaking his head with resignation, amends, "No, I don't. Ever since she came along—no, *before* she even came along—I've kind of been feeling . . . like there's something missing."

"Well, maybe it isn't about her. Maybe it's some part of yourself that you lost a long time ago, and you need to find it again."

Ryan gives a case-closed shrug and pushes aside his empty beer bottle. "Maybe. I guess I should get going. It's a long ride home on the train."

"You can stay here in the guest room if you want," she offers.

"Are you worried about being here alone at night?"

"Me? Are you kidding?" Seeing his expression, Lucy wishes she could take back her response— or at least, tone it down.

Maybe Ryan wants to feel needed. Or maybe he just wants to think that he's not the only one who feels vulnerable.

Everyone is afraid of something, she wants to tell him. *Maybe being alone at night isn't something that scares me but there are other things . . .*

Things she doesn't talk about. Ever. To anyone. That's just not her style.

"If you stay," she tells Ryan, "we can make popcorn and watch a movie."

"That's okay. I have to go."

She gets his coat, walks him to the door, and gives him a quick hug good-bye.

"Keep me posted, okay, Ry?"

"I will. You too." He rests a hand on her stomach for a moment, and she looks up at him in surprise.

She didn't say it out loud. She didn't have to.

Maybe he can't read Phoenix's thoughts, but he obviously can read Lucy's.

* * *

"Good game, guys." Jeremy high-fives the members of the basketball team—all adolescent boys whose wayward paths have intersected here, at the Bruckner Center for Behavioral Health. "Did everyone remember to fill out the menu choices for the holiday party Monday night? They were due yesterday."

Scattered affirmative head bobs, but far more dismayed head slaps accompanied by under-the-breath curses. Not surprising with this crew, though they're good kids at heart. Most of them, anyway. Jeremy doesn't judge those who aren't, too well aware that they've been through hell and back in their short lives.

That's why they're here, all of them.

It's why Jeremy's here, too. He's been to hell—and back—and wants to ensure that the boys' hellish journeys are also round-trip.

He finds it cathartic, most of the time, working with troubled kids. Maybe he can't quite relate to everyone's specific set of issues, but the big picture is pretty universal for kids like these. Jeremy knows only too well the feeling of being unloved and alone in the world. Knows, too, that he can't save all of them.

In the five years he's been working here at the center, Jeremy has lost a couple of kids.

Lost, as in dead. Usually on the streets, victims of drugs or violence.

Lost, as in incarcerated.

And sometimes, just plain lost, as in fallen off the face of the earth.

But so many of them go on to make something of themselves, to find their way back into the world beyond the group home.

It looks like Dylan is going to have a good chance to do just that. This morning, Jeremy concluded that his grandfather will be a fit guardian and started the necessary paperwork to move Dylan out of here and in with Mr. Purtell. Not in time for Christmas, but at least they can spend it together, and light the tree.

"I can't find my form—do you got another one?" asks Miguel, the scrappy runt of the group. His baby face features and gap-toothed smile make him look like a first-grader, but he's eighteen and lost a front tooth and a molar in a run-in with a rival gang member.

"I have them in my office," Jeremy tells him. "Come on upstairs with me. How about the rest of you? Anyone else lose their form?"

Yep—just about everyone else lost his form, too. Surprise, surprise.

Trooping out of the gym behind Jeremy, they trash-talk and jostle one another—for the most part, good-naturedly, though Jeremy keeps a wary eye on a couple of particularly aggressive kids.

He leads the rowdy pack up the echoing staircase and down the deserted corridor to his office—a dusty, cluttered, low-ceilinged shoe box of a room. He notices that Jack Evans, the fellow caseworker who shares the office with him, has draped a limp tinsel garland over the doorway in an attempt at festiveness.

It reminds him, yet again, that he and Lucy decided they aren't going to get a Christmas tree this year. Looking at the boys in his office—boys who are, for the most part, all alone in the world, just like Jeremy once was—he wonders, once again, if that's a mistake.

Maybe he and Lucy should do it up this year, bigger and better than ever. After all, they have each other, a roof over their heads, and a baby on the way. What's not to celebrate?

He still has to get Lucy's gift, too—and he's running out of time, not to mention cash. He'll have to charge it. She told him not to get her anything, but there's no way he'll agree to that. Especially since, when they were packing to move, he spotted several wrapped packages with his name on them.

Leave it to Lucy to have everything done in advance.

And leave it to me to wait until the last minute.

He'll have to figure out Christmas later, though. Right now, he's dealing with a gaggle of lanky teenage boys in a very small space, and the sooner he gets them out of here, the better.

"Fill these out right here, right now," he tells them as he hands out forms and pens. "All you have to do is choose what you want to eat, chicken cutlet or vegetarian pasta."

"What are the choices?"

"Are there any other choices?"

"How am I s'posed to know what I want to eat next week?"

"Wait, *what* do we do?"

Somehow, Jeremy manages to keep his patience and answer all the questions—many, more than once. His head is starting to pound as he collects the completed forms, another painstaking process. He tells the guys they're free to go but most linger, shooting the shit, accidentally toppling the pencil holder and a desk lamp that Jeremy catches before it hits the floor.

"Guys, get moving! Back to your rooms! Get your homework done."

"Ain't got no homework tonight," says Eddie, the team forward, who towers over the rest of the pack, including Jeremy.

"Then—here's a brilliant idea for you—go read a book."

"Ain't got no—"

"If you want to borrow one . . ." Jeremy gestures at the crowded bookshelf beside his desk.

"Nah, I'm good." Eddie flashes a good-natured grin and disappears into the hall.

"Good. Great. Go. All of you! Go!"

Finally, they do. Everyone but Miguel, who lingers in the doorway. "Got a second, Coach?"

Coach—it's what they all call him, though he only fills that role on Thursday nights during basketball and baseball seasons. It's his favorite part of his job, but he wonders whether that's going to change when he has a child of his own waiting at home.

It's not necessarily that these boys are surrogates for the children he's lost—or the children he hopes to have. But they do help to fill a certain void, and sometimes he worries he won't have as much time and affection to give them after the baby is born.

"What's up, Miguel?" he asks the man-boy who stands before him wearing an inscrutable expression.

Miguel pulls the door closed, and something clicks in Jeremy's brain. Only fleetingly does he entertain the thought that this kid—who's been in and out of juvenile detention facilities for violence, among other things—might be up to no good.

No. Not him. Not here and now, anyway. Not with me.

Jeremy has learned, in his life—particularly in this work—to trust his gut instincts about people. His gut tells him that despite his past record, Miguel's a good kid at heart. When you're young and unloved, you do ugly, terrible things in order to survive.

Miguel did.

So did I.

Realizing that it's utter desolation he's seeing in those big black eyes, Jeremy comes around his desk to sit on the edge facing Miguel, who stands with his hand still on the knob of the closed door.

"You okay, dude?" Jeremy asks, though it's obvious he's not okay at all.

It's not that surprising. The holidays—with all the accompanying focus on home and hearth, giving and receiving—can be particularly rough around this place. The staff tries hard to make things merry for the kids, but when you get right down to it, most of them are here because their lives are lacking in the very things the season is meant to celebrate.

Miguel shifts his weight. "My girlfriend . . ."

"Carmen?" Jeremy has heard, and overheard, Miguel wax on and on about the beguiling Carmen, who lives a few blocks from the center with her family—including an ultra-strict father who isn't crazy about his daughter's juvenile delinquent boyfriend. "What happened, Miguel? Did you guys break up?"

"No. Carmen, she's having a baby. Only she *ain't*, because she don't want to have it."

Jeremy's heart sinks. Carmen, he knows, having heard Miguel talk about her, is all of fourteen.

Fourteen. Pregnant.

This isn't the first time one of the boys has come to him in this situation—but it *is* the first time in a while. The first time since he and Lucy started trying—and failing—to have a baby of their own.

"First of all, Miguel, it's a crime for you to have intercourse with a girl her age."

"She wanted to!"

"That doesn't matter. The law—"

"What are you gonna do, Coach, report me?"

Jeremy falls silent, regroups. This is shaky legal and ethical ground and he'd better tread carefully.

"Is it yours?" he asks Miguel, who promptly nods.

"I told Carmen she's got to have it. Because, you know, our religion, it don't let us . . . you know."

Right. Jeremy knows. He also knows that religion and choice aside, an eighteen-year-old boy having sex with a fourteen-year-old girl constitutes statutory rape.

"Did you tell her how you feel about it, Miguel?"

"Hell, yeah, I did. But she don't want to listen. She says if *I* want to have the baby, I can. Yeah, right. But her, she don't want to have it."

Jeremy shakes his head. "She's young, Miguel, and I'm sure she's scared, and—"

"Nah. That's not it."

"Then what is it? Is she afraid to tell her father?"

"That, and she don't want to get fat. That's what her friend Brenda told me she said."

Jeremy stares at Miguel in disbelief, his gut clenching.

He thinks of Lucy, sick, sobbing, bleeding. He thinks of the precious new life growing inside her right now, and of how badly they both want the baby to survive, and he wants to lash out at Miguel. But that's the wrong thing to do. Dangerous. And anyway, Miguel's the one who wants to have it. It's Carmen who's infuriatingly self-centered and callous—according to her friend Brenda, anyway.

But Carmen isn't here, and she's just a kid, and Jeremy has to do his job and focus on Miguel right now.

And breathe.

He has to breathe.

"Coach, can you talk to her for me?" Miguel is asking. "Tell her she gotta have the baby, and then she can give it to me and I'll take care of it."

Give it to me.

It.

Like a *thing*, as opposed to a fully formed human being.

Think before you speak, Jeremy.

Breathe before you speak.

In. Out. In. Out.

"Unfortunately, it's not that simple, Miguel. You—"

"Maybe I ain't never had a father, but I'll figure out how to be one. A good one."

The kid is so damned earnest—and so damned misguided. He's committed a crime that could send him to jail. Look at him, just eighteen, living in a group facility, without any extended family, education, or job skills to fall back on.

And yet . . .

He so desperately wants to love and be loved.

Maybe he would be a good father. Who the hell knows?

It's not up to you to tell him he would or wouldn't be, Jeremy reminds himself. *And it's definitely not up to you to talk Carmen out of—or into—an abortion.*

"Coach?"

He sighs inwardly. "I can't talk to her for you, Miguel. But I can give you some information about resources that are available to both of you, and I need to put you directly in touch with someone who can help you make informed decisions."

Ignoring the disappointment in Miguel's eyes, Jeremy gets up, walks around the desk, and jerks open a file drawer. It's the best option—the one that will bring the least harm, if you look at it that way—yet he can't help feeling as though it's a supreme cop-out.

He thumbs through the folders, grabs handouts from several, and turns around. "Here, these are—"

Miguel is gone.

Jeremy tosses the papers aside and presses his fingertips into his throbbing temple.

Turndown is Myra Wilson's favorite time of day on the job. The hotel corridors are quiet, with most of the guests still out sightseeing or at dinner, and her shift just about over.

In less than an hour, she can trade the maid uniform for jeans and heels and head up to the Bronx to see her man. Maybe they'll hit a couple of clubs. Or maybe they'll just stay in and smoke. She wouldn't mind that. It's frickin' cold out there tonight.

She parks her housekeeping cart outside the next door and lets herself into 2715, leaving the bar latch tucked between the door and the jamb. The bed is still neatly made, not a wrinkle on the duvet, and Myra wonders if the occupant has even been here since she cleaned the room earlier. If not, she'll be out of here in no time.

In the bathroom, she finds a damp towel on the floor, toothpaste goo and shaving cream residue in the sink; hair in the tub drain. So he's been here. Whatever. He left a couple of dollars tucked with a bookmark beneath the drinking glass that holds his toothbrush and razor.

She gladly pockets the money. Tips at turndown aren't all that common. You get a lot of cheapskates, clueless tourists—especially at this time of year— and expense account travelers who aren't reimbursed out-of-pocket cash without receipts.

She checks out the bookmark. There's a photo of a man accompanied by a book cover: *I Told You So* by Richard Jollston.

Myra has never heard of the book, or of him. She tosses the bookmark into the bathroom garbage can, removes the bag, and scoops up the wet towel from the floor. About to return to her cart to dump the laundry and trash, she stops short, hearing a voice from the next room.

"Hello?"

Myra pokes her head through the bathroom doorway to see a tall, heavyset redhead. Funny— she'd been sure the room had only one occupant, and that it was a man.

"Is this your room?" she asks.

The woman hesitates slightly before nodding.

"I need you to show me that your key works in the door, then." It's a standard security procedure. Otherwise, anyone could just walk into a room that's being cleaned—and, after the maid leaves, walk right out again with whatever they feel like stealing.

"Actually, it's my husband's room. He's here on business and I wanted to surprise him." She shifts her considerable weight and a little warning bell goes off in Myra's brain. This chick doesn't look like a thief, but do they ever?

Whatever—Myra's pretty sure this isn't the guy's wife. A call girl, probably. Myra's seen them hanging around the hotel countless times before.

She's overweight for that . . . but she has a decent face, and that long red hair looks suspiciously like a wig. She's wearing glasses, like maybe she's doing some kind of naughty librarian routine. Yeah, and that tote bag she's carrying in her leather-gloved hand is probably full of sex toys.

"Sorry," Myra tells her, "I can't just let you stay here without—"

The woman reaches into the pocket of her beige trench coat. For a split second, seeing a steely glint in her eyes, Myra tenses.

But when the hand emerges, it's holding a wad of cash.

A few seconds later, the money is in Myra's pocket alongside her meager turndown tips, and the wife or call girl or whoever she is looks pleased that her little bribe was a success.

"I'll just grab a couple more towels and put a

new bag in the trash can for you before I go," she tells the woman, and starts toward the hallway.

She notices immediately that the door is now closed, and the latch that was holding it open is now fastened across the inside.

That's strange. The woman must have seen her cart outside and realized housekeeping was in the room.

The cart—Myra is stunned to see that it's inside the room, half stashed inside the closet near the door.

Myra turns, puzzled. "Why—?"

It's the last word Myra Wilson will ever utter; the last thought that will ever scream through her terrified, bewildered brain.

Whhhhyyyyy?

After Ryan leaves, Lucy changes into sweats and curls up in bed with a book. Not *What to Expect When You're Expecting*, though. When she unpacked that from the boxes they moved from the old apartment, she was initially tempted to put it on the bedside table. Instead, she placed it with the other books on the shelf in the study.

She knows some of it by heart—the first few chapters, anyway, which are organized chronologically, covering each month of pregnancy. But twice now, she's had to skip past several months to the back, where there's a section on coping with pregnancy loss.

She can't bear to open the book again until she's able to read a new chapter. Until then, it can stay on the shelf.

Tonight, she's picked up an espionage thriller she bought on a whim at Hudson News in Grand Central back when she was still commuting from Westchester. Now that she's only a couple of short, connecting subway rides away from the office, she has little time to read.

Her father, Nick, was a Robert Ludlum fan. Not long after he moved out, Lucy decided to read one of the spy novels he'd left behind, thinking she could discuss it with him. She'd never had the chance—to finish the book or discuss it with her father. She'd never seen Daddy again.

Lately, she's started reading spy novels again.

Lately, she's been thinking about her father a lot more than usual.

Not that he hasn't always been there, some-where in the back of her mind.

But specific childhood memories keep coming back to her out of nowhere. Memories of happier times, when her parents' marriage was intact. Daddy cheering her on from the soccer field sidelines. Daddy proudly snapping her picture the first time she went to school, lost a tooth, rode a pony. Daddy taking her and Ryan out for ice cream twice in one day while Mom was in the hospital after having Sadie . . .

Daddy.

I miss you, despite what you did to Mom. To all of us.

Lucy realizes she's been staring at the same page of the book for at least five minutes and it's suddenly swimming before her.

Frustrated, she tosses the book aside and plucks a tissue from the box on the nightstand to wipe her eyes. Her emotions are all over the place now that she's pregnant. Yesterday, she found herself crying over a sappy song she heard *not* on the radio, but as background music for a canned soup commercial.

Pathetic.

"Sometimes you just need a good cry," her friend Robyn said when Lucy told her about it on the phone last night.

"Not me. I never need a good cry. I hate crying."

"Oh, please, everyone hates crying. But we all have to do it sometimes."

Not Lucy. Not if she can help it.

She didn't even cry at Daddy's memorial service. She remembers sitting dry-eyed and numb in church with her mother breaking down on one side of her, tears rolling down Ryan's cheeks on the other side, and little Sadie sobbing hysterically on her lap.

Holding her little sister close throughout the service, her neck soaked with Sadie's tears, Lucy had a fierce lump in her throat, so huge and painful she could barely swallow, yet she managed not to cry.

Looking back, she isn't sure how—or why.

Maybe she was afraid that if she started, she'd never stop.

Maybe she was just trying to keep it together so that she could support the others.

Or maybe she was more angry than sad about her father back then.

Sometimes, she still is, even after all these years.

How could you?

How could you have left us?

If he hadn't gotten involved with that woman, Beth, and moved out and wrecked his marriage—their family—he'd still be alive.

Or maybe not. Maybe she'd have lost him anyway.

Chances are he wouldn't have been murdered, but things happen. People die. Dad's father did, of cancer, when he was a lot younger than Dad would've been right now.

But his mom—the grandmother Lucy didn't even meet until a year after Dad died—is alive and well. She still lives in Hawaii, where she moved after she ran off and left her husband and child when Dad was just a little boy.

You'd think, having been abandoned by his own mother, that Nick Walsh would have made sure he didn't do the same thing to his wife and children.

Or maybe it makes sense that he would. Maybe those kinds of things run in the family. Maybe . . .

No. Absolutely not. Never.

There is no way Lucy can fathom that one day, she in turn might walk out on Jeremy—let alone Jeremy *and* their child. Or that he might walk out on her and their child. Children.

Please, God, let us have a child. Children.

Again, Lucy's eyes sting with tears. Again, she takes a tissue from the box and wipes them away, shaking her head at the unfairness of it all.

Some people have everything, and throw it away.

The elegant hotel lounge is bright with twinkly white lights and crowded with tipsy tourists, post–office party revelers, nightcap-sipping business travelers, and, at the far end of the bar, a newly famous author who has yet to be recognized—

though he's been hoping and waiting for someone to come up and ask for his autograph.

Taking a leisurely sip of his single-malt scotch—a sublime eighteen-year-old Glenlivet, on the rocks—Richard Jollston keeps an eye out for other celebrities. There must be some staying here. Where do they go at night?

He feels his phone vibrate in the pocket of his Brooks Brothers blazer. He changed into it earlier, between his bookstore signing and dinner at Smith & Wollensky.

Classic, navy, gold buttons—Sondra picked it out for him.

At least two other men at the bar are wearing the same jacket, which pleases Richard. The last one he'd bought himself, probably at least five years ago, was a polyester Sears special—much more appropriate for a lecture hall than a high-class book tour.

Richard sets down his glass and pulls his phone from his pocket, wondering if it's Kristina. After the bookseller dinner—stilted conversation, but the best filet he's ever had—the publicist told him she'd be calling him with an update on tomorrow's appearances. It's the last day of his tour. This time tomorrow night, he'll be on the shuttle home to Boston for Christmas.

But it's not the publicist calling him after all; the word "home" is displayed in the cell phone's caller ID window.

Home, these days, is no longer a third floor walk-up in Quincy. Nor is it the Cape in Taunton. He and Sondra just moved into a three-thousand-square-foot house in Brookline. Far more house than they need for just the two of them, and they're not interested in starting a family at this late date, but, as Sondra says, "if you got it, flaunt it."

Finally, they've got it. *All*. He stopped at Tiffany's before dinner and bought a pair of diamond earrings for Sondra for Christmas. The little blue box, tied with a satin ribbon, is tucked into the pocket of his blazer.

"Hi, babe," Richard says into the phone, patting his blazer pocket to make sure the box is still there.

"Hi, babe. Where are you?"

"Hotel bar. Where are you?" he returns, though he knows the answer: home, sweet home. He can even picture her there in the house, perched on the family room couch with its heavenly new-leather smell. Behind her are towering vaulted glass panels overlooking the spotlighted landscaped yard. It's going to be beautiful in a few months, when they put furniture out on the patio and uncover the in-ground pool.

Meanwhile, they really do need to get curtains for the windows. As much as they enjoy looking out over the property, anyone can see in.

"So?" Sondra said when he pointed that out, right before he left. "Let them look. They can't get in."

No, that's true, thanks to the elaborate alarm system the previous owners had installed. The house is perfectly safe. Even, as far as Richard is concerned, earthquake-proof—not that another quake is statistically likely to strike that part of Massachusetts anytime soon.

But that's the thing about earthquakes. And life, for that matter.

You just never know.

"How was the dinner?" Sondra asks.

"Kind of dull. Everyone wanted to talk about himself, not my book. But the food was great."

"Good for you. I had a Lean Cuisine." He can just see her pretty face pouting.

"Next tour, I'll get them to let me take you along."

"Next tour?"

"Why not? I'm sure I've got another book in me. Maybe even a novel."

"Really?"

"Why not?" Richard repeats, and grins to himself, giddy with scotch and success.

This bustling midtown hotel has been around for years. In fact, her father used to come here sometimes on business—fitting, because it was his money that initially bought her way into this suite on the twenty-seventh floor.

After escaping from Bridgebury, she was leery about going anywhere near the vacation house that had once belonged to her father.

What if the authorities somehow suspected she was alive and had the place under surveillance? That seemed far-fetched, though. Of all the places from her past, why would anyone ever expect her to return to that one?

"They won't," Chaplain Gideon assured her. "You have to go back. You have to get it. It's the only way."

Get *it*: the money.

"It'll be our little secret," Daddy had told her on the long-ago day when he showed her the stacks and stacks of bills hidden beneath the floorboards in the carriage house loft. "Don't tell anyone."

"Not even Mommy?"

"Especially not Mommy. Promise?"

"Promise," she'd said solemnly, only ten years old, but already aware of the growing tension between her parents. "What's it for?"

"A rainy day." Daddy had flashed her a smile.

It was raining—an icy, drenching downpour—on the day she finally dared to return to the country house. She took that as a sign that she was doing the right thing.

Signs—they're everywhere, if you look for them.

The money was still there—far more of it than she had hoped or imagined.

"It will serve our mission well," Chaplain Gideon told her.

And it has, so far. And though this little detour tonight was not part of the original plan, it does fit into the greater mission.

Daddy would approve.

She's pretty confident that not all hotel staff can be bought off so easily, but she was fortunate, earlier today, to find Tony, a maintenance worker who was more than happy to find out and share with her Richard Jollston's room number—for a decent sum, of course. He had personally never heard of the author, but seemed to buy her story about being a huge fan.

Tony was wearing a wedding band and a heavy gold cross around his neck.

"Look at him," Chaplain Gideon whispered. "Look at his cross. He believes. He doesn't deserve to die. Not like the others."

She wasn't sure it was such a smart idea to let him live, though. What if, after this is over, Tony tells someone—specifically, homicide detectives—about the woman who'd been asking to get into Richard Jollston's room?

But she's well-disguised in a wig, glasses, eye makeup . . .

And even if she weren't disguised, they'd never recognize her. No one but Chaplain Gideon even knows she survived the very earthquake that heretic Jollston claims to have predicted.

Richard Jollston must die. She'd known the instant she had seen him on television this morning, smug and self-serving, talking about his so-called prophecy. As though *he* were the chosen one.

"But he isn't," Chaplain Gideon told her. "You are. You alone are the one true prophet."

Yes. And she understood what she had to do.

It's right there in Deuteronomy: *The false prophets or dreamers who try to lead you astray must be put to death, for they encourage rebellion.*

Returning to the hotel a short time ago, she managed to slip past the doorman, front desk, and lobby security by mingling with a large, boisterous group headed for the elevator bank. It wasn't hard. The hotel, decorated with white lights and fresh green boughs, was jam-packed with people.

The group on the elevator all got off on lower floors, until she was the only one left. Up on the twenty-seventh floor, she ducked into the ice machine alcove and stayed there, watching the hall.

She was waiting for Jollston, really—planning to ambush him from behind as he walked up to unlock his door.

But that wouldn't have been nearly as satisfying as the plan that popped into her head when the maid came along, pushing her cart from room to room, doing turndown service.

Myra, her name tag read.

Ah, Myra. Too greedy for her own good. Now she's lying in a pool of blood on the plush cream-colored carpet in suite 2715.

Myra is no self-proclaimed prophet, and killing her wasn't part of the original plan.

No, the maid was supposed to take the money and leave.

But the knife was so close at hand, and she couldn't help but think how easy it would be to use it . . .

So satisfying . . .

She lost control. She couldn't help it. Lost control and slit Myra's throat.

"You shouldn't have done that," Chaplain Gideon warned her, but only when it was too late.

Only when there was blood.

So much blood . . . blood everywhere. All over the floor, and all over her own clothes, and the knife . . .

Its handle was slippery in her hand. She longed to take off the glove and feel the slick stickiness of blood on her bare skin.

"That's not a good idea," Chaplain Gideon told her, and she wanted to scream at him to shut up for a change, but she was afraid someone would hear through the walls or floor or ceiling.

So she did what he said, and she left the gloves on.

"Make it look like a robbery," he said, and she took the money the maid had in her pocket.

That was a long time ago. She's been pacing, and waiting, and wondering what she'll do if Richard Jollston doesn't come back to his room soon.

She's hungry. *Starved.* She hasn't eaten in hours.

"You can't leave until you've taken care of him," Chaplain Gideon warned her. "Patience."

Now, hearing movement in the hall outside the door at last, she tenses.

He's here.

She slips quickly to the predesignated spot alongside the door hinges, where she can do what needs to be done, and make a quick escape.

Watching the knob turn, she tightens her grasp on the knife handle, tucked within the folds of her hooded cloak. She exchanged it for the trench coat that's now stashed inside the tote bag she brought with her.

The door opens.

Richard Jollston crosses the threshold.

She pounces, slashing with the knife.

The blade catches him in the arm. He turns, stunned. She swings the knife again, toward his face. His cheek is sliced open. Again, and this time she hits him in the gut. He staggers. Falls.

Again, she raises the knife. Stabs him in the leg, the neck, the throat . . .

Again and again, until she's spent.

"Thy will be done," she whispers.

CHAPTER
FIVE

Padding back from the bathroom at six-thirty A.M., her feet freezing on the bare hardwoods, Lucy finds Jeremy awake in bed. The alarm must have gone off in her absence, and he's turned on the television, as he always does in the morning. He likes to catch the early local news.

"Hey, Goose." He watches her climb back into bed and sink against the pillows. "Sick?"

"No."

"I heard you in the bathroom."

"Then why'd you ask?" She swallows hard, still tasting bile, closes her eyes, and feels Jeremy's hand on her arm.

"Why don't you call in sick today?"

"Can't."

"Why not?"

"Because I'm *not* sick. If I fall back asleep, wake me up in fifteen minutes, okay?"

"Okay."

Maybe she should tell him about the slightly crampy feeling she experienced first thing after she woke up. Very slight—so slight that right now, she isn't even sure she's feeling it.

Why worry Jeremy? I'm sure it's nothing.

She listens to the morning traffic and transit report, appreciating the rhythm of an ordinary day. Accidents, gridlock alert, bridge and tunnel bottlenecks, reporter banter. Then commercials for diapers, juice boxes, the latest must-have Christmas toys . . .

Someday I'll be buying those things.

Feeling another crampy twinge in her pelvis, she prays the Our Father and the Hail Mary, then adds a little prayer of her own.

Please, please, please, dear God in heaven . . . Please, let me carry this baby for two more months. Please.

The day after tomorrow is Sunday. She's going to miss seeing Father Les, but she's planning to join Holy Trinity, the neighborhood church where Sylvie was a parishioner. Her funeral was held there, and the whole family found comfort in the eulogy delivered by the priest, Father Bart.

Maybe Jeremy will start going to church with her. Probably not, though. Unfortunately, everything he learned years ago about his birth father, Garvey Quinn, turned him off organized religion. The ultimate hypocritical politician, the late congressman masked his wicked ways behind a pious, preachy façade.

"But it doesn't make sense for you to avoid church just because it was a big part of his life," Lucy has told Jeremy a thousand times. "You would probably find comfort and healing there, the way I have."

So far, Jeremy isn't buying it. She's not surprised. Her mother told her that Jeremy's birth mother, Marin, reacted the same way years ago, when Lauren tried to convince her to get spiritual counseling.

As far as she knows, Marin never set foot in church again—though her daughters were another story.

As usual, Lucy pushes the thought of Annie and Caroline Quinn from her thoughts.

No negative energy to start the day.

And she's no longer feeling any cramps, so that's a good sign. A great sign.

"How was your game last night?" she asks Jeremy, her eyes still closed.

"Fine. We won. I thought you were sleeping."

"Just resting. What time did you get home?"

"After ten. You were asleep."

"Yeah." She yawns. "So . . . are you going to Parkview?"

"It's Friday, isn't it?"

"Yeah, but you didn't go last week—"

"We were busy packing for the move."

"Or the week before."

"I had to go to children's court for Eddie."

"I know." Eddie is one of the kids at the center. "I just thought maybe . . ."

"Maybe I was going to stop going?"

She hesitates. "I don't think anyone would blame you."

"It isn't about anyone else. It's about me. I need to go—for me as much as for her."

Maybe more than *for her*, Lucy thinks—not for the first time.

She changes the subject. "Ryan came over after work last night."

"With his girlfriend?"

"What do you think?"

"No?"

"No. Alone. He wanted to talk *about* the girl-friend, though." She tells him, briefly, about her conversation with her brother.

"I hate to say it, but that doesn't sound very promising."

"I thought the same thing."

"Did you tell him?"

"Not in so many words. You know Ryan. Maybe he's just being . . . insecure. Maybe it's all in his head."

"Maybe. I hope so."

"She's with him, so she must care about him. Right?"

"Not necessarily."

"What, you think she has ulterior motives?" Hearing the incredulity in her own tone, she feels bad about it.

It's not as though her brother has nothing to offer a woman. He's a sweet, caring person. But Ryan Walsh is definitely not the kind of man who'd capture the attention of a gold digger or status seeker. Meaning anyone he's dating is with him because she cares about him. Right?

"It's hard to tell," Jeremy says, "without meeting her."

"That's exactly what I said to Ryan."

"And? Are we going to meet her?"

"Christmas Eve, I hope. Which is Tuesday."

"About that—I was thinking maybe we should get a tree after all."

"Really?" Lucy is surprised. "But I thought we agreed—"

"We did. But . . . I don't know, I feel like maybe

this place would be more cheerf...

tree."

...t up a

"It would. Definitely."

And maybe he's not just talking ab...
apartment. Maybe he's hoping a tree will e
him be more cheerful, too. Still . . .

"What? You're worried about the money?" Jeremy asks, and she nods.

Trees are outrageously expensive in Manhattan. It seems crazy to throw away a hundred bucks on something meant to last just a few days.

But the argument seems a little Scrooge-like.

Instead, she points out—in case Jeremy forgot—"It'll only be you and me here on Christmas Eve this year. And maybe Ryan and his girlfriend."

Not that her brother had been willing, when they talked about it earlier, to commit to spending Christmas Eve here.

"You, me, Ryan, his girlfriend, and seven fishes?" Jeremy sighs. "Why don't we just get a pizza?"

"Because you don't have pizza on Christmas Eve! You have seafood."

"I thought that was an Italian tradition. You're not even Italian."

"Jeremy!"

"Listen, how about just one or two fishes? Or even four—one fish per person. "

He's trying to be clever, she knows, but she isn't in the mood.

"It's a tradition," she tells him. "*Our* tradition. Seven fishes."

"So it shall be."

120 that to her sometimes, teasingly, when
...s she's being difficult or demanding.

...she isn't. Not right now. All she wants is for
...stmas to be the way it's always been.

Suddenly, she's homesick—not just for old holiday traditions and her old church and Father Les, but for her family.

Even when Mom gets back home to Glenhaven Park, it's going to be so much harder for Lucy to pop over to see her now that she's living in the city.

She was never the kind of daughter who relied on her mother—let alone anyone else—for help or advice. Still, there's a certain comfort in maternal affection and unconditional love.

Especially when I'm pregnant.

If her mom were nearby, she could ask her about some of these symptoms, without having to turn to the Internet or books or Dr. Courmier every time she has an unusual twinge like she did—or *thought* she did—this morning.

She supposes she could still ask her mom long distance, but speaking on the phone is much different than chatting in person.

"That's crazy," Jeremy says.

"What's crazy?" She backtracks mentally, having lost track of their conversation.

"On the news . . . shh."

She rolls over to look at the TV screen. A reporter stands on a Manhattan street surrounded by flashing police car lights. Obviously a crime scene. Or maybe an accident.

" . . . double homicide . . ."

Right the first time. Crime scene.

"What's crazy?" she asks Jeremy again.

"It's that guy who wrote that book about that earthquake."

"What guy, what book, what earthquake?"

"The one near Boston, shh . . ."

Boston . . . earthquake . . .

The relevance of *that* registers immediately, of course.

Not because of any book or the guy who wrote it, but because of the earthquake that devastated the Bridgebury, Massachusetts, prison, crushing and incinerating countless inmates—*her* among them.

Her.

That's what Jeremy calls her, as though he can't stand to utter her name.

And I don't blame him.

Following the story onscreen, Lucy discerns that an author named Richard Jollston, in New York on a book tour, had been murdered last night at his hotel, along with a maid. The police had no motive and there had been no witnesses, but they were interviewing hotel employees and studying surveillance video.

That report gives way to the announcement that the weather forecast is next, with a promise of a white Christmas for the tri-state area. Then there are more commercials for more products Lucy will need someday, after the baby is born.

She thinks about the cramping again—or is it that she's cramping again, and that brings it to mind?

She can't tell, but she's definitely feeling something. Just barely. But something.

She hasn't gotten this far in life by dwelling on

the bad stuff—and as someone who perpetually seeks order in her own little universe, she's reassured by every typical pregnancy symptom. Nausea, cravings, exhaustion . . . it's all good. Maybe this new symptom is as well.

She ponders it for a few minutes, fighting to keep the worry at bay, wondering if it's all in her head, or if it's the start of Braxton Hicks contractions, which she knows are a normal third trimester symptom.

That's probably it.

Of course that's it.

Dr. Courmier told her at her last checkup to expect to begin to feel some changes as her body starts to get ready for childbirth.

Realizing Jeremy has been silent beside her, she looks over to see him absently focused on the television screen.

"What are you thinking about?" she asks him.

"You know . . . the earthquake. The prison. *Her.*"

"She's dead," Lucy says unnecessarily.

"Yeah. I know that. But whenever I hear anything about that earthquake, it just reminds me of her and . . ." He shudders. "I hate thinking about her."

"Then don't." It's Lucy's turn to lay a reassuring hand on Jeremy's arm. "Think about something else. Something pleasant."

His eyes shift to her face, and he rolls toward her, taking her in his arms. "Guess what? I already am."

She grabs her wallet, shoves it into the pocket of her coat—a down parka, not the trench she'd worn last night—and storms out of the apartment.

She can't listen to . . . to *that*.

She can't stand to see them together, in their bed.

Striding along the carpeted corridors, she doesn't pass a single soul. Good, because she forgot to disguise herself before walking out the door.

Does it matter, though?

She no longer looks anything like the girl whose picture was splashed all over the media years ago—the girl who died long before the prison walls collapsed around her.

I hate thinking about her, Jeremy had said.

She's dead, Lucy had replied.

Good. They believe that. Let them. Good. Good! And yet . . .

The contempt in his voice, Jeremy's voice, when he spoke of her . . .

And the calming assurance in Lucy's . . .

I hate them both. They're going to pay. They're going to die.

Having reached the main elevator bank, she jabs at the down button repeatedly in time with the word screaming in her brain.

Die, die, die, die, die . . .

Frustrated, she spins and pushes through the doors to the stairs. There are seventeen flights in the squared-off spiral that goes from the first floor to the towering glass domed ceiling, still painted over from the blackout years of World War II. She descends, relishing the pounding of her feet on the wide white marble steps and the pounding of her heart against her ribs.

She has no idea where she's going, only that she has to get away.

She puts up the hood on her coat before she reaches the lobby, just in case. The weather is gray and blustery. No one will question it.

The doorman and the guard are chatting beside the security desk in the lobby. Neither gives her a second glance.

They wouldn't recognize you even if they had.

Anonymous, in New York. Who would have ever imagined that could be possible?

Obviously, people forget.

But I don't. I never forget.

When she began the hunt for an apartment to rent in Manhattan, the Ansonia was one of the buildings that had come up with a vacancy. She recognized it right away, of course.

Elsa Cavalon's mother lived in a sprawling apartment there; it was where Elsa tried to hide when she realized someone was stalking her daughter, Renny. Rumor had it that the building's illustrious tenants fought to keep its role out of the press after the story broke—to no avail. Photos of the Ansonia were splashed all over the papers, along with shots of the Cavalons' small ranch house in Connecticut, the Montgomerys' brick colonial outside Boston, and the Quinns' Manhattan apartment building.

Naturally, there weren't just pictures of the places where the crimes had occurred. The faces were captured as well, faces of the so-called heroes and the so-called victims and the so-called criminal.

She's never liked labels. It's all in how you look at things.

For instance, Elsa and Renny had slipped from La La Montgomery's grasp on that long-ago day at the Ansonia.

Or did they?

Maybe she let them go. Because she knew that she was in control. Because she didn't want it to be over so quickly.

Maybe because she had killed before, and she realized that once the moment is over, you're left with little more than blood on your hands and a hollow, anticlimactic feeling.

And you want nothing more than to experience that high again. And again . . .

You want it so badly that the need consumes you and nothing else seems to matter.

But it does matter. This mission is about so much more than personal satisfaction; about so much more than her own vendetta against the Cavalons.

"This is where you belong," Chaplain Gideon told her on that cold day when she emerged from the subway to see the Ansonia looming over Broadway. "It's close to Jeremy and Lucy—but not too close."

There were plenty of open rental apartments in the building—including this one, which happens to face the same air shaft as Sylvie Durand's place, just a few floors above.

Walking through the small one-bedroom with the Realtor, she thought about what lay ahead, and the plan became as much about the backdrop as it was about the players.

The Ansonia *was* close to Jeremy and Lucy—but not close enough.

Yes. This was where she wanted them. Here, with her, under one roof at last—a towering mansard roof that would seem more natural perched atop a haunted house than one of Manhattan's foremost historic apartment buildings. Here, where she can keep an eye on them as the time draws near.

"If you want them here with you, then you have to make it happen," Chaplain Gideon said. And then he told her how to do that.

There was no guarantee that Lucy and Jeremy would move into Sylvie's vacant apartment after being kicked out of their own. But Chaplain Gideon told her to pray on it, and sure enough, everything fell into place as neatly as those cameras fit into the nooks and crannies in every room.

Now, it's just a matter of time.

In a few days, it will all be over for Lucy and Jeremy Cavalon . . .

And just beginning for True Believers like me.

Out on the street, she walks two short blocks down Broadway, glancing repeatedly over her shoulder—a habit she picked up in prison, where you have to be on guard all the time, because you never know when violence is going to sneak up on you.

Crossing over to the newsstand on the island near the subway station, she finds that the morning tabloids that once splashed her own name and face across their pages are stacked high alongside the gum and candy.

The *Post* and *Daily News* headlines don't disappoint.

Death on the 27th Floor
Did "I Told You So" Author See It Coming?

Remembering how she felt when the taut skin of Richard Jollston's neck split open beneath her blade, she smiles to herself as she fishes a couple of dollars from her wallet.

Seeing the brown smears on them, she hesitates. These are bills she took from Myra's pocket last night. She grabbed Richard Jollston's wallet, too, before she left the room. After removing the cash, she threw it into a garbage can around the corner from the hotel, ID and credit cards intact.

"You want both papers?"

"Yes," she tells the impatient-looking vendor, "and I want the *Times*, too." She takes a copy from the pile.

The story might not be trumpeted on the front page, but she'd be willing to bet an account of Richard Jollston's demise is printed somewhere in the newspaper that was set to debut his new book on its upcoming best-seller list.

She hands over the singles, and, as she had hoped, the vendor doesn't notice the bloodstains. Good. They'll be back in circulation momentarily.

After tucking the papers under her arm, she crosses back to the west side of Broadway and hesitates, wondering where to go next. Her body is demanding to be fed, but where should she go? She keeps her back to the wall of the building on the corner—another wary tendency she learned in prison.

It's miserable out here this morning, with a

damp, icy wind blowing in from the Hudson River, cutting through her.

Maybe she'll find a coffee shop. Order a big, hot breakfast. Sit and read the papers. Try to forget what she heard back at the apartment . . .

Suddenly, she remembers something.

Are you going to Parkview? Lucy had asked Jeremy.

Where—or what—is Parkview? And why does he apparently go there every Friday morning?

She has no idea. But she sure as hell is going to find out.

She crosses Seventy-second Street and hurries back up to the Ansonia.

In twenty-five years as a homicide detective with the NYPD, Omar Meade has seen some horrific crime scenes.

This definitely ranks right up there among the bloodiest.

A hotel guest and maid, slaughtered in a fancy suite that has a hell of a view of the Chrysler building to the south and a hell of a carpet-cleaning bill in its very near future.

The bodies were discovered late last night by the housekeeping supervisor and a security guard, who went looking for the maid when she failed to return from her turndown shift.

"I'da thought she'd just walked off the job—it happens—but not with a whole cart full of stuff," the badly shaken supervisor told Meade and his partner, Lisha Brandewyne.

Both the cart and the maid are right here inside

the suite, along with the corpse of the room's occupant.

"One thing's for sure—this is no robbery gone wrong." Brandewyne shakes her close-cropped brunette head, surveying the slaughtered male victim lying just inside the door on a blood-soaked patch of carpet. The maid is a few yards away, between the bathroom and the foot of the bed.

"Hell, no," Meade agrees, "it's not a robbery."

"It was supposed to look like one, though. What are we, stupid?" Brandewyne flashes her coffee-and-nicotine-stained teeth.

Meade looks away, down at his notes.

Yes, it was definitely staged to look like a robbery. Jollston's wallet is missing, as is the maid's tip money—she'd have collected about fifteen bucks, according to the guests occupying the neighboring suites that had received turndown service before she and her cart disappeared into 2715.

But the killer wasn't very thorough. In Jollston's pocket was a Tiffany's gift box containing three-thousand-dollar diamond and platinum earrings.

Based on the estimated times of death—a couple of hours apart—Meade is betting the victims were total strangers whose paths crossed only postmortem.

He's certain this was no random crime, and that Jollston was the intended victim, considering he was hacked up pretty good—stab wounds all over his body. The Tiffany's box in his pocket was soaked through with blood.

In stark contrast, the woman was sliced open from ear to ear, execution-style, indicating to

Meade that she merely got in the way—classic wrong-place, wrong-time scenario.

With any luck, the hotel's surveillance videos—now being scrutinized down in the security office—will reveal the killer's identity. With a little more luck, Meade will track down the perp, make an arrest, and be home in time for his son Dante's holiday choir concert at school tonight.

Luck. Yeah. Wouldn't that be nice.

Meade—who doesn't go to Atlantic City, doesn't play the lottery, and hasn't made it to one of Dante's school concerts in years—has a feeling it's going to be another long day, and an even longer night.

I'd be on the train right now if we still lived in White Plains, Lucy thinks, noting the time—8:03—on the microwave in the kitchen.

She dumps half a pot of coffee into the sink and quickly turns on the tap to wash it down, her gag reflex triggered by the smell.

She puts the empty carafe into the dishwasher, along with two empty cereal bowls, spoons, and the plate she used for her toast and jam. She told Jeremy the day they moved in that she's been craving strawberry preserves, and he promptly went across the street to Fairway to buy several jars. She's already halfway through the second one.

"Should you be eating that right out of the jar with the spoon?" Jeremy asked her earlier, when they were eating breakfast. "I mean . . . that's an awful lot of jam, isn't it?"

"Cravings are good," she assured him. "Anyway . . . I just want it. I have to have it. A lot of it."

"So it shall be."

All that sugar seems to have given the baby some extra energy, that's for sure. He or she has been kicking and dancing more than usual this morning.

Lucy closes the dishwasher, wipes down the counters, and checks the clock again. 8:04.

Now what?

She's already dressed and ready for the workday, and she doesn't have to leave for at least twenty minutes.

She pours herself another cup of tea and wanders through the apartment while waiting for it to steep.

She finds herself torn between opening all the shades to let in the morning light, and keeping them drawn to shut out prying eyes. Strange, because she's never had that feeling before, and of all the places she's ever lived, this apartment in the sky is the least conducive to Peeping Toms.

Forcing herself to open the living room draperies, she peers out to make sure no one is looking back in at her. The bleak cityscape is reassuringly void of visible voyeurs, but she supposes someone could be spying on her through a telescope or binoculars.

Unsettled by the thought, she closes the drapes again. But the strange feeling that she's being watched doesn't go away.

Frustrated, she reopens the drapes, muttering, "You're losing it."

Just last night, she was scoffing at Ryan's suggestion that she's afraid to be here alone, and now look at her, in the broad light of day.

Not *afraid*, exactly, but . . .

Vulnerable. Or something.

Whatever it is, she doesn't like it.

If Jeremy were here with her right now she'd undoubtedly feel less vulnerable—or whatever it is that she's feeling. But he's on his way to Parkview.

As he got ready to go, he was even quieter than he usually is on Friday mornings with the looming visit weighing on him.

"Are you okay?" Lucy asked, watching him silently tuck his keys and MetroCard into the front pocket of the canvas bag he carries around with him.

"Yep."

That was it. Just *yep*, followed by a quick kiss good-bye, and out the door he went.

He was probably sulking because she refused to, as he put it, "christen the new bedroom."

Worried about the cramping she'd experienced, she was afraid to take any chances. She didn't want to tell Jeremy she was worried, though, about this new symptom, so instead she told him she was just nauseous. To his credit, he didn't say, "So what else is new?" but she could tell he wanted to.

Obviously frustrated, he got out of bed and went off to take a shower—most likely, a cold one.

She wishes she hadn't made plans to go out tonight with Robyn. Maybe she should cancel.

No—I can't do that to her.

She's been looking forward to seeing her friend tonight. They've been trying to get together for over a month now, but something always seems to come up at the last minute to force a cancellation—mostly on Lucy's end.

So yeah, she'd better keep the happy hour date. She and Jeremy will have the whole weekend together, and anyway, she's a firm believer in maintaining an independent social life in a marriage.

Her own mother didn't, and look what happened to her when Daddy moved out. She was pretty much abandoned by all their mutual friends.

Not that Lucy can imagine that Jeremy would ever leave her . . .

But I'm sure Mom was thinking the same thing about Daddy in the early days, before I was born.

Yeah, now *there's* an unsettling truth that's proven impossible to ignore: her parents had been happily married for a long time before Daddy's midlife crisis.

She remembers what life was like back when Lauren and Nick Walsh used to laugh together, and hold hands, and kiss. She remembers actually scolding them for acting all mushy.

Yeah, and that was nothing compared to watching Daddy fawn all over Beth the home wrecker a few years later.

Pushing that uncomfortable memory aside, Lucy unplugs her cell phone from the wall charger near the sofa. She has two calls to make today: one to her mother, and one to Carl Soto, their former landlord, to see when they can expect the return of their security deposit.

It's a little too early to call him, but Mom and Sam will have been up for a while.

She dials the number for their Vero Beach condo. It rings several times, then goes into voice mail. Maybe they went out to breakfast, or for a walk on the beach. Lucky them.

As she leaves a message, she glances at the gray December day beyond the tall rain-spattered windowpane and wrought-iron scrollwork of the Juliet balcony. Maybe the weather is responsible for Jeremy's glum mood this morning, and her own unsettled frame of mind.

Too bad we can't afford to jump on a plane and fly south for Christmas to find the sun, she thinks wistfully. It's been almost two years since they took a real vacation.

And at the rate they're going, it'll probably be a few more years until they can afford one again.

She decides it's not too early to call Carl Soto after all. And if it is . . . too bad. She dials, lets it ring.

He doesn't pick up, either. Maybe he recognizes her number on his caller ID and is avoiding her.

She sighs, waiting for it to go into voice mail, hoping they don't have to chase him down for their money. They could really use it.

He heard the phone ringing as he was stepping out of the shower and ran for it, but he was too late. He waits a few moments, dripping onto the rug, and then dials into voice mail to see if there's a message.

"Hello, Mr. Soto. This is Lucy Cavalon. Jeremy and I were wondering when we can expect to hear from you about our security deposit. Please give me a call back as soon as possible . . ."

Carl replays the message, this time grabbing a pen and paper to write down the phone number she leaves him, before remembering that it's probably in his phone's caller ID. Modern technology is a wonderful thing . . . most of the time.

He puts the number aside and returns to the bathroom to towel off, thinking about the Cavalons and about Mary, the woman who forced him to force them out of the apartment.

Well, it's not like she held a gun to his head. But she waved a wad of cash at him, and that was almost as powerful a motivator.

He'd been thinking the call might be from her. He's been hoping that every time the phone has rung for the past few days, but it never is.

Face it, Soto. You've been duped.

His friend Lee denied that he'd been behind the scheme, and although Carl had really pushed him on it, he's pretty sure Lee is telling the truth. What possible motive would Lee have to set him up that way? Besides, Lee might be a practical joker, but he's also a real cheapskate. He wouldn't find anything funny about a prank that set him back several thousand bucks.

Maybe Mary got hit by a bus and that's why he hasn't heard from her.

Or maybe something else is going on here.

Maybe the Cavalons themselves put him up to this because . . .

Because why? They wanted to force him to evict them so they could get out of their lease?

But it would have eventually been up anyway, and if they wanted to move out so badly, they'd have been better off financially just paying the rent on an empty apartment for a few more months.

Nothing about this shady deal makes sense.

But Carl can hardly go to the police to complain about a stranger coming up to him on the street and handing over a whole lot of money . . . can he?

No. You can't.

He vigorously rubs what's left of his hair with a towel and wonders what he's going to tell Lucy Cavalon when he calls her back.

Holding her umbrella and bundled in her parka with the hood up, she trails Jeremy at a safe distance as he strides along the winding path through Central Park, past Strawberry Fields and Bethesda Terrace.

The park is busy despite the raw day. Good. Less chance that Jeremy will spot her among the joggers and bikers, the businesspeople walking to work, the mothers and nannies pushing strollers wrapped in clear plastic tarp.

She looks over her shoulder every so often, as is her habit. But Jeremy never does, either because it wouldn't occur to him that he's being followed, or because he's too absorbed by his mission to pay attention to what's around him.

Back at the apartment, while devouring the hot ham, egg, and Swiss sandwiches she'd picked up at the deli, she'd plugged both "Parkview" and "Park View" into her computer's search engine. It came up with far too many hits to sort through—apartment buildings, hotels, hospitals, restaurants, stores . . .

She still has no idea which one Jeremy is visiting, but she's definitely about to find out.

He emerges from the park on Fifth Avenue at East Seventy-second Street.

Ah, familiar territory. The Upper East Side. Now what?

He turns left and walks up several blocks, then makes a right and walks two and a half blocks east.

There, he disappears into a building.

She catches up a few seconds later and looks at the placard beside the revolving door.

What the . . . ?

Parkview is a private psychiatric hospital.

After a mostly sleepless night mulling over his conversation with his sister and waiting for the phone to ring, Ryan managed to get himself to work. At least, he's here in the sense that he's physically sitting at his desk.

But really, he's not *here*. His thoughts are, as the cliché goes, a million miles away, with Phoenix—who at this point might as well be a million miles away.

Ryan's been leaving messages and sending texts since yesterday afternoon.

Why isn't she picking up her phone or texting him back?

And why can't he stop thinking about what Lucy said? Not about Phoenix—but about Ryan himself, when he told her he feels as though something is missing in his life.

Maybe it's some part of yourself that you lost a long time ago, and you need to find it again.

Maybe Lucy is right. Maybe it *is* about him. Maybe he *does* need to find himself again. He always thought that having the things that other people—normal people—his age have—like an education, a job, a relationship—would make him feel normal again, too.

He has all those things now, yet he's still incomplete, and more insecure than ever.

Especially when it comes to Phoenix.

Why is she with a guy like me?

Ryan Walsh is no fool. He can tell himself all he wants that she's attracted to his kind heart, or his sensitive soul, or that she's just new in town—a breath of fresh air compared to the women here who don't give him the time of day—but in the end, he doesn't really believe it.

Especially now that she hasn't called him back.

Traci, one of his coworkers, sticks her dark head around the corner of his cubicle. "Hey, Ryan, here's that file."

"What file?"

"The one you asked me about yesterday, when you were looking for background about that Medicare fraud case. Take a look at it and let me know if it helps."

"Right . . . I will." He takes the manila folder from her and waits for her to go.

Why isn't she going?

Where is Phoenix, dammit?

Why is she with me?

Why? Why? Why?

"Is everything okay?" Traci is asking.

"Yeah. Fine."

She looks like she wants to say something, then shrugs and walks away.

The moment she disappears, Ryan tosses the folder aside and goes back to his computer screen.

He's been trolling the local media and police blotters on the Internet, making sure there weren't any incidents overnight that might have involved Phoenix. He could find nothing about an unidentified accident or crime victim that might fit her description—although he'd stumbled across one unsettling piece that gave him pause.

There was a double homicide in a midtown hotel last night, and the name of one of the victims— the maid—hasn't been released yet, pending notification of her next of kin.

Phoenix isn't a hotel maid, Ryan reminds himself. *She's a corporate accountant.*

That's what she told him, anyway.

What if she lied?

Why would she lie?

There's that word again—*why.*

But what if she did?

What if she's really a hotel maid, and right now she's lying in the city morgue? He might never even know, because he's not her next of kin.

Who *is* her next of kin?

She's an only child and her parents are dead. She has a roommate, an ex-boyfriend, and, presumably, coworkers and friends . . .

But Ryan has never met any of them.

Why not?

What does he really know about her past, other than that she's from Arizona and her last name is Williams—which happens to be the third most common name in the United States, according to her.

Not a whole lot to go on.

He gives the computer mouse a hard shove and it skitters across his desk, colliding with the pencil cup that goes over with a clatter.

Dammit. Ryan leans his head back and closes his eyes.

She waits just outside the glass revolving door, pretending to wrestle with her umbrella as she keeps an eye on Jeremy as he speaks to the uniformed guard at the security desk, then signs in on a clipboard.

She waits until the elevator doors are closing behind him, then blows into the small lobby.

"Wow—it's nasty out there this morning!" she proclaims as the guard, a ruddy-faced older man with a shock of white hair, looks up from the newspaper he was just about to open again.

"Sure is." He knits his thick gray brows, staring at her kind of funny.

He can't possibly think she's up to something. She just walked in the door.

You're just paranoid, she tells herself, sneaking a peek at the elevator bank. The one Jeremy boarded as the sole occupant has just stopped on the fourth floor.

"I hate winter, don't you?" she asks the guard, as casually as she can.

"Nah. I like it. Good whiskey weather, as my granddad used to say."

"As far as I'm concerned, any weather is good whiskey weather *if* it's good whiskey." She grins at him and then, satisfied she's won him over, flinches. "Oh no!" she says and bends her head, rubbing her eye.

"What's wrong?"

"My contact lens . . . I just dropped it." She blinks rapidly and pats her fingertips around on the desk between them. "I hope it didn't bounce onto the floor . . ."

The guard looks down just long enough for her to take a good look at the clipboard in front of him.

"Oh! Here it is!" She pretends to pick up something from the desk and turns slightly away from him, making a show of popping her "contact" back into her eye. "There. Good thing it wasn't on the floor. I never would've found it."

"Glad you did."

"Me too. Anyway, I'm here to see Darryl Gaus. He's in 402."

"Darryl Gaus, Darryl Gaus." He scans through a directory on the computer screen. "Sorry. I'm new here. Still getting to know everyone. Yup. 402."

Across the lobby, elevator doors open and out steps an attractive woman in a dress coat, hose, and heeled pumps. "See you later, Fitzy," she tells the guard as she strides past.

"Later, Dr. Westfall." Fitzy watches her admiringly until she exits the building, then gets back to the business at hand, sliding the clipboard across the counter along with a pen. "Just sign in here and take this visitor's pass up to the nurses at the station on four."

She writes a name—not her own, and not any of her recent aliases—along with the time and the random patient's name she'd spotted toward the top of the page, listed with Thursday's patients who'd received late day visitors.

As she writes, she scans Jeremy's entry just above her own. She can make out the room number, 421, but the patient's name, like his own signature, is all but illegible.

"All set," she says cheerfully to the guard. "Have a great day, and thanks!"

"You're very welcome." Fitzy hands over a visitor's pass, then tips his hat to her as she sails onto the elevator and presses the button for the fourth floor.

"Don't tell me it's TGIF already?" Wendy Nevid comments, spotting Jeremy as he approaches the nurses' station.

"Sure is. Got any fun weekend plans?"

"That depends on how you define fun," the nurse, a petite, blue-eyed blonde, tells him. "I have to finish my Hanukkah shopping, and Ethan has karate and swimming lessons and Julia has volleyball, and they're invited to three birthday parties between them, so Mark and I will be running from one kid thing to another."

"Sounds fun to me."

Wendy shakes her head, but Jeremy means it. What he wouldn't give to be in her shoes a few years from now, with a couple of healthy, busy kids.

"How about you?" Wendy asks.

"My wife and I just moved into a new place and we've still got some unpacking to do, so that's my big weekend plan."

"Where is it?"

"Upper West Side."

"How do you like living in Manhattan?"

"So far, so good. Makes it easier to get to work, that's for sure. And to get here, too. Maybe I'll be able to come by more often." The hospital is a fairly short walk across Central Park. In better weather, it will be a nice stroll. Today, he didn't enjoy it in the least.

"It means a lot to her that you're here every Friday morning."

"I missed last week. And the week before." And the week of his grandmother's funeral, too, back in November.

"Really?" Wendy shrugs, and he wonders if she really didn't notice that he wasn't here. Or is she just trying to make him feel less guilty?

"Well, things come up," she says. "You come when you can, and when you do, she's glad to see you."

He nods, but he's not so sure, most of the time, that she even knows he's there with her.

He comes anyway, because he wants to see her. Because he *has* to see her. Because if it weren't for her, he wouldn't be here.

Here, as in alive.

And if it weren't for me, she wouldn't be here, he can't help thinking. Here, as in *here*: at Parkview.

It's taken him years to realize that he isn't directly responsible for the tragic series of events that destroyed her life and so many others that touched it. He knows that he's a victim, too. But no one can erase the fact that a lot of people might have been much better off if he'd never been born.

Might *have been better off?*

Would. Would *have been better off.*

He thinks of Miguel and his pregnant girl-friend, Carmen, as he has many times since last night, then pushes them from his head. They have nothing to do with this. With him.

"How has she been this week?" he asks Wendy.

"Just fine. She rolled herself down the hall to bingo last night and won a stuffed animal. She was thrilled."

Thrilled about winning a toy while playing bingo in a wheelchair.

Not just any toy. A stuffed animal.

Wendy Nevid might not grasp the irony, but Jeremy does. It was a stuffed animal—containing a hidden memory stick full of damaging evidence—that triggered Garvey's deadly rampage fifteen years ago.

He forces a smile. "That's . . . great. That she won bingo, I mean. That she was so happy . . ."

"Simple things matter a lot in this world, Jeremy."

She's not talking about the world in general, he knows—because in the real world, who gives a crap about bingo? She's talking about the world of Parkview.

Wendy touches his arm, her pretty face sympa-thetic. "I know it's not easy for you to see her like this, but—"

"I'm sure it's not easy for anyone who visits this place." *Please don't feel sorry for me. I don't want to start feeling sorry for myself. Or angry . . .*

"No. But our patients are in good hands. I hope you know that."

"I do." This time, his smile is genuine. "Have a great weekend, Wendy."

"You too." She gives a little wave and he heads down the hall.

Standing with her back against the wall, right around the corner from the nurses' station, she absorbs what she just overheard.

At first, she thought Jeremy and the nurse were talking about Elsa Cavalon, or possibly Renny. Maybe one of them finally went off the deep end, a delayed response to all they had been through years ago . . .

But then, analyzing what Jeremy had said—that he'd missed last week, and the week before—she realizes it can't be Elsa.

She, as of a few days ago, had been perfectly fine, living in Connecticut with her husband, Brett. And Renny is in college at NYU, downtown.

She knows. She's been keeping tabs on them—along with everyone else in Jeremy's world.

The nurse was clearly talking about someone who's been here for a long time. Long enough for Jeremy to have established a regular visiting routine. Long enough for him and the nurse to be all first-name chummy and—

"Excuse me!"

Jolted by a voice right beside her—the same voice that was just chatting with Jeremy—she turns to see a pretty blonde clad in pastel scrubs. Ah, Nurse Wendy.

"Can I help you?" she asks—not exactly unpleasantly, but not in nearly as friendly a tone as she used with Jeremy.

"I—I think I'm lost. I'm here to visit my uncle."

"Who's your uncle?"

"Darryl Gaus."

Immediately, Wendy's blue eyes take on a wary expression. "Darryl Gaus is your . . . *uncle*?"

Hearing the slight hesitation and incredulous emphasis on the last word, she realizes she's just made a terrible mistake.

Darryl. It's an unusual name for a woman, but not unheard of.

Wendy bounces back quickly, but there's no denying that she's suspicious. "Hang on a sec, I'll check the room number for you." She disappears around the corner—undoubtedly to call security.

There's no time to wait for the elevator. She rushes toward the adjacent stairwell instead, praying there's no alarm on the door.

Luck is with her.

She hurtles herself down four flights and emerges in the lobby.

Fitzy, the guard, looks up in surprise from his *New York Post* with its *Death on the 27th Floor* headline. "Hey, what's going on? Are you okay?"

She blows past him and out the door, and she doesn't stop running until she reaches the subway station several blocks away.

Fishing a MetroCard from her pocket, she scurries down the stairs and through the turnstile. Panting, she pushes her way along the subway platform, crowded with rush hour commuters.

The train pulls in almost immediately.

Safely on board, wedged into the car with dozens of oblivious strangers, she sighs with relief.

That was a close call.

Now that it's over, she turns her attention to a far greater concern: Who in the world is Jeremy Cavalon visiting in a mental hospital?

With his bearded chin resting in his hand, Omar Meade stares at the last few seconds of the grainy video, taking it in without comment.

"Talk about *bizarre*," Lisha Brandewyne murmurs, seated beside him in the small back office.

They're accompanied by a couple of uniformed cops, a security guard, and the nervous Nellie hotel manager Stanley Reiner, who looks like he's going to faint at any given moment—though he has yet to even see the gory crime scene upstairs. He won't, if Meade has any say in the matter.

After watching the snippet of video through to the end, Meade commands, "Play it again."

"Play it again, *Sam*," chirps Brandewyne, and Meade shoots her a look that of course she doesn't catch.

The security guard obediently presses a button and Meade pushes Brandewyne and her stupid, inappropriate quip out of his head.

Onscreen, a long shot of the hallway on the twenty-seventh floor.

Elevator doors open.

Out steps a heavyset woman in a hooded trench coat. Her head is bent, her face hidden from view.

She walks swiftly down the hall and disappears through a door at the end.

"No cameras in the stairwells?" Lisha asks unnecessarily, and the security guard shakes his head, pressing another button as Reiner wrings his hands.

A new scene—the maid emerging from suite 2713 and rolling her cart down to the next one, 2715.

She unlocks the suite and reaches inside to fold the security latch out onto the jamb, using it to prop open the door to the hall.

Moments later the door to the stairwell opens and the figure in the trench coat emerges. Hood still up, head still bent, she walks purposefully down the hall to 2715. She opens the door, pushes the maid's cart inside, slips in after it, and closes the door.

A new scene: Richard Jollston stepping off the elevator, strolling to his room, swaying a little. He'd been drinking in the bar—they've established that. Three whiskeys, and he was obviously feeling no pain.

Yet.

In silence, they watch him disappear into his suite, never again to be seen alive.

"Okay, one more scene . . ." The security guard pushes another button and the onscreen image advances.

Now—and this freaking sends chills down Omar's spine—the door to the room opens and a figure slips out into the hallway. Still hooded—but this time, not by a trench coat. Now she's wearing some kind of long, flowing cloak.

"She looks like a damned monk," Lisha mutters, shaking her head.

Exactly.

Omar rubs his beard thoughtfully. "Play it again."

"Play it again, S—" Brandewyne breaks off, this time catching his glare.

"Hi, you've reached Phoenix. Leave a message and I'll be sure to get right back to you."

No, you won't.

Ryan hangs up, resisting the urge to stand up and pace. There's nowhere to go in this tiny cubicle, and he doesn't want to leave it in case she tries to reach him on his direct office line instead of on his cell.

But he doubts that's going to be the case. No, he's becoming more and more convinced that something catastrophic has happened. Either to her—or to him.

If nothing terrible happened to her that would prevent her from getting in touch, then she's not getting in touch because she doesn't want to. Because she's finished with him.

That would be catastrophic—and not entirely unexpected. The more he's thought about the way she keeps him at arm's length, the more he's come to realize that not only does she probably not feel the same way about him that he does about her . . .

But maybe *he* doesn't even feel the way he thought he did about her.

How can you love someone you don't trust?

And when you get right down to it, how, in this world, can you trust *anyone*?

Look at what happened to Ryan's parents. To his grandparents on his father's side. And to countless other marriages.

Shattered lives, broken homes, cheating spouses . . .

This is crazy. What made Ryan think he had a shot at happily-ever-after when even people who have everything going for them can't guarantee success?

You'd be better off alone.

And it's a good thing, because that's where you've always been, and it looks like that's where you're going to be from here on in, and that, my friend, will give you plenty of time to find yourself.

Jeremy finds the door to room 421 ajar, as usual. Taped to it is a paper Christmas stocking, her name written on it in silver glitter glue.

Not her real name, of course, but the alias Jeremy used for her when he registered her here a few years ago, after the final blow to her psyche. The assumed name was a last-ditch effort to protect what little was left of her privacy and dignity. He didn't think it would work, but it very well may have.

Only a handful of people here at the hospital even know the true identity of the frail woman in room 421.

The rest of the world seems to have bought the story Jeremy planted in the press with the help of her longtime friend Heather Cottington: that Marin Hartwell Quinn had gone into seclusion somewhere in Europe, hoping to put her heartbreaking past behind her.

CHAPTER SIX

Lucy is on her office phone troubleshooting a PC with an employee when she feels a buzzing vibration in her purse beneath the desk.

She quickly reaches down, pulls out the phone, and checks the caller ID.

"I'm sorry, I need to put you on hold for a moment," she tells the woman on her office line, and presses the hold button before the inevitable protest.

She answers her cell with a brisk "Hello?"

"Mrs. Cavalon?"

"Yes. Who is this, please?" she asks Carl Soto, not quite sure why she's pretending she doesn't know—maybe so that he won't think she's been waiting breathlessly for his return call.

Truthfully, she hasn't. It's been a busy morning so far, and the few times she's been able to take a breather and focus on something other than work, her former landlord hasn't even come to mind. Jeremy has. She tried calling his cell a little while ago, but it was turned off, as it usually is when he's at the hospital visiting Marin. She left him a message to call her when he leaves Parkview.

That crampy feeling she had this morning is

also in the back of her mind. She hasn't felt anything further, though, so she's going to take that as a good sign.

"This is Carl Soto, Mrs. Cavalon," the landlord is saying over the phone. "I wanted you to know that I do have your security deposit, and I'll be happy to put it into the mail if you want to give me your new address."

"Thanks. It's 2109 Broadway—"

"Or—I just thought of something," Carl Soto cuts in so promptly that she realizes he didn't *just* think of it at all. "I can drop off the check in person tomorrow."

In person? That's a bizarre offer, coming from a man Lucy's seen perhaps twice in all the time he's been their landlord.

"I have to be in the city anyway. That way you don't have to wait for it to come in the mail next week."

"That's really not—"

"I'd like to do that, if you don't mind, Mrs. Cavalon. There's actually something I wanted to talk to you about."

She frowns, glancing at the red hold light on her desk phone, conscious of the waiting client. "Is it about the apartment? Because we made sure that we left it clean."

"No, no, you did. Spotless. I appreciate that. And it is about the apartment, but I—"

"It's okay," she quickly cuts in as the other line on her desk phone lights up with a call. "You can stop by tomorrow anytime. We'll be home."

"Good. I'll see you at around eleven."

She hangs up and tosses her cell back into her

purse, then quickly presses the button for line two. "Lucy Cavalon."

"Hi, Lucy, I think one of the computers on our network down here has a virus . . ."

"All right, hang on just a second, I'm on the other line."

As she juggles phone calls, her thoughts drift back to Carl Soto. She isn't particularly anxious to see the man in person after what he did—but they *do* need the money, the sooner the better . . .

Plus, he's definitely piqued her curiosity.

What could he possibly say to them about the apartment at this late date, other than to apologize for kicking them out?

If that's all he wants, they can certainly live without it.

But Lucy has a feeling there might be more to it than that.

Occasionally Jeremy finds Marin still in bed when he arrives; but when he doesn't, he finds her precisely where she is today: sitting in her wheelchair, facing the room's lone window. It overlooks an alley between the hospital and the office building next door. Not long ago, she was in a smaller room across the hall, facing a different alley.

Despite the hospital's bucolic name— Parkview—Jeremy's noticed that most of the patient rooms and visitor areas look out on concrete walls of other buildings.

But he suspects the view matters very little—to her, anyway. Though she gravitates to this spot, facing the glass, she never really seems to be seeing what's out there.

HELL TO PAY 155

Hell, half the time, when she looks at him, she doesn't seem to know who he is.

No. It's even more complicated than that. Looking into her vacant blue eyes, he often thinks she has no idea who *she* is, either.

On the deep windowsill before her sits a marble notebook that serves as the journal patients are encouraged to keep. Spiral-bound notebooks aren't allowed here. When Jeremy mentioned that to Lucy the first time they visited together, she didn't understand why.

"You could hurt yourself with the wire," Jeremy told her, and saw the sad comprehension filter into her green eyes.

She knew, of course, about the final tragedy that had pushed Marin Hartwell Quinn over the edge and sent her to a mental health facility in a psychotic state. It happened shortly after two milestone incidents in Jeremy's life took place within a few months of each other: his own wedding, and Garvey Quinn's death. Yes, just when he thought he might be able to put the past behind him and make a fresh start at last, all hell broke loose again.

As a result of that final blow, Marin may very well be here at Parkview for the rest of her life. Given a choice, it's not what she ever would have wanted. Her own father had been diagnosed with early-onset dementia and lived out his days in a facility near Boston—talking to people who weren't there, Marin once told Jeremy, and ignoring people who were.

"It's heartbreaking to see him like that," she said sadly, "stuck in that place, not even knowing where he is most of the time."

And now, it's her turn.

"Do you know if this kind of thing runs in the family?" Jeremy asked Wendy a while back.

"That's something you need to discuss with the doctor."

Probably. But he can't bring himself to do it. Maybe he's afraid of what he might find out.

As Jeremy crosses the room toward her, he notes the framed photograph on the sill beside the marble notebook—which for all he knows is probably blank.

There's no glass covering the picture. Glass, of course, can be broken into shards that can slit wrists.

In the photograph are Caroline and Annie, Marin's two daughters—Jeremy's sisters.

He doesn't like to look at it, and he isn't sure it's a healthy thing that she carries it around the room with her, holding it in her lap, or setting it on the nearest surface.

He has no doubt that when she played bingo last night, the photo was propped alongside her card and chips. It will be on her nightstand tonight when she goes to bed—that's where it is every night, as though the two girls are guardian angels watching over her.

That was Lucy's take on it, anyway.

Jeremy's just glad she didn't say it in front of Marin, who would have started wailing hysterically about how it should be the other way around. Sometimes when she gets going like that, they have to stick her with a needle to calm her down. Jeremy witnessed it once—his frail, frantic mother being strong-armed and tranquilized by a couple of nurses—for her own good, he knows—and he never wants to see it again.

His mother.

Technically, that's what Marin is—his birth mother. Twice, she mourned his loss: when she gave him up as a newborn, and when she found out he'd been kidnapped and left for dead by his own father.

He doesn't doubt that she loves him—or rather, *loved* him, when she was capable of it.

But Elsa Cavalon is the mother he remembers for the three precious years of his childhood before he was abducted. She's the one who tucked him into bed and bandaged his knees and believed in him when the whole world was against him.

She's the mother who tried desperately to find him, hiring a private detective, Mike Fantoni, when the police got nowhere.

She's the mother who sat in the front pew when Jeremy and Lucy were married, the one who will rock their child in her arms—the one their child will call Grandma.

She's the one—the only one—Jeremy calls Mom.

It's different with Marin. By the time Jeremy found his way back to her, she'd been ravaged; she was so fragile he sensed that she was on the verge of a breakdown long before it actually happened. They bonded, yet not as mother and son in the sense that she would look after him, as a parent would; as Elsa and Brett have since the day he came back into their lives.

No, it's more that he looks out for Marin, makes sure she's taken care of, makes sure—with the aid of her longtime friend, Heather—that Marin is "sighted" overseas from time to time—just often enough to keep anyone from looking for her closer to home.

"Marin?"

She doesn't respond. Maybe he spoke too softly, not wanting to risk anyone overhearing her name. Or—he notes her slumped posture—maybe she's asleep.

Stepping around the front of the wheelchair, he sees that her eyes are open, staring dully out the window.

Once the epitome of graceful beauty, Marin Hartwell Quinn bears little resemblance to her oft-photographed former self. Her straggly blond hair is streaked with gray, her skin like faded, crumpled tissue paper from a forgotten drawer.

"Marin?"

She blinks, looks up at him without recognition.

"It's me. Jeremy."

"I know." Almost dazed, she nods and reaches out with a thin, blue-veined hand that looks as though it belongs to a much older woman. Resting it on the sleeve of his jacket, she asks, "Have you seen her?"

He sighs inwardly.

He'd been hoping, somehow, that today, she wouldn't ask.

He should have known better. She always asks. And his answer is always the same.

"No. I haven't seen her."

Still wondering about the patient Jeremy was visiting at Parkview, she rides the subway home: first the Number Six train downtown, then the shuttle across Forty-second Street to Times Square, and finally an uptown Number Two express.

Every train car is crowded with rush hour commuters, but not a single person makes eye contact with her, or even glances her way.

That's the beauty of New York City. You can get lost here.

And found, too.

Yes—found, the way she found Lucy and Jeremy after she got out of prison.

But not right away.

Chaplain Gideon told her to leave Massachusetts immediately after she escaped, so she took an Amtrak train to Washington, D.C., and changed there for another train that took her all the way south to Miami.

It had been winter in the Northeast, but the Florida weather was beautiful—warm and sunny, with a salty breeze that reminded her of her childhood, and Daddy.

Miami is a transient place—particularly at that time of year. She quickly found an off-the-books job waiting tables and rented a room not far from the beach. They fed her well at the restaurant where she worked. She ate conch fritters and key lime pie. She let her prison-shorn hair grow long. The sun bleached it and made her skin weathered and ruddy, but she liked it that way. She liked to be outside after all those years in prison. Winter turned to spring, summer, and finally fall, and Chaplain Gideon told her it was time to return to the Northeast.

She located Jeremy and Lucy without a problem—that's the beauty of the Internet.

It wasn't immediately obvious to her that Lucy was pregnant, though. Not until the day she trailed her after work to a maternity store on Lexington Avenue.

Standing out there in the cold, watching Lucy through the plate-glass window as she browsed the racks of clothes . . .

Lucy Cavalon was pregnant. Through her, the bloodline would endure.

Enraged, she realized that Jeremy's wife had stolen the life she herself could have—should have—had.

But then Chaplain Gideon explained to her what was going on, and he quoted from the book of Revelation.

Behold, I am coming soon! My reward is with me, and I will give to everyone according to what he has done . . .

Suddenly, it all made sense.

Lucy was with child, just as the Virgin Mary had been—but this baby would not belong to her and Jeremy any more than Mary and Joseph's baby belonged to them.

Interviewing the widow of a murder victim is one of Meade's least favorite parts of this job. It's hard enough to sit in a room with a shell-shocked stranger who's just suffered an unimaginable loss; torturous to gather as much information as possible while weeding out details that seem important to the widow but are often irrelevant to the case.

Richard Jollston's wife, Sondra, arrived in Manhattan just twenty minutes ago, predictably distraught. Now, seated in a private interview room at the precinct, she wants to tell Meade and Brandewyne about the new house she and her dead husband just bought—how it has a pool and professional landscaping and is right down the street from one of the Red Sox players.

Meade—a die-hard fan of the rival New York Yankees—isn't interested in that, unless the Red Sox are behind Jollston's murder, which he highly doubts.

But he lets Sondra talk and sob and wail, "Why, why, why?" because that's the humane thing to do.

And because it gives him a chance to study Sondra's demeanor and make sure her grief is genuine. He's already aware that the Jollstons' marriage was troubled; that they had recently reconciled. But only, as he and Brandewyne privately noted, after Richard stumbled into fame and fortune.

"This guy was like a modern-day Chicken Little," Brandewyne said—though, mercifully, not in front of Sondra Jollston, who had yet to arrive at that point.

"That doesn't make sense," Meade told her.

"Of course it makes sense. Chicken Little went around saying the sky was falling, and no one believed him until all of a sudden—"

"But 'modern-day' implies that Chicken Little was real," Meade cut in, "and he wasn't."

"Where do you get that?"

"You think he's real?"

"No! I mean, that is not what 'modern-day' implies."

It was stupid, arguing about an imaginary character from a children's fable, and he knew it, but he couldn't help himself. Brandewyne pushed his buttons.

At the moment, though, watching her hand a box of tissues to the weeping widow and pat her arm, Meade has to admit that she's got just the right female touch here.

"Did your husband have any enemies, Mrs. Jollston?" she asks after a minute or two.

Sniffling, Sondra shakes her head.

"Any weird encounters with readers?" Meade puts in. "Bizarre fan mail? Anything like that?"

Again, she shakes her head. "Not unless you consider religious freaks weird or bizarre."

Meade and Brandewyne look at each other, and he knows she, too, is thinking about the footage of Jollston's presumed killer.

"What do you mean, Mrs. Jollston?" he asks.

"Just—I don't know, there are a lot of people out there who think that the earthquake—that earthquake, because it was so strong, and not in a place where anyone but R-Richard would expect it—" Her voice breaks on her husband's name, and she goes off again on a trail of tears.

Meade lets her cry, but only for a moment. "What do people think about the earthquake, Mrs. Jollston?"

She wipes her eyes, blows her nose, shakes her head. "That it meant the end of the world is almost here. Richard got a few letters from people quoting the Bible and talking about Judgment Day and the Second Coming—that sort of thing."

Common religious ideology, Meade knows.

But they might just have found the connection to a possible motive.

As usual, Jeremy has a busy day ahead. But on Friday mornings, he always builds in a little decompression time before the first appointment, knowing he'll need it after the weekly ordeal at Parkview.

He checks his voice mail as he heads down Lexington Avenue on foot. Two messages: one work-related, and one from Lucy checking to see how his visit went.

He opts to put both on the back burner for the time being, and instead dials his parents' Connecticut home number. Calling Elsa when he leaves Parkview has become a habit for Jeremy—possibly because he craves the maternal contact that is so sorely missing when he's with Marin.

Elsa answers cheerily on the first ring. "Hello?"

Hearing her voice, Jeremy immediately feels better. "Hi, Mom."

"Hi!"

She's always so happy to hear from him. What a great feeling.

"I thought you might call," she says, "so I waited to go out."

"Do you have to be somewhere? Go ahead, I can call back later."

"No, it's nothing urgent. I just have to get some food into the house because Renny's coming home from college tonight with a friend."

"Boyfriend?"

"She says no, but you know Renny."

Yes. His sister the flirt. Guys have been falling in love with her since she was in middle school, and she still—as far as he knows—flits from one to the other like a hummingbird.

"You and Lucy are still planning on driving up on Wednesday morning, right?"

"Right." They've barely talked about Christmas plans, but he's pretty sure they're still going to Connecticut.

"Good. It's going to be sad this year without Maman. She was planning on being away for Christmas, but still . . ."

"I know."

"Is it hard for you to be there in the apartment, Jer?"

"It's only been a few days, but I do think about her a lot."

"Well, I'm glad you and Lucy are there, partly for selfish reasons. It means I can delay going through Maman's things and getting the place ready to sell. I'm dreading that."

Jeremy was once in her shoes, after Papa died, when he had to settle his affairs. But there wasn't a shred of sentimentality about that process. He'd boxed up everything in the house for Goodwill—*everything*. He didn't want a single reminder of what he'd endured there.

He sold the house quickly, took the check, and left California without looking back. Went to Texas and had plastic surgery to fix all the damage Papa's fists had caused—and that was when bits and pieces of his old life started to come back to him. It was when he remembered Elsa, and knew he had to find her. If he hadn't, would she have found him anyway? Mike Fantoni had figured out that he was still alive . . .

Mike, whose murder was yet another senseless tragedy.

I wish I had known him. I wish I'd had a chance to thank him for never giving up on finding me, Jeremy thinks as Elsa chats on about the holidays—about which gifts she still needs to buy, and what she's planning to serve for dinner.

"The only thing is, the weather forecast is looking pretty stormy for the middle of next week. Maybe you and Lucy should come up ahead of time, before it gets bad."

"I don't know . . . we always spend Christmas Eve with Lucy's side of the family."

"I thought everyone was in Florida."

"Ryan's not. I don't think Lucy would want to leave him alone for Christmas."

"Bring him—the more the merrier."

Jeremy smiles. It's still wonderful, after all those years alone, to talk to someone whose main concern is making his life easier and happier. Elsa always has his back, as does Lucy.

He's aware that his father is also there for him, but there's always been a little bit of tension between Brett and Jeremy. Before the kidnapping, and after, too. It's as if Brett can't quite forget what Jeremy did to La La Montgomery, and is always a little worried that Jeremy might snap again.

Who can blame him?

"Do you want me to call and invite him?" Elsa asks, and Jeremy has no idea what she's talking about.

"Ryan," she explains. "Should I call to invite him for Christmas?"

"Oh—I'd better talk to Lucy about it first. I'll let you know what she says. Listen, Mom—I should go."

"All right, just first tell me—how was everything today?" Elsa asks, and he knows she's talking about Marin.

"Pretty much the same."

"Did she ask you—"

"Yes. She always does. Sometimes I wonder if it's right not to tell her."

"She *was* told," Elsa points out gently. "More than once, back in the beginning. Remember?"

Who could forget something so traumatic? Every time Marin asked for her daughter and was told she had died, it was like the first time she was hearing the news. She went crazy with grief—then, according to the doctors, blocked out the truth because it was just too painful to accept.

"It was so hard for her," Elsa says quietly. "For all of us."

"I know. But this is hard, too."

"On you. I hate that you've had to go there alone every week and face this."

"I'm her son."

"You're my son, too. I worry about you."

Warmed by the concern in her voice, Jeremy says, "I know you do, but you don't have to. I'm fine."

"Good. And Lucy? How is she feeling?"

"Great, other than the fact that she has her head in the toilet most of the time."

"Poor thing. I read somewhere that ginger helps with morning sickness. Maybe I'll bake some gingerbread boys for Christmas."

That reminds Jeremy of the cookie platter that turned up at the apartment door the day they moved in. They have yet to come across the neighbor who left them. That bothers him on some level. It probably shouldn't. It's certainly not bothering Lucy.

"I really need to hang up," Jeremy tells his mother, checking his watch. "I have a few other calls to make, and then I've got to get busy with work."

"Sorry, I didn't mean to keep you. I just miss you."

"I miss you, too. But I'll see you in a few days, for Christmas."

"I can't wait." She signs off with her usual, "Remember—I love you."

Jeremy smiles. That's something he'll definitely never forget.

There it is again—that slightly crampy feeling.

In the midst of a network configuration, with her coworker Patrice standing beside her desk, Lucy winces and stops what she's doing.

"Lucy?"

"Mmm hmm," she tells Patrice, "just a second."

She's definitely not imagining it. There's a little ache in her lower midsection, and then it's gone.

"Braxton Hicks contraction?" asks Patrice, who's had three children, and Lucy looks up at her in surprise.

"I'm not sure."

"What's going on?"

"I don't know . . . it's like a little cramp or something . . . but it's gone now."

"Welcome to the third trimester. Those are Braxton Hicks contractions. Kind of like a trial run for the real thing. But believe me, this is *nothing* compared to labor. Now that's pain."

"Great. I can't wait."

"Sorry." Patrice grins at Lucy's wry expression. "Just telling it like it is. But the agony is totally worth it—you'll see."

I hope I will, Lucy thinks, and goes back to the network configuration.

* * *

As she emerges from the subway at Seventy-second Street, her thoughts once again shift back to the mystery patient.

She has a feeling she knows who it is, but . . .

Can it be?

The lovely and enigmatic Marin Quinn—in a loony bin right here in New York City?

Possibly.

Probably.

The woman was a basket case years ago. With all that's happened since, it should be no surprise to anyone that she's been committed.

But I'm not just anyone. I should have known.

She'd been told, not long after she found herself in prison, that Marin had moved to Europe to get away from the media fallout.

To find out now that it was a blatant lie—and that Jeremy, her cherished son, visits her weekly . . .

Out of nowhere, squealing tires. She looks up to see an angry cabdriver honking the horn. She just wandered into an intersection without bothering to check the light.

The cabdriver rolls down his window, sticking his head out to yell, "Jesus, lady, I almost ran you over!"

She just looks at him.

"You're lucky you weren't killed," he shouts.

"We're all going to die. Soon." She points to him. "*You're* going to die. It's time to repent."

"Freaking lunatic," the cabbie mutters, and rolls up his window, shaking his head.

CHAPTER
SEVEN

Lunchtime, and Ryan still hasn't heard a thing from Phoenix. He's gone through the motions of his workday, because really, what else is there to do?

Call the police?

Go home?

Put his head down on his desk and cry?

Without Phoenix, this job is all he has. He can't afford to risk it.

Shoving his cell phone into the pocket of his overcoat, he leaves his cubicle. Maybe he can at least just step outside to get some air and clear his head.

"Going out to lunch?" asks Barbara, the elderly receptionist, sitting there as always with her stack of tabloids and her bowl of candy—usually butterscotch, but this week, it's miniature candy canes.

Before Ryan can reply, his cell phone starts to ring in his pocket, nearly making him jump out of his skin. He fumbles for the phone, bumping the bowl. It topples over, scattering cellophane-wrapped candy canes all over the floor.

Ignoring it for the moment—along with Barbara's dismayed reaction—Ryan hurriedly pulls out his phone, sees the number, answers immediately.

"Hi, Ryan."

"Hi." Ignoring Barbara and the litter of candy, he walks swiftly back toward his cubicle with the phone pressed against his ear.

"How are you?" Phoenix asks.

The fear and worry evaporate. Steeped in indignation and disgust, he echoes, "How *am* I? Where *are* you?"

There's a pause. "At work."

"Where have you *been*? Yesterday, last night, this morning . . ."

"Home. Why?"

"Because I haven't heard from you since yesterday morning, that's why." Back in his cubicle, he sinks into his chair. "Didn't you get my messages and texts?"

"What messages and texts?"

That gives him pause. Is it possible that she really didn't get them, due to some kind of technical glitch, or . . .

Or just not checking? Not bothering to check?

Not caring enough to call you regardless of whether she knew you'd been trying to reach her?

"You know, Ryan," she muses, "I *thought* it was strange that you hadn't been in touch."

"Then why didn't you call me?"

"I am! I'm calling you now."

"But it's been over twenty-four hours. I mean . . . here I am reading about a woman who was killed in some hotel room last night, and all I'm thinking is that it might have been you."

There's a moment of silence on the other end of

the line. Ryan is certain she's going to accuse him of being too clingy, and frankly, he won't blame her.

But then she laughs a little and asks, "What would I be doing in a hotel?"

"I have no idea. I just kept thinking—"

"Well, just stop *thinking*. I'm fine. Are we going to meet later, after work?"

He sidesteps the question with one of his own. "I don't know . . . are we?"

"It's Friday night, isn't it?"

"Yes . . ." Maybe he was too quick to judge her. Maybe, because he's always been so insecure, he smothers people.

Not *people* . . .

There is no one, really, that he could possibly smother but *her*. Phoenix. The woman he loves.

Lucy was right.

He needs to get a life. He needs to give Phoenix some space, learn to trust her. Otherwise, he's going to snuff out their relationship.

"Ryan?"

"Sure," he hears himself say, and he sighs inwardly.

Oh well. Guess I'll give her space another day.

"Where do you want to meet?" he asks. "How about if I come your way for a change and we—"

"Actually," she cuts in, "I was thinking it might be nice to try a new restaurant I heard about."

"Where is it? Near your apartment? Or your office?"

"No," she says, "near yours—right over on Sixth Avenue. I'll see you on our usual corner, okay? At five-thirty?"

Sixth Avenue?

"Ryan? Five-thirty?"

"Okay." His hand trembles as he hangs up the phone.

Sixth Avenue.

New Yorkers call it that.

Newcomers and tourists usually call it Avenue of the Americas.

Maybe not all . . . but most of them. Enough to make Ryan wonder about Phoenix. About how she told him she's only been in the city for a few months.

Maybe that's true. Maybe she just doesn't want to sound like a tourist and call it Avenue of the Americas. Maybe . . .

Maybe she lied.

Oh hell.

But why would she lie about where she was born and raised? That doesn't make sense.

He's being ridiculous. Paranoid. Insecure.

Still . . .

Ryan looks at the computer. Maybe he should do some digging around. Just to make sure she is who she says she is.

As he reaches for the mouse, though, a shadow falls across his desk and he looks up to see Traci.

"Hi. Did you figure it out?"

"Figure what out?" he asks, wondering how long she's been standing there.

"You know . . . the file I gave you. The Medicare fraud case. Did it help?"

"Oh. Uh, I haven't figured it out yet."

"Do you want me to go through it with you? It might be kind of confusing."

He shakes his head. "No, thanks. I'll be fine on my own."

"He knows," she tells Chaplain Gideon, pacing the herringbone hardwoods. "He knows."

"Why do you think that?"

"Because he brought up what happened in that hotel room last night. Why else would he have mentioned it?"

"He was worried that something had happened to you. That's all."

"No. He was baiting me."

"Maybe. But it doesn't matter. You didn't give anything away."

"But if he knows—or even suspects—then I have to get rid of him. It's getting too dangerous."

"Not just yet. You need him. That's why you're with him. Hold on a little longer."

"I don't know if I can."

"You must. This isn't about him. It's about the baby."

"I'm well aware of that."

She squeezes her eyes shut.

She's the prophet, the chosen one, the one who will deliver the child to the waiting world.

She didn't want to believe Chaplain Gideon when he first explained that Lucy Cavalon was carrying the child she herself should have borne. The child she would gladly have borne, had she been able. But then she realized that of course it was true, that it made perfect sense, and—

"Patience."

Her eyes snap open.

Patience. She hates that word. Hates hearing it over and over, hates the sound of Chaplain Gideon's voice when he says it, but she can never drown it out. He just keeps talking. Constantly, talking to her, talking *at* her. Telling her what to do.

"You have to get this right, or it will all be for nothing. Do you understand?"

She looks down at her hands.

Just hours ago, they were covered in sticky red blood.

Now, they're clenched into hard, angry fists. *Impatient* fists.

"Yes," she tells Chaplain Gideon. "I do. I understand."

"So either Jollston told the perp what room he was staying in, or she found out some other way," Brandewyne muses aloud, and Omar resists the urge to shoot back, *No shit, Sherlock.*

Instead, he finishes his second hot dog in a single bite, washes it down with a swig of Pepsi, and brushes the crumbs from his black slacks.

"Coming?" he asks Brandewyne, who's still seated on the low wall beneath the overhang of the adjacent office building, munching away at her sloppy street cart falafel.

"Can I finish my lunch?"

"Sure. Go ahead." He tosses his hot dog wrapper into the nearest trash can and carefully props the Pepsi bottle on top to be discovered by the next homeless person to come along.

Brandewyne takes another bite, chews, swallows. The woman loves to eat. Nothing wrong with that. And she's in decent shape—not *shapely*, by any means, but not hugely overweight. Just solid.

With that short hair and strictly functional wardrobe, she obviously doesn't spend much time worrying about her looks. Nothing wrong with that, either.

It's just . . .

When Meade first found out that his longtime partner Ben Tarrant was going to be replaced with a female detective, he was admittedly intrigued. With his schedule, it's not easy to meet women at his age. He might have briefly entertained the fantasy of an on-the-job tryst with a partner who looks more like Charlie's Angels than Baretta.

Okay, to be fair, Brandewyne's not quite as . . . as masculine, or as . . . swarthy as Baretta. And she's probably a charming—all right, that's a stretch, but at least a *decent*—human being when she's not on the job. But sometimes, he really doubts it.

Looking at his watch, he thinks about Richard Jollston and Myra the maid and the murderous woman in the monk robe.

Brandewyne looks at Meade looking at his watch. Some kind of creamy sauce is smeared in the corner of her mouth. He does his best not to make a face.

With a sigh, she stands and dumps the rest of her lunch, including her half-full Diet Pepsi, into the trash can.

"Why'd you do that?" Meade asks.

"Because I can't eat with you breathing down my neck."

He's hardly breathing down her neck, but . . .

"No, I mean why'd you throw away the bottle? Someone can return it for a nickel."

"So let him work a little to find it." Brandewyne wipes her mouth on the sleeve of her coat, already mucked up with food stains, and takes a pack of cigarettes from her pocket.

God, he misses Tarrant—and not just because the guy was a good-hearted, fastidious non-smoker.

Tarrant was more efficient, if that was even possible, than Omar Meade himself. Together, they were a well-oiled machine.

Now Tarrant spends his days golfing in the South Carolina sunshine, and Meade is saddled with a woman whose slovenly habits—along with just about everything else about her—have been driving him nuts. None of it should matter as much as it does, but he can't seem to help it. After six weeks, she's wearing on him. Too bad his own retirement is still a few years off.

He's not one to give up on anything—even his marriage. He stuck it out till the bitter end. But he's starting to think that this partnership might not work out.

Brandewyne puffs away on her cancer stick as they head back toward the hotel a few blocks away.

It's a crappy day—cold, misty, rainy—and the sidewalk is a sea of umbrellas and trench coats. Plenty of Burberry plaid on this particular stretch of Park Avenue, and glossy paper shopping bags from fancy stores.

"You think it's some kind of cult killing?" Brandewyne asks.

"That, or Little Red Riding Hood's gone psycho."

Little Red Riding Hood assassinates Chicken Little. Yeah, that's good.

Veiled in smoke, Brandewyne coughs a smoker's cough before asking, "You think the cloak was red?"

He shrugs. The surveillance tape was black and white. Anyway, he was kidding.

Pretty much.

Then again, if all these years on the job have taught him anything, it's that you just never know who you might be dealing with: serial killers, terrorists, cult leaders, random nutcases . . .

He's seen 'em all. A psycho Red Riding Hood isn't that big a stretch.

Omar's phone rings just as they reach the hotel entrance, which is festooned with a wreath the size of the Rockefeller rink. "Silver Bells" is piped over a speaker above the doorman's post. Ah, life goes on. You'd never know a gory murder took place here last night.

Not even breaking his stride, Meade answers his phone immediately with his customary "Yeah."

"Thought I'd check in and see how you two lovebirds are making out today. Pun intended." Doug Alden, a fellow detective down at the precinct, loves busting his chops about Brandewyne.

Meade responds with an expletive, which brings a laugh from Alden—and then it's down to business.

"Some bum found Jollston's wallet in a garbage can and turned it in looking for a reward."

"Really." Meade stops walking and raises an eyebrow. "That was noble."

"No kidding."

Brandewyne, too, has stopped walking. She mouths, *What up?*

Not *what's up. What up.* Fortysomething middle-class white woman gangsta talk. That kind of crap drives Meade crazy.

"Listen, we might have to give him one hell of a reward," Alden is saying, "because we lifted some prints off the leather."

"Yeah? They probably belong to the bum or Jollston." After all, there wasn't a single print at the murder scene. The killer monk had been wearing gloves that were plainly visible in the surveillance video.

"It looks like there are three different sets of prints on the wallet, Meade."

"Now you're talking."

Of course, random prints only tend to be helpful if whoever left them has a prior criminal record on file in the system. Hopefully that will be the case.

"So listen, they're running them now at the lab."

"Let me know what comes up, Alden."

"Will do."

Meade ends the call and turns back to Brandewyne in time to see her grind out a cigarette on the sidewalk a few feet away from the doorman, who sees it, too.

"What up?" she asks aloud this time, and this time, Meade tells her.

"Know what, Omar? This might just be our lucky day."

"I wouldn't count on it."

"Yeah, well, *you* never want to count on anything."

Thinking of all these years on the job, and the

kid he rarely sees, and the wife who left him for another man—one who has time for her—Meade doesn't argue with that.

At four o'clock, Lucy closes the door to her office, picks up her cell phone, and dials her mother's number in Florida.

Lauren Walsh picks up on the first ring. "There you are. We've been playing phone tag."

"Hi, Mom. Sorry I couldn't pick up when you called me back earlier. I was on the other line." Actually, she'd been on both other lines when her mother buzzed in on her cell phone. She's spent the day juggling phone calls, as usual. And being relieved that she hasn't had the slightest hint of a cramp all afternoon.

"Aren't you still at work, Lu?"

"Yes, but I figured I'd better call before you and Sam head out to the early-bird special or something." Lucy smiles.

She can hear the smile in her mother's voice, too, when she replies, "We might be snowbirds, but we're not quite that stereotypical just yet. Although Sam did say he wants to give me golf lessons for Christmas so that I can join him on the course."

Golf.

Lucy's smile fades.

Every time she hears the word, she thinks of Jeremy wielding a bloody seven-iron over a helpless little girl.

No matter how you look at it, La La Montgomery, regardless of whom—of *what*—she grew up to be, was once a helpless little girl.

Lucy makes appropriate comments as her

mother talks on about golf lessons and the great weather they had for last weekend's visit from Lucy's Aunt Alyssa and Uncle Ben and her cousins Trevor and Courtney, who are still in high school.

But mostly, Lucy's thoughts are settled again on Jeremy.

She doesn't know why, but she's still feeling uneasy—mostly about him. About the way he was acting this morning. Dark, distant.

Something's bothering him. Possibly something other than the fact that she rebuffed him this morning in bed, even something other than his Friday visit to Marin, which is always a downer.

Lucy frequently offers to accompany him, but she didn't today. Anyway, he usually doesn't want her there. He said it confuses Marin.

He's right about that. On one recent occasion, Marin lit up as she walked in the door with Jeremy—before she realized who Lucy was. Or rather, who she *wasn't*. Then Marin started sobbing in despair and had to be tranquilized.

"It's not that she didn't want to see you," Jeremy later explained. "It's just that she thought you were my sister."

"Which sister?"

He just looked at her. "I don't know. Does it matter?"

No. It didn't. Either way, it was heartbreaking.

Earlier, Jeremy called to say that he was headed from Parkview to a family meeting for one of his "guys," as he refers to the troubled youths at the group home. From there, he was going to a children's court hearing and then on up to the Bronx to put in some time on the grant he's writing, capped off by a group session at six-thirty.

"I'll try to get home before eight," he'd told Lucy, who then reminded him that she's going out tonight with Robyn.

"I won't be home too late," she promised. "Do you want me to bring you some Mexican takeout from the restaurant?"

"No, it's okay. I'll figure out something for dinner. See you later." She couldn't tell if he was disappointed or just in a hurry to get off the phone, but again, he didn't seem quite like himself.

Now, hearing her mother chatter on about what a nice time she and Sam are having in Florida together, Lucy feels a pang. Between the lost pregnancies and Sylvie's death and the move, it's been so long since she felt as though she and Jeremy were really in sync, enjoying life.

Then she reminds herself that Mom and Sam went through a lot before they got to this place—and not just the usual second marriage/blended family stressors. Sam was shot right after they met, for Pete's sake, trying to help Mom protect her family from Garvey Quinn.

Yeah, they deserve some happiness.

So do Jeremy and I. I just hope we can get back to that good place soon.

"How have you been feeling?" her mom is asking.

Should she mention the cramping? No. Patrice said it was probably just Braxton Hicks contractions, and when Lucy looked that up on the Internet at lunchtime, the symptom matched.

"So far, so good," she tells her mother.

"Good. Everything's going to be okay this time, Lu."

Of course, Mom doesn't know that for sure, but there's a certain comfort in her words, in hearing her voice.

"I really think it will," Lucy agrees.

"That's my girl. How's the new apartment?"

"Big. Fancy."

"I can't wait to see it—and you. Don't forget—I'll be on a plane the second you go into labor, unless you need me sooner."

"No, I'm fine." And even if she weren't, she would never ask her mom to cut short her time in Florida.

"What about Ryan?"

Lucy hesitates just long enough for her mother to ask, "Lucy? Is Ryan okay?"

"Yeah, he's . . . I mean, he's . . ."

Something tells her not to get into Ryan's relationship with their mother. She doesn't know how much her brother has told Mom, and it's not up to her to complicate his life.

"He's good, Mom. Actually, he came over last night after work."

"How did he look?"

"Like Ryan."

"And Sadie? Have you heard from her?"

"No, but I never hear from her."

"I don't, either. Not as much as I want to, anyway."

Hearing the worried note in her mother's voice, Lucy points out, "She's away at school, Mom, and it's finals time. Did you hear from *me* regularly when I was in college?"

"Pretty much. But you were the model child, remember?"

Lucy is smiling again, until her mother adds, "I just hope Sadie's not involved in anything she shouldn't be . . ."

Drugs.

Mom doesn't bother to say the word, but Lucy hears it loud and clear.

Sadie was only four when their father moved out, and she had a hard enough time adjusting to that, let alone everything that came after. When she got to middle school, she fell into the wrong crowd—the crowd with a lot of money and no supervision.

It happens to a lot of kids—but Sadie, given what she had already been through, was especially vulnerable.

Lucy's always thought that if she had still been living at home then, she might have been able to help Sadie work through her horrible memories, rather than resort to chemical attempts to block them out.

But who knows? Mom couldn't get through to her, nor could Sam. They looked for help in every direction—Sadie's guidance counselor and teachers, her child psychiatrist Dr. Rogel, even Father Les.

In the end, Sadie's badly needed wake-up call came in the form of a tragedy that hit much too close to home.

Sadly, it was too late for Jeremy's sister, but not for Lucy's.

"I'll give Sadie a call over the weekend," she promises her mom.

"Do that. And give Ryan a hug for me when you see him. Jeremy, too. How is he? It must be hard for him to live in his grandmother's apartment so soon after losing her."

Hmm . . . maybe that's it, Lucy thinks. Maybe Jeremy is just mourning the loss of Sylvie, and that's why he's seemed so down.

Maybe they shouldn't have moved into the Ansonia after all.

Sitting on the hardwood floor in front of the tall living room window, staring bleakly at the monochromatic skyline beyond the iron scrollwork of the Juliet balcony, she remembers waking up one morning to find herself in prison.

Andrew Stafford came, of course—only the very best legal representation for her family—and they talked about why she was there, and she could tell he suspected she was faking when she claimed she didn't remember any of it . . .

She *was* faking.

She remembers everything: the fury bubbling up inside her, and feeling as though she was going to lose control and do something horrible—

And then you did.

But she learned long ago that you don't necessarily have to own up to anything. If you've been through what she's been through in her lifetime, people tend to give you a pass.

Unfortunately, as it turned out, no one gives you a pass for committing murder—even if the murder was justified. Even if the brilliant Andrew Stafford fights for an acquittal after you've been deemed mentally competent to stand trial.

Chaplain Gideon was right. What she did last night was dangerous.

She has to tread carefully from here on in.

Has to suppress the fury once again stirring inside her, and the overwhelming desire to kill again.

Williams might be the third most common surname in the United States—an odd thing for someone to have mentioned, now that Ryan thinks about it—but Phoenix is one of the most unusual first names. You'd think that would help, when it comes to tracking down information about her past.

Nope.

He hasn't had much free time at work this afternoon, as his boss, Rachel, has pretty much been breathing down his neck. But as the day winds down, he's finally able to get on the Internet and look for his girlfriend . . . only to find that she isn't there.

There are plenty of hits for Phoenix, and Williams, and even Phoenix Williams, but none of them is *his* Phoenix Williams.

Which means she isn't.

She isn't what? he asks himself, annoyed with his own paranoia.

Isn't yours?

Or isn't Phoenix Williams?

Maybe both. Oh hell.

In this day and age, if you plug a name into an Internet search engine, chances are you're going to come back with something relevant. The person's Facebook page or LinkedIn profile, or the fact that they broke a high school track record—*something*.

His own name, for example, generates pages and pages of hits. Yeah, there are a lot of Ryan

Walshes out there, but there are plenty of links to
Ryan himself.

In his case though, most of them have something to do with Garvey Quinn's terrible crimes.
There are press photos of him and Lucy and
Sadie when they were kids, after the kidnapping and their father's murder. The pictures ran
again when the whole La La Montgomery thing
happened, and again after that, when Garvey
was tried and convicted and sentenced to life
in prison, when he died, when his daughters
died . . .

Every Quinn tragedy generates press coverage
and renewed interest in the Walshes—nowhere
near as many photos of Ryan as there are of Garvey himself, and his own family, but still—Ryan's
face, his name, are out there.

Phoenix Williams—*his* Phoenix Williams—is
not.

What, if anything, does that mean?

And what, if anything, is he going to do about it?

He has yet to figure that out when his cell phone
rings at a few minutes before five. Seeing that it's
Phoenix, he lets it ring into voice mail.

The moment it stops ringing, though, he regrets
doing that. He should have just picked up. What if
she didn't leave a message? What if she did? What
if she's in some kind of trouble and needs him?

*Idiot. You could have just answered the phone to see
what she wants. You didn't have to get into anything
serious right now.*

He waits an agonizing minute, then checks for
messages, not sure whether he's hoping she left
one, or that she didn't.

She did. When he hears it, he's glad he didn't pick up.

"Hi, I just wanted to let you know I'm stuck at the office working late, so I have to cancel tonight. Sorry. I'll talk to you over the weekend."

Short and not all that sweet.

But at least it buys him a little more time to figure out how he's going to break things off with her.

Wow. So that's it, then. That's what he wants to do.

The realization brings only mild surprise—and surprising relief.

Even if she didn't lie about any of it—her name, or who she is, or where she's from . . .

And even though he loves the way he feels when he walks around with her on his arm, loves being alone with her, loves waking up with her . . .

He doesn't love *her*.

He doesn't trust her, either.

In fact, right here, right now—he's almost afraid of her.

Maybe it's just that seeing those old news accounts and photos online brought back all the fear and uncertainty he'd experienced as a child whose life was in jeopardy.

A child whose parent was murdered.

A child who learned the hard way that people aren't necessarily who they seem—or claim—to be.

CHAPTER
EIGHT

Going through the familiar routine of his workday—an intense family meeting on behalf of one boy, a court appearance for another that was disappointingly canceled after a long wait—Jeremy finds that his thoughts keep wandering to Marin, and to Miguel and Carmen, and to Lucy.

Why does it all have to be so complicated? Why can't things just work out for a change?

Yeah? Work out how, exactly?

Marin wakes up tomorrow feeling all better and walks out of the psych hospital to live a fulfilling and productive life?

Miguel and Carmen have their baby and live happily ever after?

Lucy has our baby and we live happily ever after?

Why does that last scenario suddenly seem as unlikely as the others?

Why can't he be the eternal optimist like his wife?

Because I've been through hell and—

And Lucy hasn't?

Not fair. She, too, has been through hell.

But Lucy's more resilient than most people.

Somehow, she always manages to go right on living and hoping, no matter what life throws at her.

Meanwhile, Jeremy, more and more often lately, wonders if he lacks a certain coping mechanism that would enable him to do that. And if so—is it any wonder? Look at his biological parents and siblings . . .

Not every human condition is hereditary, he reminds himself, as he often does.

So many *are*, though. He did a lot of reading on that topic when he was getting his masters . . . and afterward, too. In fact, quite a few of the books he'd carried with them from the old apartment were on the topic of mental health. Books he's been thinking, lately, he should probably reread. Again.

So, yeah, in addition to worrying about Marin's mental state, he worries about his own, too. And he worries about his unborn child.

Maybe I need to make an appointment with Dr. Kitzler. Or find someone new to see in the city.

That's probably the better option. It wouldn't be easy to get up to Westchester for a psychiatry appointment anymore—especially after the baby comes.

But starting over with someone new isn't very appealing, either. Dr. Kitzler had known him so well . . .

Just not well enough to realize what's really been bugging me all these years.

And that, in a nutshell, is why he can't find a new shrink. He doesn't want to go through that again—the constant fear that he's going to slip up, say too much—and lose everything.

He's got to get through this on his own.

He has a pounding headache by the time he finishes his last home visit and gets on the north-bound Number Six train to the Bronx, where he has a group session scheduled for six-thirty. He'd been planning to head home right afterward, but maybe he'll stick around and keep working on the grant he's been writing.

After all, Lucy won't be waiting for him tonight. When he called her to check in a little while ago, she reminded him that she's going out after work with her friend Robyn.

She also told him that Carl Soto wants to come by tomorrow with their deposit check. "And he said he wants to talk to us about something."

Jeremy's guard went up. "About what?"

"He wouldn't say."

"Did you tell him to go screw himself?" he asked—only he didn't say "screw," and regretted it immediately. He might be in a pissy mood, but he didn't have to talk that way around Lucy.

There was a pause on the other end of the phone before Lucy said, "We need to get our money back first. *Then* we'll tell him to go screw himself."

She didn't say "screw," either.

Jeremy grinned, loving his wife, and feeling his pissy mood brighten just a bit.

That didn't last long, though. Not on a rainy winter Friday on the heels of a depressing workday and an even more depressing visit to Parkview.

As if those visits can possibly be anything *but* depressing.

What's he supposed to do, though? Stop going? If he doesn't visit Marin, who will?

Her friend Heather used to come, but she spends most of her time traveling abroad now that her physician husband is retired. Jeremy's mother, Elsa, and his mother-in-law, Lauren, occasionally visit—though not lately. Lauren is down south with Sam, and Mom—well, it's not like she's right around the corner. Anyway, she's had her hands full lately, dealing with the holidays and Sylvie's death.

It's up to Jeremy to keep up the Friday visits to Parkview.

"You're all I have left," Marin sometimes sobs, clinging to him like a frightened little girl.

She hasn't done that in a while, though. And today when he saw her, he noticed that she was much more withdrawn than she was even a few weeks ago.

Jeremy wanted to talk to Wendy about that before he left today, but she was tied up with some kind of security issue.

"An unauthorized person tried to get up here," Alice, the nurse tending the desk, told Jeremy, who considered—and refrained from—making a bad joke about the irony of someone trying to break *into* a mental hospital. Wendy might have appreciated it, but Alice looked as though she hasn't cracked a smile since her mother tickled her baby feet—if then.

After stepping off the subway at the Soundview Avenue station, Jeremy descends the stairs to the street and raises the collar of his jacket against the wet wind. The Kinks' song "Father Christmas" is running through his head again.

He stops at a pizzeria a block away in the

shadow of the elevated subway tracks. Colored lights, a plastic menorah, and an Italian flag share equal space in the plate-glass window.

"Jeremy! Bro, how's it going?" The young man behind the counter—whose family owns the place—gives him a high five.

"Girardo, how've you been?"

"Pretty good. Did I tell you I enlisted?"

The military is one way out of this poverty-stricken neighborhood—and Jeremy prays it won't be a one-way ticket for Girardo, who tells him he's hoping to see active service in the Middle East.

Patriotic, brash, convinced of his own immortality . . . Girardo wants to be a hero.

Don't we all.

Standing at the counter, Jeremy gobbles a couple of slices of pizza before heading over to the group home.

Boys' voices echo in the corridors, whooping it up as is typical on a Friday night. Quite a few of them greet him with a jovial "Hey, Coach" as they pass, while others barely acknowledge him, lost in their own troubles. More of the usual.

The garland-draped door to his office is closed and locked. Opening it, he notices that things are looking buttoned up on Jack's side of the tiny room. He must have left for the day, eager, as always, to get home to his wife and newborn son, whose pictures decorate Jack's cluttered desk and bulletin board.

"You'll be doing the same thing pretty soon," he recently told Jeremy, aware of Lucy's pregnancy—though not of the two miscarriages. The first had taken place before Jack started working here, and the second early in a pregnancy that Jeremy had not yet shared with his colleagues.

Ordinarily, he enjoys the camaraderie with Jack, but today, Jeremy welcomes the solitude. His desk is stacked with paperwork as usual, and he has to prepare for the scheduled group meeting, and—

What's that?

He spots a piece of paper on the floor just past the threshold. He picks it up, unfolds it, and sees that it's a note, scrawled in pencil on a ragged-edged sheet of spiral-bound notebook paper.

> *Coch I am working till 8 but I need u to*
> *tawk to Carmen 4 me be4 its to late.*

The period at the end of the sentence is the lone punctuation, and the only signature is a seven-digit phone number.

Miguel's cell phone?

Or Carmen's?

Suddenly, Jeremy wishes Jack were here after all. He wouldn't mind running the circumstances by someone other than his supervisor, Cliff Sutter—without using names, of course. Miguel came to him privately with personal information, and Jeremy, as a social worker, is bound to uphold that confidence. Technically, though, Miguel has committed a crime, complicating the ethics of the situation and Jeremy's role in it.

"Coach?"

Jeremy looks up to see one of his basketball players standing in the doorway. "Hey, Leland, what's up?"

"When is that form due for the team dinner? Because I can't find mine . . ."

With a sigh, Jeremy folds Miguel's note in half

and shoves it into his pocket. It will just have to wait until later.

Lucy met Robyn Gillery—now Robyn Hanover— on their first day of kindergarten at Glenhaven Park Elementary School. They looked so much alike that the teacher thought they were twin sisters. At least, that's what she claimed, and it broke the ice.

These days, Robyn—who works in fashion merchandising and married serious money—dyes her hair blond, wears full makeup, and dresses in designer clothes.

While no one would ever mistake her and Lucy for sisters at a glance, their friendship has endured. But that's how it is with Lucy. She's always taken her relationships seriously; she doesn't let people in unless they're keepers.

"Do you realize we've known each other for a quarter of a century?" Lucy asks Robyn as they settle into a back booth at La Margarita, their favorite place to meet for . . . well, margaritas. Not that Lucy will be having one tonight.

"*A quarter of a century?*" Robyn echoes. "When you put it that way you make me feel old."

"How do you think I feel? I'm even older."

"By three whole weeks."

"Two weeks and five days." At Robyn's arched brow, Lucy grins. "Hey, when you get to be my age, you'll realize that every day counts."

"Ladies, long time no see." Hugo, their favorite waiter, turns up with menus and ice water. "Can I get you started with some drinks?"

Robyn orders a margarita, straight up, with salt.

Lucy orders seltzer with lime.

"You know, one cocktail won't kill you," Robyn tells her as Hugo walks away.

"You're kidding, right?"

"I'm sorry. I just thought—you look tense."

"Bad day at work." Lucy shrugs, not wanting to get into what's really bothering her. It isn't that she doesn't trust Robyn, but what she really needs right now is an escape.

"I'm sure it didn't help that you and Jeremy found yourselves homeless at Christmastime with a baby on the way."

"Yeah, well . . . I'm not the first woman that's ever happened to," she quips. "And it worked out pretty well for Mary and Joseph, so . . ."

Robyn smiles and shakes her head. "Your optimism never ceases to amaze me, Lu. How have you been feeling lately?"

"Nauseously optimistic or optimistically nauseated, depending on the moment."

"That's good."

"Yeah. It is good."

"When I was pregnant, I was so miserable that I was seriously worried Tom was going to leave me."

"That would never happen." Robyn's husband, a financial analyst, is as crazy about her as she is about him.

"No, because he knows that if he left, I'd last about two seconds on my own."

"That's not true."

"You know it is."

Lucy grins. "Okay—maybe it is."

"Good thing I'm not like you, Lu, or he really might have left."

"Gee, thanks."

"No, what I mean is, you're totally self-sufficient. If Jeremy walked out the door tomorrow and never came back, you'd survive on your own without a problem. And I mean that as a compliment."

"Thanks again—I think. So tell me . . . how's Ardyn?"

"Are you trying to change the subject?"

"Absolutely, because—I know this is hard to believe—but I don't really feel like talking about what would happen if my husband walked out the door tomorrow."

"I'm sorry—I'm such a clod. Consider the subject gladly changed—to my favorite subject, as you know. Ardyn is amazing."

"Do you have any pictures?"

"Are you kidding?" Robyn reaches into her enormous purse and pulls out her iPhone. She presses a button and hands the phone across the table.

Lucy scrolls through a gallery of pictures of her friend's baby, now eight months old. She can't help but feel a pang, seeing Ardyn smiling, sleeping, sitting up, playing with blocks . . .

The first time Lucy got pregnant, Robyn was, too. Their firstborns were supposed to be the same age. They were supposed to play together, go to school together, become BFFs, just like Lucy and Robyn are.

"She's so beautiful, Robyn." Lucy hands the phone back across the table.

"You're the best, Lu. I mean, I know how hard it must be for you . . ."

It is. Excruciating. But she's not going to show it.

If the tables were turned, she'd want to share pictures of her own beautiful baby and she'd want Robyn to be happy for her, wouldn't she?

Absolutely.

And someday, you're going to have that chance, just you wait.

Yeah . . . she's getting sick of waiting. But that's all she can do. Wait, and hope, and do everything in her power to stay pregnant until her February due date.

Pacing, she waits for some sign of life to appear in the apartment above, but her computer screen shows only silent, empty scenes. The Cavalons should have been home from work by now—Lucy, at least. Where is she?

What if something went wrong with the pregnancy? What if she lost the baby?

"Don't think that way," Chaplain Gideon scolds. "This child is strong enough now to survive outside the womb. It will be born in just a few more days."

Yes. Just a few more . . .

Five, to be exact.

"But you have to control yourself until then. You can't take any more chances. Not like last night."

"That had to be done! Matthew 24:11! 'And many false prophets shall rise, and shall deceive many.' He had to be destroyed!"

"Yes, but you took needless risks. The maid—"

"I silenced her so that she won't talk."

"And now you're thinking about doing it again. Admit it."

"*No.*"

"Yes. You're thinking about doing it to Ryan. That's why you didn't want to see him tonight.

You were afraid you wouldn't be able to control yourself."

She couldn't argue with that. It was true.

But Chaplain Gideon is right. She needs Ryan Walsh around—for five more days.

On Christmas Eve, he's going to lead her right to his sister Lucy—and the baby.

Hopewell Junction is about seventy-five miles and an hour and a half's drive—two hours, with traffic—away from Parkview Hospital. Some days, that's not nearly enough distance between the two.

Wendy Nevid would love to put this particular Friday behind her and enjoy the weekend, but she can't seem to get past the nagging memory of what happened this morning.

That woman . . . the one who tried to get onto the fourth floor . . . there was something about her . . .

"One more story, Mommy?" Ethan begs, and Wendy obliges. But the whole time she's reading, she's hearing that voice.

I'm here to visit my uncle.

If she hadn't said that—if she hadn't mistakenly assumed Darryl Gaus was a man—Wendy would have let her go about her business in 402.

Which was . . . what?

The hospital's security people contacted Darryl's sister Kyle, who visits nightly, and told her about the incident. Kyle had no idea who the woman might have been—or why anyone would be trying to see—or harm—Darryl, a paranoid schizophrenic with no close friends and no other living relatives.

"One more story, Mommy?"

Realizing she's just read "the end," Wendy smiles and shakes her head. "You have to get up early tomorrow morning for swimming lessons, Ethan."

After kissing him good night and looking in on Julia down the hall, she goes to the kitchen to fix a cup of tea. Decaf. She has a feeling she might have a hard time getting to sleep tonight.

Why is this bothering me so much?

Actually, she knows why.

But maybe she's wrong. Maybe her mind is just playing tricks on her.

She couldn't take it anymore—being in that cramped little apartment, watching still-life frames on her computer screen, waiting for the Cavalons to appear.

So she bundled herself up, and she left, not certain where she was going until she got outside into the raw, misty December night.

Then she knew where she wanted to go. Where she *had* to go.

Now, for the second time today, she strides through Manhattan with a purpose, shouldering her way past pedestrians, scurrying across Broadway just before the light changes so as not to break her stride.

Up one block, over one, across another broad avenue . . .

This time, unlike this morning, she's not following anyone.

The pavement is shiny from the earlier rain and

bustling with people and traffic. Holiday shoppers tote bags from one store to another, and festive noise and sidewalk smokers spill from restaurant doorways. She passes rows of fragrant, fresh-cut evergreen trees lined up in sidewalk stands that are strung with overhead bulbs. She passes plate-glass storefronts decorated with tinsel and lights, as are some apartment balconies and windows high above the street.

Holy Trinity Church is located a stone's throw from the Museum of Natural History, on a relatively quiet side street lined with stately brownstones.

She pauses for a moment, looking up at the old stone church, with its stained glass windows and towering spire. Massive double doors, at the top of broad concrete steps, are hung with matching Christmas wreaths—fresh boxwood, with red velvet bows.

She climbs the steps, heaves open one of the doors, and slips into the vestibule. It smells of incense and wet coats, but evening Mass ended almost an hour ago, and the place is deserted, as she had known it would be.

Sometimes, she comes here when it's crowded with people. She sits among them, and she listens to them pray, and she wonders how they can be so oblivious.

"So many people are," Chaplain Gideon tells her. "So many people don't see what's right there in front of their noses."

But *she* sees. *She* knows.

She just has to stay focused on the task ahead, and her own salvation.

She can't get sidetracked by other things. Not even . . .

Parkview. Marin.

All day, she's been wondering about that.

She did some checking on the Internet. Found references to Garvey Quinn's widow having been spotted, over the past few years, in Italy, in France, in Spain . . .

There are photos, too.

Purportedly.

In all of them, the woman identified as Marin is clearly trying to be incognito in hats and enormous sunglasses. It definitely looks like her. But it also looks like thousands of other beautiful, wealthy women who rub shoulders with the beautiful people in Europe.

Quite an elaborate ruse, if that's what it is. If Marin is, indeed, occupying room 421 at Parkview Psychiatric Hospital.

I'm going to find out. As soon as it's safe to go back there. I'll give it a day or two. Monday. I'll go on Monday.

But for now, tonight, she has other things on her mind.

In the dimly lit sanctuary, she steals up the aisle, past a tiered display of flickering candles and rows of wooden pews, all the way to the front of the church.

She kneels in the front pew, but she isn't here to pray.

She's here to remind herself of the plan—just in case she's tempted, in the days ahead, to get sidetracked again.

There, on the altar, is the familiar Nativity set

composed of familiar life-sized figurines. All the pieces are there: Mary and Joseph, the shepherds and angels, lambs and camels . . .

All but one.

The straw-filled manger is empty.

According to church tradition, on Christmas Eve at midnight, the baby will be placed there.

The baby. The Messiah.

But this time, the child will be real—and the priest won't be the one delivering him to the manger.

I will.

Holding her mug of hot tea, Wendy sticks her head into the living room, where her husband, Mark, is watching a basketball game.

"What's up?" he asks, still focused on the screen.

"I'm going to check e-mail and then go to bed early."

He glances over at her, takes one look at her face, and picks up the remote to mute the TV. "Bad day, Wen?"

She shrugs. "Better than others. Worse than some."

"Why? What happened?"

She tells him, quickly, about the woman who'd tried to gain access to the patient floor. When Wendy had returned with a security officer, the woman had disappeared. Fitzy, the new lobby guard, said she'd run past him and out onto the street.

"I don't know why it's been bothering me all day," Wendy tells Mark now. "There was just something about her . . ."

"What?"

"I keep picturing her face, and . . . I don't know. Maybe I'm wrong."

"*You?*" Mark asks dryly. "Since when?"

She grants him a little smile. "First time for everything."

"What are you wrong about, Wen?"

"It's just . . . you know what? I don't think I'm wrong."

"Surprise, surprise."

"Seriously, there was something familiar about her. That woman. I could swear I've seen her someplace."

"Maybe she's been at the hospital before. Maybe she was visiting a patient, or maybe she worked there or something. Maybe she got fired and she was coming back to shoot up the place," he says, aiming a finger pistol.

"No—I mean, it wasn't recent, when I saw her. I'm positive of that. It was a long time ago. And that's the weird thing."

"What is?"

"Fitzy said the exact same thing—that she looks vaguely familiar. But he's only been working at the hospital for a couple of weeks."

"Jeremy?" Lucy calls, feeling around for a switch on the wall as she steps into the circular foyer. "Jeremy!"

Maybe he isn't home yet. The apartment feels very still, and the overhead chandelier she just turned on seems to be the only light.

Jeremy should be here by now, though.

"Jeremy!"

No reply.

She locks the deadbolt behind her, but not the chain. Clearly, her husband isn't home yet. Maybe he stopped off on the way to get something to eat.

She kicks off her shoes and pads down the hall, turning on lights as she goes. In the bedroom, she digs her cell phone out of her bag, drops the bag onto the floor, and calls Jeremy.

The call goes into voice mail after several rings. Suddenly a little uneasy, she leaves a message. "Hey, it's me. Where are you? I thought you'd be home by now. Call me."

After hanging up, she stands there for a minute, holding the phone. Maybe they're doing track work on the subway and he got stuck somewhere. Or maybe he stopped to grab a burger in a loud restaurant where he couldn't hear his phone ringing.

Frowning, she decides she might as well text him, too.

Where r u?

She hits send, then sets her phone on the nightstand and heads toward the bathroom.

Scrubbing her hands at the sink, she glances at the tub. It occurs to her that it would feel good to run a hot bath before bed.

Why don't you?

She's never been a bath person, lacking the patience to sit around soaking when she could be getting things done. But tonight, she's weary from a long week.

Besides, when she mentioned the slightly crampy feeling to Robyn over dinner, Robyn said it sounded like Patrice was right and it was Braxton Hicks contractions.

"That, or you might be overdoing it, Lu, on your feet and running around too much," she said.

Lucy wanted to protest that that wasn't the case, but when she thought about it, she realized it hadn't exactly been a relaxing week.

"Look, I know you hate to sit still," Robyn said, "but you really need to take it easy, no matter how hard it is."

"Do you think I should call the doctor and tell her about the cramps?"

"You said it was just this morning? At home and then again after you got to work?" At Lucy's nod, Robyn shook her head. "I think you need to go home, take a bath, and get into bed. Sleep in until noon tomorrow."

"Noon? Yeah, *right*," Lucy said, but the way she's feeling right now, it doesn't really seem like a stretch.

She reaches out abruptly and turns on the hot water tap. Then, just as abruptly, she turns it off.

Sylvie drowned in this tub a month ago. How could Lucy possibly think it would be a good place to soak away her troubles?

Remembering Jeremy's vibrant grandmother, Lucy feels her eyes well up with tears.

Sniffling, she wipes them away, half crying, half laughing at what an emotional wreck she's become lately.

She's going to be a real basket case by the time the baby is born.

Shaking her head, she changes into her pajamas and returns to the bedroom, where she spots a light blinking on her cell phone, indicating that she has a message.

She picks it up. There's a text from Jeremy. Good.

Stopped 4 food. Don't wait up. Luv U. J.

"Don't worry, I won't," Lucy whispers aloud. Yawning deeply, she quickly texts back a four-letter reply—**OK, U2**—before climbing into bed, too exhausted to go back out and turn off all the lights—too exhausted to even think.

All she wants to do is sleep. Maybe even till noon.

"Hi, honey . . . how are you feeling tonight?"

Marin opens her eyes to see one of the night nurses standing beside her wheelchair.

How are you feeling?

Why do people persist in asking that stupid question every day of her life?

How do they *think* she's feeling?

How would they feel in her shoes?

Slippers, she amends, glancing down at her feet, propped on the chair's footrests.

Once, she lived in designer high heels, the fashion-plate wife of a promising politician destined for the governor's mansion. She woke up every morning in a showplace apartment, surrounded by a loving husband and three beautiful children . . .

No, two. *Two* children. Two daughters.

Her firstborn, Jeremy, had never been part of the picture-perfect family she and Garvey paraded along the campaign trail. He was their dark secret, born before they were married and given up at birth.

But I never stopped longing for him . . . never stopped looking for him . . .

Only after Garvey was gone—the picture-perfect illusion shattered—did Jeremy come back into her life.

Even then, Marin was fool enough to believe they could somehow live happily ever after, she and her three children, together at last.

But it wasn't meant to be. Such a cruel twist of fate that a woman who had only ever wanted to be a loving mother to all her children was robbed of every single one of them.

Only Jeremy came back to her.

Now, he's all she has.

Her girls . . . Annie—Annie's gone. Dear God, Annie's gone.

As always, the realization—the memory of that awful morning—brings a fresh wave of grief.

And Caroline . . .

Why doesn't she come to see me?

Where is she?

A swell of panic rises up along with the grief—the instant, terrible kind of panic a mother feels when her toddler disappears for a few seconds on the playground, or a teenager is submerged beneath a wave at the beach. The kind of panic that gives way to blessed relief when the child resurfaces safe and sound.

But Caroline has yet to turn up.

And so, when anyone—like this stupid, smiling nurse—asks Marin how she's feeling, she ignores the question.

She ignores just about everything now, wasting away the endless days in this quiet institution where she's been living for what, a year now?

Maybe two.

Five?

She doesn't know. She doesn't care. She only wants to be left alone—and for the most part, she is.

Sometimes, though, she gets visitors: Jeremy, usually. Once in a while, Heather will come, or even Lauren Walsh and Elsa Cavalon—usually together, two-thirds of a tragic team of female survivors that once included Marin as well.

She no longer thinks of herself as a survivor.

This existence . . . this isn't surviving.

This is merely waiting.

Waiting for the nightmare—her *life*—to be over at last.

Every light in the place is on when Jeremy walks through the door, and for a moment, he wants to walk right back out again, thinking Lucy is still up. Even though he told her to go to bed. Even though she said she would.

Drained, exhausted, he just doesn't want to see her right now. Doesn't want to let *her* see *him*. She'll start asking questions that he doesn't want to answer—about where he was, and what he was doing, and why . . .

But the apartment feels absolutely still as he stands there in the foyer. Maybe he was wrong.

No, she's not awake, because if she were, she'd have heard him come in, and she'd be calling out to him. She always does—so happy to see him whenever he comes home. So sweet. Lucy. The mother of his child.

Lucy, who doesn't know what kind of man she really married.

Jeremy walks through the apartment as quietly as he can, turning off lights as he goes. When he reaches the bedroom, he sees her there, in bed, sound asleep. Her lips are slightly parted and she's lying on her side, her arms cradling her stomach beneath the comforter as though she's protecting her child even in slumber.

For a long time, Jeremy stands looking at her. Loving her so much it hurts. Knowing she loves him in return—but only because she doesn't know the whole truth about him.

If she did—

But she won't.

Jeremy turns away, and turns out the light.

Sitting at his kitchen table in Queens, fork in hand, Meade picks at the cold fried rice in the cardboard container before him. The grains are hard and the preternaturally red pork slivers chewy, and it might be better if he heated it up, but he doubts it. It's got to be three days old, at least. Maybe four.

When did he last order Chinese?

Oh, crap. Last weekend. Saturday night, when his son Dante was here with him for weekend visitation and his mother—Meade's ex-wife, April—was out on the town with Meade's ex–best friend, Johnny.

Disgusted—and not just by the stale food—he stands and crosses the entire length of the kitchen in two steps. He jabs his foot on the pedal to open the garbage can, dumps the container inside, and lets the lid bang closed. It echoes through the apartment, but that doesn't matter.

There's no one trying to sleep in the bedroom, shouting at him to keep it down in here. Back when there was, he'd grimace at the sound of April's voice and fantasize about what it would be like to have his own place.

Now he knows; has known for a few years.

It's hard to come home to an angry wife, but even harder to come home to an empty place.

Yawning, aching with exhaustion, he pours himself a scotch and takes it to his easy chair in the living room. Sinking into it, leaning back, and raising the footrest, he thinks about Richard Jollston, about how scotch and blood were the last thing he ever tasted.

Maybe it beats the hell out of cold, stale Chinese food.

The last thing Meade ate before that was . . . what?

He thinks back over the day. Right. Street cart hot dogs, a few minutes before Alden called to tell him about the fingerprint. And then he and Brandewyne went back into the hotel and discovered there had been a new development: one of the maintenance guys who'd been working yesterday—his name was Tony—had come forward to say he'd been bribed yesterday afternoon by a woman who wanted to know which room Jollston was staying in.

That established that she didn't know the guy—or at least, that she hadn't been invited to his room.

Apparently, she said she was a fan of the author. Meade wouldn't buy it, but Tony did. Pretty unbelievable, since it's usually movie stars and rock stars who attract groupies trying to bribe hotel staff—not paunchy middle-aged literary newcomers.

But it's Christmas, and Tony's kids still believe in Santa Claus, and that's what he was thinking about when the woman offered him a handful of cash that would go pretty damned far at Toys "R" Us.

Poor guy was terrified he was going to go to jail, or get deported—yet he came forward as soon as he heard about the double murder.

"I know I need to do right thing," he told Meade in broken English.

Too bad there aren't more crime witnesses like Tony.

Then again, the dollar signs in Tony's eyes seemed to have temporarily obscured his vision, because he couldn't tell them a whole lot about the mystery woman that they didn't already know from the videotape. She was heavyset with red hair, wearing dark glasses—not unusual, even on a rainy day, in a celebrity-frequented hotel.

Meade's phone rings, startling him. He glances at the clock on the DVR as he reaches to answer it. This is going to be—if not bad news, then, at least, news. You don't call someone after midnight to shoot the shit.

"Meade. You up?"

"I'm up," he tells Alden. "What's going on?"

"You know that print?"

"Yeah . . ."

"We got a match."

"Yeah?" Meade sets down his drink and reaches for a pen and paper.

"Yeah. There's just one thing . . ."

"What is it?"

"The person it belongs to?"

"Yeah?"

"She's dead."

"When did she die? What happened?" He imagines a bloody showdown between the suspect and the police somewhere in Manhattan and wonders how the hell all this could have gone down since he left the precinct less than an hour ago.

"She's *been* dead. For a long time, Meade. Way before last night."

"*What?* I thought you said it was a fresh print."

"It was."

"Then how—" Meade is already on his feet, looking for his keys, his wallet, his badge. "Never mind. I'm on my way down there."

CHAPTER
NINE

On Saturday morning, Lucy awakens early, heart pounding from a nightmare.

Jeremy snores beside her as she lies in bed staring at the ceiling, remembering . . . She was here in the apartment, at night, alone—but not really alone, because as the action went on, it shifted and she was playing hide-and-seek. Her opponent wasn't just hiding, though—he was invisible. Lucy could hear footsteps, and breathing, and she felt his presence—knew he was standing right in front of her at one point. But she couldn't see him.

Creepy.

She rolls over and closes her eyes, trying to fall back to sleep, but it's no use. Once she's up, she's up; she's always been that way.

With a sigh, she sits up—not too fast, though, because that tends to make her feel sicker. Right now, the nausea is there, but not raging. Yet. And she's not the least bit crampy, either. Good.

Checking the clock, she sees that although it's not noon, it's not that early after all—well past eight. She'd have been out of bed long ago if this

were a weekday—or an ordinary weekend morning if she weren't pregnant.

Hard to believe, now that she's so sluggish, that
she used to wake before dawn without an alarm
on Saturday mornings. She'd go for a long run,
shower and change, and go back out for bagels
and coffee to bring home to Jeremy—all before he
raised an eyelid.

She misses having that kind of energy. She
misses running, too, she thinks wistfully as she
heads gingerly toward the bathroom, feeling like
she's going to throw up any second.

Yes, and she misses her old strong, lean body—
a body she could count on not to betray her.

Always athletic, she kept up her morning
runs—though at a much less intense level than
usual—through much of her first pregnancy, with
her doctor's blessing. When she lost the baby, she
questioned everything she had done—including
exercise.

The second time she was pregnant, she didn't
run at all—and miscarried anyway, early on.

There was no question that this time, she would
take it easy. Dr. Courmier—a fellow marathon
runner—was empathetic, but absolutely ruled
out vigorous physical exertion. She suggested
that Lucy try yoga, which Robyn swears by—and
brought up again last night when they were talking about how Lucy needed to relax.

"Do you not remember that I tried a couple of
classes with you, and hated it?" Lucy asked.

"You might like it better now," Robyn told her,
but Lucy seriously doubts that.

She's not a yoga person. She's just not. Sitting

there, stretching and chanting, not even breaking a sweat, she couldn't seem to clear her mind as she was supposed to. She kept thinking about all the interesting, productive things she could—should—be doing instead. It stressed her out.

She flips on the bathroom light, wondering if she's actually going to make it through the morning without throwing up for a change. She's feeling queasy, but if she can manage to brush her teeth and get some food into her stomach . . .

As she starts to reach for her toothbrush, a sudden wave of nausea sweeps over her and she turns abruptly toward the toilet instead.

Vomit, flush, brush, rinse . . .

It's all good. Pregnancy hormones.

Only about two months to go.

Back in the bedroom, she glances at Jeremy, still in bed asleep. She didn't hear him come in last night. It must have been late.

His dark hair is sticking up in tufts here and there as though it got wet in the rain and dried that way, and his jaw is shaded with razor stubble. But he's no longer snoring.

Is he asleep?

"Jer?" she whispers.

He doesn't stir.

She pulls on a robe and walks out of the bedroom, quietly closing the door behind her.

Jeremy's eyes snap open the moment Lucy leaves the bedroom.

"See? I told you he wasn't really sleeping," Chaplain Gideon gloats.

"I knew that. I could tell he was just pretending." Sitting in front of her computer, watching the action in the Cavalon apartment a few floors above, she works the mouse, expertly zooming in so that the screen shows a close-up of Jeremy's face.

His expression is troubled.

Ah, so maybe he, too, is a prophet.

Maybe he senses the coming apocalypse.

Or maybe he's just thinking about his troubled past.

She zooms out on that image and zooms in on another: Lucy in the kitchen.

She's just standing there between the counter and the stove, resting a hand on her rounded stomach.

Judging by the dreamy expression on her face, she isn't thinking about the past, and she hasn't a clue that the future will be anything but happy.

As she waits for the toast to pop up and the teakettle to whistle, Lucy allows herself to imagine what her mornings will be like this spring, after the baby is born.

Will she be so exhausted from late night feedings that she'll want to sleep in?

Or will motherhood energize her to get up early and hit the winding pathways in Central Park?

That seems much more likely. When this burden of worrying and waiting has finally been lifted, she'll be her old self again, raring to get up and go. Will she take the baby with her, strapped into a jogging stroller?

Probably not at first. It's probably not good for

a newborn to be out when the weather is still raw
and chilly. Or do they need fresh air?

I don't have a clue.

She hasn't allowed herself to think beyond the
pregnancy. She can't bear to read the next chapter
in *What to Expect When You're Expecting*, let alone
research what comes after the baby is born: motherhood, caring for an infant . . .

Maybe it's time, though.

Maybe she can at least picture herself just
like all those other moms she sees—moms who
go contentedly about their daily lives with their
healthy babies in tow.

The phone rings, breaking into her pleasant
thoughts. It's early for a Saturday morning phone
call. *Too early.*

Lucy thinks of Ryan as she goes to answer it.
He'd been in the back of her mind all day yester-
day. And, after the phone call to Mom in Florida,
Sadie had been in her thoughts as well.

Well, one thing is for sure—no college kid is
going to pick up the phone to call family at this
hour on a Saturday morning.

Not unless something is wrong . . .

Lucy picks up the phone and, in the next terrible moment, learns that something is, indeed,
very wrong.

Not, however, with her sister. Not this time.

The moment she heard the ringing telephone
blast over the computer speakers and saw the way
Lucy's expression transformed from peaceful to
concerned, her heart started racing in anticipation.

Now, as she watches Lucy rush toward the bedroom clutching the phone, she edges her chair a
little closer to the computer screen and rests her
chin in her hand, like a courtside fan leaning in
for a better vantage.

Though the other end of Lucy's conversation
was of course inaudible, she can tell by the look on
Lucy's face that this was no chatty morning call.

No, it's clearly bad news.

And I'll bet I know what it's about.

Someone must have found the body.

If Brandewyne gets on Meade's nerves in New
York—and she sure as hell does—he should have
considered what it would be like to spend five
hours with her in a car, stuck in traffic.

Then again, even if he had anticipated this living hell, there's not much he could have done to
avoid the situation. They had to drive up here to
Bridgebury today, where they're going to interview various prison officials who had survived
the deadly earthquake.

"I would kill for a cigarette," Brandewyne
announces for what seems like the hundredth
time, tapping her fingernails on the armrest
between them as Meade stares in frustration
at the brake lights strung out ahead of them on
Interstate 95.

He thinks about pointing out that the exit is just
a mile away. But at this rate, it could be an hour
before they reach it.

Instead, he says, "Maybe you should just quit.
It's not good for you."

"No . . . really?"

It occurs to him, hearing the sarcasm in her voice, that he might just get on her nerves the way she gets on his. Hard to imagine, but he supposes that could be true. When you spend a lot of time with someone, it's inevitable. His long-wed parents bicker all the time, but their marriage works.

Then again, they love each other.

Meade and Brandewyne most definitely do not love each other. They don't even like each other, unless Brandewyne is concealing a secret well of affection for him.

And yet . . .

And yet, like an old married couple, when they're actually working together as a team, they do manage to get things done.

After the print match came back, they spent a sleepless night together at the precinct, digging up old press clips on the suspect, and tracking down the names and addresses of pretty much everyone who had known her personally. There's a trove of information, and they might just get somewhere with it if they can pinpoint someone from her past who might have been willing to help her if she really did escape last year.

If *she really did?*

She did.

Absolutely. She must have. Fingerprints don't lie.

And the quake is a clear-cut connection to Jollston, who wrote a book about it. There must be some motive for murder there—well, in the killer's twisted mind, anyway, though Meade isn't entirely convinced that's all there is to it.

He lifts his foot from the brake and lets the car

roll forward along with the cars in front of them, then jams the brake again as traffic stops moving abruptly.

"There are going to be people who need to be warned that she's alive," he comments to Brandewyne, still tapping her nails. "People she might go after the way she did Richard Jollston."

"Well, I'm pretty sure he's the only one who wrote a book about that earthquake."

"No kidding."

She shrugs. "Just saying."

"Yeah, I know, but . . ." Meade keeps going back to the surveillance camera image of her fleeing the crime scene in that weird, flowing cloak. "I have a feeling things might be a lot more complicated than they seem."

"Aren't they always?" Brandewyne asks, and he nods in agreement, inching the car toward the exit up ahead.

Most days, Marin loses time.

She'll be sitting right here in her favorite spot, in front of the window, and it's as though she blinks and the sky behind the city skyline goes from sunny blue to starry black, or from starry black to sunny blue—or at least, milky gray, as it is today.

Sometimes, she'll learn from the staff that a visitor was here with her, yet she finds that she can't remember the visit—even though she was reportedly right here and wide awake the whole time. Scary, the way she forgets so easily; the way her mind plays tricks on her these days.

Sometimes, she swears she's glimpsed Garvey here with her—though everyone swears that's impossible. They say he's dead. She'll never see him again.

Deep down, she knows that's a good thing—not that he's dead, but that he's out of her life forever. Yet there were times, even after all he'd done, when Marin missed him desperately. Garvey was always in control. He always knew what to do. When he was gone, leaving Marin alone to raise their children . . .

I just didn't know what to do. Ever. About anything.

And now—there's nothing she *can* do. Locked away from the world, she's helpless.

Really, there's only one person Marin longs to see . . .

Why doesn't she come?

And why, when I ask for her, won't anyone tell me where she is?

"So . . . which one was Miguel?" Lucy is asking gently, sitting on the edge of the bed beside Jeremy.

Which one *was* Miguel.

Not *is*.

Was, past tense, because Miguel, the baby-faced young man with the quick grin and missing teeth and fatherhood dreams, is dead.

According to Cliff Sutter, Jeremy's boss, who just called with the news, Miguel's body was found on West End Avenue just a few blocks from here—not far from the coffee shop where he'd eaten his last meal.

But of course, Cliff didn't mention that part, because he didn't know about it—yet.

Jeremy knows, though. He knows exactly what

Miguel ate: cheeseburger, fries, Cherry Coke. He knows because he was there. With Miguel. He was there as Miguel ordered his food and ate and talked . . .

He was there right before Miguel died.

Numb, Jeremy pictures him, lying facedown on the sidewalk in a pool of blood . . . or was he faceup, his eyes fixed and vacant? Was there a pool of blood, or did it wash away in the rain?

So many questions . . .

How long before it comes out that Miguel spent his last hours with Jeremy Cavalon?

Is it better to tell someone now, or wait until the police come knocking at his door, asking questions?

Does he start with telling Lucy? Or Cliff? Or does he go straight down to the precinct and talk to the police? Where *is* the precinct? He doesn't even know. How would he know?

Feeling Lucy's hand on his arm, he flinches.

"Sorry," she says, "I know this is hard."

She has no idea *how* hard.

His thoughts are spinning, his stomach churning.

Who saw him with Miguel? The coffee shop waitress, the other patrons—it was pretty crowded last night. The whole damned neighborhood was crowded; it's the last weekend before Christmas.

Out on the street afterward—it was late. Really late. Not as crowded. Who might have seen them together then?

Even if no one had seen them, there are Miguel's phone records. They'll show that he received a call from Jeremy.

He should have told Lucy last night when he

got home that he'd met Miguel after work. But she was asleep. And even if she hadn't been . . .

I wouldn't have told her.

"Jeremy? Are you okay?"

"I need to get up there," he tells his wife. "Up to the center. The other kids—they're going to be upset when they find out."

"You should go."

He nods. He should go.

And yet, for some reason, he can't seem to make his legs start moving. All he can do is sit here and think about Miguel and wonder what he's going to tell the police when they come knocking.

And they will.

They're going to start asking questions, even just routine questions, and they'll investigate his past, just a routine investigation . . .

And then the red flag will go up, and God only knows what will happen.

"Lu," he says, turning to her—but she's already up, on her feet, running. Running to the bathroom, where he hears her getting sick, and it's his turn to call, "Are you okay?"

"Yeah," she calls back weakly, after another minute or two. "I'm fine."

Then she gets sick all over again.

Jeremy sits there listening, and then he hears a high-pitched whistling sound and his blood runs cold. It takes him a moment to realize it's the teakettle.

At first, he thought it was . . . sirens.

That's crazy, of course, because the teakettle sounds nothing like sirens, and anyway, it would be hard to hear actual sirens from way up here, with these thick walls, and anyway, it's not like they'd be coming for him . . .

Yet.

Ryan sits at the kitchen table in the house where he grew up, eating a bowl of Cocoa Puffs. If you took away his morning beard and the fact that the house is empty and silent, this could be unfolding fifteen or twenty years ago.

Except, fifteen or twenty years ago, Ryan Walsh didn't know what it was like to feel so anxious and lost. And this gabled Queen Anne Victorian on Elm Street in Glenhaven Park was a happy, busy home back then, with a normal family living here.

Normal.

What the hell does that even mean anymore?

He doesn't know what it means—but he does know what it doesn't mean: a grown man eating Cocoa Puffs and wondering if the woman in his life actually even exists.

At times like this, Ryan desperately misses his father.

He needs a confidant. Someone who knows him well, a straight-shooter who won't get all caught up in worry and emotion . . .

Someone like Lucy, really.

But *not* Lucy. •

Because when it comes to him, Lucy gets all protective and territorial. And if he tells Lucy about his suspicions about Phoenix, and they turn out to be unfounded—then Lucy will always harbor a shred of doubt about her.

What does it matter? It's not as though she's ever going to meet her, right?

Right?

Ryan shoves the last spoonful of cereal from his bowl into his mouth and chews glumly.

Yesterday, he was absolutely convinced he had to break things off with Phoenix. Last night, he even thought about how he would go about it, and how he would pick up the pieces and move on.

But this morning, when he woke up in his lonely bed in his childhood bedroom, he had second thoughts.

If she really is who she claims to be—despite the fact that Ryan can't find any trace of her in any Internet search engine, nor in the public records he accessed for a fee—then why break up with her?

Why not just work on getting over his own insecurities—insecurities that have obviously cost him the ability to trust another human being and have a healthy relationship?

After all, he's not the first man to ever fall in love with a woman who seems too good to be true.

Ryan grabs the cereal box and dumps what's left in it into his bowl, including the chocolaty dust from the bottom of the waxed-paper liner.

He needs to talk to someone else who's been there—or at least, someone else who's fallen in love with a woman, any woman.

So where is he supposed to turn?

He has casual male acquaintances, but none he would call a friend.

There's always Sam, he supposes—but he's too far away, and too close to Mom. Ryan doesn't want to involve her in this.

And then there's Jeremy—the closest thing Ryan's ever had to a brother. Jeremy's right here in New York. And Ryan has a feeling that if he asks his brother-in-law not to talk to Lucy about this—because he doesn't want to cause her any undue stress while she's pregnant—Jeremy won't tell her.

Yeah. He'll call Jeremy. At least it's a start.

Riding the local train up to the Bronx, Jeremy stares absently at the overhead subway map and remembers what it was like when the man he knew as Papa—the man who had tormented and nearly destroyed him—died.

It was an awful lot like this.

Fifteen years ago, in the immediate aftermath, Jeremy had the same terrible feeling of guilt, the same panicky fear that he was going to be incriminated by the police.

That was different, though, in so many ways . . .

He was so young, then—just twenty-one, and living in California, in Papa's house. He had no friends. Papa had seen to that.

For fourteen years, he kept Jeremy isolated from the world. For fourteen years, he abused Jeremy—physically, emotionally, sexually. Fourteen years of hell.

There was no one to turn to for help.

And that meant that when Papa died and the police asked questions, there was no one to protect but himself. Had they found out the truth and sent him to jail, he was the only one who would suffer.

Now he has Lucy, and a baby on the way. If the truth ever came out . . .

But it won't now, after all these years, if it didn't back then.

No one questioned Jeremy's story. No one ever learned that Papa didn't have to die that day out on the lake.

That's the thing about drowning. It's hard for anyone who wasn't there to prove that it wasn't an accident.

If, say, a person can't swim . . . and that person rents a fishing boat and forces the young man he *claims* is his son to go out on the lake with him . . . and the person drinks too much and accidentally falls overboard . . . and the so-called son doesn't jump in after him, or even throw him a life ring . . .

Well, the so-called son who didn't rescue him is the only one who really knows what happened.

The irony that his grandmother Sylvie also drowned has not been lost on Jeremy. She was here alone, slipped, fell, hit her head. That's what the coroner ruled, anyway, and there's no reason for anyone to question it. Of course no one did.

But when it happened, Jeremy couldn't help but worry, somewhere in the back of his mind, that someone might make a connection to Papa. That someone might question whether Sylvie's death really had been an accident, or whether Jeremy might have had something to do with it.

He didn't, of course. He loved her. He'd have no reason to harm her. No one would have reason to harm her.

Sylvie Durand's death was an accident.

Papa's was not.

He, however, deserved to die. He deserved to rot in hell for what he'd done to Jeremy for all those years—and, he suspected, to other boys. Boys who never came forward.

The train has arrived at Soundview Avenue.

Jeremy gets off, descends from the elevated platform, and heads toward the Bruckner home.

It was only about twelve hours ago that he made this trip in reverse, calling the number on Miguel's note as he walked, and praying it didn't belong to Carmen. Miguel, he knew, would be finishing up his shift at the warehouse where he works—*worked*—part time.

Miguel. Past tense. Miguel. Dead.

Last night, he answered his cell phone on the first ring. "Coach, can you meet me? I need to talk to you."

"Did you go through the information I gave you?"

"Yeah."

No, he hadn't. Jeremy could tell by his tone.

"But I need to talk to you, Coach."

"Maybe on Monday," Jeremy started to say, "we can—"

"Monday will be too late. I need help. Tonight. Please."

"I'm on my way home, Miguel."

"I'll come there. I'll come anywhere you are."

"You can't come to my apartment, Miguel," Jeremy said quickly.

"Then I'll meet you someplace else. Where you living now? Upper West Side, right?"

Wondering how he knew that—then realizing the kids probably know a lot more about him than he realizes—he hesitated.

"Coach, come on, please. There's no one else who can help me."

"All right," Jeremy said, against his better judgment, and told him about the coffee shop.

Miguel arrived five minutes after he did. By that time, Jeremy was angry—at himself for agreeing to be there, and at Miguel for talking him into it. Angry, exhausted, tense, emotional . . .

Had anyone in the coffee shop noticed his mood, or overheard what they were talking about?

Even if anyone had . . . it wasn't necessarily incriminating evidence against him.

No . . . but it won't help his case. If, during the investigation, the police make a connection between this and Papa's death . . .

Jeremy's cell phone rings in his pocket, startling him.

Checking the screen, he sees that his brother-in-law is calling. It's unusual for Ryan to get in touch directly with Jeremy. Elsa must have called to invite him for Christmas.

But Jeremy can't pick up the call. Not right now.

Whatever Ryan needs will just have to wait.

"So you agree that it is absolutely possible, then, that an inmate could have walked out of Bridgebury prison that night?" Meade looks from Brad Vecchio, the prison superintendent, to Damien Hammill, the corrections officer, who agreed to this interview with him and Brandewyne today.

The meeting is taking place in a depressingly damp Quonset hut that reminds Meade of his late grandfather's Sears shed. It serves as temporary headquarters for prison staff, not far from the site they refer to as, not surprisingly, ground zero.

"It's possible," Vecchio says carefully, "but unlikely."

"We're not interested in likely," Brandewyne speaks up. "We're just interested in *possible*. And if it's possible . . ."

"It's possible," Vecchio repeats reluctantly.

It might just be the circumstances, but Meade is having a hard time imagining the superintendent, given his ho-hum demeanor, mustering the slightest bit of enthusiasm for anything at all. With his gray crew cut, fleshy face, and no-neck physique, he's the kind of man who seems decidedly ill at ease in the suit he's wearing, ill at ease in the metal folding chair—which he also appears to be wearing—and naturally, ill at ease answering questions posed by a couple of NYPD detectives.

You can't really blame the guy. It was bad enough that Bridgebury's aging infrastructure was partly responsible for the deaths of so many inmates and staff members. But if one of those inmates walked away from that tragedy and murdered two innocent people—and goes right on killing—Vecchio is going to have a real problem on his hands, and he knows it.

Reminding himself that this is an interview and not an interrogation, Meade looks at the superintendent. "Tell me what you remember about this particular inmate."

"Not a thing."

"Did you know her?"

"Do you know how many inmates there were at Bridgebury, Detective Meade?"

"I do. And I'd say that she was among the most notorious, wouldn't you?"

"They're all notorious. That's what I'd say. Wouldn't you?"

Meade gives up on him for the time being and turns to the corrections officer, a fellow African American. Sometimes, the shared-culture thing helps to put a brother at ease.

"Officer Hammill."

"Detective Meade."

"You worked on Cellblock B, correct?"

"Correct."

"And you remember this particular inmate?"

"I do. She was quiet—during the day. At night, though, she'd talk. A lot."

"To the other prisoners?"

"Nah."

"To herself?"

Hammill shakes his head. "To someone she called Chaplain Gideon."

"Who's that? The prison chaplain?" Brandewyne guesses.

"The prison chaplain's name was Harry Connelly," Vecchio speaks up. "He died in the collapse."

"Then who's Chaplain Gideon?" Meade looks from Vecchio, who shrugs, back to Hammill.

"Well, at first I thought maybe it was her nickname for one of the other inmates," Hammill says. "They have nicknames for each other, you know?"

Meade nods.

"Crazy nicknames. Like there was this one hard-ass—built like a linebacker, if you know what I mean? And her cellmate calls her Tinkerbell. There's another one, they call her Beanpole, and believe me, she's no beanpole."

"They used to call me Wino back in high school," Brandewyne says unnecessarily. "And I didn't even drink."

Meade sighs inwardly. "So . . . Chaplain Gideon? Is that a nickname, do you think? Something she called one of the other women on the cellblock?"

Hammill shakes his head. "I looked in on her whenever she'd start talking to this Chaplain Gideon person, and there was never anyone there. Guess he was just a figment of her imagination."

"Mrs. Cavalon? I have someone here to see you," the lobby security guard announces over the intercom, startling Lucy for the second time in the space of a few seconds—the first time being when security buzzed up in the first place.

Her nerves have been on edge ever since Jeremy left, well over an hour ago, to head up to the Bruckner home to deal with the fallout from last night's tragedy.

She'd have gone with him if he'd have let her, but he wasn't about to do that.

"It's work for me, Lucy."

"But it's going to be hard on you."

"I don't come with you to work when you're facing a tough day," he told her with a shrug, "and you don't have to come with me."

She could have argued that this was different, but she could tell he wasn't in the mood for reason, much less company—or sympathy.

Nor was he in the mood to talk about what had happened to Miguel.

That's how Jeremy is, sometimes, in a crisis. He simply shuts down.

She had no choice but to let him go, out the door, off to face what is bound to be a difficult day in a lifetime that's been overloaded with difficult days.

After he left, Lucy realized she was feeling crampy again. She'd been so caught up in what was going on with Jeremy that she's not even sure when it started. She only knew that she felt it.

She made herself sit down and put her feet up, and it's definitely subsided.

Braxton Hicks?

Please, God, let it be Braxton Hicks.

As she tries to process what the security guard's voice is telling her—*someone here to see you*—the rest of her brain is preoccupied with what her body is feeling and with her husband's latest challenge.

Miguel.

She's heard the name before, but she can't remember specific details about him, and Jeremy wasn't in any frame of mind to share them when she asked.

One thing is certain: Miguel was little more than a child—a child whose short life had seen a lot of pain—and now he's dead, just days before Christmas.

When Jeremy's boss, Cliff, told Lucy why he was calling, he mentioned that one of the boys had been mugged and killed.

Lucy assumed it had happened in the South Bronx near the Bruckner home. When she discovered that Miguel had been slain right here, in their own neighborhood, she'd been shocked and dismayed.

"Mrs. Cavalon?"

Lobby security. Right. "Yes? I'm sorry . . . who did you say was here to see me?"

"Mr. Soto. Carl Soto."

She gasps. How could she have forgotten all about the landlord's visit this morning?

How, indeed?

"Carl Soto? Oh—that's fine. Go ahead and send him up. Thank you."

What?

Why on earth is Carl Soto here to see Lucy Cavalon?

She glares at the computer screen, where Lucy is hurriedly brushing her hair into a ponytail and checking her reflection in the mirror.

She seemed surprised when she heard his name.

Almost as surprised as I was.

Now what?

There's no doubt that the landlord is going to discuss the apartment he forced the Cavalons to vacate. Why else would he be here?

Her thoughts racing, she wonders if there's any way to intercept him on his way upstairs.

And what will you do to him?

Slit his throat right then and there?

"No risks," Chaplain Gideon booms at her, and she winces, closing her eyes. He keeps on talking to her—talking *at* her, the way he always does.

"You know better. Last night was foolish enough—and the night before, at the hotel. You're letting temptation get the better of you. If you're not careful, you're going to ruin everything."

She takes a deep breath and opens her eyes. Onscreen, Lucy is smoothing her maternity top over her bulging belly.

They're close, now . . . so close . . . to Judgment Day.

Chaplain Gideon is right. He always is.

"Don't worry," she whispers to him. "I'll control myself this time."

Opening the door to her former landlord, Lucy wishes Jeremy were here with her, or at least, that she'd had time to compose herself before the visit.

Carl Soto is wearing a dress shirt and dark slacks and leather jacket, and he reeks of cologne—decent cologne, probably, but to Lucy's pregnancy-sensitive nostrils, pretty much any scent is unappealing.

"Hi, Mrs. Cavalon."

She sees his eyes go straight to her stomach, and realizes he didn't know she was pregnant. Well, of course not. How would he? They never saw him, and they didn't tell him about it when they got the eviction notice.

If they had, Lucy realizes, it might have made a difference, because when the man looks up again, it's with an expression of consternation.

"This—uh—this is for you." He thrusts something at her—a cellophane-wrapped poinsettia in a tinfoil-wrapped pot, the kind you buy at the supermarket. It's red and a little sickly-looking, but it's the thought that counts, Lucy reminds herself, and thanks him for it.

"This is for you, too." He hands her a package. "UPS left it for you at the apartment."

"Thank you." Checking the label, she sees that it's a Christmas gift she ordered from a catalog a while back—a sweater for Jeremy's sister Renny. It was out of stock at the time, and she forgot all about it. "I filled out a mail-forwarding form at the post office. I guess I should let UPS know that we moved, too. And maybe tell the downstairs tenants to keep an eye out for packages."

"They left last night to go away for the holidays," the landlord tells her, "but I'll stop by again and make sure nothing else shows up this week."

"Thank you. That's nice of you. Come on in. I'm sorry Jeremy isn't here," she says, leading him into the living room, "but he, uh, got called into work."

"It's all right." He looks around, clearly impressed. "Well, you two landed on your feet, didn't you?"

Immediately irked, Lucy sets the package and the plant on the coffee table, hard enough so that several petals drop off.

"This is my husband's grandmother's apartment," she informs him.

"Oh. Well, uh, it was nice of her to let you move in with her, huh?"

She shrugs, not about to bother to tell him that Sylvie happens to be dead. Better to just get this visit over with, security deposit back in hand, and put the whole experience behind her.

He looks at the sofa, clearly waiting to be invited

to sit down. She was about to do just that before he made that comment about landing on their feet.

Might as well stay on my feet, she decides, *and make him do the same.*

Petulance isn't usually Lucy's style, but it's been a rough morning already and Carl Soto rubs her the wrong way.

He clears his throat. "Mrs. Cavalon, I've been feeling really bad about what happened. About— you know."

Kicking us out on the street during the holidays— especially now that you know I'm pregnant? Yeah, I'll bet.

He shoots another glance at her stomach, and, feeling suddenly vulnerable, she resists the urge to wrap her arms around it.

"For what it's worth . . . I didn't know."

Lucy shrugs.

"Really . . . I didn't know you were expecting."

"I believe you."

"But anyway—it wasn't my idea for you to move out."

She raises an eyebrow and resists the urge to point out that it wasn't exactly her idea, either.

"I'm not proud to admit this, but . . . well, some-one wanted to move into the apartment before your lease was up, and I—I couldn't turn her down."

Lucy just looks at him, not quite getting it.

He takes a deep breath. "She offered me money—a lot of money—for the place."

Okay, now she *definitely* doesn't get it.

The apartment was decent—as urban duplexes go—but there are countless places just like it in White Plains. Better places.

"Sentimental reasons," Carl Soto explains, as if reading her mind. "She said she lived there when she was growing up, and she wanted to move in again."

Resting a hand on the small of her back, Lucy absorbs that, and offers him an *okay, whatever* shrug, wishing he would just give her the check and go.

"I felt bad about it, but, you know, I really needed the money—who doesn't?"

If this is an apology, Lucy thinks, he just needs to come out with it. She sneaks a peek at the antique Jeux d'Olympe marble clock on the mantel and wonders what Jeremy is doing right now; whether he's okay.

"And you have to know, Mrs. Cavalon, I thought this woman really wanted to live there . . ."

He *thought* she really wanted to live there?

Something in his tone alerts Lucy that this isn't just about an apology. She looks sharply at Carl Soto's face.

"What?" she asks, seeing his obvious guilt along with an oddly anxious—perhaps even frightened—expression. "What is it? What's wrong?"

"She never moved in. I let her know you were out, that the place was all hers, and I never heard from her again."

"But—what does that mean?"

"I don't know." He shakes his head. "You tell me."

Lucy's mind races through various possibilities.

That she didn't really want to live there after all?

That she was just a kindhearted stranger who wanted to hand Carl Soto a lot of money—at Lucy and Jeremy's expense?

That she wanted them out?

But why? It makes no sense. None at all. Unless they have an unknown enemy who's trying to make their lives difficult . . .

"Who was she?" she asks Carl Soto. "What was her name?"

"It was Mary. That's all I know."

Mary . . .

The name triggers a memory in her brain—something she said to Robyn just last night.

It worked out pretty well for Mary . . .

As in, being pregnant and homeless at Christmas.

As in, no room at the inn.

Which, of course, has nothing to do with this.

"She didn't give you a last name?" she asks, and Carl shakes his head. "What did she look like?"

"It was dark out. I didn't get a good look at her face. She did give me a phone number, but I've been calling and texting her to let her know she can move in, and I haven't heard a word."

"Maybe it wasn't even a real number."

"No, it is. She did respond from it early on—before I let her know the apartment was ready for her to move into."

"I guess she changed her mind."

"I guess so."

"It happens." Feeling a tightening in her pelvis, Lucy knows she needs to sit down. But she definitely doesn't want to ask Carl to sit now that he's said what he wanted to say. "Listen, Mr. Soto—"

"Carl."

"Carl. It's okay. You made a mistake. It's not like we're out on the street—we're doing all right here, so . . . no harm done."

"I hope not."

She frowns. "What do you mean?"

"There was something *off* about her . . ." He hesitates. "The more I think about it, the more I feel like she might have been . . . up to something. Something . . . bad."

"You mean you think she wanted to hurt you?"

"Or you."

His words send a chill down Lucy's spine.

"Do you have her phone number?" she asks Carl.

"It's in my cell phone." He reaches into his pocket and pulls out the phone. "I can give it to you if you want, but I doubt she'll call you back, either."

Lucy doesn't bother to tell him she isn't planning to call the number. She's planning to see if it can be traced, just in case . . .

You know that's crazy, though, don't you? You know this is probably about Carl, and it has nothing to do with you and Jeremy.

Yes, she knows. Absolutely.

She's just a little uneasy this morning, that's all—what with Miguel's death . . .

Which also has nothing to do with this.

Still, she writes down the number, and thanks Carl Soto for coming by. Twice. He keeps talking, though—talking about how sorry he is, and how he didn't mean to cause them any trouble . . .

At last, he gets the hint and hands over the check for the security deposit.

Relieved, Lucy walks him to the door.

"Good luck with the baby," he says, "and . . . everything."

"Thank you."

"Merry Christmas, Mrs. Cavalon."

"You, too, Mr.— Carl."

He smiles, shakes her hand, and disappears down the hall.

Whew—glad that's over.

It went better than Carl expected, though. Mrs. Cavalon seemed to be very understanding, and not overly concerned, which put him at ease.

In the lobby, the security guard at the desk says, "Have a good day."

The doorman who opens the door for Carl tells him the same thing, tipping his hat.

Wow—this is some place. Carl no longer feels so guilty about making the Cavalons move out on such short notice, whatever the reason. Baby on the way or not, they're much better off here. Who wouldn't be?

As he walks back down Broadway toward the subway station, he thinks again about Mary, wondering what her deal was.

Oh well—he has a feeling he'll never see her again.

But five minutes from now—the last five minutes of Carl Soto's life—he will learn that he couldn't be more wrong.

Jeremy sinks into the chair behind his desk and exhales shakily.

His office mate, Jack, looks up at him from his own desk a few feet away. "That was pretty rough, wasn't it?"

"*Rough* doesn't begin to describe it."

Telling a roomful of kids that one of their friends had been murdered last night may not be the absolute worst thing Jeremy's ever had to do— not by a long shot—but it was horrible.

The boys' reactions ran the gamut of emotions: disbelief, anger, sorrow, and even what appeared to be indifference on some faces.

Some of these kids are so damaged that they're numb to loss.

Others are determined not to reveal a crack in the façade, terrified of what might seep through.

Trying hard not to bare his own emotions, Jeremy handled the questions, comments, and outbursts the best he could, with support from his supervisor, a couple of caseworkers, and a trained grief counselor brought in for the occasion.

"Miguel was a good kid," he tells Jack, whose hands are steepled beneath his clean-shaven chin, eyes somber behind a pair of aviator glasses.

"He *was* a good kid."

"I just can't believe that after everything he'd been through in his life, something like this happened to him."

Jack nods. "It's unfair."

Unfair—not a word that's typically part of Jeremy's own vocabulary these days—mostly because it's not a part of Lucy's.

In this world, some people are made to suffer far more than others, and she believes it's useless to analyze or try to make sense of it.

It is what it is, she often says. *You just have to deal.*

Yeah. Jeremy's dealing.

"What about Miguel's family?" Jack asks.

"His aunt raised him after his mother disappeared. He didn't have a father."

"He *had* one," Jack points out. "They all had one, somewhere along the line."

Yeah, and some of these kids probably wouldn't be here if their fathers hadn't bailed out on them somewhere along the line—if they even were aware of their sons' existence in the first place.

Jeremy thinks of Miguel, wanting so badly to do the right thing for his own child.

Last night, they talked about what would happen if he succeeded in talking Carmen out of an abortion. It didn't look likely. Miguel was even thinking of going to her father and telling him she was pregnant, knowing he'd forbid her to terminate the pregnancy.

"I'd already have done it," he told Jeremy, "if I didn't think he might kill me."

Those words have been ringing in Jeremy's ears ever since he found out about Miguel's death. As far as Miguel knew, Carmen's father didn't know she was pregnant—but he could have been wrong.

And last night, after they left the restaurant, Miguel seemed a little jumpy. He kept looking over his shoulder, as though he thought they were being followed.

Probably just an old habit, Jeremy thought. A lot of kids who emerge from a world where violence is prevalent—a world of drugs and street gangs—are hypervigilant.

Jack breaks into Jeremy's grim thoughts. "So did someone get ahold of the aunt and tell her?"

Jeremy nods and tells Jack that Miguel's aunt

had reacted, predictably, with hysteria and self-recrimination. She was a single mother with three kids of her own, and she couldn't handle her nephew once he reached adolescence and got himself into trouble—but that didn't mean she didn't love him.

"I wonder who the hell did this to that kid. I thought he was through with gangs and drugs," Jack comments, "but maybe not. Maybe it wasn't a random mugging."

Jeremy shrugs. Time is running out. Even now, he knows, the police are investigating the murder, looking for witnesses. They're going to come across someone who saw something, because someone always does.

And when that happens, they're going to come to Jeremy wanting to know why he didn't tell anyone that he was with Miguel last night.

They'll think he might be guilty—of something other than bad judgment.

They're going to start probing his own façade, and God only knows what might seep through.

"Jack," he says, before he can change his mind, "I need to run something by you."

"What's up?"

"It's about last night."

Lucy hadn't planned on doing anything at all today, but after Carl Soto left, she realized she'd better take the check to the bank. It might take a few extra days to clear with the Christmas holiday this week, and the sooner they have access to the money in their checking account, the better.

She pulls on her coat, grabs her purse, and heads out the door.

On a Saturday morning, there's a little more evidence of life in the corridors of the Ansonia. On the way to the elevator, she exchanges greetings with a pair of men juggling grocery bags as they unlock their apartment door, and when the elevator stops on the way down, a family of four are already on board: mother, father, and toddler wearing a Santa hat and pink-swaddled infant in a double stroller.

"Hi!" the toddler says. "Hi!"

Lucy smiles. "Hi."

"Hi! Hi!" He squirms and strains against the seat buckle. *"Out! Out!"*

"No, Cameron, you have to sit, like Emory is. See?"

"Out! Out!"

"Sorry," the mom tells Lucy, as her husband ignores the kids and taps away on his BlackBerry. "Terrible twos."

"It's okay."

"When are you due?"

"Oh . . . um, February."

"Not too far to go then."

"No . . . not too far."

"The last few months are the hardest. I'm Laurie, by the way."

"Lucy."

"Nice to meet you."

"You too."

The elevator reaches the lobby and Lucy trails the family *out, out,* past the security desk. She can't help but think that if she didn't have a belly sticking out in her coat, Laurie might not have been as sociable.

This isn't the first time lately—well, since she started showing—that Lucy's been engaged in friendly conversation by fellow pregnant women or moms of young children. It's almost as if she's been welcomed into a special club—one that she's been longing to join.

As she heads out into the overcast Saturday morning—almost afternoon—she notices that Broadway is positively teeming with women and children. Again, she allows herself to imagine her future—pushing a jogging stroller, or holding a small hand in the crosswalk.

The nearest branch of their bank is only about ten blocks south of here. Good thing, because there's a tremendous commotion at the subway station at Seventy-second Street. Police cars and ambulances surround it with lights flashing, and a pair of uniformed officers are stationed at the entrance, turning people away.

Lucy will just have to walk down.

She shoulders her way past the scene on a sidewalk crowded with bystanders who are speculating about the situation. The mass consensus seems to be that someone committed suicide on the tracks. She overhears the word "jumper" a few times, and one person says, "It's that time of year."

Her thoughts turn to Miguel, and to Jeremy.

Poor Jeremy. Poor Miguel.

Suddenly, the world seems like a precarious place.

As if to punctuate the thought, the baby kicks.

It's all right, little one, Lucy tells her child. *I'll take care of you. I promise.*

"So now at least we know that she's nuttier than a fruitcake," Brandewyne comments, and takes a deep drag on her cigarette as she and Meade head back to the car. "Talking to people who don't exist. Classic."

"Hallucination is an indicator for all kinds of conditions." Meade ticks them off on his hand. "Schizophrenia, psychosis, psychotic depression . . ."

"Nuttier than a fruitcake," Brandewyne repeats, exhaling a film of smoke into the foggy New England air. "That's my diagnosis. Perfect for this time of year, don't you think?"

Ignoring the smoke and her question, Meade goes on, "That doesn't mean this guy, this Chaplain Gideon, doesn't really exist. Maybe he wasn't there talking to her in her jail cell—"

"He *wasn't* there."

"No, I get that! But he might be real."

Brandewyne raises a bushy eyebrow. "Why do you think that?"

"Gut feeling."

She doesn't question that. As a fellow detective, she gets it—that sometimes, you operate purely on instinct.

"Okay." She stubs out her cigarette in the dirt with the toe of her scuffed black shoe. "Then let's get back to New York and check it out."

Jeremy finds his supervisor's office door open. From the threshold, he can see Cliff sitting at his desk in front of the computer, staring into space.

He immediately jerks to attention at Jeremy's knock. "Come on in."

"Can I close this?" Jeremy rests a shaky hand on the doorknob.

"Go ahead. Have a seat."

Jeremy closes the door, sits, and takes a deep breath. Telling Jack about last night was daunting enough.

Telling Cliff—which was, of course, Jack's immediate and predictable advice—is downright scary.

Jeremy's supervisor is an intimidating guy—not just physically, though at six-foot-four and close to three hundred pounds, Cliff certainly cuts an imposing figure. But his no-nonsense demeanor gives him an air of authority that has been known to thwart even the toughest kids around here. Of course, he has a soft spot for them, or he wouldn't be in this job.

But Jeremy isn't one of the kids. He's an employee, one who might be in trouble.

"Is this about Miguel?" Cliff asks, before he can say a word.

"How do you know?"

"What else would it be about?" Cliff shakes his head. "It's a damned shame. I can't stop thinking about that poor kid."

"I can't, either. Listen, Cliff . . . I was with him late last night."

Cliff levels a look at him but doesn't say anything, obviously waiting for him to go on.

"He's—he *was*—going through some personal problems and he asked me to meet him. I bought him dinner at the coffee shop near my house."

"What time was that?"

"I met him there at about ten. We stayed until almost midnight. I said good night to him on the street, went home, and . . ." Jeremy swallows hard.

"Did you tell the police?"

"Not yet. I thought I should tell you first."

"What kind of personal problems was Miguel having?"

Jeremy tells him about pregnant Carmen. Of course Cliff immediately grasps the statutory rape issue.

"But if that's what you're worried about—that you didn't report it—you know it's not—"

"That's not what I'm worried about," Jeremy cuts in. "I'm worried that I'm going to become a suspect because I was with him."

"But you're innocent."

That's not a statement, Jeremy knows—it's a question. He answers it with a vigorous nod.

"You know the cops are going to want to interview you."

Yeah. Jeremy knows.

"They would have anyway, since you work closely with Miguel. They're going to talk to me, too. All of us. It's routine."

"I know."

"But if you're worried about being a suspect . . ."

He gives Jeremy another questioning look, and Jeremy nods.

"Then you might want to have a lawyer present when they talk to you."

Lawyer.

Just hearing the word brings Andrew Stafford to mind, and that makes him sick.

But Cliff is right.

First, Jeremy has to go home and tell Lucy, and then he has to call a lawyer.

Not Stafford, though.

Anyone but Stafford.

* * *

Back in the apartment, her heart racing, Lucy forces herself to sit as she dials her doctor's office. Really, all she wants to do is pace—but moving around too much is probably why this is happening.

This . . . crampy ache, low down, in her pelvis.

She noticed it again as she was leaving the bank.

It's probably just Braxton Hicks, but . . .

"Dr. Courmier's office."

"Hi, this is Lucy Cavalon." She recognizes the receptionist's voice. It's Andrea, who's new, and young. "I'm a patient, and I'm having . . . an issue. Is she there, please?"

"She's at the hospital right now . . . is this urgent?"

"Not urgent." *I don't think. God, I hope not. But . . .* "Do you know when Dr. Courmier will be back?"

"She's with a patient—doing an emergency C-section—so I'm really not sure. But I'll transfer you to the nurse-practitioner if you want?"

"Thank you."

Lucy waits, nervously tapping her foot. A more seasoned medical receptionist would undoubtedly have known better than to mention a fellow high-risk patient's emergency.

She thinks about the poor woman enduring an emergency C-section, and she says a quick, silent prayer for her and her baby.

Then the nurse-practitioner, Gloria Rivera, is on the line. "Hi, Lucy. What's the matter?"

"I'm not sure it's anything at all, but it's a new symptom, so I thought I'd better call."

She describes what she's been feeling—and

then, in response to Gloria's questions, what she's been doing, and eating. She also answers a series of questions about other possible symptoms of preterm labor—lower back pain, spotting—none of which she has, thank God.

"Okay, first of all, you need to get off your feet," Gloria instructs Lucy. "And I mean off. Lie down for the rest of the weekend and see what happens. If the cramping continues, or if anything changes at all, you need to call us. Meanwhile, I'll have Dr. Courmier get back to you as soon as she's available."

Lucy thanks her, hangs up, and heads straight to her bed.

It's been an hour now, at least, and yet she keeps reliving, over and over, the exhilaration of pushing Carl Soto to his death.

Standing on the edge of the crowded subway platform as the train roared into the station, he had turned his head in the split second before she put her hands on his back.

It was almost as though he sensed, in that final moment, that she was there, right behind him. Or at least, that *someone* was there.

Almost as though he sensed the danger—just as she had the night she felt the earthquake coming right before it hit.

There was no glimmer of recognition in Carl's eyes when he looked at her. Of course not.

She had made sure he hadn't gotten a good look at her that first night in the shadowy gas station parking lot, when she handed over the money in exchange for his eviction of the Cavalons.

She had been filled with rage up there in her

apartment, sitting there at her computer screen, watching Carl, listening to Carl, as he told Lucy Cavalon what had happened.

Lucy didn't seem overly concerned, and yet—

There was something about her reaction that set off a warning alarm. She was curious, and maybe a little bit disturbed.

Damn Carl Soto. Damn him to hell.

Chaplain Gideon was talking to her—shouting to her—about being careful. But she knew what she had to do.

When Carl Soto left the building, she followed him to the subway, down the steps, past the turnstiles, through the sea of people. Saturday morning in Manhattan. Christmastime. Everyone had someplace to go. Everyone was caught up in his or her own business.

She was positive no one noticed when she shoved Carl Soto, hard, as the train pulled into the station.

All they saw—if they noticed anything at all before the chaos erupted—was a man falling onto the tracks. A tragic accident, but one that happens once in a while, like elderly women slipping and falling and drowning in the bathtub.

And most likely, all Carl Soto saw—the very last thing he would ever see—was the face of a stranger.

Hearing the key turn in the lock, Lucy looks up from the spy novel she's been holding open to the same page for God knows how long. In the four hours since she picked up the book and crawled into bed, she's read maybe a dozen pages—and absorbed none of them.

"Lucy? Are you here?" Jeremy calls.

Not *Goose*, but *Lucy*. That's not a typical greeting. But of course, his day has been anything but typical.

She sets the book aside and gingerly gets off the bed.

Thankfully, the cramping subsided hours ago. When Dr. Courmier called back, she told Lucy to continue to take it easy.

"Do you think it could have just been Braxton Hicks?" Lucy asked before they hung up.

"It could have been. But let's be on the safe side. No marathons for you this weekend, okay?"

She laughed, and so did Lucy, feeling a little more at ease now that she'd touched base with the doctor herself. She wanted to ask about the other patient—the one who'd had the emergency C-section—but she thought better of it.

Did she really want to hear that things hadn't gone well, if that was the case?

In the foyer, she takes one look at Jeremy's jacket and hair and exclaims, "You're soaked!"

"The Seventy-second Street station is closed because of some incident. I had to ride up to the next stop and walk back down. It's miserable out."

"Rain, or snow?"

"Rain."

"It's supposed to start snowing at some point, though," she tells him. "Tomorrow, I guess."

She watched the television news earlier, wondering if there would be a story about Miguel. There wasn't—but there was plenty of coverage about the "guaranteed" white Christmas, a rare enough incident in New York City that it's eclipsed all but the most pressing items.

Jeremy doesn't bother to comment. His face is drawn. He looks . . .

Well, as though someone has died.

And someone has, Lucy reminds herself. Clearly, Jeremy is taking it hard.

"Was it brutal?" she asks, resting a hand on his shoulder.

He nods and shrugs out of his coat.

"Here, give me that." She takes his jacket and drapes it over the antique coat tree. Damp fabric probably isn't good for old wood, but who cares.

"Do you want some tea?" she asks her husband, following him through the apartment to the kitchen. "Or something to eat? Did you eat?"

He shakes his head.

"No, you didn't eat, or no, you don't want anything?"

"Both." He takes a glass, fills it with tap water,

and drains it as though he's been dying of thirst. Then he puts the glass into the sink and turns to her. "Sit down. We need to talk, Goose."

Something in his tone—in the forced, unfamiliar way he utters her nickname—strikes a fearful note.

She studies his face, but she can't read his expression. All she knows is that something is wrong—and that this is not the time to tell him about her own troubling symptoms.

Chewing thoughtfully, she watches the computerized image of Jeremy and Lucy in their kitchen several stories above. She doesn't have to be there in person to notice that the tension between them is thicker than the peanut butter spread on the hunk of bread in her hand.

Having heard Lucy's side of the telephone conversation with Dr. Courmier this afternoon, she watches Lucy's face as she waits for Jeremy to tell her whatever it is that he's going to tell her.

She's probably wondering whether she should, in turn, tell him that she might be going into premature labor.

If that's the case, everything is in jeopardy. Everything.

"It's all your fault," Chaplain Gideon tells her now, again.

There's no way of proving that the twenty-block walk had anything to do with the cramping Lucy described to her doctor. But it wasn't a good thing—that's clear.

"This could ruin everything," Chaplain Gideon warns. "If she's admitted to the hospital—"

"I know that!"

"If you had controlled yourself, none of this would have happened. Jeremy would have been at home with her today. He wouldn't have let her walk to the bank. And even if she had gone herself, she could have taken the subway."

"Shut up!" she screams at him, throwing the piece of bread against the wall. She closes her eyes and clamps her hands over her ears. "Just shut up! Do you think I don't know that?"

But she couldn't help herself. She's been under so much pressure, and she just snapped.

If only she hadn't spotted Jeremy with that kid Miguel last night, on the street, when she was on her way back from Holy Trinity. She followed them—at a safe distance, of course.

But she saw the kid turn around—not just once. Twice.

She was sure he'd spotted her. She had her hood up, and she was pretty sure he couldn't have seen her face, but what if she was wrong? What if he'd seen her and recognized her? What if he told Jeremy?

She couldn't take that risk.

After they parted ways, she followed Miguel down one dark street, and then another.

He looked over his shoulder a few times and picked up his pace, expertly turning corners. He definitely knew he was being tailed, and he was trying to shake her.

He couldn't.

After it was over, she felt better.

She just had to get it out of her system. Better some random kid than Ryan Walsh.

And yet, she can't keep taking chances like this. This afternoon with Carl Soto, and last night with Miguel, and before that, in the hotel . . .

"It won't happen again," she tells Chaplain Gideon now. "I promise."

But he doesn't reply, and when she opens her eyes, he's gone again.

"Bingo," Brandewyne says, and Meade looks up from his laptop to see her focused on hers.

They're back in New York after a hellacious drive back down I–95, which Meade has decided is his least favorite road in the world. Tailgaters, rubberneckers, speed demons. He'll take the FDR at rush hour any day.

"Bingo, what?" he asks Brandewyne.

"You were right."

"About . . . ?"

"Chaplain Gideon. He's a real person."

Meade waits for her to elaborate.

But Brandewyne, who enjoys dramatic announcements, seems to be waiting for him to ask her to elaborate.

Meade has no choice but to oblige. "Who is he?"

"Was, actually."

"Is he dead?"

"No. He's retired now, but he *was* the prison chaplain at Hazelton, which is—"

"I know what Hazelton is," Meade cuts in, his thoughts spinning.

Hazelton is the prison where Garvey Quinn was serving his life sentence before he died.

* * *

Jeremy takes a deep breath.

Maybe, he tells himself, *you're making too big a deal out of this.*

He looks at Lucy, perched on the kitchen stool, wearing an expression of anticipation and concern, her hands folded over her round belly.

"Last night, I was with Miguel before he died."

She blinks. No other reaction, though. She's cool, his wife. She doesn't overreact, or even react, unless there's a good reason.

Quickly, Jeremy explains the situation—including the bit about Carmen being pregnant. Miguel told him in confidence, but Miguel's dead now, murdered, and the truth is bound to come out. If not in public, then at least in the police investigation, in which Jeremy is about to become involved.

Tell wife . . .

Check.

Call lawyer . . .

Next on the list.

"So you met Miguel to talk to him about whether his girlfriend should have an abortion?"

"I met him because he was upset that she wanted to, and he wanted to know if he had any legal rights as the baby's father."

"What did you say?" Lucy asks, and he sees her glance down at her stomach.

"I told him that it's her choice, not his," Jeremy says wearily, "and I reminded him that he had committed statutory rape, so when you start talking about legal rights . . . he didn't have much of a leg to stand on."

Lucy shakes her head sadly. "And then what?

He walked off into the night and someone killed him?"

"Yeah. Pretty much." Jeremy swallows hard.

"How did it happen?"

"He was stabbed on the street. His wallet was gone."

"So it was a robbery."

"It looks that way, but Lucy, I was probably the last person to see him alive—other than who-ever killed him. The police are going to want to talk to me."

She nods. It makes sense.

But of course, she doesn't know that he has something to hide. She doesn't know that he once killed a man.

Chances are, she never will.

"I think I should call a lawyer," he tells her.

"Why?" she asks, looking startled.

"Just to be safe."

"Who? Andrew Stafford?"

"Are you kidding me?"

"He's a good defense attorney, Jeremy, and he—"

"No. I'm not calling him." Jeremy shakes his head resolutely. "I'll call anyone but him."

"He's the best."

"You sure about that?"

She shrugs. "When you're guilty, you're guilty. He couldn't help what happened to—"

"Do you think I don't know that?" he bites out, and sees her flinch.

Dammit. His anger is getting the best of him.

Jeremy shoves both hands through his hair, pressing on his scalp. His head is throbbing again.

"Jeremy, if you want a lawyer—"

"We can't afford Andrew Stafford, that's for damned sure. We can't even afford a regular lawyer. What was I thinking?"

She hesitates, then offers him a little smile. "I don't know. It's not like you're guilty of anything. You're not on trial. You're just a witness to a crime."

She's right. That's all it is—this time.

And even if it weren't . . .

Andrew Stafford is the last person he'd ever call to his defense.

A ringing phone startles Ryan awake.

He opens his eyes and sees that the living room has grown dark since he lay down on the couch.

What time is it?

Nine o'clock?

Five o'clock?

This is pretty much the shortest day of the year; it could be either.

He grabs the cordless phone on the end table behind his head. "Hello?"

Dial tone, and the ringing continues.

Wrong phone. Groggy, he pulls his cell from the pocket of his jeans.

It must be Jeremy, calling him back at last.

"Hello?"

"Hi! What are you doing?"

Phoenix.

Dammit, he should have checked the number before he picked up.

"Hi," he says tentatively. "Not much. What are you doing?"

"Wondering why I haven't heard from you all day. Is everything okay?"

"Why wouldn't it be?"

There's a long pause.

"I thought maybe we could get together tonight, if you weren't doing anything and felt like coming into the city . . ."

"No, thanks."

Ryan surprises himself with that reply, but it's true.

Not only does he not feel like going into the city, but he doesn't feel like seeing Phoenix.

"Are you sure?" she asks.

"Positive."

There's a pause. "What about Christmas?"

"What about it?"

"It's this week and we haven't even talked about it . . ."

A couple of days ago, he'd have made this easy for her. Not anymore.

"What did you want to talk about?"

"Well . . . what are your plans for the holidays?"

"I'm going to my sister's for Christmas Eve."

He wonders if she's going to ask about spending Christmas Day together, but she surprises him again. "Would it be all right if I came with you, do you think?"

"To my sister's?"

"It's my first Christmas far from home . . ."

"But I thought you weren't comfortable around family."

"I never said that."

He thinks back. He could swear she did say it. Or something like it.

Why the sudden change of heart?

"It's just that I don't have any family of my own, so the holidays are kind of hard."

His heart goes out to her. He can't help it. It's Christmas, and she's alone, orphaned . . .

"I'm sure my sister would love to meet you," he says, "if you're up for it."

Sucker, a little voice says, and he cringes.

Okay, maybe he is. He can't help it. It's not like she stepped out of a Dickens tale, but she *is* an orphan, and she *is* alone for the holidays . . .

And so am I.

He does have his sister and brother-in-law, but they're a couple, and they're going away to Connecticut on Christmas Day, and that leaves Ryan to spend a solitary holiday for the first time in his life.

"Really, Ryan? You want me to come?"

He does. Dammit, he really does.

"Sure. You'll love Lucy and Jeremy." He wishes he were as sure about that as he sounds.

"I'm sure I will," Phoenix tells him, and Ryan can't help but note that she doesn't sound convinced, either.

Hanging up the phone, she shakes her head.

"I don't think so, Ryan," she mutters. "In fact, I already know that I *don't* love Lucy and Jeremy. You either. Far from it."

But he doesn't have a clue about that. No, things are back on track now with their relationship.

She was so preoccupied last night and this morning that it had taken her a while to realize that Ryan had failed to call her since she left that message last night. It's not like him not to get in touch.

She wondered if she'd gone too far yesterday, canceling their date. But what else could she have done? She knew she'd better keep her distance from him; she could feel the tension building inside her.

In that mood, if she'd been with Ryan last night, there's no guarantee that he'd have lived to see Christmas Eve.

But now everything has fallen into place. Everything is going to work out the way it's supposed to—as long as Lucy doesn't wind up in the hospital.

She's been keeping a close eye on her, watching her face and her body language for signs that she's going into labor. It's hard to tell.

For both of us, apparently.

Now it's a waiting game.

If things seem to be escalating and she hears Lucy say anything about going to the hospital, or even to be checked out by her doctor, she'll just have to put the plan into motion early.

"But that's not how it's supposed to be," Chaplain Gideon warns her. "It has to be right. On Christmas Eve."

"It will be. It *has* to be."

"Jeremy—one last thing . . ." Standing in the kitchen doorway, Lucy watches him glance up from the sandwich he reluctantly agreed to eat, seated at the granite breakfast bar.

"What is it?" he asks wearily.

Poor Jeremy. He's so rattled by Miguel's death.

But it's not as if he's going to wind up a suspect in the murder just because he was with the kid right before it happened. At least he agreed that Lucy was right about that.

Case closed, it seems, for the time being.

"I just thought you should know about something that happened today." Not about her new symptoms, though. She's feeling fine now and he doesn't need one more thing to worry about. There's no need to tell him the truth unless the cramping starts up again. Lucy chooses to believe that it won't.

But he should know what Carl Soto told her about the strange woman who bribed him to get them out of their apartment.

Quickly, she explains the situation.

"What does that mean?" he asks, looking troubled.

"I don't know. Maybe nothing—to us, anyway."

"I don't like it. I want to talk to Carl about it."

"I talked to him. He told me everything he knows."

Jeremy is already dialing his cell phone. "Maybe he remembered something else after he left. Or maybe he's heard back from her today."

"I'm sure he would have called if—"

Jeremy holds up a finger, shushing her. The landlord must have picked up on the first ring.

"Hi, Carl, this is Jeremy Cavalon. My wife told me what happened with the apartment, and I'd appreciate it if you'd call us back here as soon as possible. I have a couple of questions for you."

"Voice mail?" Lucy asks as he hangs up after

leaving both his cell number and the phone number for the apartment.

"Yeah—the call went right into it."

"I really am sure it's nothing, Jeremy."

He shrugs, examines his phone. "I need to charge this. The battery is low."

"Do you want me to plug it in for you?" She holds out a hand.

"No!" He puts the phone back into his pocket. "I'll do it. Later."

Lucy studies him for a moment as he picks up the sandwich and takes a bite. He chews and swallows with all the pleasure of a child taking pink penicillin.

Lucy wants to tell him he doesn't have to force himself to eat, but realizes he can make that decision for himself. Obviously, he doesn't have the patience today for his wife's controlling tendencies, and frankly, she doesn't blame him.

"I think I'm going to go lie down in the bedroom for awhile, okay?"

Jeremy nods, not bothering to ask why. If he had, she'd have given him a vague answer about needing a nap.

About to leave the room, she turns back. "Maybe we can get some takeout for dinner later—I'm in the mood for udon."

She waits for him to say, *So it shall be,* but he doesn't.

"Sure. Fine. Whatever. I'm going to go into the den with my laptop and work on that grant I'm writing."

She isn't quite sure she believes him. Grant writing on a Saturday evening, after the kind of day he's had today?

Maybe he's going to look up the details of Miguel's murder in the press. Or maybe it's not about that at all. It's possible he's doing some last minute online Christmas shopping—though that doesn't seem likely in his current frame of mind.

Whatever the case, she can tell he needs some alone time, and she respects that . . . even though she's personally had much too much alone time today.

But . . . doctor's orders.

Back in the bedroom, she leans back against the pillows and picks up her book again. She forgot to mark the page she was on when Jeremy came home—and after searching through the first two chapters, realizes she can't even find it.

Frustrated, she tosses the book aside, realizing she isn't in the mood to read, or even to pretend to read.

Maybe she can find something to watch on television. An old movie like *The Homecoming* or *A Christmas Story* would take her mind off everything. When she was a little girl, she and Ryan used to curl up between their parents in the living room lit only by the glow of tree lights and watch the holiday classics on TV.

Then their parents separated, and Daddy died, and nothing was ever the same—especially the Christmas season.

Maybe that's why I try so hard with my own Christmas Eve tradition. And now we don't have a tree or any decorations other than that pathetic grocery store poinsettia, and Ryan isn't even sure he'll come . . .

She sighs, picks up the remote, and aims it at the cable box, pressing the power button.

The TV is still tuned to the local news channel, where a meteorologist is standing in front of a map of the tri-state area.

" . . . and I think we're talking heap big snow here, folks," he's saying.

Heap big snow? Seriously?

Lucy rolls her eyes.

"Areas north and west of the city could see over two feet of accumulation by Tuesday morning. In the city itself and on south, if this other system merges as we think it may, we're looking at about thirty inches with considerable blowing and drifting."

Okay, that *is* a heap big snow. Especially considering that the city tends to come to a standstill for six inches.

If the forecast is correct, she and Jeremy aren't going to be driving to Connecticut on Wednesday for Christmas. Ryan might not make it here even if he wants to. The commuter line usually runs like clockwork, but if enough snow falls on the tracks, the trains can be paralyzed.

"Bottom line," the meteorologist says, "is that you'd better watch out, and you'd better not pout, because we're going to have one heck of a white Christmas here in the tri-state area. Katie, back to you."

As the scene shifts back to the news desk, Lucy mutes the sound and reaches for the phone. Better give Ryan a heads-up, in case he doesn't know what's going on. Sometimes, he seems to dwell in a media-free bubble.

He answers right away. "Hey—I was just going to call you."

"Really? About what?"

"Christmas."

"Great minds think alike. That's why I'm calling you. Did you hear about the snowstorm?"

"What snowstorm?"

She sighs and explains the situation. "So listen, why don't you come here and stay after work on Monday night so you won't have to try to get back down to the city on Tuesday for Christmas Eve—you *are* planning to be here, right?" she adds, and waits for him to tell her he'll have to let her know.

"I'll be there. With Phoenix."

Lucy's jaw drops. That was too easy.

"What's up with you guys, Ry?"

"What do you mean?" he sounds defensive.

"I mean you were worried, and . . . I take it everything's going well now?"

"I just told you she's coming for Christmas Eve, didn't I?"

"Yes. You did. But . . ."

"We're not engaged, if that's what you're wondering, and we didn't break up, either. Okay?"

"Okay." She gives up. Obviously, he doesn't want to talk about it.

That's all right. Neither does she. She's had enough conflict for one day.

Sitting at an antique desk in the small den off the hall, Jeremy waits impatiently for his laptop to boot up.

As he waits, he finds himself glancing repeatedly at the wall behind him, and wonders why. It's not as though someone's going to be there, looking over his shoulder. Lucy's down the hall in the bedroom. Her door is closed, and so is the door to the den.

The lyrics of an old Kinks song run through Jeremy's mind, and he shakes his head.

Yeah, paranoia. It's a self-destroyer all right.

Between Miguel's death and what Lucy just told him about the woman who paid off their landlord to get them out of their apartment . . .

Why would anyone do that?

Sentimental reasons, my ass.

Maybe if it were a charming old house like the one where Lucy grew up, or even a nice apartment in a historic building that has some character, or right across from the train station or bus stop . . .

Or maybe, Jeremy thinks, if the woman had actually moved in after he and Lucy moved out . . .

Granted, it's only been a few days. But according to the secondhand information from Carl Soto, it was some kind of scam and she's gone.

Where does that leave us?

Here in the Ansonia—for no apparent reason.

Jeremy pushes the thought aside as his laptop finally opens to the home screen. He opens a search engine and quickly types in his own name, something he hasn't done in years.

He wants to see exactly what the cops are going to see when they do the same.

Predictably, there are thousands of hits. Scrolling through them, he sees that—aside from a few that have to do with his work at the Bruckner home—they're all links to press related to his kidnapping and his connection to the Quinns and La La Montgomery.

A few of the articles refer to the fact that he was "rescued" by a rumored pedophile who raised him in seclusion in California. But since there was never any proof of the abuse, and Papa was never charged with anything, and wasn't alive to defend himself, his name was kept out of the press.

Nowhere is there any mention of how he died, or when, or where. For all anyone knows, reading the articles, he passed in his sleep of old age.

But what if the police want to know more? If they ask Jeremy what happened to Papa, and he tells them—not the whole truth, of course—will they sense that he has something to hide?

Maybe he should call a lawyer.

No. You can't afford one, remember? You can't even afford to get your wife a Christmas gift.

Irritated, he closes out of the screen and wonders how long it would take—and cost—to buy something online. Something special. The kind of gift that Lucy deserves.

Is it too late?

Jeremy swallows hard over a sudden lump in his throat. He loves her so much it actually hurts.

But that's okay. He'll take the pain.

Better me than Lucy.

Meade's vision is starting to blur and his shoulder blades are on fire as he sits typing up his notes on the case. This is exactly how he felt last night when he sat down in his chair at home. Then Alden called and he had to get right back up and on the case.

This is crazy. He's got to go home and get some

sleep or he's going to crash and burn right here at his desk.

Not only has he been up for almost forty-eight hours, but in that period of time he hasn't ingested anything other than gallons of coffee, a rest stop microwave burrito, cold week-old Chinese food, and a couple of dirty-water dogs.

Brandewyne is in pretty much the same boat, if you add a couple of packs of Marlboros. Apparently, they're her secret weapon, because at this particular moment, Meade's feeling a lot worse than she's looking. Seated at her own desk across from his, she's talking on the phone—presumably, still trying to track down Chaplain Gideon.

Brandewyne sees Meade looking in her direction, grins, and gives him a big thumbs-up. Does that mean she's found him?

Too burned out to do much more than give her a nod, he returns to his keyboard, making one typo after another and not bothering to correct them.

A minute later, she's off the phone and standing over his desk. "Found him, Meade."

"Where?"

"Pretty close by. He's living in Jersey. Want to take a road trip?"

"Where in Jersey?" Parts of it, like Hoboken, are closer to the precinct, even, than Meade's Queens apartment. But South Jersey—Cape May, Atlantic City—is a few hours away.

"He's down near Trenton. And he goes to a ten o'clock church service on Broad Street every Sunday morning without fail."

Meade nods thoughtfully. "Good. We'll be waiting for him when he comes out tomorrow morning."

"Think we should let him know we're coming?"

"Not if he's involved in this."

"You think he is?"

Meade leans back, stretching his aching shoulders. "I'm not convinced that he isn't. Not with the connection to Garvey Quinn."

He's done some reading up on the crooked politician today.

He remembers the case, of course, though he didn't work on it.

Back then, he was just a young cop—a newlywed, with a pregnant wife and a loyal best friend. Johnny had been Meade's best man and was soon to be godfather to his only son. Meade never dreamed he'd become Dante's stepfather as well.

"Do you think we should warn the Quinns?"

His thoughts spin back to the case—nothing like someone else's misery to make you forget your own. Maybe that's why he's so good at this job—and why he sucks at his personal life.

"There's not much family left around here to tell. Quinn's widow went to Europe a few years back. Lives over there like a recluse, according to what I read. I'm one step ahead of you, though—been trying to track someone down to get in touch with her."

"What about the son and his wife?"

"Them, too. Jeremy Cavalon, and—get this—he's married to Lucy Walsh—she's the one whose father Quinn killed. He had her kidnapped, too, with her brother and sister. Luckily, there was a happy ending."

"We don't see enough of those. Where do they live now?"

"Up in White Plains. I called, got their voice mail, left them a message."

"Guess you really are one step ahead of me."

"Guess so. Or maybe a few steps ahead of you." Meade flashes her a fake-smug grin.

"Do you think she might go after them?"

So much for the grin—fake or not.

"With someone like this, we can't even guess what she'll do next," he tells Brandewyne grimly, thinking of the bloodbath in that hotel suite, "and I just pray to God we don't have to see the results."

CHAPTER ELEVEN

Sunday morning, Lucy wakes up early. Not *early*-early, though; once again, it's past eight o'clock.

But early enough to have a good, long debate with herself about the wisdom of attending Mass at Holy Trinity.

Though it's only a couple of blocks from here, she wouldn't walk over. Not after what happened to her yesterday.

She hasn't had a pelvic twinge since, meaning she probably really was suffering from overexertion, or undigested Mexican food. Possibly both.

She and Jeremy had a relaxing Saturday night eating takeout Japanese noodle soup from a place around the corner, then watching TV together in bed.

She noticed that Jeremy seemed less anxious and more attentive than he had earlier. It was his idea that they watch a couple of DVDs from Sylvie's vast collection.

The two vintage French films sounded interesting from the descriptions, but Lucy lasted through only about five minutes of the first before dozing off.

Looking at Jeremy, still sound asleep, she considers waking him to ask whether he thinks she should go to church.

No. Let him sleep.

Especially considering he still doesn't know there's a valid reason why she might want to avoid going out.

Later—she'll tell him later about the cramps she had and doesn't have now.

For the time being, she's going to take a cab over to church. She could really use a dose of comfort and healing right about now.

Meade wouldn't call what he had last night a "good night's sleep." He had nightmares—gory ones. Occupational hazard. But it was sleep, more or less, and it was certainly night—one of the longest nights of the year.

Waking up to drive to Trenton with Brandewyne is almost as much fun as yesterday's trip up to Massachusetts after no sleep at all. And he loves the Jersey Turnpike about as much as he loves the New England corridor of I–95 . . . but at least traffic is moving here at this hour on a Sunday morning.

"Did you finish your Christmas shopping?" Brandewyne asks. She's behind the wheel this time. So far, she's pulled over for two smoke breaks, but who's counting?

"My kid just wants iTunes gift cards," Meade tells her. "That, or a laptop, which I can't afford." He hopes Johnny can't, either, and he hates himself for that. Hates that he wants to begrudge

Dante a new computer just because he doesn't want his stepfather to be the one who gives it to him.

"No one else to shop for?"

"My mother. I got her one of those vacuum cleaners without the bag." Seeing Brandewyne's eye roll, he says, "What? It's what she wanted."

"You might want to rethink that. I don't care what she told you, Omar. No woman really wants a vacuum cleaner for Christmas, with or without the bag."

"Yeah? How do you know?"

"Gut instinct. It's never wrong."

"Never?"

"I'm a detective. *And* a woman."

Not the most womanly woman he's ever met, that's for damned sure. And yet—there's an unusual hint of wistfulness in her tone, and in her expression as she looks out at the road ahead.

"What do *you* want?" he asks her.

"You really want to know?"

"I asked you."

"I want my kids to spend Christmas with me this year. But one is somewhere in Afghanistan and the other one is God knows where—probably going with my ex and his third wife on a fabulous tropical vacation—no joke, I'm totally serious, last year they went to Cabo. So that's not gonna happen."

Meade absorbs that, wondering if maybe he and Brandewyne might have more in common than he thought.

She rarely talks about her personal life. Maybe because he doesn't ask. All he knows is that she's divorced with two grown sons, one on active duty, the other a slacker. And that she lives on the Lower East Side in a rent-controlled apartment. That's it. Pretty much the same bare-bones details he's shared about his own life.

"If that's not gonna happen," he says, "do you by any chance want a free bagless vacuum instead?"

Brandewyne grins and slaps the steering wheel. Her teeth are still yellow with coffee and nicotine, but for some reason, it bothers Meade a little less.

J—I went to Mass at H.T.—Love, L

Jeremy plucks the yellow Post-it note from the mirror above the bathroom sink and stares at his reflection.

You look like shit.

He'd better pull himself together, though, because Cliff just called to say that the cops want to interview them both, along with several boys who were close to Miguel, and other members of the staff.

"I'll get there as soon as I can," he promised Cliff.

"With a lawyer?"

"Nah—I realized that's not necessary."

"Didn't think so. In fact, the more I think about it, if you're lawyered up, it might make them think you have something to hide."

"Well, I don't, and I won't."

Now, as Jeremy runs the water for a shower, he assures himself that there's nothing to worry about. This isn't about him. He owes it to Miguel to help the police find out who murdered him.

All he has to do today is go up there, answer some routine questions just like everyone else.

He has to go buy his wife a Christmas gift, and a tree, too. They're going to celebrate this holiday the way they always have.

Jeremy isn't sure when he came to that conclusion.

Was it just now, when he looked at himself in the mirror and decided he doesn't want to be this miserable person?

Or maybe it was last night, when he was watching Lucy sleep, lying on her side facing him, her forearm resting on her rounded stomach.

No matter what happened in the past, he's spent the last fifteen years doing the right thing—and he's going to keep on doing it.

Maybe I ain't never had a father, but I'll figure out how to be one. A good one.

With Miguel's words ringing in his ears, Jeremy steps into the bathtub and lets the hot water wash away yesterday's grime.

Holy Trinity Church, a beautiful old cathedral in the heart of the Upper West Side, is standing room only on this last Sunday morning of Advent.

Wedged into the end of a pew halfway down the aisle, surrounded by the familiar rituals of Sunday Mass—organ music, incense, prayer—Lucy is still waiting to be swept by the usual feeling of comfort and healing.

She does her best to keep her attention focused on the priest and the beautifully decorated altar. There are dozens of white poinsettias and flickering white votives, and three tall evergreens are strung with simple white lights.

Off to one side is a life-sized crèche.

Lucy can't help but fixate on it—on the empty manger positioned at the forefront, between the Mary and Joseph statues.

Lots of churches set it up this way, she knows, so that the baby Jesus figurine can be carried in on the Christmas Eve procession and symbolically placed on the bed of straw.

Lucy always thought it was a beautiful tradition.

But today, a strange feeling of foreboding came over her the moment she saw the empty manger, and she's grown increasingly uneasy.

Relieved when the Mass comes to an end, she exits the pew and faces the altar to cross herself.

Turning her back on the unsettling Nativity scene, she joins the parishioners making their way toward the rear of the church. The organist is cheerfully playing "Joy to the World," one of Lucy's favorite carols, but even that doesn't help to dispel the nagging sense of uneasiness.

Reaching the back of the church, she turns to dip her hand into the font of holy water. As she does, she glimpses a familiar face in the crowd funneling toward the door.

Lucy stops short, stunned.

It can't be.

Someone bumps into her, hard, from behind.

"Pardon me, I'm so sorry," an elderly man says.

Lucy just looks at him and then turns, dazed, back toward the face in the crowd.

It's gone, of course.

Because it was never there.

Because it couldn't have been there.
Because she's dead.

"Are you joining us for bingo today?"

Marin looks up to see a nurse's aide standing behind her. Lost in thought as she stared out the window, she didn't even hear anyone come into the room.

"Bingo . . . no, not today."

"Are you sure? You won big the other day, remember?" The aide points to the stuffed monkey propped on Marin's bedside table. Beside it, a towering red bloom has sprung from the ceramic flowerpot Wendy Nevid gave her a while back.

"It's an amaryllis," she said, as Marin inspected the stub of a stalk poking up out of the dirt. "Watch it grow, and it'll be blooming by Christmas, I promise."

It's blooming. It must be Christmas.

"No bingo today," Marin tells the aide, "but thank you for asking, Jackie."

She smiles. "You remember my name."

Marin nods. She remembers a lot of things. Today is one of those days when her mind is feeling sharp.

She wishes Jeremy would come visit. There are so many questions she wants to ask him.

She picks up her marble notebook and rifles through the pages, filled with her own handwriting.

When she's feeling lucid, she writes things down—things she doesn't want to forget.

But it doesn't do her much good. When she's

having a bad day, she never thinks to look inside the notebook.

She opens to a random page and starts reading.

> *When Jeremy showed up after all those years,*
> *I worried about how Caroline would adjust to*
> *her long-lost brother . . .*

Yes, Marin well recalls those troubled days . . . and the bizarre circumstances under which Jeremy had come into Caroline's life.

Driven by a misguided effort to get to know the sister who had no idea he even existed, Jeremy hadn't revealed his true identity to Caroline when they met. Marin can't really blame him for that—like Caroline, Jeremy was oblivious to La La Montgomery's vicious manipulation of their relationship. Both Marin's children were unwitting pawns in La La's vengeful game.

In the end, it was Jeremy who saved Caroline at La La's hands.

But he couldn't save Annie.

No one, not even Marin, could save her tender-hearted younger daughter.

Through all those years, Annie quietly shouldered the unfair burdens she'd been handed: her father's emotional abandonment, his unspeakable crimes and the resulting public scandal, her sister's resentment, her brother's reappearance—and, worst of all, her mother's reliance on prescription medication to cope with everything.

I failed her.

Marin stares down at the page, where fresh teardrops have fallen on words that are as difficult to read now as they were to write months ago:

If only I had realized how Annie was struggling.

But Marin never knew.

She was too swept up in the tragic maelstrom and the vicious cycle of chemical dependency to see what was right there before her: a child in crisis. A child who went from self-medicating with food to self-medicating with drugs.

A few days after learning that her father had died in prison, Annie swallowed a handful of sleeping pills stolen from Marin's bedside table. Then she got into bed, clutching her teddy bear, snuggled beneath her quilt, just as she had every night of her life.

The next morning, she didn't wake up.

"Chaplain Gideon."

Car keys in hand, about to head toward the parking lot adjacent to the brick church, the lanky old man turns instead toward the sound of Meade's voice.

"I'm Detective Meade, and this is Detective Brandewyne. We're with the NYPD."

Chaplain Gideon glances at the badges in their hands, pale gray eyes wide in his withered face. "Is there something I can help you with, Detectives?"

"There is," Meade tells him. "We'd like to talk to you."

"I'm on my way to meet friends for brunch. They're already at the restaurant, waiting for me."

"We'll try not to take up too much of your time."

"It's supposed to start snowing soon."

Meade follows the old man's gaze to the overcast sky. He can definitely smell snow in the frigid

air. The storm is coming from the southwest, forecast to hit Trenton before it makes its way up to
New York City later tonight.

"Would you come with us, please, Chaplain?"

"Do I have a choice?"

"You do," Meade admits, his breath puffing
white in the air. "But we really need to talk to you."

The chaplain tilts his head, studying Meade,
then Brandewyne.

"We're investigating a double homicide," she
tells him, and he seems to consider that before
making up his mind abruptly.

"All right. Let's go."

She's sure Lucy spotted her in church, just before
she slipped out the door.

There's no question about it; no mistaking the
look of shocked recognition on Lucy's face.

Huddled in the last booth of a diner around the
corner from the church, she's broken one of the
first rules she learned in prison: Never sit with
your back to the door. But in this case, it's okay.
Her seat faces a mirrored wall that reflects the
entire place. In it, she can keep an eye on the room
behind her, just in case.

Not that she can imagine, in her wildest dreams,
that Lucy possibly managed to follow her here
without being spotted. Still, she keeps her guard
up, because you just never know.

"Hi there, what'll it be?" The waitress, bored,
nearing the end of her shift, doesn't bother to
make eye contact.

Having grown accustomed to maintaining

invisibility in the heart of a crowded city, she orders scrambled eggs, white toast, bacon, hash browns, orange juice, black coffee—nothing requiring additional questions or conversation.

The waitress disappears.

Her thoughts turn back to what happened in church just now.

She should have resisted the temptation to show up at Mass, having known Lucy was going to be there. Thanks to the camera she'd planted in the bathroom—one that shows Lucy miserably hunched over the toilet bowl every morning, sick as a dog—she'd seen the note on the mirror. It was easy, so easy, to zoom in on the Post-it and read Lucy's large, legible script.

> *J—*
> *I went to Mass at H.T.*
> *   —Love, L*

The thought of Lucy in Holy Trinity—sitting in a pew facing the altar, with no idea what lies in store for her there—was too tantalizing to ignore.

She dressed quickly and walked over, arriving just before Mass started. Sitting several rows behind Lucy, she wondered if maybe Lucy *did* have some kind of awareness after all. If not an inkling about what was going to happen on Christmas Eve, then perhaps just a hunch that she wasn't completely among strangers in that church.

She kept turning to look over her shoulder, as if she were searching for a familiar face.

From a distance, mine wouldn't have been.

But close up—looking into my eyes for just that split second by the door—she knew it was me.

What is she going to do about it?

As long as I don't take another risk—not the slightest risk—everything is going to be all right.

There's only one way to avoid risk: by spending the next forty-eight hours alone in the apartment, emerging only on Christmas Eve, when it's time.

But what about tomorrow?

She was planning to return to Parkview, to see if Marin really is there.

If she doesn't go, she might never know.

But if she does go . . . there's no telling how she might react.

Is she willing to take a chance?

"Snowing out there yet?" the lobby security guard asks as Lucy hurries toward the elevator.

"Not yet."

"Looks like it's going to be a white Christmas, though."

Lucy smiles and nods and is relieved to step onto an empty elevator.

Is she going to tell Jeremy what she saw at church?

Rather, what she *imagined* she'd seen?

That's about as logical an explanation as Lucy can come up with. Other than . . .

No, she doesn't believe in ghosts.

There was a time when she might have—or at least, when she wanted to. After Daddy died, she kept hoping his spirit might appear to her. She and Robyn even spent a couple of sleepovers trying to contact him with a Ouija board, succeeding only in scaring themselves so that they had to sleep with the lights on.

The elevator reaches her floor and the doors slide

open. Lucy pushes through the doors leading from
the elevator bank to the quiet, carpeted corridors.

Unlike yesterday, when the Ansonia's halls
were relatively teeming with activity, Lucy doesn't
encounter another soul—living or dead—before
she turns off onto the short hallway that leads to
their door.

But it's not all that difficult to imagine an old
building like this being haunted.

If she *did* believe in ghosts—now, as a level-
headed adult—would it mean that this particular
spirit has a message for her from the great beyond?

If so, nothing good, that's for sure. Lucy had felt
the bad energy from the moment she walked into
Holy Trinity and saw that empty manger.

*Maybe that's why I imagined seeing her. Maybe
she was in the back of my mind. Because if she isn't—*
wasn't—*the queen of bad energy, well, she's—she
was—pretty close.*

Unlocking the door, she wonders again if she
should tell Jeremy what happened.

Maybe she'll mention it in a joking kind of
way—like, "You'll never believe my latest crazy
pregnancy symptom . . ."

No . . . she won't take that approach. There's
nothing the least bit amusing about *her*.

Stepping over the threshold, she calls Jeremy's
name.

No answer.

Thinking he's still asleep, she makes her way
into the bedroom. The bed is made—Jeremy-style,
anyway, meaning he pulled the comforter up to
cover the sheets and blanket and picked up the
stray pillows that had fallen onto the floor. Maybe

he's in the den on his computer again. She quickly smooths the sheets, blanket, and comforter, re-arranges the pillows Lucy-style.

"Jeremy?" she calls, going out into the hall, the kitchen, through the apartment room by room. "Jeremy?"

Where is he?

Ordinarily, she wouldn't be thrown, but seeing that face in church . . .

"Jeremy!"

Backtracking to the bedroom, and finally into the master bathroom, she sees that her yellow Post-it note is still on the mirror.

Then she realizes that isn't the one she left.

It's a note from Jeremy.

Relieved, she plucks it off the mirror.

> *L—Cliff called and I had to go into work*
> *for a few hours.*
>
> Love, J

A few hours should be enough time for Lucy to figure out what the heck happened—or didn't happen—back there at Holy Trinity.

The greasy spoon off Broad Street in Trenton is overheated and overcrowded with locals wearing their Sunday best, lingering over their after-church breakfasts.

Meade and Brandewyne managed to snag a small, semi-private table where they can talk to Chaplain Gideon in relative privacy.

"I take it this isn't where you were planning to meet your friends?" Brandewyne asks, watching him examine the spoon he's about to use to stir his coffee. He makes a face and sets it aside.

"No. We go to Denny's."

Brandewyne arches a brow. "Now that's a step up."

It definitely is, at least from this place, Meade thinks, noticing some dried crud on his own spoon.

But they're not here for the fine cuisine or atmosphere, or even for a hot cup of coffee—good thing, because the sludge the waitress poured into his cup is lukewarm at best.

They're here to see if Chaplain Gideon can shed any light on the Jollston murder. So far, they've told him just the basic details of the crime. Not a hint of recognition on his face about any of it.

They've also established that he has a very good alibi for the night of the murders. He was leading a prayer group at the church here in Trenton. Plenty of people will be able to vouch for him, and Meade fully intends to speak with them.

"Tell us about Garvey Quinn," he says abruptly.

The old man doesn't look particularly thrown by the name.

"I wondered if this might have something to do with him." He nibbles the crust of a piece of toast that was probably dry before it was dropped into the toaster.

"Why is that?" Meade asks.

"Because you're NYPD. That's where he was from. New York City."

"A lot of inmates at Hazelton are, though, aren't they?"

"Yes. But I didn't get too close to many of them. Not like Garvey. We prayed together all the time.

He repented for his sins. He was saved, you know, before he died."

"Too bad no one saved all those people he murdered," Brandewyne mutters—loudly enough to be overheard by Meade.

Not, apparently, by Chaplain Gideon, though. He goes on without missing a beat

"Garvey was very passionate about his faith, and he wanted to share his beliefs with everyone he met. That turned off some of the other inmates, but not all of them. He was frighteningly charismatic."

"Frighteningly?"

"He had a dark side. And he displayed serious delusional behavior toward the end. All that time in prison—I think it just got to be too much for him."

"Poor guy."

Meade shoots Brandewyne a warning look, and asks Gideon, "Delusional, how? What happened?"

"He had apocalyptic fantasies. He started to talk about the end being near . . ."

"*His* end?" Maybe he'd sensed that he was going to die. It happens. Meade's father, who—like Garvey Quinn—dropped dead of a sudden heart attack—reconciled a longstanding feud with his brother about a week before it happened.

But Chaplain Gideon is shaking his head. "Not *his* end. The End of Days. The Second Coming. He was obsessed. He talked about it all the time, wrote about it."

"What did he write?" Meade asks. "Did he keep a journal?"

"Not that I know of. He wrote letters—long letters."

"To who?"

Meade resists the urge to correct Brandewyne's grammar. To *whom*. It should be to *whom*. He sips his coffee. Ugh.

"To everyone. His family, his friends, his enemies . . ." Chaplain Gideon sighs. "If he had channeled all that energy toward changing this world for the better, imagine what he could have accomplished."

"That's something I think about every day doing the work I do, Chaplain," Brandewyne says, as Meade looks around for the waitress. He's chilled through after waiting outside on the church steps in the bracing wind, and he really could use some hot coffee.

"People like you—both of you—you're doing just that."

"Doing just what?" Brandewyne asks.

"Changing this world for the better."

The two NYPD detectives, both of whom are balding, bespectacled, slightly overweight, and wearing wedding rings—are barely distinguishable from each other or countless other middle-aged men Jeremy's ever met. Not the least bit intimidating; in fact, they've been surprisingly pleasant so far.

Why wouldn't they be? This isn't an interrogation, Jeremy reminds himself. It's an interview. He's not a suspect, he's here to help.

"Mr. Cavalon, did Miguel say or do anything that made you think he might be in some kind of danger on Friday night?"

"No."

They're meeting in the center's large confer-

ence room, decorated with paper snowflakes sus-
pended on strands of monofilament fishing line
from the drop ceiling. The boys made them in art
class. Some are barely more than rectangles with
a few haphazard holes cut in them; others, elaborate three-dimensional filigrees.

Jeremy's gaze keeps drifting toward the
snowflakes, wafting a bit in the air blowing
through the ceiling vents. But he does his best
to stay focused on the detectives, not wanting
them to think he has any reason not to look
them in the eye.

"Did Miguel mention anything about a plan to
meet anyone after he left you that night?"

"No."

The detectives take turns asking the questions,
writing down his answers.

"Did he receive any phone calls or texts while
you were with him?"

Is it a trick question? They'd have to know that,
wouldn't they? Unless the mugger—if it was a
mugging—stole Miguel's phone . . .

But still, the cops would be able to access the
phone records.

Yeah, they must know. If not yet, then they will
soon.

"His girlfriend texted him quite a few times,"
Jeremy tells them.

"Do you know what it was about?"

"He didn't tell me, and I didn't ask."

"Did he talk to you about their relationship at
all?"

Jeremy contemplates that.

Do they even know Carmen is pregnant? They
might not. Miguel mentioned last night that he

hadn't told anyone but Jeremy, and if Carmen hasn't told her parents yet . . .

But her friends know. At least one friend—Brenda. Brenda, who said Carmen didn't want to have the baby because she didn't want to get fat.

Have the detectives talked to Carmen yet? To Brenda? How much do they know?

How much should Jeremy tell them?

Least harm . . . what would cause the least harm? That's your obligation.

"Mr. Cavalon? Did Miguel talk to you about Carmen?"

The truth. Just tell the truth. You have nothing to hide—not when it comes to Miguel, anyway. He's already been harmed.

Jeremy swallows hard. "He did talk to me about her."

"What did he say?"

"It was told to me in confidence . . ."

"We understand that. But we're talking about a dead child, Mr. Cavalon, and if he told you anything that might have led to his murder—in confidence or not . . ."

Miguel is dead.

A dead child . . .

Powerful wording.

A child who technically raped a child who is now expecting a child . . .

But Miguel can no longer get into trouble for that.

Trouble—it's a relative term.

"Carmen was pregnant. He wanted her to have the baby. She didn't want to."

The detectives exchange a now-we're-getting-somewhere glance.

Jeremy looks at the snowflakes dancing in the hot air and hopes that Carmen, wherever she is this morning, has changed her mind.

Ryan doesn't go to Mass every week the way Lucy does. Whenever he has attended, though, his sister has always been here.

Today, he finds himself looking around the church expecting to see her, even though he knows he won't find her.

He came on a whim, and probably for the wrong reason. He's not opposed to spiritual healing, but he's really just looking for a way to fill the weekend.

He was worried that if he stayed at home with nothing to do, Phoenix might call and he'd jump at the chance to see her.

He was even more worried that she wouldn't call, and he'd spend the day sitting by the phone.

Pathetic. Yeah, he knows. But at least he's trying to do something about it.

"Ryan Walsh—good to see you," Father Les greets him, standing by the door after Mass is over.

In his mid-forties, tall, athletic, and charismatic, Father Les has been with the parish for about ten years now. He always shakes hands with his parishioners as they exit, making Ryan feel vaguely guilty whenever he hadn't been here for a while. *Like now.* But if Father Les is taking attendance, he doesn't chide Ryan for his absences. He just seems genuinely glad to see him.

"Has Lucy settled into her new apartment in the city?" he asks, after inquiring about Ryan's new job.

"She has."

"We're going to miss seeing her here. Be sure to wish her a merry Christmas for me, and remind her to let me know when the baby comes. I'm keeping her in my prayers."

"I'll tell her," Ryan promises.

"And a merry Christmas to you, too, Ryan. Remember—God is in control."

Those are, and always have been, Father Les's standard parting words to everyone.

Ordinarily, Ryan lets them go in one ear and out the other.

But today, for some reason, the phrase resonates. He starts to walk away, but then turns back to the priest.

"Father?"

About to shake the hand of the next parishioner, the priest turns expectantly back toward Ryan.

"If God is in control, does it mean that your life is predestined and your fate is out of your hands? That nothing you do—or don't do—will matter?"

"Not at all. We all have free will, Ryan. We all make choices every day of our lives. It's up to us to listen to what God is saying—to let God guide us down the right path. Do you understand?"

Ryan doesn't—not at all—but he nods politely. "Thank you, Father."

He turns again to go.

"Ryan?"

"Yes?"

"I'm here if you need me." Watching him intently, the priest raises a hand and makes the sign of the cross over Ryan, blessing him.

Why?

Does he see something? Know something? Feel something?

A chill slips down Ryan's spine and he hurries away.

Snowflakes are starting to swirl as Meade steers the car onto Interstate 95, heading back toward the Jersey Turnpike. Brandewyne wanted to drive, but he insisted, in no mood to stop every half hour so that she can smoke a cigarette, hacking away the whole time from inhaling smoke and cold air. That's what happened just now, when she insisted on lighting up before they hit the road.

"You know, she could be long gone from New York by now," she muses, turning up the fan on the passenger's side vent to blast some heat in her direction.

"Let's hope so. But it's still only a matter of time before she snaps and hurts someone else."

"Like that old guy."

"Who?"

"Chaplain Gideon, who do you think?"

"She's never even met him," Meade reminds her.

"Exactly—but obviously, she spent a whole lot of time thinking about him. And talking to him," she adds pointedly.

True.

"What if she comes looking for him? It sounds like she's living out some kind of apocalyptic fantasy herself."

"I agree. But I don't think she'll try to harm Chaplain Gideon."

"Who do you think she has in mind?"

Meade shakes his head grimly. "I'm not sure, but I wish Jeremy Cavalon and his wife would return my phone call."

"Maybe they have."

"No. I checked a few minutes ago, before you got into the car. Not a word from them. I hope . . ."

"What?" she prods, when he trails off.

"I just hope she didn't get to them before we did."

"Goose? Where are you?"

Startled awake, Lucy opens her eyes. It takes a groggy moment for her to get her bearings—she's in the bedroom, but it's not morning; the light is wrong: long shadows falling through the windows across the brocade rug.

Oh—that's right. She was lying on the bed, resting, and she must have fallen asleep. A glance at the clock tells her it's late afternoon.

At her side is her copy of *What to Expect When You're Expecting*. She'd been reading through it, looking for information about daydreams and hallucinations, wondering if by any chance they were a symptom of pregnancy.

Sure enough, there was a section in the book about vivid dreams and fantasies, both at night, and during the day, when you're wide awake—or think you are. There wasn't much information, but it was enough to convince Lucy that she'd definitely imagined the "ghost" she'd seen this morning at church.

"Goose!"

"In here." She sits up and the baby kicks, seemingly in protest.

"C'mere!" he calls over a thumping racket in the front hall.

She makes her way in and her eyes widen at the sight of Jeremy juggling an enormous pine tree through the door.

"What are you doing?"

"What does it look like I'm doing?" He drops the tree, closes and locks the door, and grins at her. "Merry Christmas, Goose."

She throws her arms around him. "I don't want to know how much that cost."

"No, you don't."

"It's huge! How tall is it? Are you crazy?"

"I had to get a tall one with these twelve-foot ceilings. Oh, and I got you a present, too."

"You mean that isn't it?"

"No, it's in my coat pocket. No peeking," he adds with a laugh as she playfully pokes his pocket.

"What made you decide to do this?"

"It Christmas, and we're having a baby." Jeremy puts his hand on her stomach. The baby obliges with a swift kick. "Whoa—did you feel that?"

"Did I feel it? Are you kidding?" Lucy rests her hand over his, leaning her head on his shoulder, and finally, there it is: that feeling of comfort and healing that eluded her at Mass this morning.

Earlier worries try to push their way into her head, but she learned, years ago, how to keep troubling thoughts at bay. Sometimes, no matter what's happened in your life, you just have to be in the moment.

"Come on, Goose," Jeremy says, giving her stomach a final pat. "Let's get this tree decorated. Christmas Eve will be here before we know it."

"Well, I guess Lucy didn't recognize me after all at church," she tells Chaplain Gideon, watching Lucy stand by, laughing, as Jeremy wrestles the tree into the living room.

"You don't know that for sure."

"If she had, she would have done something about it. At least have told Jeremy. Instead she went to bed and slept all afternoon."

"True. Maybe she thought you were a figment of her imagination," Chaplain Gideon suggests.

"You don't think she can tell the difference between something real and something that's only imagined?" She smiles, relishing the thought of Lucy Cavalon thinking she might be delusional.

She's almost tempted to pop up again and tease Lucy a little—make her think she's really going crazy.

Chaplain Gideon's response to that idea is loud and clear. "No! Absolutely not! You heard what Jeremy said just now, didn't you?"

Yes. She did.

Christmas Eve will indeed be here before we know it.

All she has to do is get through another two days, and it will be time. A whole new world will begin for her—and this one, this miserable world, will end for Lucy and Jeremy Cavalon and so many others.

Just as Daddy promised it would.

Two more days, and then she'll see him again— after the baby comes, when the dead will rise up to be judged alongside the living.

Just like Daddy said.

Turning away from the computer screen, she yanks open a drawer and pulls out a treasured packet of envelopes. Dozens of them, with thick, folded sheets of paper inside, all tied together in a satin ribbon she'd worn in her hair as a child— back when she was Daddy's little girl.

A snowstorm of historic proportion struck the tri-state area late Sunday night, bringing significant accumulation, high winds, and drifts several feet high. City public schools are closed this week for the holiday break, but many businesses let their employees leave early on Monday and will remain closed through Christmas Day tomorrow. Air travel is snarled with thousands stranded at the airports, and still, the snow keeps falling—"

"Can we please watch something else, Lu?" Ryan asks, sprawled in an antique chair with his legs dangling over the arm. "A soap opera, a game show, anything? This 24–7 storm coverage is getting old fast. I mean, it's just snow."

"A *lot* of snow," Lucy points out, sitting on the sofa with her feet propped on the marble coffee table.

"I know, but still . . ." Ryan gestures at the TV, where the scene has shifted to a reporter out in the blizzard-blown tundra—could be the Dakota prairie, could be Times Square—poking a yardstick into a snowbank.

"All this drama—you'd think we were at war

or something. Can't they cover anything else? Is weather all that's happening in this city?"

"Pretty much." Lucy glances toward the tall windows, where snow is coming down hard against a bleak urban winterscape.

Stretches of I–95 are closed up and down the East Coast, and she's already informed Jeremy's parents that they won't be able to make it to Connecticut tomorrow. Good thing, because the news desk just reported that there are power outages and jammed phone lines all over Eastern Connecticut.

When Lucy called Elsa early this morning to cancel, her mother-in-law was disappointed but already anticipating the inevitable. "We'll have a belated celebration this weekend. Just stay safe, both of you. How are you feeling?"

"Fine," Lucy told her, but the truth was, she had awakened feeling a little crampy again this morning.

She's done nothing but rest for more than twenty-four hours now, so it isn't due to exertion. Her company and Ryan's were among the businesses that closed early yesterday and didn't open at all today. The two of them have spent the better part of the last twenty-four hours in this room, lit only by the tiny colored bulbs on the Christmas tree standing tall between the windows. They've been cozily watching TV, eating, talking, and reading . . . just like old times.

If only Jeremy were here . . .

But she hasn't seen much of him during waking hours since he left for work yesterday morning, an hour before she did. He was out till late last night for his basketball team's holiday dinner. It took him over two hours to get home due to snow on the elevated tracks in the Bronx. Nonetheless, he braved the weather again today to head back up again.

Lucy knew better than to try to talk him out of it—not just because she knew she wouldn't succeed, but because she knew how much it meant to Jeremy to spend at least part of the holiday with his "guys." Plus, he was supposed to pick up a couple of bags of donated gifts for the boys on the way to the group home, and there was absolutely no way he'd miss doing that.

When she reached him a little while ago on his cell, he promised to leave by five o'clock to head home, and said he'd pick up something for dinner along the way.

"What did you have in mind?" Lucy asked.

"Whatever I can get. Pretty much everything is closed."

Including the fish market. Lucy called to check first thing this morning.

"Wait, Jeremy, do you want me to call around and see if I can have something delivered so you don't have to stop?" she asked.

"No, I'll take care of it. I'll probably just get a pizza or some Chinese, okay?"

Pizza or Chinese. So much for her seafood dinner. From seven fishes down to one: a can of tuna Ryan found in the cupboard and made into sandwiches for their lunch.

"I miss you, Jeremy."

"I miss you, too," he said, but he sounded distracted. Well, of course. He was at work. "Look, I've got one bar left on my phone. I forgot to charge it last night and it's about to die. So don't worry if you don't hear from me. I'll get there—with dinner."

Takeout on Christmas Eve seems wrong, as does

the thought of missing midnight Mass, but at this rate, Lucy doubts she and Ryan will attempt to get there. The mayor has already announced that there should be no unnecessary travel in the city, prompting a number of churches to cancel Christmas Eve services. Lucy's been keeping an eye out for Holy Trinity to appear among them on the cancellation crawl along the bottom of the screen.

"And now, let's head out to Central Park, where our reporter Sammy Nguyen is braving the elements."

Ryan groans and throws a pillow at the TV screen. "Lu—please change the channel."

She tosses him the remote. "Here. All yours."

"Got any movies we can watch on DVD?"

"There's a whole library of them in the other room. Go pick something out. *It's a Wonderful Life* is there."

Ryan grins. "Hmmm. . . . I think I've seen that."

Yeah, no kidding. They used to watch it over and over on Christmas Eve when they were both living at home.

"I'm going to send Phoenix a quick text," Ryan says, taking out his phone, "and then I'll find that DVD."

Ever since he arrived here yesterday, he's been going back and forth with his girlfriend, who's stuck at work. Hers, apparently, is one of the few companies in the city that hasn't closed due to the weather or the holiday.

Lucy leans her head back, stretches, and notices a tightening, again, in her lower stomach.

It's been happening on and off all morning, though she's done nothing but rest with her feet up.

"Another pain?"

She looks up to see Ryan watching her worriedly. "Not pain, just . . . it's probably Braxton Hicks."

Ryan—newly well-versed in obstetrical terminology—suggests, "Maybe you should call the doctor again."

Lucy contemplates that. She called the office this morning, spoke to both Gloria and Dr. Courmier, and was told to stay off her feet.

"If it gets any worse, we need you to come down to the hospital and get checked out," Dr. Courmier told her, and Lucy could hear the concern in her voice. "But I'd just as soon have you stay put for now. It's so hard to get around the city, I don't want you going out if you don't have to. If you slipped and fell, it would be bad."

Lucy wholeheartedly agreed. The storm coverage has shown endless footage of accidents at slippery Manhattan intersections. Cabs are reportedly scarce due to the weather and the holiday, buses are stranded, and even the subways are delayed due to buried tracks in outlying boroughs.

"It hasn't gotten worse," Lucy tells Ryan now.

"But it hasn't gotten better, either?"

She shakes her head, not knowing what to do, which isn't at all like her. If it were just about her own physical well-being, she'd simply sit tight and wait out any nondrastic physical symptom, assuming it will pass.

But it's not just about her. It's about another person, a tiny, fragile person whose life is in her hands.

She doesn't want to take any chances.

But when you weigh the risks . . .

Leaving the apartment in the storm to get to the doctor is a definite risk—dangerous, even.

Staying here—especially since this symptom has been coming and going for days now, and there's been no lull in the baby's usual movement—seems to be the better choice.

She never even told Jeremy about the earlier cramping, or the phone calls to the doctor. She didn't want to put a damper on Sunday afternoon and evening. They spent hours decorating the tree, talking and laughing as though they hadn't a care in the world.

A few times, she saw a shadow cross Jeremy's eyes, and knew he was thinking of Miguel. But he seemed determined to keep sorrow at bay that day, and Lucy was only too happy to go along with that. She was feeling absolutely fine at that point—no cramps—and she had already concluded that the face she'd glimpsed in church had been a hallucination.

What else did she have to worry about?

There *was* just one thing . . .

Before they went to bed, she heard Jeremy on the phone in the next room. He was leaving another message for Carl Soto, who had yet to return Saturday's call.

But Carl didn't respond to Sunday's call, either. Nor did he get in touch yesterday.

Every time Lucy allows herself to think about that woman—Mary, Carl said her name was—she feels vaguely uneasy.

She was already asleep late last night when Jeremy finally came home and crawled into bed, but woke up to snuggle next to him. She told him briefly about her day and mentioned that there hadn't been a response from the landlord yet.

Jeremy seemed so exhausted that he didn't even seem to want to talk about it.

"Maybe he just went away for the holidays," she said with a yawn, and drifted back to sleep.

She didn't remember until this morning that Carl had promised to keep an eye out for packages at their old address this week. If he'd gone away, it must have been a last-minute plan.

Lucy sighs, watching the snow fall. It's Christmas Eve, always her favorite day of the year, filled with traditions. Yet right now, the only thing that's familiar is her brother's company.

"I'm glad you're here with me, Ry," she tells him, and sees that he's still holding his phone, texting again.

"Yeah, I'm glad I'm here, too," he mutters.

"Is Phoenix still coming over later?" Maybe having company will make it feel a little more festive.

Ryan nods. "She says don't worry, nothing would keep her away."

Seated at his desk, Meade thrums the fingertips of his right hand on his mouse pad and holds the phone to his ear with his left.

"Mrs. Cottington," he says patiently, "I understand all of that, completely. I wouldn't be asking you for this information if I didn't think your friend might be in danger."

There's silence on the other end of the line, and for a moment, he thinks the call might have been lost.

That wouldn't be surprising. It's taken him the better part of two days to track Marin Quinn's friend to a yacht in the Mediterranean. It's all very glamorous and exclusive—the yacht belongs to a Saudi businessman whose security is ridiculously tight. Meade probably would have had an easier time arranging to have Christmas dinner tomorrow with the first lady.

But at last, he's got Heather Cottington on the line—at least *had* her on the line. The ship to overseas-shore connection has thus far been patchy and static-ridden.

But not disconnected; Heather Cottington speaks again, and he notes that she sounds groggy, or drunk, or both. It's closing in on midnight in her corner of the world.

"How do I even know that you're with the NYPD?" she asks. "For all I know you're a reporter. Or someone who's trying to hurt Marin yourself."

"Omar!" Meade looks up to see Brandewyne standing over his desk and frowns, indicating that he's in the middle of a call.

"It's important," she hisses, and he waves her off. So is this.

"Look, Mrs. Cottington, I don't blame you for being cautious. I understand that you're trying to protect your friend. I'm doing the exact same thing. Here's what I propose. We hang up. You call the main switchboard number for the NYPD and ask them to put you through to me. Then you tell me where I can find Marin Quinn. Is that a deal?"

Another hesitation.

He drums the mouse pad. Brandewyne waits impatiently by his desk, shifting her weight from one foot to the other.

"Deal," Heather Cottington says, and hangs up before he can get in another word.

He sighs and looks up at Brandewyne. "What's up?"

"You know how I've been trying to track down the Cavalons' landlord?"

Meade nods. Having failed to hear back from the Cavalons over the weekend, he and Brandewyne have been concerned. Yesterday morning, they made the treacherous trip up to the White Plains duplex, only to find it apparently deserted, upstairs and down.

Assuming the Cavalons might have gone to work, Meade tracked down their workplaces and attempted to reach them there. A call to Lucy Cavalon's company went into an automated message that they had closed due to the weather.

And although he got through to someone at the group home where Jeremy Cavalon worked, he was told that Jeremy had left for the holidays. But he had been there, so at least they know he was safe. As of yesterday, anyway.

"I found him," Brandewyne announces triumphantly.

"Jeremy Cavalon?"

"No! The landlord!"

Oh. Right. They were hoping to gain access to the apartment without having to get a search warrant.

"Where is he?"

"He's—"

She breaks off as Meade's desk phone rings. They both look at it.

"That's Heather Cottington," he says, reaching for it. "Just tell me—where's the landlord?"

"In the morgue."

Every time Jeremy thinks about what he did yesterday afternoon, he feels sick inside.

He was right here, in this very spot—sitting at his desk in his office, working on the grant—when the phone rang. Not his cell, but the desk phone, the line he and Jack share.

"Hello?"

He was greeted by an unfamiliar male voice. "This is Detective Meade from the NYPD. I'd like to speak to Jeremy Cavalon, please."

His heart stopped.

"Is this . . . is it about Miguel?"

"Excuse me?"

"Miguel—is it about Miguel?" His head was spinning.

"I'm afraid it's a confidential matter."

Confidential—then it wasn't about Miguel. The police had spoken to just about everyone here about his murder, which remains unsolved. It wouldn't be a confidential subject.

They must know, Jeremy thought, as panic swept through him, about Papa. They must have done some searching into his past.

"May I please speak to Mr. Cavalon?"

It hit him only then—the detective didn't realize he was actually talking to Jeremy.

In that moment, he reacted in much the same

way he had that day on the boat fifteen years ago, when Papa fell into the water.

He saw an opportunity—an immediate escape—and he seized it without thinking about the consequences.

"I'm sorry," he heard himself say, "Jeremy's left for the day."

"So he *was* there today? You saw him?"

"Yes." His stomach was churning.

"Do you know where he can be reached?"

"I'm sorry, I don't. He's . . . off until after Christmas."

There was a pause.

The detective thanked him and hung up.

What he'd done—lying to the police—was wrong. But in the grand scheme of things, does it really matter? All he wanted—all he *wants*—is to buy himself a little more time.

Time to spend with his guys.

Time to spend with his wife.

Time to spend preparing himself for what inevitably lies ahead: punishment for a crime he committed fifteen years ago.

"Coach?"

He jumps, startled by the voice, and looks up to see one of the boys in the doorway of his office.

"Sorry—I didn't mean to scare you."

"No, it's okay, Dylan. What's going on? I thought your grandfather was going to pick you up."

The boy has talked of nothing but the holiday visit to his grandfather. Jeremy's heart sinks and he wonders if maybe the weather kept Mr. Purtell from coming to get Dylan. And here he is with his hair neatly combed to one side, wearing a red sweater.

"My grandfather is waiting for me downstairs," he says proudly, and Jeremy can't help but smile. "But before I go, I just . . . I wanted to give you this."

He holds something out.

It's a clay ornament. All the boys made them in a crafts workshop last week, cutting them out with cookie cutters, baking them, painting and glazing them.

This one is shaped like an angel, painted in silver glitter, with the word "Coach" painstakingly lettered across it.

Speechless, Jeremy looks from the ornament up to the boy's face.

"I know it's stupid"—Dylan shuffles his feet—"but I wanted to thank you for making sure everything worked out with my grandfather, and . . . I don't know, you've been kind of like a guardian angel to me."

He mutters the last part, looking down at the floor, as though he's embarrassed by his own sentimentality.

"Dylan—" Jeremy's voice breaks. He tries again. "I'll treasure it. Thank you."

Every year, Wendy Nevid and her fellow Jewish colleagues volunteer to work an overnight shift on Christmas Eve and Christmas Day so that their Christian coworkers can spend the holiday with their families. In return, they work shifts on Rosh Hashanah and Yom Kippur, two of the most important holidays in the Jewish calendar.

The system works out well for everyone.

This year, though, Wendy can't help but worry about Mark and the kids, snowbound in Hopewell

Junction. Julia has been coughing since yesterday, and when Wendy called to check in a little while ago, Mark said she was running a low-grade fever. Meanwhile, Ethan kept begging to go outside and build a snowman.

"Last night, Daddy said we could today, and now he won't."

"That's because Julia is sick and Daddy is taking care of her."

"I can go out by myself."

"No. No! Put Daddy back on the phone."

Of all the days for her to be working and Julia to be sick . . .

"Whatever you do, don't let him out by himself," Wendy told Mark. "He might wander off and get lost."

"I won't let him go out by himself or get lost, don't worry."

"And make sure there's enough Dimetapp in the medicine cabinet to get Julia through the night."

"There is."

"And if you're not sure what to make for dinner, there's some—"

"I've got it all under control, Wen," her husband assured her. "Just worry about what you have going on there."

The truth is, there isn't much going on here.

Ordinarily, Parkview is bustling with holiday visitors on Christmas Eve, but the weather is keeping most people home.

Sitting at the fourth floor nurses' station, Wendy bites into lunch—a slice of homemade gingerbread a patient's daughter dropped off earlier for the staff—and flips through the *New York*

Post, with its front-page blizzard photo and towering headline *WHITEOUT!*

For a change, the tabloid is almost devoid of the usual urban dramas—knifings, drive-by shootings, bridge suicides—in favor of snowstorm coverage.

Caught up in a feel-good article about a Good Samaritan who welcomed a busload of stranded tourists into her home, Wendy is barely aware of the elevator's *ding*, signaling a fourth floor stop.

Then she hears a man clearing his throat and looks up to see a pair of strangers standing over her, flashing police badges.

Wendy immediately closes the newspaper and brushes the gingerbread crumbs off her hands.

"I'm Detective Meade," says the distinguished-looking African-American gentleman with salt-and-pepper hair and beard, "and this is Detective Brandewyne." He gestures at his stocky female partner.

"Wendy Nevid. What can I do for you?"

The female detective leans closer, her voice a near whisper. "We're here about one of your patients, Marin Quinn."

The name hits Wendy like an avalanche of ice. No one is supposed to know she's here. *No one.*

She just looks at the woman, not saying a word.

Detective Meade clears his throat. "We understand that Mrs. Quinn is registered under an assumed name to protect her privacy, Ms. Nevid."

Does he want her to confirm that?

The few staff members who share this privileged information are under strict orders never to reveal the true identity of the woman in room 421.

What should she do?

"Maybe we could talk in a private room?" Detective Meade suggests. "We understand that this is a sensitive matter."

"We have reason to believe your patient might be in danger," Detective Brandewyne adds.

Danger.

The magic word, given what Wendy knows about Marin Quinn's past.

She nods briskly and stands. "Just let me find someone to cover the desk."

"Good—you're still here," Cliff says, sticking his head into Jeremy's office as he's packing to head home—Dylan's precious gift wrapped in layers of tissue and stashed in his pocket.

Jeremy looks up, alarmed—then sees that Cliff is smiling. He wouldn't be, if the police were here to take Jeremy away.

"I just called and Garrett's is open. How about coming down with me for some Christmas cheer? We could use it, I'd say, after the last few days."

It's so unlike Cliff to be jovial that under ordinary circumstances, Jeremy might almost be tempted to accept the invitation.

But today, his circumstances are anything but ordinary.

"Sorry, Cliff, but it's Christmas Eve—I'd better get home." Jeremy can't help but think that Cliff—with a wife and three children at home in Brooklyn—should want to do the same.

"I don't know how you're going to do that," Cliff tells him. "I've been checking the MTA Web site and there are massive delays on all the elevated lines in the Bronx."

Jeremy contemplates that. "What about the underground lines?"

"They're running, but the closest B and D station is a couple of miles from here. How would you get over there?"

"Cab?"

"You're kidding, right? There's no way you're going to find a cab around here on a night like this."

"I don't know, then. I guess I'll try my luck at the Soundview Station. There has to be a train through eventually."

"I wouldn't be so sure."

Jeremy shrugs. Never in his life has he wanted so badly to be at home.

"All right," Cliff says. "Get home safe."

"You too. Want to walk with me to the subway?"

"No, thanks. I think I'll head over to Garrett's anyway and wait it out."

Wondering what makes a man choose a pub filled with strangers over home and his family, Jeremy wishes Cliff a merry Christmas and pulls on his coat.

"There *was* something unusual," Wendy Nevid tells the detectives, seated at a table with them in the break room.

They've been asking mostly routine questions until this one—about whether anything unusual has occurred here at Parkview in the last couple of days.

Now, as she nods vigorously, Detective Meade leans toward her with interest. "What happened?"

"Friday morning," Wendy says, "someone tried

to get onto the floor. She said she was here to visit one of the patients, but she was lying."

"*She?*" Meade and Brandewyne exchange a glance. "What did she look like?"

Wendy thinks back. "She was heavy, medium height, with dark hair."

"Wait a minute." Meade pulls something out of his pocket.

A photograph. No—a mug shot. He slides it across the table to Wendy. "Is this her?"

Wendy looks at it. "Yes. That's her. Who is she?"

But then, all at once, before Meade even tells her, she knows. Knows why that woman looked so familiar, and knows where she's seen her before: in a framed photograph in room 421.

She's much younger in it, and pretty, and slender, but still . . .

"She's Marin Quinn's daughter."

C-U-Soon. Love, R

C-U-Soon. Love, P

After sending the return text message, she puts her phone aside and glances up at the computer screen. There, she watches Ryan do the same, courtesy of the hidden camera concealed in Lucy Cavalon's living room a few floors above.

She'd been dreading these last twenty-four hours, holed up in her tiny apartment, just waiting until it's time. But actually, it's proven quite entertaining to watch the two of them, Lucy and Ryan, lounging around without a clue that this is their last day on earth.

If they knew, would they be doing anything differently?

Would they be calling their parents, or praying, or trying to escape?

Is that why Lucy is having those cramps she keeps talking about? Because she's anxious?

She even called the doctor, who seemed to reassure her.

She hasn't said much about it to her brother, but concern is blatant on her face.

What if something's wrong with the baby?

"The baby will be fine," Chaplain Gideon croons. "Just a few more hours. Patience."

Patience!

It's always about patience. Always.

But not for much longer.

She paces, nervous with anticipation—like a child on Christmas Eve, she thinks, much to her own amusement. Only she's not waiting for Santa.

Just a few more hours, and it will be time for her to show up at the apartment door upstairs. They'll let her in. Of course they will.

Once she's in, Lucy will recognize her. But by then it will be too late. By then, the end will have begun.

Just as Daddy said it would.

Again, she pulls out the packet of letters— the ones Garvey Quinn wrote her from prison. They've given her the fortitude, these last few days, to resist temptation. The end is in sight now. Her reunion with her father is in sight. Tonight . . .

She pulls the topmost letter from the stack, carefully unfolds the yellowed pages, and begins to read what Daddy wrote to her years ago.

Dear Caroline . . .

* * *

Seeing the obvious concern on the petite blond nurse's face, Meade offers her a reassuring smile. "You've been really helpful, Ms. Nevid."

She nods, still clearly shaken by that photograph.

"We're going to station a uniformed officer in the lobby and another one up here on the floor, just like we talked about. In fact"—he looks over his shoulder toward the hall outside the break room, where Brandewyne is on the phone, making the necessary arrangements—"someone should be here shortly, and we won't leave until that happens, I promise."

"You really think Caroline Quinn would want to hurt her own mother?"

"She's a sick woman. We don't know what she might try to do, or where she'll surface next. In fact, that's what I wanted to ask you about. Mrs. Quinn has a son—"

"Jeremy."

"You know him?"

"He visits her every Friday."

"Was he here this Friday?"

"Yes."

"Well, we haven't been able to get in touch with him and his wife." Or their landlord, who, it turns out, was struck by an express train on Saturday afternoon and was killed.

The platform was crowded, and no one saw exactly what happened in the moments before Carl Soto fell, jumped, or was pushed onto the track. It's not clear which of those scenarios took place.

They might never find out. Though the MTA has, in the years since 9/11, installed surveillance cameras over a good portion of the subway system, that particular section of that particular station wasn't covered.

"Do you know," Meade asks Wendy Nevid, "if the Cavalons went away for the holidays?"

"Not that I know of. They had just moved, and—"

"They *moved*?"

The nurse nods. "A week or two ago, I think."

"You mean they're not living in White Plains now?"

"No, they moved to the city."

"Do you know where?" Meade's thoughts are racing. No wonder.

"Upper West Side."

Upper West Side . . .

It's where Carl Soto was hit by that subway train—and that's looking less and less like a coincidence—or an accident.

"Do you know *where* on the Upper West Side?"

Wendy shakes her head. "I'm afraid I don't. I should have asked."

"It's okay. We'll find them."

"Why? Do you think they might be in danger, too?"

Yes, Meade thinks grimly. *I think that anyone who's ever crossed Caroline Quinn's path might be in danger.*

Aloud, he says only, "Do you think we can speak with Mrs. Quinn now? We'll go easy, I promise," he adds, seeing the worried look on the nurse's face.

"It's just that she's very fragile."

"I understand."

"What is it that you're hoping to find out?"

"Anything that might shed some light on

where her daughter is, or where she might turn up next."

"But she doesn't even know what happened to Caroline in the first place."

Meade's eyes widen.

"It's not that she wasn't told," the nurse goes on, "just that she couldn't really accept it."

"That Caroline died in the earthquake?"

"No, long before that. She couldn't accept that Caroline went to prison for killing her own sister."

Ryan hands Lucy a cup of tea. "Careful—don't spill it. It's hot."

"Thanks, Ry. It's decaf, right?"

"Right."

"Are you sure?"

He just looks at her.

"Okay, I'm being a nagging sister. Sorry."

"It's okay. That's just you."

She sticks out her tongue at him, then picks up the remote and aims it at the television screen, frozen on an image of a despondent George Bailey standing on a snowy bridge in Bedford Falls. Thumb poised to press the play button, Lucy asks Ryan, "Aren't you going to sit down?"

"Are you sure you don't want me to make you something to eat?"

She shakes her head. "Jeremy should be coming soon."

He called from his office phone a few minutes ago to say that he was leaving, and that his cell phone actually had died.

"I hate to say it, but it might take him a while to

get here," Ryan tells his sister. "Maybe you should at least sip some soup or something."

"'Sip some soup'? I'm not sick, Ry, and you're not Florence Nightingale."

He manages a smile, glad to hear her sounding like her old self, but he can see the worry in her eyes.

He's worried, too. So worried that just now, when he was in the kitchen, he even texted Phoenix about what's going on.

Maybe she's never had a baby but at least she's a woman, and Ryan figures some female advice might be helpful. He's utterly clueless when it comes to this stuff, and Lucy adamantly refuses to let him call their mother in Florida.

"All she'd do is worry, and it would ruin her Christmas," Lucy told him.

"But at least you can ask her if this is normal."

"I already asked my doctor. She said that it probably is."

Ryan knows that, but still . . .

My sister is having some cramps or something, he texted Phoenix while he was in the kitchen, waiting for the teakettle to whistle. **Do you think it could be early labor pains?**

She must have been busy at work. The response took a few minutes to come back: **When is she due?**

He quickly replied: Not until February.

Only a few seconds this time for the response: **IDK.**

IDK—*I don't know.* So much for female advice.

A moment later, she sent another message: **Try not to worry.**

Try not to worry? Easy to say if you've never met Lucy and aren't here to see the way she's just lying around brooding. That's completely unlike his sister.

Ryan just wishes Jeremy would hurry up and get here.

Or Phoenix, who told him that even if she has to walk through the storm to spend Christmas Eve with him, she'll do it.

It's such an about-face from the way she was acting last week that he can't help but wonder if something might be wrong with her. First hot, then cold, hot, cold—it can't be normal behavior.

Ryan isn't familiar with the symptoms of, say, bipolar disorder, or depression, but he's pretty sure drastic mood swings are among them. Maybe . . .

Maybe he'll talk to her about it. After the holidays, though.

Right now, we all just have to get through Christmas Eve.

The dark thought takes him by surprise. The holidays are meant to be joyful, not something to be endured.

But he can't help it.

Trapped in a strange apartment with Lucy in this condition, and the city paralyzed by snow . . .

But really, it's just more of the same, isn't it? It's like he was telling Lucy last week.

There's some big, heavy dark thing hanging over my head . . . I feel like something's going to go wrong. Like it's got to.

Every restaurant between the Bruckner home and the Soundview Avenue subway station was closed when Jeremy passed. So much for the city that never sleeps, he thinks, trudging up the steps to the elevated train. They're drifted over with snow, not the most promising sign for the impending commute home to Manhattan.

Reaching the platform, he finds it snow-swept and deserted.

Apparently the rest of the world—the whole world, judging by the eerie stillness—is already safely at home for the holidays. That, or in the corner pub drinking shots with Cliff.

A cold west wind blows tufts of snow into Jeremy's face. He bends his head and turns his back. After a momentary reprieve, the wind seems to circle around and come at him from the other direction, as if to prove that there's no escape.

There never is.

He looks up the tracks to the north, hoping to spot the headlight of an oncoming train, but all is dark and desolate.

Cliff was right about the dearth of cabs tonight. Maybe Jeremy should brave the weather and walk the couple of miles over to the Grand Concourse, where he can pick up the underground subway line back to Manhattan. The B is a local. It stops at the Museum of Natural History on Central Park West. From there, it would be a short walk home.

A short walk through a raging blizzard, after a long walk through a raging blizzard.

Jeremy thinks about Lucy waiting for him, and wonders when or how he's ever going to get there.

He thinks of his parents, cozy at home in Connecticut with his sister Renny.

My sister . . .

Jeremy thinks about his other sister, the one who died just days after Garvey Quinn's fatal heart attack in prison.

Annie's short life was so difficult and her death—if she grasped what was happening to her—was brutal.

But maybe she didn't realize it. Maybe she just swallowed that drug-laced cocoa that Caroline gave her, and went to sleep.

Or maybe she was high before she even drank it, too high to realize that she was about to die.

Jeremy hopes that was the case, and according to the coroner's report, it seems likely. Annie had other drugs in her system that morning: marijuana, cocaine, booze.

The usual.

Sleeping pills—*that* was unusual. Finding those in Annie's system—coupled with the fact that there was no suicide note—raised a red flag.

For Jeremy, anyway.

The police thought it was reasonable that she might have killed herself in the wake of her father's death.

Jeremy knew that wasn't the case. From the moment he got the terrible call that Annie was dead, he knew she hadn't killed herself, despite Garvey's death and despite her addiction. He suspected—no, he *knew*—that Caroline must have done it.

Both girls had dutifully come home to be with their widowed mother.

Jeremy was there, too. He witnessed Caroline's cruel treatment of Annie, saw the hatred and contempt in her eyes whenever she looked at her.

After Annie's death, he told Marin that Caroline could have been capable of killing her. He told the police, too.

Marin hadn't believed him.

Even before Annie died, Marin had descended into her own little world, numbing the pain with drugs the way Annie did. Losing her child sent her into a grief-stricken abyss from which she would never emerge.

But the police believed Jeremy. Enough to open an investigation.

Caroline was questioned. Arrogant, delusional, she didn't think to call a lawyer. Not until she was charged with murder after her fingerprints were found on the prescription bottle on Marin's nightstand.

Circumstantial evidence, Andrew Stafford later argued. Maybe Caroline had picked up her mother's prescriptions from the pharmacy.

She hadn't.

And she had said just enough to the police before her lawyer arrived to ultimately incriminate herself.

Convicted, sentenced to prison.

Bridgebury, as fate would have it.

The prison wasn't far from the Montgomery home in Nottingshire, where Jeremy had saved Caroline's life years ago. Saved her life, and taken La La Montgomery's. She'd died of massive head injuries.

Hers was the second life Jeremy had taken, but it was in self-defense. He was saving his sister, never dreaming that in doing so, he condemned his other sister, Annie.

When he learned last year that Caroline had died in the prison collapse, he felt nothing but relief. She—like Garvey Quinn, and like Papa—deserved what she got.

It was Lucy who said it best, quoting from the Bible: "As ye sow, so shall ye reap."

At the time, those words brought Jeremy comfort.

Now, however, they haunt him.

The police want to talk to him. Not about Miguel.

Time is running out, just as he always knew it would.

Leading the two detectives into room 421, Wendy sees that Marin is in her wheelchair beside the window, watching the curtain of falling snow.

"Someone is here to see you, sweetie," Wendy says gently.

Marin's head swivels and her blue eyes are wide as she looks from Wendy to the detectives and then, expectantly, around the room.

"Where is she?"

Wendy's heart sinks. "No, it's not—"

"Where *is* she?"

"No, sweetie, it's these nice people who came to see you—their names are Omar and Lisha." Wendy rests her hands on Marin's shoulders and clears her throat, looking at the detectives, sending them a silent message to say whatever it is that they need to say and then leave Marin Quinn in peace.

Detective Brandewyne clears her throat. "Mrs. Qu—"

"*No!*" Wendy says sharply, shaking her head to indicate that they don't call her that here.

Quickly grasping the situation, his dark eyes laced with sympathy, Meade speaks up. "I'm sorry, ma'am, we just wanted to come by and . . . wish you a Merry Christmas. That's all."

For a long time, Marin says nothing, just staring at his face. Then she shakes her head a little, as if coming out of a trance. "Have you seen her?"

"Seen who?"

"My daughter . . . Where is she? It's Christmas, and I thought she'd come."

Watching the tears roll down Marin Quinn's pale cheeks, Wendy aches for her.

"Where is she?" she asks again, clutching the detective's sleeve.

Meade shoots Wendy a questioning look; she nods at him.

He clears his throat and then he speaks the truth—as much of the truth as Marin Quinn can handle.

"I don't know where she is. I'm sorry."

Standing in front of the open refrigerator in her apartment, Caroline tilts her head back and chugs eggnog straight from the carton, savoring the rich creaminess as it coats her throat and slides into her full stomach.

Now that the time is near, her mind is beginning to cloud with uncertainty about what lies ahead.

What will it be like—the new world?

Will there be earthly pleasures? If there aren't, will she miss them?

One thing is certain—it would be impossible to

miss anything in the next world as deeply as she's missed her father in this one.

At least when Daddy was alive, he was still a part of her life. She was able to visit him in Hazelton. As soon as she graduated from college, she rented an apartment located just a few miles from the prison gates, so that she could see her father whenever there were visiting hours.

During that precious time together, they talked about Chaplain Gideon, the man who had come to him in prison to teach him about salvation.

Salvation meant that Daddy and Caroline would be together again, forever.

It seemed too good to be true, but when Caroline started reading the Bible, as Daddy told her to do, she saw for herself. It *was* true, right there in black and white.

In the letters he sent between visits, Daddy steered her to the relevant passages and reminded her, as he had from the time when she was a little girl, that she was special.

The day she learned that her father had died in prison—that was the end of her world. *This* world.

But tonight . . .

Tonight, the dead will rise up.

Tonight, she'll be reunited with her father.

She closes her eyes and quotes one of his favorite passages, from Luke 21:22.

For these be the days of vengeance, that all things which are written may be fulfilled.

When she opens her eyes, Chaplain Gideon is there. "It's time, Caroline."

CHAPTER THIRTEEN

Startled by a loud knock at the apartment door, Ryan jumps to his feet. "That must be Phoenix. It's about time!"

He and Lucy have been sitting here for hours, watching *It's a Wonderful Life* over and over, just like they did when they were kids. Watching, waiting, worrying, wondering . . .

Why is it taking so long for Jeremy to get home?

And Phoenix—she'd texted long ago to say she was on her way. Where is she?

"It can't be her," Lucy tells Ryan as he starts for the door. "Security would have to buzz from the lobby to tell us she's here. It must be Jeremy."

"But why would he knock?"

"I don't know, maybe he lost his keys or something. Or maybe it's one of the neighbors."

"I thought you don't know any of them."

"I don't, but one of them left us cookies and—just go see who it is, Ryan," she says impatiently.

"All right, all right."

Ryan goes into the circular foyer, looks through the peephole, and grins.

"It's Phoenix!" he announces triumphantly,

unlocking the door and throwing it open. "Thank God you made it. How is it out there?"

She steps inside, bundled from head to toe in a long, hooded coat. No—not a coat, Ryan realizes as she steps over the threshold. A *cloak*. What the . . . ?

She pulls the door closed, turns the lock and the deadbolt, and then slides the chain. It's all accomplished in one swift, furtive movement, such an odd thing to do that Ryan instinctively takes a step back from the door.

"Phoenix? What are you—"

He breaks off suddenly, realizing something.

She's bone-dry. How can that be? She just walked forty blocks in a storm, and yet she's dry.

Bewildered, he looks at her face.

Seeing the icy gleam in her eyes, he takes another step back as dread steals over him.

"What are you doing?"

She laughs—a guttural, humorless sound.

His mind races back to the day he looked for her on the Internet—her name, her face, anything at all about her—and couldn't find it.

"Who *are* you?"

"You mean you still haven't figured it out?" She shrugs. "I guess that's because you and I never met, years ago. But I'll bet your sister will know me. Let's go try her, shall we?"

"Get out," Ryan tells her fiercely, and starts to reach for the door.

She stops him, her hand jerking out from the folds of the robe.

Ryan stares in horror at the knife in her hand . . .

A knife that's encrusted with dried blood.

* * *

"How long is this going to *take*?" Brandewyne paces in front of Meade's desk, sucking on a candy cane.

She can't smoke here inside the precinct, and it's so nasty outside that even she isn't willing to brave the weather long enough to smoke an entire cigarette. Instead, she's gone through almost the entire package of candy canes someone left by the coffeepot.

"We're waiting for a federal agency to come up with restricted information on Christmas Eve, in the middle of a blizzard," Meade reminds her. "It'll be a miracle if we get our hands on the Cavalons' new address before New Year's."

"You're kidding, right?"

He shrugs.

"There must be another way."

"There isn't, unless the phone company beats the post office to the punch and provides us with those unlisted numbers."

Aside from cutting through the red tape necessary to get restricted information from the postal service, their only other option is to contact other family members who might know where to find Jeremy and Lucy Cavalon.

But Meade's repeated calls to the Walsh house in Glenhaven Park went unanswered, and Elsa and Brett Cavalon's Connecticut town is currently in a blackout zone, hard hit by the storm.

"That's the problem with cordless phones," Brandewyne muses, and Meade realizes that her thoughts have traveled along the same path as his.

It used to happen all the time, with Tarrant.

Meade would be sitting there mulling an angle on a case, and Tarrant would voice it aloud.

"When the power goes out," Brandewyne goes on, "so do communications. That's why everyone should have a good old-fashioned landline."

"Do you?"

"Absolutely. Do you?"

He nods and notices that her tongue is unnaturally pink. And that she's whittled the candy cane tip so that it resembles an ice pick's deadly point.

They go back to waiting in silence.

She bites off the ice pick tip. Crunching it, she asks, "What would you be doing tonight if you weren't here, Omar?"

"Same thing I do every night. Eating. Sleeping."

"What about Christmas?"

"You mean tomorrow? Before I come here, I'm picking up my son and going down to Staten Island to see my mother."

But thanks to Brandewyne, his mother's gift is going to be late this year. He's planning to return the vacuum and get something a little more special for the only woman in his life.

"What are you doing for Christmas?" he asks Brandewyne—the only *other* woman in his life, he realizes.

"No plans. Maybe I'll see an early movie."

He nods. He, too, has spent many a lonely holiday in a darkened theater.

For an awkward moment, he wonders if Brandewyne is expecting him to invite her to come with him to Staten Island. But that would be weird, wouldn't it? Hell, yes. It's not like she's his girlfriend. It's not like she could ever *be* his girlfriend.

No . . . but she's your partner, and maybe she could turn into a friend . . .

No, thanks. Meade doesn't need any more friends.

More friends?

Thanks to Johnny and April, Meade has been keeping people at arm's length for years now. Everyone except Tarrant, because they worked together every day and there was no avoiding him.

Kind of like Brandewyne.

The phone rings, and he seizes it gratefully. "Yeah."

"Detective Meade? This is Ivette Lynde with the United States Postal Service. We have that forwarding information you requested."

Lucy sits up expectantly and runs a hand over her head to smooth her hair, trying to remember the last time she brushed it.

Under ordinary circumstances, she'd have made herself presentable and her home as welcoming as possible before meeting her brother's girlfriend for the first time. But these are extraordinary circumstances, to say the least, so here she is in sweats and slippers. She kept thinking she might change her clothes and pull herself together, but when she found out a little while ago that Christmas Eve services at Holy Trinity have been canceled, she decided not to bother.

Meanwhile, the living room is cluttered with books, papers, snack wrappers, empty cups . . .

Earlier, when she'd suggested to Ryan that he straighten the place up a little, he'd brushed a litter of potato chip crumbs onto the carpet and made a haphazard attempt at stacking the magazines he'd discarded onto the floor beside his chair.

Lucy had to bite her tongue to keep from going into bossy big-sister mode, much as she longed to order Ryan to get the magazines off the floor, and vacuum the rug, and take the dirty dishes to the kitchen . . .

There are just some things she can't control, and people she shouldn't try to control. If being in this situation has taught her anything, it's that she needs to lighten up, that she can't do everything herself.

Hearing a thumping crash in the other room, she calls out, "Ry?"

No reply.

"Ry! What's going on?"

Still no reply.

Oh no. Did he knock over one of Sylvie's prized pieces of art?

Frowning, Lucy starts to hoist herself up, calling, "Ryan?"

All at once, a cloaked figure swoops into the doorway.

Stunned, Lucy tries—and fails—to make sense of what she's seeing.

"Hi, Lucy. Remember me?"

That face—that face inside the hood—it's the same face Lucy thought she saw on Sunday morning at church.

No, she *did* see her.

She *was* there, and now she's here, and . . .

And in her hand is a knife dripping with fresh red blood.

* * *

As the nearly empty B train approaches the station at Eighty-first Street and Central Park West, Jeremy stands and holds the pole with one hand as he raises the already damp collar of his coat with the other.

Time to go back out into the cold.

That's the last thing he wants to do after his earlier ordeal.

It had taken him well over three hours to trudge two miles across the Bronx, from the Soundview Avenue elevated station to the underground 167th Street station on the Grand Concourse. He was relieved when he made it, glad to descend from the howling blizzard into the warm, dry underground tunnel—dingy tiles, scurrying rodents, and all.

The ride downtown might have lulled him to sleep, if he weren't chilled to the bone, wet and uncomfortable. Good thing.

The doors slide open and Jeremy steps out onto the platform, the lone passenger to disembark here.

The B train disappears into the southbound tunnel, its clattering wheels giving way to the sound of a smooth clarinet playing "Silent Night."

Jeremy can see the subway musician sitting cross-legged on the floor at the far end of the platform, at the foot of the exit stairs.

As he heads in that direction, he reaches into his pocket, feeling for some loose change. His fingers encounter a wad of tissue and in that moment, touching the carefully wrapped angel ornament as the mellow musical notes wash over him, he experiences a sudden aura of peace.

It's Christmas Eve, and he's almost home, and Lucy is there, pregnant with his child.

Right now, that's all that matters.

The musician, a wizened man in a porkpie hat, looks up as he approaches.

Jeremy reaches into his other pocket and finds his wallet. Opening it, he takes out the lone bill inside—a twenty he got from the ATM yesterday at lunch hour. The twenty he wasn't going to spend unless it was absolutely necessary.

It is, he decides. *It is necessary.*

The musician sees the bill, and his eyes smile at Jeremy, but he doesn't miss a note.

Jeremy stoops to place the money into his open, empty case.

As he starts up the steps, the man stops playing just for a moment. Just long enough to call, "God bless you."

Jeremy smiles. *He already has.*

Meade lightly taps the brakes to come to a stop well in advance of another red light. Sixth Avenue. So close and yet so far.

It's taking forever to drive across the city. It isn't because of the traffic, though. Not in the traditional sense. Cars are everywhere they shouldn't be—buried in no-parking zones, front-ended in snowbanks, sliding through intersections directly in front of the patrol car.

"You know, it's a good thing this isn't a matter of life and death," Brandewyne comments from the passenger's seat.

"It might be," he tells her grimly, staring

through the windshield at the blowing snow. "If Caroline Quinn has figured out where Lucy and Jeremy are, and if she's decided she wants to get to them . . ."

"But that building, the Ansonia, has good security. It would be hard for her to get past the lobby."

"She managed to do it at Parkview Hospital."

"True. Let's just hope she learned her lesson that time."

"I doubt it. She didn't learn her lesson when she went to prison for murder. I have a feeling that the only thing that's going to stop her is . . ."

Meade doesn't bother to say the word.

She knows what it is.

Death.

Somewhere, someone is screaming.

Lucy.

Lying on the floor in the foyer, Ryan struggles to call out to her, to tell her that he's here, that he's coming to help.

But he can't speak, and he can't help, because he can't move. There's an agonizing pain in his side.

She stabbed me.

Phoenix stabbed me with that knife and then she went into the living room and now she's stabbing Lucy.

"Please, nooooo, no!" Lucy is shrieking, sobbing, and no one is coming to help. No one but Ryan can hear, because the damned apartment is soundproof. Lucy told him that a long, long time ago.

The night he came to tell her he felt like something bad was going to happen.

Phoenix . . . dear God.

Why are you doing this?

Who are you?

Lucy is screaming and he's in agony and he closes his eyes to block it all out . . .

And then, mercifully, it all fades away.

At last, Meade pulls the police sedan beneath the portico of the Ansonia.

Before he and Brandewyne can even step out of the car, a doorman appears beside it.

"See? I told you. Great security," Brandewyne murmurs.

"What can I do for you?" the doorman asks as they flash their badges.

"We're looking for a couple who live in this building. The Cavalons. Do you know them?"

He shakes his head. "Talk to Bobby at the desk. He'll know them. He knows everyone. You can leave the car right here. It's okay."

"Thanks," says Meade, who was already planning to do just that.

Technically, it isn't an emergency, and yet . . .

Something tells him that it might be.

And like Brandewyne's, his gut instinct is rarely wrong.

Once again, Jeremy finds himself enveloped in a swirling wall of white. To the east, across Central Park West, the park is a beautiful, frozen wasteland. To the west, shrouded in falling snow, are tall buildings with windows that glow like festive twinkle lights.

Jeremy heads down West Eighty-first Street, past the Museum of Natural History.

All he can think about is getting home to Lucy.

The elegant Ansonia lobby is deserted, other than a security guard sitting at a desk beside the elevator bank.

Meade and Brandewyne show their badges; he introduces himself as Bobby and asks how he can help them.

"We're looking for Jeremy and Lucy Cavalon. They moved in about a week ago."

"Sylvie Durand's grandson and his wife." Bobby nods. "Yeah, that was such a shame, what happened to her."

Narrowing his eyes, Meade echoes Bobby's last four words as a question.

"She drowned. Right up there in her apartment. Slipped, fell, drowned. A couple of days went by before anyone found her."

Meade and Brandewyne exchange a glance.

Another sudden death in the Cavalon circle. And Meade's infallible gut instinct tells him that Sylvie Durand didn't fall into her bathtub any more than Carl Soto fell onto the subway tracks.

"We need to speak to the Cavalons right away," he tells Bobby. "Do you know if they're home?"

"I don't know, but let's buzz the apartment and find out."

A couple of days went by before anyone found her . . .

Meade sincerely hopes that the Cavalons are safe and sound in their apartment.

Because if they aren't, it might take a couple of days to secure a warrant to get in there—and by then, it will be too late.

It's a boy, of course.

Just as Caroline had known it would be. A boy with her father's blood, and her own—Quinn blood—pumping through his veins.

Clasping the warm, wet bundle against her racing heart, wrapped in the folds of her cloak, she rides the elevator down to the ground floor, below the lobby.

The laundry room is there, along with storage rooms and exits to the parking garage and an alleyway behind the building. The area is deserted, as she'd known it would be.

It had gone well. Better than expected. Jeremy wasn't there to get in the way. Only Ryan, and he'd gone down easily with one jab of the knife.

He was lying dead in a pool of blood when she'd walked past him just now on her way out the door. At least, she was pretty sure he was dead. She thought of stopping to make sure, but it's almost midnight, and the baby is so tiny and fragile, she's afraid he might not make it. When she first cut him from Lucy's womb, he was so still she thought he had already died.

But then he made a faint, crying sound, and she rejoiced.

"You will live," she whispers to him now as she pushes through the door, out into the street. "You have to."

* * *

Something is buzzing, far off . . .

Ryan reaches for his alarm clock but his arm isn't moving, and then he remembers . . .

She stabbed me.

And Lucy . . .

Oh, Lucy. Oh no.

Mustering all his strength, he manages to call out to his sister. His voice is hoarse, weak. Much too weak to be heard.

That's why she's not answering him. It has to be why.

Oh please. Oh, Lucy.

The buzzing sound again, somewhere overhead.

Ryan forces his heavy eyelids up.

He can see the door, the wall beside it . . .

Red on white.

Why . . . ?

Ryan closes his eyes again.

Blood . . .

That's what it is. Blood smeared on the wall, and on the doorknob.

But something else . . .

He forces himself to look again.

There's the intercom.

The intercom . . . buzzing . . .

Ryan strains to get up, but the pain in his side is so fierce . . . he can't lift his body without leverage.

He needs something to hold, a way to pull himself up toward the intercom . . .

If he stretches his arm, he can almost reach the doorknob. *Almost, almost . . .*

His fingers brush the knob. It's slick with blood. His own?

Please not Lucy's. Please . . .

He grasps the knob, pulls himself up . . . up . . .

Jeremy forces himself to keep walking toward home, walking straight into the ferocious west wind off the Hudson a few blocks away.

He keeps his head bent against it, watching his own feet blaze a trail along the blanketed sidewalk, looking up every once in a while to make sure he hasn't wandered into the street.

It wouldn't matter, though. There's not a car to be seen, or a person. The only soul Jeremy passed was a fur-bundled man standing in the shadow of a stoop, holding a dog on a leash. He didn't even glance in Jeremy's direction.

Jeremy's coat and gloves are soaked through, his teeth are chattering, his cheeks and ears are stinging in the vicious cold, and every step is a tremendous effort.

If only there were someplace to stop for just a few minutes. Just to get out of the incessant wind, catch his breath, regroup, warm up . . .

But this is a residential block, lined with elegant brownstones, many with festive white lights in the windows and snow-fringed greens on the doors.

From somewhere, though, a silvery hint of sound—other than the wind and a distant siren—reaches Jeremy's frostbitten ears.

Church bells.

Holy Trinity, Jeremy realizes. It must be. His grandmother's parish is right around here someplace.

He tries to scan the block ahead, but a harsh gust tosses snow like fine sand into his eyes, forcing him to bend his head.

He walks on, looks up again.

There it is—the church steeple, looming overhead.

He's going in. Just for a minute or two. Just to get warm, and maybe . . .

Maybe to see if he can find some comfort and healing.

"I guess they're not there," Bobby informs Meade and Brandewyne, shaking his head.

Meade curses inwardly.

It's Christmas Eve. The entire city is snowbound. The Cavalons should be home.

"Maybe they went away for Christmas," Brandewyne suggests.

"How?" Meade snaps. "Do you think they hitched Rudolph to a flying sled?"

"Geez, Omar, you don't have to—"

"Wait, shhh!" Bobby waves at them. "I hear something!"

They fall silent as Bobby stands with the intercom receiver pressed hard to his ear, his head tilted in concentration. "I think someone might be in there. I can hear . . . It sounds like . . . moaning."

Meade immediately starts for the elevator bank with Brandewyne right behind him.

"Wait, Detective!"

"We're going up."

"But you can't just barge in without—"

"We have good reason to believe that someone

is hurt in that apartment." Meade jabs the up button and checks the elevator indicators.

The closest one is on the ground level; it's on its way up.

"Just give me a minute," Bobby calls, hurrying across the lobby toward the doorman.

"We don't have a minute."

The elevator arrives.

The doors slide open.

Brandewyne starts to step inside first, then gasps.

Meade follows her gaze. His stomach turns over.

Blood.

Blood on the floor of the elevator.

Fresh red blood.

"' . . . the sun will be darkened,'" Caroline mutters as she makes her way through the street, clasping the newborn inside the folds of her cloak, "'and the moon will not give its light; the stars will fall from heaven . . .'"

She tilts her face upward. The stars are falling now, millions of stars, cold and glittering in the light of a streetlamp.

She resumes reciting the quote from the Book of Matthew, her words growing frenzied as she turns the corner and sees Holy Trinity ahead.

"' . . . when ye shall see all these things, know that it is near . . .'"

She arrives at the church and a worrisome thought darts into her brain, bringing with it a flicker of panic.

What if the doors are locked?

Masses are canceled. She heard Lucy say it, earlier.

But then she notices fresh footprints in the snow, leading from the street to the door.

Someone is inside.

It doesn't matter who it is, or what they're doing there. She doesn't care. In a few moments, everything will be over.

" . . . Heaven and earth shall pass away . . ."

Still reciting the Bible passage, she climbs the steps, opens the door, and slips inside.

The trail of blood leads from the elevator to the apartment door, but Meade knows the droplets fell in the opposite direction.

He knows Caroline escaped, covered in blood.

Brandewyne is already on the elevator following the trail wherever it leads, having immediately called for backup downstairs and EMTs up here.

"Hurry." It's all Meade can do not to impatiently push Bobby aside as he turns the key in the lock.

"I am hurrying, Detective."

Meade clenches his jaw.

Bobby opens the apartment door.

"Oh God . . ."

"Stay back." Meade draws his pistol and crosses the threshold.

Blood. More blood, a lot of it, pooled on the herringbone hardwoods and smeared on the wall. There's a bloody handprint on the intercom.

A man lies on the floor below it, just inside the door.

Meade quickly bends over him, finds a faint pulse. "Jeremy?"

His eyes are wide; he's in shock, bleeding from a gash just below his rib cage. "Lucy . . . help her . . ."

Meade takes off his jacket, wads it into a ball, and presses it over the gaping hole in his flesh.

"Here, get in here," he calls to Bobby. "Put your hand on this. Keep pressure on it."

Wide-eyed, Bobby crouches beside the wounded man, pressing his hands over the bloody wound.

Meade runs through the apartment, looking for Jeremy's wife, calling her name. Bedroom, bathroom, kitchen, dining room . . .

Living room.

Dear God.

Blood everywhere.

She's lying faceup on the carpet in a pool of it.

Her midsection has been cruelly slashed; her eyes are wide open.

But they're not vacant, Meade realizes in relief.

No, they're awash in tears.

"Please . . ."

Meade kneels beside her. Her eyes close, open, close again.

"Stay with me, Lucy." He holds her hand. It's cold. Her wedding and engagement rings are sticky with blood.

He can hear voices in the hall.

"In here!" he hollers to the EMTs. "Hurry up!"

"My baby . . ." Lucy's eyes are open, locked on Meade's. "Please, she took my baby."

"Where, Lucy? Where did she go? Do you know?"

Kneeling in a pew at the front of the church, Jeremy clasps his hands beneath his chin, talking to God.

Praying to God.

He knew, from the moment he entered the sanctuary, that it's no accident he took this route home.

He needs to be right here, right now. There are things that need to be said at last. Even if he's only saying them inside his own head, and in his heart.

Thank you for sparing me years ago, and for letting me find my way back home to Elsa and Brett and Marin and my sisters . . .

Thank you for giving me Lucy, and for the child growing inside her.

Please let our child grow up safe and strong.

Please let me be there to see it, to take care of my wife and child.

Please . . .

I'm sorry for what I did. I'm sorry for not saving Papa that day. I know it was wrong. I'm sorry for hating him; I know hate is wrong, too.

I promise to teach my child not to hate.

I promise—

Hearing a whisper of sound at the back of the church, Jeremy turns to see that he's no longer alone.

The church is dark. Quiet, other than the distant chiming of the bells in the steeple and the wind rattling the stained glass windows.

The pews are empty; the altar lit by Christmas tree lights and flickering candles.

Caroline starts up the aisle with the baby, his little body warm and still—perhaps too still—in her arms.

* * *

Jeremy stares from the shadows of the side pew.

Someone is here . . . someone in a hooded robe, moving up the aisle.

A priest?

Arms outstretched overhead, the figure is clutching a white bundle.

Long ago, Lucy told Jeremy about the meaningful Christmas Eve processional at her old church, in which the priest delivered the figure of the Christ Child to the empty manger at the altar at midnight Mass.

That's the way they do it at her old church.

But here, the baby Jesus figurine is already in the manger—probably placed there earlier by the priest when midnight Mass was canceled.

So then what's going on now? Jeremy wonders, staring at the spectacle in the aisle.

The way this priest is holding the bundle up in the air—like some kind of sacrifice, or offering . . .

As he comes closer, Jeremy realizes that the swaddled object in the priest's hands is streaked in red.

Then, in shocked horror, he spots it—a tiny hand, a human hand, flailing.

And he realizes that it's a baby, a live baby, and that the red streaks are blood.

Jeremy leaps to his feet, but the priest doesn't seem to be aware of him.

He draws closer, into the light, and all at once, Jeremy glimpses the face beneath the folds of the hood.

It isn't a priest.

It isn't a man.

Caroline.

Dear God, it's Caroline, and she's holding a baby . . .

A tiny baby . . .

A blood-covered newborn . . .

"Noooooooooooooooo!" Jeremy screams, and he races toward her.

Someone is here, Caroline realizes at the last minute, before she jerks around.

But it isn't Chaplain Gideon.

It isn't Daddy.

No, it's . . .

"Stay back."

"Give me my child."

"This isn't your child. 'Behold, he cometh with clouds; and every eye shall see him.' See him, Jeremy? See him?"

He looks up, up at the baby in her hands. She can feel his horror and his fear, and she smiles.

"Where is my wife?" he asks hoarsely.

" 'And woe unto them that are with child . . .' "

"What did you do to her?" He takes a step closer.

"Don't do it. Don't touch me. If you come any closer to me, I'll drop him."

She won't, of course.

She needs to put him on the bed of straw. Now.

Ignoring the question, she throws her head back and shouts to the heavens, "Here he is!"

She walks toward the altar and stops, staring at the manger in astonishment.

The baby is already there.

How can that be?

* * *

She's insane.

And she took my child—ripped my child from Lucy's . . .

No.

Jeremy can't allow himself to think of it, can't focus on anything but what's happening here and now.

The baby. Tiny, helpless . . .

"What do you want?" Caroline cries out, and seems to be listening for something, waiting for something.

The church is silent, but for the slightest creaking . . . the wind?

Jeremy is afraid to breathe, much less turn his head toward the sound.

"He's yours!" Caroline screams. "Take him! What are you waiting for?"

She walks up onto the altar, peers down at the manger, gives it a sudden, vicious kick.

It topples over, and the baby Jesus figurine shatters on the floor.

"You promised!" Caroline rails. "I don't understand! What do you want me to do?"

She goes still, listening again, eyes closed.

Jeremy is about to make a move toward her when suddenly, she bends over and sets the bundle on the altar. She's muttering to herself. He tries to make out the words.

"' . . . and they shall have no pity on the fruit of the womb; their eyes shall not spare children . . .'"

Her hand disappears into the folds of her robe.

Jeremy watches in horror as she draws out a knife.

"What are you doing? No!"

She whirls on him. " 'Cursed be he that keepeth back his sword from blood!' " She lifts the knife high over her head, poised over the newborn child.

With an anguished cry, Jeremy hurtles himself toward the altar.

It's no use, though. He's too far away. The knife is already making its deadly descent.

Jeremy saved Caroline's life fifteen years ago.

But he won't be able to save his son.

"We're taking you outside to the ambulance now, okay?"

Who is that?

Who's talking?

Ryan struggles to open his eyes.

He can feel movement, as though he's being carried.

"Hang in there. We're taking you to the hospital."

The voice is unfamiliar.

The air is cold.

He struggles to open his eyes.

He does, just for a moment, and sees snow, and a red light flashing.

Red . . . white . . .

Blood on the wall . . .

"It's going to be okay, Jeremy," the voice says.

No . . . my name isn't Jeremy . . .

But Ryan doesn't have the strength to correct them.

If he could speak at all, he'd ask about his sister.

But he remembers her terrible screams, and the darkness is slipping over him again, and maybe it's better not to know.

* * *

A gunshot resonates through the church.

Caroline falls to the floor, a crimson stain spreading across her robe.

Stunned, Jeremy turns to see a tall, African-American man with gray hair and a beard, still holding a pistol outstretched in both hands.

"Stay where you are!" he calls to Jeremy, and strides toward the altar.

Jeremy starts toward it, too.

The man turns. "I said stay where you are!"

"But that's—"

"Stop!" He takes aim at Jeremy.

Jeremy stops, bewildered.

He can hear sirens outside.

"Who are you?" the cop asks, coming toward him, the gun still trained on him.

"My name is Jeremy Cavalon, and that's—" He gestures helplessly toward the altar. "That's my son."

"*You're* Jeremy Cavalon?"

He nods. "Please. My son . . ."

"Do you have ID?"

"In my wallet. My pocket."

"Don't go for it. I'll get it." He walks closer, warily patting Jeremy until he finds the wallet. He takes it out.

"Jeremy Cavalon. Hell, that's you. I'm sorry, I didn't—"

Suddenly, the doors are thrown open. Cops and paramedics swarm the church, the altar.

"I'm Detective Meade." The man takes his arm and leads him toward the altar, calling, "This is the baby's father. Let us through."

A cluster of EMTs are already working furiously on the baby.

Jeremy takes it all in . . . the tiny figure, the blood, the tubes and needles, all those strangers, working to save his life . . .

"Vital signs are good," a female paramedic announces, and begins rattling off numbers.

Jeremy's legs wobble in relief.

His son. His precious son.

Oh, Lucy. I wish you could see him.

He feels a steadying hand on his shoulder and turns to see Detective Meade still beside him.

"I'm sorry," he says. "I really didn't know who you were . . . before. We thought you were back at the apartment with . . . your wife."

Jeremy's heart stops.

"Lucy," he whispers.

"Do you know who was there with her?"

"My brother-in-law—her brother, Ryan. Is he . . . ?"

"He was injured pretty badly." The detective's expression is somber. "He's on his way to the hospital."

"And . . . my wife?" Jeremy braces himself for what's coming.

I'm not ready to hear it.

He closes his eyes, knowing he'll never be ready to hear it.

He had everything.

So much to lose . . .

"She lost a lot of blood, but we got there in time."

A sob escapes Jeremy's throat. "She's alive?"

"Hell, yes, she's alive. She told us right where to find the baby."

"Lucy." He laughs through his tears. "Lucy's . . . she's always telling people what to do."

"What I want to know is, how did *you* know to find him here?" Detective Meade asks.

Jeremy shakes his head in wonder.

"I guess I just . . . I decided it was time I started praying."

Yawning, Meade pushes back his chair at last, the case paperwork wrapped up—for the time being, anyway.

Caroline Quinn was DOA, but Lucy Cavalon, Ryan Walsh, and Lucy's infant son are all stabilized. Jeremy is at children's hospital with his child. Born at thirty-four weeks, the kid is amazingly sturdy.

And the doctors who were working on Lucy said that she had already been in the early stages of labor. He'd have been a preemie anyway.

But it should never have happened like this. Never.

If Meade had gotten there a split second later . . .

But he made it. Thanks to Lucy, who managed to stay conscious throughout the barbaric procedure Caroline performed on her, listening to her ranting and raving.

Apparently, she thought the baby was the Messiah, here to save the world.

Meade shakes his head.

Ordinarily, it would be his duty to notify the next of kin. Perhaps someday, Marin Quinn will officially have to be told.

But not now. Not on Christmas. Not in her condition.

He'll leave the final decision up to her doctors, and Nurse Wendy, and Jeremy.

Brandewyne appears at Meade's desk, pulling on her coat, an unlit cigarette ready in her hand. "I'll walk down with you, if you're ready, Omar."

"Sure."

Together, they make their way through the office.

"Merry Christmas, guys," Alden calls as they pass his desk. "Great work."

"Merry Christmas," they call back in unison.

"Jinx." Brandewyne punches Meade in the arm.

He sighs inwardly and holds the stairwell door open for her. He thinks about saying, *Ladies first*, but really, that doesn't quite apply here.

"You know," Brandewyne says through a yawn, "when I was a little girl I always knew Christmas Eve was the longest night of the year."

"December twenty-first is the longest night of the year. Not the twenty-fourth."

"I'm not talking about science. I'm talking about the way it feels when you're a kid, waiting for Santa. But I have to say, none of those long Christmas Eves were anywhere near as long as last night was."

"I have to say you're right."

"I want to go home and sleep for a week." She yawns again.

"Are you sure about that?"

"Well . . . maybe two weeks. Why?"

"Because I was going to ask you if you wanted to come to my mother's in Staten Island with me and Dante."

"You were?"

He wasn't. But for some reason, it popped out.

"What if your mother thinks I'm your girl-friend?"

"She won't." *Trust me.*

"I hope not. Because I have a boyfriend."

"You *do*?"

"Yeah. His name's Kenny. He's stationed in Guam. We've been together for three years—a long-distance relationship."

"I never knew that."

"You never asked."

Meade tilts his head, contemplating that.

"Please tell me you weren't thinking of asking me out."

"I wasn't," he promises her truthfully. "So . . . Staten Island?"

"You got it. As long as we're not bringing your mother a vacuum cleaner with a bow on it."

He grins, holding the door for her.

"Ladies first," he says, and follows her out into the glare of morning sun on fresh Christmas snow.

"Lucy . . ."

The voice is far away.

"Lucy?"

She opens her eyes.

The light is so bright.

Jeremy. Sweet Jeremy, smiling at her with tears in his eyes. Why?

"Hi," he says softly.

"Hi." She manages to lift her hand to his cheek, brushing away a tear. "What's wrong?"

"Nothing, I just . . ." He shakes his head, wipes his eyes with his sleeve. "You're going to be all right."

"Of course I am."

"And Ryan is, too."

Ryan . . . what is he talking about?

Confused, she lets her eyes close.

She's sleepy, and the darkness is peaceful.

Jeremy is still talking.

"The baby . . . he's beautiful, Goose."

"The baby," she murmurs, wondering if she's dreaming. "Yes."

"He's strong. Really strong. Just like his mommy."

Strong. Yes.

She forces her eyes open again. She's strong. She is.

Jeremy is there again, or maybe still there, holding a little box. "This is your Christmas present."

"Christmas . . ."

"It's today. We'll celebrate when you come home," Jeremy tells her. "You and the baby. Here, look."

He lifts the top of the box and pulls out a delicate gold chain with an oval locket.

"Beautiful," she murmurs.

"I'll put it on you, but first . . ." He pries open the locket's hinged face and holds it close to her. "Do you see him?"

There's a picture.

A baby.

She wasn't dreaming.

"Yes," she tells Jeremy. "I see him."

"That's our son."

"Our son," she echoes in wonder, taking in every detail of his tiny face. "When can I hold him?"

"He's so little. He's in the neonatal ICU. I

haven't held him yet, either, but they said we can. Soon."

"I want to see him." She swallows hard, and it hurts. Everything hurts.

"You will, Lu. You'll see him, and you'll hold him. You're his mom."

"He needs a name," she tells Jeremy. "Our son."

"I know, and I was thinking . . ." He clears his throat. "I know we haven't even talked about names yet. And you might have a strong idea yourself . . ."

"Hey," she manages, and he grins.

"Admit it, Goose. You've been known to have a strong idea or two in your day."

It hurts to smile, but she does. "What are you thinking? Names . . ."

"Michael."

"Michael." She contemplates it. "After Miguel?"

"Yes. And for Mike Fantoni, the detective who—"

"I know," she whispers, reaching for Jeremy's hand. She finds it. Squeezes it.

So many tragedies in their lives. But now it's time to look ahead.

"And you know," Jeremy goes on, "Michael is an angel."

"Yes. Michael Walsh Cavalon. I love it."

"Michael *Walsh* Cavalon?" her husband echoes.

"Michael *Walsh* Cavalon."

Jeremy kisses her gently on the forehead. "So it shall be."

And so it was.

Turn the page for a sneak peek of

NIGHTCRAWLER

Coming 2012 from

Wendy Corsi Staub

and Avon Books

September 10, 2001
Quantico, Virginia
6:35 p.m.

Case closed.

Vic Shattuck clicks the mouse and the Southside Strangler file—the one that forced him to spend the better part of August in the rainy Midwest tracking a serial killer—disappears from the screen.

If only it were that easy to make it all go away in real life.

"If you let it, this stuff will eat you up inside like cancer," Vic's FBI colleague Dave Gudlaug told him early in his career, and he was right.

Now Dave, who a few years ago reached the Bureau's mandatory retirement age, spends his time traveling with his wife. He claims he doesn't miss the work.

"Believe me, you'll be ready to put it all behind you, too, when the time comes," he promised Vic.

Maybe, but with his own retirement seven years away, Vic is in no hurry to move on. Sure, it might be nice to spend uninterrupted days and nights with Kitty, but somehow he suspects that he'll never be truly free of the cases he's handled—not even those that are solved. For now, as a profiler with the Behavioral Science Unit, he can at least do his part to rid the world of violent offenders.

"You're still here, Shattuck?"

He looks up to see Special Agent Annabelle Wyatt. With her long legs, almond-shaped dark eyes, and flawless ebony skin, she looks like a supermodel—and acts like one of the guys.

Not in a let's-hang-out-and-have-a-few-laughs way; in a let's-cut-the-bullshit-and-get-down-to-business way.

She briskly hands Vic a folder. "Take a look at this and let me know what you think."

"Now?"

She clears her throat. "It's not urgent, but . . ."

Yeah, right. With Annabelle, everything is urgent.

"Unless you were leaving . . ." She pauses, obviously waiting for him to tell her that he'll take care of it before he goes.

"I was."

Without even glancing at the file, Vic puts it on top of his in-box. The day's been long enough and he's more than ready to head home.

Kitty is out at her book club tonight, but that's okay with him. She called earlier to say she was leaving a macaroni and cheese casserole in the oven. The homemade kind, with melted cheddar and buttery breadcrumb topping.

Better yet, both his favorite hometown teams—the New York Yankees and the New York Giants—are playing tonight. Vic can hardly wait to hit the couch with a fork in one hand and the TV remote control in the other.

"All right." Annabelle turns to leave, then turns back. "Oh, I heard about Chicago. Nice work. You got him."

"You mean *her*."

Annabelle shrugs. "How about *it*?"

"*It.* Yeah, that works."

Over the course of Vic's career, he hasn't seen many true cases of MPD—Multiple Personality Disorder—but this was one of them.

The elusive Southside Strangler turned out to be a woman named Edie . . . who happened to live inside a suburban single dad named Calvin Granger.

Last June, Granger had helplessly watched his young daughter drown in a fierce Lake Michigan undertow. Unable to swim, he was incapable of saving her.

Weeks later, mired in frustration and anguish and the brunt of his grieving ex-wife's fury, he picked up a hooker. That was not unusual behavior for him. What happened after that *was*.

The woman's nude, mutilated body was found just after dawn in Washington Park, electrical cable wrapped around her neck. A few days later, another corpse turned up in the park. And then a third.

Streetwalking and violent crime go hand in hand; the Southside's slain hookers were, sadly, business as usual for the jaded cops assigned to that particular case.

For urban reporters as well. Chicago was in the midst of a series of flash floods this summer; the historic weather eclipsed the coverage of the Southside Strangler in the local press. That, in retrospect, was probably a very good thing. The media spotlight tends to feed a killer's ego—and his bloodlust.

Only when the Strangler claimed a fourth victim—an upper-middle-class mother of three living a respectable lifestyle—did the case become front page news. That was when the cops called in the FBI.

For Vic, every lost life carries equal weight. Even now, when he thinks of the heartbroken parents he met in Chicago, parents who lost their daughters twice: first to drugs and the streets, and, ultimately, to the monster who murdered them.

The monster, like most killers, had once been a victim himself.

It was a textbook case: Granger had been severely abused—essentially tortured—as a child. The MPD was, in essence, a coping mechanism. As an adult, he suffered occasional, inexplicable episodes of amnesia, particularly during times of overwhelming stress.

He genuinely seemed to have no memory of anything "he" had said or done while Edie or one of the other, nonviolent alters—alternative personalities—were in control of him.

"By the way," Annabelle cuts into Vic's thoughts, "I hear birthday wishes are in order."

Surprised, he tells her, "Actually, it was last month—while I was in Chicago."

"Ah, so your party was belated, then."

His party. This past Saturday night, Kitty surprised him by assembling over two dozen guests—family, friends, colleagues—at his favorite restaurant near Dupont Circle.

Feeling a little guilty that Annabelle wasn't invited, he informs her, "I wouldn't call it a *party*. It was more like . . . it was just dinner, really. My wife planned it."

But then, even if Vic himself had been in charge

of the guest list, Supervisory Special Agent Wyatt would not have been on it.

Some of his colleagues are also personal friends. She isn't one of them.

It's not that he has anything against no-nonsense women. Hell, he married one.

And he respects Annabelle just as much as—or maybe even more than—anyone else here. He just doesn't necessarily *like* her much—and he suspects the feeling is mutual.

"I hear that it was an enjoyable evening," she tells him with a crisp nod, and he wonders if she's wistful. She doesn't sound it—or look it. But for the first time, it occurs to Vic that her apparent social isolation might not always be by choice.

He shifts his weight in his chair. "It's my wife's thing, really. Kitty's big on celebrations. I mean, she'll go all out for any occasion. Years ago, she actually threw a party when she potty-trained the twins."

As soon as the words are out of his mouth, he wants to take them back—and not just because mere seconds ago he was insisting that Saturday night was *not* a party.

Annabelle isn't the kind of person with whom you discuss children, much less potty-training them. She doesn't have a family, but if she did, Vic is certain she'd keep the details—particularly, the bathroom details—to herself.

Well, too bad. I'm a family man.

After Annabelle bids him a stiff good night and disappears down the corridor, Vic shifts his gaze to the framed photos on his desk. One is of him and Kitty on their twenty-fifth wedding anniversary last year; the other, more recent, shows Vic with all four of the kids at the high school graduation last June of his twin daughters.

The girls left for college a few weeks ago. He and Kitty are empty-nesters now—well, Kitty pretty much rules the roost, as she likes to say, since Vic is gone so often.

"So which is it—a nest or a roost?" he asked her the other day.

She dryly replied, "Neither. It's a coop, and you've been trying to fly it for years, but you just keep right on finding your way back, don't you."

She was teasing, of course. No one supports Vic's career as wholeheartedly as Kitty does, no matter how many nights it's taken him away from home over the years. It was her idea in the first place that he put aside his planned career as a psychiatrist in favor of the FBI.

All because of the Night Watchman.

Ah, the one that got away.

It's been almost thirty years since the series of murders terrorized New York and captivated a young, local college psych major.

"Back when I first met him, Vic was obsessed with unsolved murders," Kitty announced on Saturday night when she stood up to toast him at his birthday dinner, "and since then he's done an incredible job solving hundreds of them."

True—with one notable exception.

The Night Watchman disappeared into the shadows years ago when the New York killings stopped abruptly.

Vic would like to think he's no longer alive.

If by chance he is, then he's almost certainly

been sidelined by illness or incarceration for some unrelated crime.

After all, while there are exceptions to every rule, most serial killers don't just stop. Everything Vic has learned over the years about their habits indicates that once something triggers a person to cross the fine line that divides disturbed human beings from cunning predators, he's compelled to keep feeding his dark fantasies until, God willing, something—or someone—stops him.

In a perfect world, Vic is that someone.

But then, a perfect world wouldn't be full of disturbed people who are, at any given moment, teetering on the brink of reality.

Typically, all it takes is a single life stressor to push one over the edge. It can be any devastating event, really—a car accident, job loss, bankruptcy, a terminal diagnosis, a child's drowning . . .

Stressors like those can create considerable challenges for a mentally healthy person. But when fate inflicts that kind of pressure on someone who's already dangerously unbalanced . . . well, that's how killers are born.

Though Vic has encountered more than one homicidal maniac whose spree began with a wife's infidelity, the triggering crisis doesn't necessarily have to hit close to home. Even a natural disaster can be prime breeding ground.

A few years ago in Los Angeles, a seemingly ordinary man—a fine, upstanding boy scout leader—went off the deep end after the Northridge earthquake leveled his apartment building. Voices in his head told him to kill three strangers in the aftermath, telling him they each, in turn, were responsible for the destruction of his home.

Seemingly ordinary. Ah, you just never know. That's what makes murderers—particularly serial murderers—so hard to catch. They aren't always troubled loners; sometimes they're hiding in plain sight: regular people, married with children, holding steady jobs . . .

And sometimes, they're suffering from a mental disorder that plenty of people—including some in the mental health profession—don't believe actually exists.

Before Vic left Chicago, as he was conducting a jailhouse interview with Calvin Granger, Edie took over Calvin's body.

The transition occurred without warning, right before Vic's incredulous eyes. Everything about the man changed—not just his demeanor, but his physical appearance and his voice. A doctor was called in and attested that even biological characteristics like heart rate and vision had been altered. Calvin could see twenty-twenty. Edie was terribly nearsighted. Stunning.

It wasn't that Calvin *believed* he was an entirely different person, a woman named Edie—he *was* Edie. Calvin had disappeared into some netherworld, and when he returned, he had no inkling of what had just happened, or even that time had gone by.

The experience would have convinced even a die-hard skeptic, and it chilled Vic to the bone.

Case closed, yes—but this one is going to give him nightmares for a long time to come.

Vic tidies his desk and finds himself thinking

fondly of the old days at the Bureau—and a colleague who was Annabelle Wyatt's polar opposite.

John O'Neill became an agent around the same
time Vic did. Their career paths, however, took
them in different directions: Vic settled in with
the BSU, while O'Neill went from Quantico to
Chicago and back, then on to New York, where he
eventually became chief of the counterterrorism
unit. Unfortunately, his career with the Bureau
ended abruptly a few weeks ago amid a cloud of
controversy following the theft of a briefcase containing sensitive documents on his watch.

When it happened, Vic was away. Feeling the
sudden urge to reconnect, he searches through
his desk for his friend's new phone number, finds
it, dials it. A secretary and then an assistant field
the call, and finally, John comes on the line.

"Hey, O'Neill," Vic says, "I just got back from
Chicago and I've been thinking about you."

"Shattuck! How the hell are you? Happy birthday. Sorry I couldn't make it Saturday night."

"Yeah, well . . . I'm sure you have a good excuse."

"Valerie dragged me to another wedding. You
know how that goes."

"Yeah, yeah . . . how's the new job?"

"Cushy," quips O'Neill, now chief of security at
the World Trade Center in New York City. "How's
the big 5-0?"

"Not cushy. You'll find out soon enough, won't
you?"

"February. Don't remind me."

Vic shakes his head, well aware that turning
fifty, after everything O'Neill has dealt with in
recent months, will be a mere blip.

They chat for a few minutes, catching up, before O'Neill says, "Listen, I've got to get going. Someone's waiting for me."

"Business or pleasure?"

"My business is always a pleasure, Vic. Don't you know that by now?"

"Where are you off to tonight?"

"I'm having drinks with Bob Tucker at Windows on the World to talk about security for this place, and it's a Monday night, so . . ."

"Elaine's." Vic is well aware of his friend's longstanding tradition.

"Right. How about you?"

"It's a Monday night, so—"

"Football."

"Yeah. I've got a date with the couch and remote. Giants are opening their season—and the Yankees are playing the Red Sox, too. Clemens is pitching. Looks like I'll be channel-surfing."

"I wouldn't get too excited about that baseball game if I were you, Vic. It's like a monsoon here."

A rained out Yankees-Red Sox game on one of Vic's rare nights at home in front of the TV would be a damn shame. Especially since he made a friendly little wager with Rocky Manzillo, his lifelong friend, who had made the trip down from New York this weekend for Vic's birthday dinner.

Always a guy who liked to rock the boat, Rocky is also a lifelong Red Sox fan, despite having grown up in Yankees territory. He still lives there, too—he's a detective with the NYPD.

In the grand scheme of Vic Shattuck's life, old pals and baseball rivalries and homemade macaroni casseroles probably matter more than they should. He's rarely around to enjoy simple pleasures. When he is, they help him forget that somewhere out there, a looming stressor is going to catapult yet another predator from the shadows to wreak violent havoc on innocent lives.

September 10, 2001
New York City
6:40 p.m.

"Hey, watch where you're going!"

Unfazed by the disgruntled young punk, Jamie continues shoving through the sea of pedestrians, baby carriages, and umbrellas, trying to make it to the corner before the light changes.

Around the slow-moving elderly couple, the dog on a leash, a couple of puddle-splashing kids in bright yellow slickers and rubber boots . . .

Failing to make the light, Jamie silently curses them all. Or maybe not silently, because a prim-looking woman flashes a disapproving look. Hand coiled into a fist, Jamie stands waiting in the rain, watching endless traffic zip past.

The subway would have been the best way to go, but there were track delays. And God knows you can't get a stinking cab in Manhattan in weather like this.

Why does everything have to be such a struggle here?

Everything, every day.

A few feet away, a passing SUV blasts its deafening horn.

Noise . . .

Traffic . . .

People . . .

How much more can I take?

Jamie rakes a hand through drenched hair and fights the reckless urge to cross against the light.

That's what it's been about lately. Reckless urges. Day in, day out.

For so long, I've been restrained by others; now that I'm free, I have to constantly restrain myself? It's so unfair.

Why can't I just cross the damned street and go where I need to go?

Why can't I just do whatever the hell I feel like doing? I've earned it, haven't I?

Jamie steps off the curb and hears someone call "Hey, look out!" just before a monstrous double city bus blows past, within arm's reach.

"Geez, close call."

Jamie doesn't acknowledge the bystander's voice, doesn't move, just stands staring into the streaming gutter.

It would be running red with blood if you got hit.

Or if someone else did.

It would be so easy to turn around, pick out some random stranger, and with a quick, hard shove end that person's life. Jamie could do that. It would happen so unexpectedly no one would be able to stop it.

Jamie can feel all those strangers standing there, close enough to touch.

Which of them would you choose?

The prune-faced, disapproving biddy?

One of the splashing kids?

The elderly woman or her husband?

Just imagine the victim, the chosen one, crying out in surprise, helplessly falling, getting slammed by several tons of speeding steel and dying right there in the gutter.

Yes, blood in the gutter.

Eyes closed, Jamie can see it clearly—so much blood at first, thick and red right here where the accident will happen. But then the gutter water will sweep it along, thin it out as it merges with wide, deep puddles and with falling rain, spread it in rivulets that will reach like fingers down alleys and streets . . .

Imagine all the horror-struck onlookers, the traumatized driver of the death car, the useless medics who will rush to the scene and find that there's nothing they can do . . .

Nothing anyone can do.

And somewhere later phones will ring as family members and friends get the dreaded call.

Just think of all the people who will be touched—tainted—by the blood in the street, by that one simple act.

I can do that.

I can choose someone to die.

I've done it before—twice.

Ah, but not really. Technically, Jamie didn't do the choosing. Both victims—the first ten years ago, the second maybe ten days ago—had done the choosing; they'd chosen to commit the heinous acts that had sealed their own fates. Jamie merely saw that they got what they deserved.

This time, though, it would have to be different. It would have to be a stranger.

Would it be as satisfying to snuff out a life that has no real meaning in your own?

Would it be even better?

Would it—

Someone jostles Jamie from behind.

The throng is pressing forward. The traffic has stopped moving past; the light has changed.

Jamie crosses the street, hand still clenched into an angry fist.